Spellbound

The Scarlett Vampire Chronicles—Vol 2

Rebecca S.

ISBN: 0692379304
ISBN 13: 9780692379301
Library of Congress Control Number: 2015903593
Rebecca S. Stratford, CT

Dedicated to
Anibal Rodriguez, Jr.

Special Thanks
To
Sigrid Martinez
Rey Rodriguez
Frankie Rivera
Jackie-Lynn Valentin
Samantha Arrow
Leslie Plaza

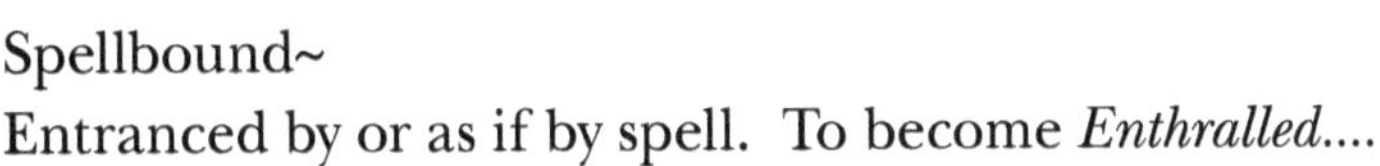

Spellbound~

Entranced by or as if by spell. To become *Enthralled*....

PROLOGUE

The two young girls sit quietly together on a pink, knitted blanket, each playing with her dolls. The sun shines brightly on their freckled faces. They both wear matching green dresses, which in turn match their beautiful emerald eyes.

"Flora, Ezarbet…come, it is time for our daily lesson," their mother calls out, her long red hair flowing softly in the breeze.

The twin girls run earnestly to their mother, both racing to see which will get to her first. Even at the young age of eight, they are very competitive, each one vying for the attention of their mother. Ezarbet gets there first, giving Flora a smirk. Ezarbet always wins.

"Come, let's have a seat, my girls," their mother says to them, patting the disappointed Flora on the back.

She leads them to the seating area by the pond of their home. It is breathtakingly beautiful; with flowers blooming and the sun shining off the water, it is a surreal surrounding. The girls come out here often with their mother to recite chants and become one with nature.

"OK, what is the first rule of thumb before summoning?" she asks her children.

"To respect nature for what it is—to never take advantage of its beauty," Flora says, looking at her mother while smiling shyly. Ezarbet rolls her eyes.

"Yes, my love. We must always respect nature. We must ask its permission before chanting," she says softly, looking at both of them.

"Mother, this is so boring. I want to learn other things," Ezarbet complains, crossing her arms across her chest.

"Every witch must learn the basics first," she scolds Ezarbet, who rolls her eyes again. "Come," their mother says, continuing where she left off. "Let's join hands and summon nature."

Ezarbet lets out a sigh of frustration and joins hands with Flora, who grabs her mother's hand.

Closing their eyes, the girls begin to chant in unison with their mother, each whispering softly, summoning nature. A wind starts to pick up, flowing magically around them—an open invitation from nature. They open their eyes, and there are white butterflies surrounding them. Flora lets out a laugh as one lands on her nose. Ezarbet, annoyed, swats at the butterflies.

"You see, my loves, this is nature granting us permission," their mother says to the children.

"What else can we do, Mother?" Flora asks earnestly.

"It is limitless, my love." She leans down and touches Flora's face softly.

"Well, I want to learn now. I hate summoning nature; it is so boring," Ezarbet says.

"Patience is a virtue, my love. You must first learn to become one with nature, and then we can move on to more."

Ezarbet rolls her eyes again.

"Mother, why are warlocks our enemies?" Flora asks, changing the subject.

"Well, my love, it happened very long ago. It is said that a witch by the name of Sorsha had a grand love affair with a man by the name of Zander."

Both girls start to giggle at the mention of a love affair.

"It is said that Zander used Sorsha and her affections. He took advantage of the love that she gave so freely and used it against her. He left her powerless and heartbroken. So that began the war of the warlocks and witches."

"I would never fall in love. But I bet Flora would fall in love with a warlock," Ezarbet says sarcastically.

"I would not," Flora says, arguing back.

"Yes, you would," Ezarbet counters, sticking out her tongue.

"Girls, girls…enough of that." Their mother scolds them both, making them fall silent. "Now that we are done for today, you can both go run off and play," she says, patting them both on the head and walking back toward the house.

"You are such a baby," Ezarbet says to Flora, giving her a nudge as she walks by.

"I am not," Flora says, following her.

"Oh yeah? Prove it," Ezarbet says, turning around with a look of challenge in her eyes.

"What do you mean, 'prove it'?" she asks.

"Let's summon some magic."

"No. We cannot do that without Mother." Flora shakes her head, looking back toward the house.

"See, I knew it. You are such a baby," Ezarbet says again, stomping away from her.

"I am not," Flora says after her.

"Baby girl, baby girl," Ezarbet calls out, taunting in a baby-like voice.

Flora crosses her arms and watches her sister walk off toward the far end of the pond. She lets out a huff and walks after her in defeat, following her into the wooded area behind the pond. Flora catches up soon enough, but she accidentally bumps into Ezarbet as soon as she does. "Shhh," Ezarbet says.

"What are you doing?" Flora whispers.

In the distance, they watch a fawn standing by itself, almost blending into the woods.

"I want to try something," Ezarbet says.

Flora says nothing but watches as Ezarbet begins to chant, lifting her small hands up. The air seems to shift around them, growing still. Flora pauses in alarm, knowing exactly what her sister is doing.

"Ezarbet, stop," she whispers, looking between her and the fawn.

Ezarbet keeps chanting, ignoring her. Flora watches as the fawn starts to shake its head as if trying to clear it. Then it makes a sound as if in agony, falling to the ground on its side, and lies still as if dead. Ezarbet stops chanting and opens her eyes, smiling as she sees the magic she's created. The fawn is dead.

"What did you do? Why would you do such a thing?" Flora whispers with tears in her eyes.

"I have been experimenting. I am sick of asking permission, and I have become quite bored. Being bad is so much more fun," Ezarbet says, smirking at her.

Flora looks dumbfounded at her sister. It's as if she's seeing her in a new light—a light Flora fears will become all too familiar. A casting of blackness looms over her identical twin sister…a casting of evil. "You have been experimenting?"

"Yes, and you better keep this little secret to yourself, or else." Narrowing her eyes, Ezarbet turns to walk away. The dark aura around her follows.

"Or else what?"

She pauses as if surprised Flora had the nerve to speak up.

"Well, I wouldn't want to use my spells on you accidentally, now would I?"

She turns and stalks off, leaving Flora with that silent threat. Ezarbet always makes good on her threats. Shoulders slumping, Flora begins to follow her sister but decides to turn back. Slowly she walks over to the dead fawn, feeling very sorry for it. Kneeling down, she touches its head, tears coming to her eyes once again.

Flora has always had the ability to feel someone's pain or happiness. Her mother calls it an extraordinary gift. It's one of the many gifts of becoming a witch, but not all witches have this ability. Why would her sister take such a precious life, just to experiment? Flora puts her hands over the fawn's body and begins to chant softly, begging the spirits to give life once more to the innocent fawn. With her body rocking back and forth, she feels a power sweep through her, overwhelming her, knocking her small body backward. Opening her eyes, she watches in amazement as the fawn sits up, alive. Very slowly, almost hesitantly, the fawn moves forward, meeting her eyes with its gentle brown ones. She lifts her small hand gently, petting it on the head, its fur tickling her hand.

"I am so sorry, my friend," she whispers.

The fawn takes one last touch from her and then runs off deeper into the enchanting forest.

Flora looks left and right, making sure she is not caught, slightly smiling as she walks back to her home. Ezarbet isn't the only one holding onto a secret; Flora is also experimenting on her own.

1

"Scarlett..." I hear Hugo's gentle voice call out to me and the faint sound of a knock at the door.

Digging myself out of the very comfy duvet covers and moving my hair out of my face, I peek around my room. It's completely dark except for an alarm clock that stands on the nightstand, the big neon numbers reading 8:00 p.m. Holy crap—I slept through the whole day. Sitting up, I notice I still have on the white robe I was wearing this morning. I must have just knocked myself out from complete exhaustion.

"Scarlett," Hugo calls out again, this time starting to knock impatiently.

"Sorry, come in," I say, sitting up and rubbing my eyes. I clear my throat, which sounds very raspy.

He opens the door and stops, possibly because he notices my room is in complete darkness.

"Are you dressed?" he asks before turning on the lights.

"Yeah, sorry," I say, apologizing again as I pull the robe closer to my body.

The bright lights hit my eyes fast; I close them momentarily, feeling my vision adjust itself. Hugo sits on the bed with me just as I open my eyes again, his soft brown eyes still looking at me as if I might break down at any moment. I grab his hand, which is long and lean against mine. It's warm and soft compared to Ian's cold hands.

"I'm OK," I say, reassuring him. He nods his head and looks down at our hands, not saying anything.

And I'm not lying. I feel more than OK. I feel free. Free of feeling, free of fear, and free, most of all, of myself. No longer will I let my emotions get the best of me. If I come across as a coldhearted bitch, then so be it. Ian's words come back to me: "Emotion is a weakness."

God, he was so right. As much as I hated him, he was right. Not wanting to think of him, I change the subject.

"Have you gotten in contact with the Xs?" I ask Hugo.

"The only one I have been in contact with is Bastian."

"OK, let's have him come here. There's plenty of room for him."

"I've already invited him; he will be arriving shortly."

"OK, great," I say, letting go of his hand and swinging my legs off the bed. "Hugo, who is Opal?" I ask, turning to face him.

"Opal," he says softly, displeasure in his voice as he gets up from the bed. "What do you know of her?"

"She has the other half of the prophecy. Who is she?"

He looks away for a moment, deep in thought, before turning back toward me. "She is one of the most powerful witches; she spells with the deepest of black magic."

"We have to find Flora. And I know just the person who is going to help us. Michael Pearson," I say, heading to the bathroom.

"How will Flora help? She is powerless," Hugo says, looking annoyed for the first time ever at the prospect of dealing with Flora.

"Hugo, you and Flora..." I trail off. I don't want to say too much and risk him getting upset, but in my vision, there was more than just a connection between Hugo and Flora; it was something more powerful. I knew this was something I had to let him explore on his own.

"You just have to trust me on this," I say instead, shutting the door to the bathroom.

"You just have to trust me on this," Scarlett says, walking into the bathroom, leaving me with just that.

I saw her struggle with what she wanted to tell me; I know, of course, that there is more to what she said. I hear the shower start to run. Letting out a frustrated breath, I walk out of her bedroom. I know that Flora is a piece of the puzzle, but it still annoys me beyond belief that I will be working side-by-side with a witch—and the queen's identical twin sister, no less.

Of course, there was the backstory of why witches and warlocks became enemies; the story always seemed to change as the years went by. Witches took from the warlocks, and warlocks took from the witches. One always bumped the other out. It was a big game of chess; they were always trying to checkmate one another. The bottom line was that each believed the other was the enemy who dealt with black magic. Witches and warlocks picked sides, and those sides were always opposing.

Heading over to the window, I look out into the night. The tall buildings are still lit with Christmas lights, and crowds of people walk up and down the snowy streets. They aren't wrong, those who call this "the city that never sleeps."

A banging at the door breaks my stare from the beautiful view. I know who it is right away. I can only imagine what he had to do to get into the hotel. All the Xs are impressive, but Big Red is the most distinctive, with his huge physique and flaming red hair.

I swing open the door, and an impatient Big Red stands there in all his glory.

"About time you opened the damn door, pretty boy. What took you so long? Couldn't you have you used your magic to open it?" he says sarcastically, waving his hand as if he were a wizard.

I smile at him and open the door wider for him, regretting that along with his presence comes the annoyance of his mouth. However, as soon as he takes his first step through the doorway, he's automatically zapped, his big body falling to the floor and jerking as if stunned by a stun gun.

"Motherfucker," Big Red moans, trying to get up but tripping over himself instead.

The smile I give him doesn't quite reach my eyes.

"Oh…I must have forgotten that I spelled the doorway. My apologies," I say, faking innocence.

Holding my hand up, I unbind the spell, letting it know who to let in and who to keep out.

"Yeah, I'm sure you're sorry, Warlock," he says, brushing off his knees and walking into the suite.

"Whoa, just look at this fucking place," he says, admiring the lavish surroundings.

Rolling my eyes heavenward, I have to agree with him. This is the best hotel New York has to offer. The place is marvelous. It gives off an age-old romantic appeal.

"Come, this is a four-bedroom suite. I will show you where you can stay. The curtains are thick, and with my help you can keep the sunlight out."

Big Red follows me and I show him his room. Each room has a fireplace and the same matching décor of gold and ivory.

"This is it," I say to him, waving my hand for him to enter.

He walks in and the room looks instantly smaller.

"It's a little fruity for me, but I guess this will do."

I turn to walk out and he stops me.

"Where are Scarlett and Ian?"

"He didn't come with her," I say, not wanting to divulge. Big Red nods his head in silent understanding.

"I knew that asshole couldn't be trusted."

"What asshole?" Scarlett asks from behind me.

I turn to see her, fully dressed in a white sweater that falls off the shoulder, showing off her pale skin, and black leggings with long black boots that make her look taller. Her long hair is still wet from the shower. She is breathtakingly beautiful, a young woman who would stop any man dead in his tracks. I can't imagine having a physical attraction to her myself—I can tell she's stunning, but I only have the feeling one might have for a sister, if I had any.

"Ian…" Big Red trails off, seeming for once in his life at a loss for words.

"Ian who?" she says, walking away—but I catch the flash of pain that runs across her face just for the briefest of moments.

Walking out of the room and offering no explanation, I head toward the doorway, knowing they'll follow me. I don't have the energy to talk about what happened with Ian. I don't want to think about him. It's better this way.

"Where are we going?" Hugo asks, cutting into my thoughts.

"There's a bar downstairs; I want a drink. We can discuss the next phase of the mission," I say, grabbing my jacket before heading out the door. They're behind me instantly. I have to say it feels great having them both at my side. I press the button for the elevator and take a peek at Hugo, who has his lips pursed as if he wants to argue.

The elevator dings open, and the elevator operator welcomes us with a warm smile, his eyes going wide as he looks at Big Red. We all squeeze into the tight space and wait patiently for the door to close. I watch as he nervously presses the button to the main floor. I still need to come to grips with the fact that someone actually does this for a living. The guys let me out first; I can imagine what we look like. As soon as we're out in the lobby, people start to stare. Shit!

"If anyone asks, I'm a celebrity from the UK, and you two are my bodyguards."

Big Red lets out a cough. "Sure, Britney fucking Spears with an accent, of course," he says behind me, his voice heavy with the joke.

Shit, he's right. I can't pull off an accent. "OK, scratch that. I'm some rich heiress, and you two are my bodyguards."

We walk over to the bar and have a seat. Looking at the drink menu, I decide I want something strong. The waitress comes over. She looks to both Hugo and Big Red, smiling shyly and flushing a little. She's attractive enough, with light brown hair pulled back in a ponytail, her hazel eyes straying toward Big Red. He grins knowingly at her. His expression says, "Yeah, I'm fuckable."

"Hello, welcome to the Plaza. What can I get you?" she asks with a pen and pad in hand as her blush deepens.

"Get us three shots of tequila," I say before either of the men can speak.

"Sure, coming right up," she says. She gives Big Red one last lingering glance before walking off, swaying her hips.

Hugo gives me a disapproving look.

"What?"

"Nothing," he answers shortly.

"It's a day of celebrating. I want to celebrate," I say.

We sit in silence before the waitress comes over with the tequila shots, placing them each down in front of us.

I wait for her to leave before I hold up my glass. "OK, here is to the small battle we just won and to many more." I toast each of them and take the glass to my mouth, gulping the tequila down. It doesn't burn the back of my throat like last time. They both drink with me. Hugo excuses himself to go use the bathroom. So here we are, Big Red and me. He lets out an uncomfortable cough; I know he wants to discuss Ian.

"Listen, I am not a man who apologizes easily…" he starts off, not meeting my eyes, clearly very uncomfortable.

"It's OK," I say simply, cutting him off.

"You're different," he says softly to me after a moment's pause, his beautiful green eyes looking at me with wonder.

"Yeah, well, I guess I decided it was time to grow up," I say, smiling at him.

He smiles back. Once again we have this silent understanding between us. He is impulsive, and I know he is going to have to learn the hard way. Something is going to make him change, just the way I have changed. Then a thought occurs to me. My vision of Chayton.

I lean forward. "Big Red, who's Chayton?"

"Chayton…I've never heard of a Chayton," he says, shaking his head and shrugging his huge shoulders.

"Really?" I ask.

"No, I think I would remember someone by the name of Chayton," he says matter-of-factly.

The waitress comes over again, interrupting us. She smiles at Big Red. "Can I get you guys something else?"

"Yes, love. How about another round?" he says, giving her a dashing smile.

Big Red is not only an impulsive, charming asshole, but also a flirt. *He doesn't know who Chayton is either*, I think with frustration. *Who are you?* I have to get to the bottom of this.

Hugo comes back from the bathroom and takes a seat. "What did I miss?" he asks.

"Well, Big Red is sorry for being a dick. But what I really wanted to discuss is Michael Pearson. He's our ticket to finding out where Flora is; I'm sure of it. The sooner I get close to him, the better."

"OK, what's the plan?" Big Red asks, looking game for a mission.

"Well, I plan on calling him and asking for investment advice, of course. New Year's Eve is coming up, and there's going to be a big gala. Guess who will be getting invited?"

"We have to be careful. The queen most likely will have him spelled so he cannot become entranced," Hugo says, playing with his empty shot glass.

"All right. Mind if I go in too, just to be the lookout?" Big Red says.

I look over to him and smile. "I thought you'd never ask. Hugo, I'm going to need you to produce a fake ticket for Big Red to get in. This is like an exclusive party only for VIP guests. After the gala, I plan on making a pit stop at Mr. Pearson's apartment."

The waitress comes over with another round of shots. We all clink our glasses together before swallowing.

"Wait a second—you want to go to his apartment? Do you think that's safe?" Hugo asks.

"Don't worry; I think I can handle myself with a sentinel. Whatever he has on the queen must be in his personal files. He's not going to leave that around just anywhere."

"What if the queen alerts him?" Hugo asks.

"I don't think she has any idea we're here."

"But it's just a matter of time before she will," Big Red counters.

"Well, it's not as if I'm trying to hide," I say, leaning back in my chair as I feel the liquor begin to take its effect on me.

"OK, well, let's get this plan started. Con and the others have contacted me; they're searching for another location," Big Red says, getting up from the table. He glances toward the waitress, who keeps giving him the eye. "Duty calls," he says, leaving us and walking over to her.

Hugo is quiet, his hand playing with the empty shot glass.

"What's wrong?" I ask him.

"Nothing, I just don't want you to make reckless decisions," he says, meeting my eyes.

"Reckless? What do you mean?" I ask. I purse my lips together, a little offended.

"Losing all your humanity. That is what makes you so special, Scarlett. I don't want you to lose that."

"Special? Listen, I just have one thing on my mind, and that is to avenge the death of my parents. Look at where their love got them. Death," I say harshly.

"Scarlett..." Hugo trails off, seeming at a loss for words.

I get up from my seat, aggravated by this whole conversation. I don't want to feel or think; I just want to do. Hugo quickly stands up and follows me. I look over to Big Red; he has the waitress raising her head in laughter in response to what he's saying, clearly smitten with him. Rolling my eyes, I walk out of the barroom. Zipping up my jacket, I head out the doorway and walk toward the hotel's exit.

"Where are you going?" Hugo asks, stopping me before I can make my exit.

"Sightseeing," I say, dodging around him and going through the door.

The cold wind hits my face first. God, I can't get enough of this weather. Thankful that Hugo is not following me, I make my way into the night, my six-inch-heeled boots stomping away against the snow. The streets aren't too packed with people. I look up at the tall buildings in wonder. This is my new home. There's no place on earth like it, with the different kinds of people, food, culture. All walks of life are in this city.

I'm also keeping company with all of the biggest names in fashion. Each store is closed, of course, because it's late, but I stand longingly in front of the window of Chanel. The mannequin is all decked out to the nines, wearing a pair of black sunglasses and a red trench coat that's accessorized with the brand's signature black, quilted handbag. She's the epitome of the chic New York woman. Chanel is one of my favorite designers, even though it used to be that I couldn't afford any of their pieces. But all of that's changed so drastically now—I can afford anything I want. "The sky's the limit…"

I walk slowly away, heading farther down the block and keeping my head down. I don't really know where I'm going, but at this point I don't really care. I feel like my feelings are starting to catch up with me. Hugo's voice keeps running through my head, shooting back at me rapidly. "Don't lose your humanity."

"Shut up, Hugo," I whisper back, wondering if he can hear me.

I feel the hairs on the back of my neck start to stand; it's the familiar feeling that I'm starting to become accustomed to when vampires are near. I stand still for a moment, letting the feeling come over me slowly, my senses awakening. From my fingertips to my toes, my body comes alive for action. I close my eyes and focus, breathing in the cold air, feeling the wind hitting my face. I can smell the copper scent of blood.

Curling my hands into fists, I set off into a run, my speed picking up. I couldn't give two shits who's going to meet me on the other end. All I know is I'm going to fuck up his or her night.

2

The scent of blood envelops me first. I stand in front of Grand Central Station, watching people come in and out of the place. *Whoa, vamps are getting pretty ballsy to feed in such a public place,* I think as I enter one of the most famous landmarks in New York City. It feels a bit unreal as I look around, sensing that the blood is coming from the top floor. In the distance I can hear the sound of trains coming to a halt. The station is huge and has many intricate features. From food stands to small boutiques, the place is a great space to just walk around in, even if you have nowhere to be. Except that I did.

Purposefully making my way through the thick crowd, I find a stairwell leading to the upper level. There are fewer people up here; in fact, it's surprisingly empty after the crowd downstairs. Taking the steps slowly, I can smell the blood more pronouncedly. The hairs on the back of my neck stand strong as I zero in on my target. There are at least five men and one woman, ancients, all of whom appear to be sharing a young couple. Two of the ancients are on the lookout while two feed from the man, one at the wrist and one at the neck. The female ancient is at the girl's throat, sucking away roughly. The young couple looks oblivious to what is taking place, their eyes hazy as if drugged, and their skin graying from the loss of blood. The ancients' nostrils flare as they sense me, just as I had sensed them. They all turn toward me, releasing the humans. They fall to the floor, their bodies weakened, but I can still hear their hearts beating. Looks like I got here just in time.

Giving the vampires the finger, I set off in a run, trying to get them out of public view. Taking the steps two at a time, I run through the crowd, leading them out of the station, and head toward a small bridge. One of the ancients closes in on me, and I flip forward before he can make his grab. Now facing him, I see that he has a small knife in his hand as he launches himself at me. I reach for his extended arm, quickly placing it above my shoulder so I can snap it. He screams out in pain, releasing the knife in agony. The female ancient charges at me, her face still bloodied from the meal she didn't get to finish. I jump just before she can get to me, my legs going around her neck, snapping it. She falls to the ground, her body dissipating to black ash. I flip the other ancient over my shoulder, grabbing his knife quickly and stabbing him in the heart. In my peripheral vision, I see another ancient running my way. Flipping the knife in my hand, I toss it with all my might, aiming perfectly at his heart and turning him to black dust in midstride.

The two other ancients come at me fast, one grabbing me from behind while the other approaches me from the front. I kick out with my leg, making contact with the front one's abdomen. While he falls to the ground, gasping, I grab hold of the ancients' arms around me, breaking their holds and spinning so I am facing the vampire behind me. I grab him by the jugular and rip it out, turning him to ash.

"Ugh...you fucking bitch, you're going to pay for this," the wounded ancient behind me hisses, still on the ground and holding his abdomen.

I walk over to him slowly, almost taunting him. I want him to feel as humans do; I want him to feel what it feels like to be hunted. Inches from him, I kneel down slowly so we're almost eye to eye.

"Do you know who I am?" I ask him.

"Why the fuck would I know who you are?" he says, his black eyes narrowing at me.

I focus, clearing my mind. I'd wanted to experiment more with this power that was new to me anyway. *"Because I am the prophet,"* my mind whispers to him.

His mouth gapes open, and his black eyes widen in recognition. Before he can move again, I stab him with a dagger I had hidden in my pocket. He lets out a gasping breath, his body convulsing as the dagger meets his heart. He begins to fade before me slowly, the cold wind making the black ash rise around me. I stand with the dagger still in my hand, looking up at the dark sky, feeling the edge that had built inside me dwindle.

"Freeze," a man yells from behind me.

I slowly turn toward the voice that holds such strong authority. He's a young cop of Spanish descent. He's tall and lean, and his glare is narrowed as he stands there, holding out his gun pointed straight at me. As I turn fully toward him, I watch as he ever so slightly lowers the gun.

"Ma'am, I am going to ask you to lower the weapon, very slowly. No one has to get hurt," he says, eyeing the dagger in my hand. He has that awesome Bronx accent that I always find so sexy.

"I think you're the one who should lower your weapon, Bronx," I whisper to him with my mind.

He looks momentarily taken aback, his eyes widening as he hears my voice float ever so softly to him. Before he can blink, I fling my dagger right toward his gun, aiming it perfectly into his barrel before he can let out a shot. He stares at the gun and back at me, his eyes widening.

"What the fuck?" he says, dropping the gun and coming toward me.

Nodding in agreement, I turn toward the railing of the bridge, looking down. I climb over it. I've always had this fear of heights, but now with this new power I hold, I don't feel an ounce of terror. Only a pure adrenaline rush.

"Lady, don't jump," he yells frantically, his eyes wide, running toward me.

Before he can reach me, I free fall fifteen feet down, landing perfectly on my boots. I take a look up, and I see the cop looking down at me incredulously, his mouth open from being out of breath. I can almost imagine his heart racing. I used to feel that fear. Smiling up at him, I head back to the hotel.

"What the fuck?" I mutter to myself, wiping off the cold sweat that is forming over my brow.

Watching the woman with the glowing eyes free fall off the bridge, I sure as fuck thought she was a goner. But when she landed on her feet and smirked up at me, I couldn't believe what I'd just seen—or could I? Things were getting strange as fuck in this city. People were going missing and then reappearing in the hospital half-dead from blood loss but with no evident injuries. When questioned, they couldn't give a how, when, or where. It was as if their memories had been wiped clean.

Turning away from the bridge, I rub my tired eyes and take a deep breath. Walking away from the ramp, I look at the ground and notice her footprints on the snow—and that isn't the only thing I notice. There's also what appears to be black ash scattered over the entire area. Kneeling down on my haunches, I pick up one of the thicker pieces with my fingers. It begins to break apart into dust. "No fucking way," I say to myself, getting up quickly and heading back over to the ramp. I've tried so hard to forget, but now it all comes rushing back to me. The childhood that was taken from me, the death of my mother, seeing doctors who would tell me that what I experienced was posttraumatic, the clear fantasy of a child who was too young to comprehend what had really happened. I remember that black ash…

"Antonio, it's time for bed," his mother called out to him from the kitchen.

"But Mama, it's almost done," he begged his mother, watching his favorite baseball team, the Yankees, play against one of their biggest rivals, the Red Sox.

"Agh, niño—OK, you have five more minutes. I don't wanna hear you complaining when it's time to get up for school, though, and remember to say your prayers," his mother said, going into the living room and making sure to get his word that he would not disobey her. She had long, dark hair that was starting to gray at the sides. She was medium built, and she always wore either her uniform from the diner or the one from the hospital.

This time, she was wearing the green scrubs from the hospital. It was tough for her being a single parent, but she made it a point that he would never do without. His father was not in his life; he remembered his grandmother always muttering under her breath, "He chose the streets over his family," but his mother never dwelled on the what ifs. She worked toward giving him a life where he wouldn't get sad when he saw a father and son together. She would be enough. Being a tough Puerto Rican mother from the Bronx, she played both roles well.

"I promise, Mama," he said, knowing she couldn't resist his charming smile. She smiled back, leaning over to plant a kiss on his head and combing his dark hair away from his forehead.

"OK, I'm going to take a shower," she said to him, walking off toward the kitchen again.

Watching the rest of the game, he was thrilled that his Yankees won. As he headed over to his room, he heard something drop in the bathroom and the faint sound of a whimper. Pausing by the bathroom, he knocked softly.

"Mama, are you OK?"

There was no answer, just the shower running.

"Mama," he said again, now knocking harder on the door. He opened the door to find his mother's lifeless body on the floor with a pool of her blood surrounding her. He dropped onto his knees in front of her, unaware of the danger that now surrounded him. Sensing someone behind him, he turned and looked up to see eyes as black as night, fangs protruding from a vicious mouth, his mother's blood all around the monster's lips.

Antonio balled his tiny hands into fists and stood, tears rolling down his face. "What did you do to my mama?" he asked bravely.

The monster chuckled at him.

"Looks like I will have two meals tonight," the monster said as he made a grab for him. Antonio quickly went under the monster's legs,

making a run for his room, but the monster was quick—too quick. He made a grab for Antonio's ankle, dragging him back into the bathroom. Antonio screamed out, kicking and scrambling, before he made a grab for the plunger by the toilet and attempted to hit the monster with it. The monster caught the plunger midswing and laughed.

"What the fuck you going to do with this, kid?" he yelled as he broke the plunger easily with his hands. The monster tossed the broken pieces to the floor and grabbed Antonio by the neck, lifting his small body off the floor.

"Poor little human—I once wished I could have saved my mother too. I will end your pain here and now," he said evilly to him.

Before the monster could take a bite at his throat, Antonio reached down to his chest and yanked, breaking the sterling silver necklace with the Yankee pendant his mother had bought him for his birthday last year. He shoved it into the monster's mouth out of pure desperation. The monster coughed and dropped him to the floor, stunned. He hit the floor hard and watched as the monster went down onto his knees, holding his throat. It looked like there was smoke coming from his mouth, as if he was having some sort of reaction to the silver.

Antonio wasted no time looking for the closest weapon there was: the broken piece of the plunger, which now looked like a wooden stake. "I'll tell you what I'm going to do with this. I'm gonna kill you," he said as he rushed over to the monster and stabbed him with it straight in the heart.

The monster didn't have a chance to react. He stared at him once again, stunned—stunned at the turn of events, at being outsmarted by an eight-year-old human. The monster started to convulse, and his body began to fade, becoming black ash.

Antonio sat there for what seemed like forever; he distantly heard knocks on the door, the cops rushing in, grabbing him from the bathroom floor as he clung to his mother's lifeless body. He pounded on the officer's back as he took him away from the scene that he would remember for the rest of his life: the scene of his mother's blood and the black ash that surrounded it.

I close my eyes from the memory that I have worked so hard to forget—the memory that I'd wanted not to be real. It is all coming back to me as if I've been hit with a four-by-four. What the fuck is going on? And what was that lady doing out here? Is she one of them? With her dark hair and glowing eyes, she looked like one, but I can't help feeling an instant attraction to her. *Hell, I would have to be a dead man not to be attracted to her.*

If she's one of them, though, why didn't she just kill me? Did she kill them? Is that why she had the dagger in her hands? There are so many questions left unanswered. I vow to myself I'll find out one way or another.

3

"Mother, why must you leave?" I asked her for the thousandth time, pouting my lips as I watched her carefully packing her clothes in a suitcase.

"Darling, you know I must leave—but not for long, I promise you. It will just be a few days. They will go by quickly," my mother said as she walked over to me and touched my face lightly.

"But it seems like so far from here. You know Ezarbet likes to pick on me. Who will help me when you are gone?" I looked at her earnestly, wishing she would take me with her. I felt tears start to well up, and I bit my lip to keep them from falling. Ezarbet always called me a baby for crying.

"Oh, Flora..." My mother stopped what she was doing and came over to the side of the bed where I was sitting. She looked beautiful. With my matching red hair and green eyes, I got a glimpse of what I would look like when I was older. If only I could be as graceful.

"You are stronger than you think," my mother said, tucking my unruly hair behind my ear.

"I am a baby," I said, disagreeing with her. I looked down and began to fiddle with a string that was hanging from my dress.

"My baby..." she said, lifting my face so our eyes met. "One day, you will be a force to be reckoned with, but you must believe in yourself."

I didn't disagree with her that time. She got up from the bed and went over to her bureau, opening her wood-carved jewelry box. Coming back over to the bed, she held a gold necklace with a heart-shaped locket.

"This was my mother's," she said a little sadly. She unclasped it and leaned over, putting it around my neck.

I gently picked it up. Its simplicity was beautiful. I tried to open it, but it wouldn't open.

"It is said that only your true love can open it," she said, smiling.

"Mother..." I said, rolling my eyes, embarrassed at just the thought.

She let out a laugh and tickled me, making me fall back against her plush pillows as she fell over me and kissed me on the cheeks. We lay there on the bed for a moment, spent and silent. I turned to her. "Do you really have to go?" I whispered.

"You know I must, my darling," she said, moving my hair from my forehead. "I will be back soon, I promise..."

That was when I realized, at the young age of ten, that promises are never kept. She never returned to me. She died of what doctors said was a brain aneurysm.

For the first time, I open my eyes and feel them begin to water. Clasping the locket that still hangs around my neck, I try to gather my strength not to break down. Hearing the sound of a key rattling, I turn over, slowly wincing, trying to lift my body from the cold, hard ground. A guard comes in, one of the ancients the queen hired to watch over me. His name is Alexander. He has pale, long blond hair and is built to perfection. Like the queen, he is very attractive, but he has a soul that is blackened.

He opens the door, carrying a tray of food that he drops down carelessly, the food falling to the dirty floor. "Dinner is served, my lady," he says sarcastically, his pale green eyes gleaming.

I don't answer him, and that seems to anger him. He is at me in a flash, yanking me up by the hair and flinging me against the wall. I gasp in pain, my weakened body sagging to the floor. He grabs me again, this time holding me up, his face close to mine and his fingers digging into my flesh. I can smell his reeking breath.

"One day, the queen will give me the permission I need to have my taste of you," he whispers close to my ear. "And when she does, I promise you it will be the last day you live."

I close my eyes against his warning. He's been hungry for me since the beginning. I feel it every time he comes in to serve me my food. He lets me go and I sag to the floor, not with relief but because I'm just too weak to stand. I watch as he closes the door, locking it as he walks away. *What am I going to do?* It is just a matter of time before Ezarbet makes up her mind about what she wants to do with me, and letting me go free is something I know is not going to happen. There's only one way I'm leaving here, and that's in a body bag.

Lying back down on the floor, I contemplate just giving up—at least I'll die on my own terms. I feel the tears start to spring to my eyes. This is it. My final moments of life.

I think back to the life I once led before becoming imprisoned…my magic becoming the thing I loved most, and the sheer beauty it held. But at the same time, my life had become my sister's. I was her shadow, putting my own life to the side. I was as frightened of her as everyone else was. No one wanted to feel her wrath. As soon as I found out her plan for the king,

I had to intervene. She set her own fate, just as I have. And afterward, I felt her wrath like no other. My fate has been to be trapped in a cage, no better than an animal, for twenty-one years. My life is over.

Feeling my lips begin to tremble, I quietly beg the spirits to take me. I'm ready to surrender. If I were strong enough, I would wave a white flag.

"Take me," I whisper. "I am ready."

I close my eyes, letting my tears fall freely, whispering over and over again, "Take me." I began to feel a presence with me. Warm arms wrap around my cold, broken body, giving me comfort. This is it. They are ready to take me, and I am ready to be taken. I snuggle closer, finding the warmth comforting. Feeling the presence come closer to me, I hear the voice I have not heard for many years.

"You are not ready, my child," my mother whispers in my ear.

Gasping, I try to sit up and open my eyes, but the force of my mother's presence won't let me.

"I do not have much time. So you must listen and not speak," she tells me, her voice sounding far away but still close enough that I can hear her.

I nod my head furiously, scared to speak.

"You have come too far to give up. I won't let you. You are stronger, so much stronger, than you can imagine. You have to fight. Do you hear me, Flora? You fight."

Her voice begins to fade, and the comforting warmth that I feel vanishes with it. I have longed to hear her voice again, and never would I have imagined it would be in these circumstances. Turning over on my side, I wrap my arms around myself. I can't let my sister win. I have to fight. I feel my eyes begin to close from exhaustion, until I feel something crawling on my shoulder, going up my knotted hair, its tiny whiskers tickling my face. Opening my eyes, I see my first sign of salvation. My mouse. I set him on my palm; he has the most beautiful key I have ever seen attached to his tail. With my heart in my throat, I sit up slowly.

"Thank you, my friend," I whisper to him, meeting him at eye level.

He gives me a squeak in response, releasing the key into my hand. Setting him down, I stand up, feeling rejuvenated. I now have purpose. I walk over to the food that's become dirty from being on the floor, my mouse at my heels.

"Come, I will share this with you," I say to him. Sitting back down, I break a piece of bread, trying to wipe as much dirt off of it as I can. I give him a generous piece, and he eats greedily. Eating with him, I know I have to eat as much as possible to gather my strength. Clutching the key to my heart, I smile for the first time in twenty-one years.

Entering the hotel room and watching Big Red and Hugo watching television is a sight to see. They're watching *Dracula.*

"You know these movies got it all wrong. I mean, who the hell thought it was OK for us to be scared of crosses? What a bunch of pussies," Big Red says, shaking his head in disgust as he polishes his knife collection.

"Well, he is a ladies' man," I say, taking off my jacket and avoiding Hugo's probing stare.

"Yeah, too bad the real guy wasn't such a ladies' man," Big Red says.

"The real guy?" I ask curiously.

"Yeah. We started from somewhere...just like you humans. There was a first of our kind. A man by the name of Draken."

"What happened to him?" I ask.

"Who knows? It was way before my time. There are a lot of versions out there—one of them being that he sleeps until the day he can be awoken," he says dramatically.

"Ha. I think you're watching way too many movies," I say, turning to go. Hugo gets up, blocking me.

"Where did you go? I know something happened."

"Nothing happened. Let it go," I say, clenching my teeth. Since when do I become angry with Hugo?

"Whoa, whoa now. He's right. You reek of fight," Big Red says, getting up and coming over to me.

"If you must know, I met up with a couple of ancients," I say, rolling my eyes at the both of them before passing Hugo. I walk toward my room, not wishing to discuss what took place.

"What do you mean, you took on a couple of ancients?" Hugo says, his eyes widening. He grabs me by the arm and stops me from entering my room.

"I'm fine. I can take care of myself," I say, hating to see the look of disappointment in his eyes. I look over to Big Red, daring him to challenge me. Holding his hands up, he wisely backs off.

"Scarlett..." Hugo shakes his head, at a loss for words.

"Don't," I say, stopping him. I yank my arm away and open my door. I slam it shut as soon as I'm in my room.

Frustrated, I go over to my bed and fling my body across it, turning so I'm lying on my back. Looking at my hands, I see the telltale signs of black residue—of the ash. My nails look dirty and chipped. I'm in desperate need of a manicure. Closing my eyes, I put my hand to my forehead, feeling the pulsing drum of a headache coming on.

I know why Hugo is upset—he's my guardian after all—but I'm a big girl. I can handle myself. After all, wasn't I born to do this? Taking a deep breath, I feel myself begin to drift. I know exactly what I want to see. There's no point of looking into the future if you don't have a glimpse of the past.

I was in a home that was dark and had the overwhelming feeling of evil. Opal's home. I noticed right away that her back door was open, leading to the backyard. It was daylight out. The sun shone brightly, and the heat of the summer made my brow sweat. The backyard looked just as haunted as the home. It was partially surrounded with tombstones, and the grass was brown from not being watered.

I saw her right away. It was pretty hard to miss—someone dressed in a black cape in the middle of summer. She was talking to someone. I made my way over and noticed she was talking to a little girl no more than ten years of age, with bright red hair. Queen Ezarbet.

"What brings you here, little girl?" she asked Ezarbet. Her voice sounded raspy. If I had to give a witch a voice, that would be it.

"You know why I have come. I have something you want, and you have something I want," Ezarbet stated very sarcastically, putting her hand on her hip. Even at a young age, she sounded very entitled.

Opal cocked her head. She seemed taken aback momentarily.

"What is it you think I need?"

Ezarbet stepped forward bravely, coming to stand in front of her. She was not at all intimidated by Opal's haughty look and white eyes.

"I think you want my mother's powers."

Opal let out a laugh.

"What makes you think I would need the help of a child—her daughter, no less? I can take her powers, just like that," she said, snapping her fingers, her eyes narrowing in anger.

"No, you can't. I mean no offense. You are powerful, but she has the spirits of the light on her side. To break that you would need a link—her other half. Me."

I watched as Opal quietly debated what Ezarbet had just told her.

"Why would you betray your own mother, child?"

Shrugging her shoulders, Ezarbet started to walk away.

"I am sick of being told what's right and what's wrong. I want to spell of my own free will. When I want. I shouldn't have to ask permission to do it. I want you to teach me magic that is black."

"I cannot teach you black magic, child, because you have already been touched by it."

"Then this should be easy…"

Her voice began to fade out, ending my vision of the past. I felt myself getting jolted into the future. My body was being thrown off the seat of a car, a really fast car. Brushing my hair out of my face, I tried to sit up straight, but the car swerved to the right, throwing my body to the other side. The car was zooming left to right. I felt the gears being shifted quickly. Finally the car zoomed straight, and I could get my bearings. I was driving the car. And whoa, what a car. I noticed right away the steering wheel stamped with a yellow label bearing a black prancing horse. A Ferrari. What the hell was I doing driving a Ferrari, and more importantly, why the hell was I driving like a maniac? It was pouring rain outside, the fog so thick I could barely see.

I looked at myself in the rearview mirror: my eyes were narrowed and glowing. My hair was drenched from the rain. I was holding the steering wheel so tightly that my knuckles were going white. I was clearly pissed off beyond belief. Was I being chased? I tried to look back again, but my future self swerved the car, cutting off another car. I pressed on the gas fully, which threw my body back. Agh! I grabbed hold of the front seat, swinging my body around so I was now sitting in the front and I had a better view of the car. Holy shit! It was amazing.

"Dammit!" I heard myself shout, causing me to focus on what was actually going on. I watched as my eyes shifted upward to the rearview mirror and I slammed my hand down on the steering wheel in frustration, pressing on the gas more fully, shaking uncontrollably either from the cold or anger. Maybe both. I looked back; there was a car right on our heels, flashing its lights. It was difficult to see with the pouring rain. The car swerved to the right, coming up side-by-side with the Ferrari. I inhaled sharply as soon as it pulled up, my heart slamming in my throat. It was a very familiar blue-silver Aston Martin. It looked like I was being chased by none other than Ian.

4

Bringing the goblet to my lips, I savor the taste of blood. I let it linger in my mouth before swallowing. The taste is exquisite, but I do prefer drinking from the vein. With a sigh, I set the goblet down and stood, walking over to the burning fireplace. There is a knock at my door.

"Come in," I call.

The guards come in, bowing before me. A woman with a dark cape enters, and I instantly smile.

"Queen Ezarbet, we have the guest you requested," a guard says as he stands.

"Yes, you may leave us," I say, waving them off.

As the door closes, she smiles at me, lifting her cape, her white eyes looking amber from the fire. Opal. "Look at you," she says. "You got everything you want, it seems."

"Not quite. We have to stop her," I say, knowing she knows who I am speaking of. *Scarlett.*

"Are you willing to upset the balance yet again?"

I let out a chuckle, walking to stand in front of her. *Upset the balance again? I could give two shits about the balance!*

"I would do whatever it takes to bring her down and secure what legacy I have. I will watch her people suffer."

"That's exactly what I wanted to hear," Opal says. Reaching into her cape pocket, she produces a piece of ivory paper that has been folded into four. She hands it to me, and I carefully open it. It is the other half of the prophecy. Just reading the first line brings a smile to my lips. Not reading the rest, I gently fold it back into place.

"I take it you are pleased."

"More than pleased. When do we get started?" I ask. Going over to the bureau, I put the prophecy down and turn back to her. I'm almost giddy with excitement.

"The third full moon from now. Did you not read the whole prophecy?"

"Why would I read the whole thing, if I have you to tell me about it?" I say, shrugging.

"They speak of two," she says simply.

"Two..." I say, deep in thought. If there can be two...I can't and don't want to think of yet another problem. No. I am clearly the one. I know without a doubt that this is my destiny. I need it to be. "Well, I am not concerned about the other. Once I have Scarlett cornered, she will regret the day she was born."

Opal says nothing for a long while. Either she fears disagreeing with me, or she just wants to see my plan through. She knows I hold no fear and most likely respects me for it. She is just as bloodthirsty as I.

"As you wish. So what will be your next plan of action? The longer that girl lives, the more problems await," she says, bowing her head.

Before I can respond, there is a knock on my door.

"Come in," I half yell.

The two guards come rushing in, their heads bent in fear of meeting my eyes. Behind them walks Matthias, a trusted ancient known to be the one to get a job done right. He has his dark hair pulled back into a ponytail. He has piercing green eyes and is very tall. He reminds me of a python. I've heard many stories about him—he plays dirty, and I know without a doubt that we'll get along just fine. I'm willing to pay handsomely for someone to do the things that I need done, whatever his methods.

"My queen," he says, going on one knee and bowing his head.

Walking over to him, I give him my hand. He looks up and gently brings it to his mouth, his soft lips leaving a shadow of a kiss. My body automatically heats. *Yes, he will do just fine.*

"You know why I have summoned you. I want you to go get the prophet and bring her to me. Do whatever you need to do to see this is done. I don't accept failure easily."

"Of course. I wouldn't want to disappoint," he says, standing.

"The travel preparations have been made. You will leave here in two days' time. Make yourself at home until then." Smiling, I walk over to the door and open it to let him out. I lean forward so he gets a good view of my breasts.

"I intend to," he says, walking out.

I shut the door and turn. Opal is shaking her head. "You have not lost your touch with men, it seems."

"Boys will be boys," I say, shrugging my shoulders. I walk over to Opal and grab her hand. Her fingers are long, and her nails are painted black.

"I think it's time I pay our dear friend Scarlett a visit, don't you think?" I ask softly, touching her hand gently with mine, silently telling her I need her spell to make that happen.

Flipping her hand over, I touch the scar that was made by her own hand, the marking of a witch who had touched the blackest of magic. A circle with a star, a demonic marking. My nail trails over the scar that has marred her skin. She's in a league of her own. Yes, I'm a witch, but I'm not as powerful as Opal. That day when I first approached her—when I'd decided to make a deal with the devil—I knew I'd made the right choice. Taking my mother's powers forever linked me to Opal. It's as if we are now sisters. It is too bad we're not identical, because with our powers, we're unstoppable.

She smiles at me, evilly ready to play whatever wicked game I have planned.

"As you wish..."

"I would not go after her if I were you, pretty boy." Big Red stops me from knocking on Scarlett's door.

I turn, letting out a frustrated curse. I put my hand through my newly cut hair and turn away from the door.

"I know women, and trust me when I say you don't want to go in there."

"What if she'd gotten hurt? We should have been there."

He shrugs his massive shoulders, going back to the couch. He sits on its plush pillows and continues polishing his knife.

"But she didn't. I mean, come on, you saw her defeat Abel. Fuck, we all did! She wants to blow off steam. Let her."

I shake my head in frustration. "She's not like that."

"She's more like us than you."

I turn away in pure frustration and walk toward my room. What would Big Red know? He knows nothing of Scarlett. She is not the cold being she's portraying herself to be. And all due to that stupid fool, Ian! I feel my fingers clench at the mere thought of him. He'd hurt and changed her all at the same time. The power of love! Ha! That's why I'm always guarded against such things; there's no room for romantic idealization. Of course, that doesn't mean I'm dead below the waist. Any woman I might seek would seek the same. No conversations, no strings attached. No complications.

Slamming my door shut, I snap my fingers, turning on the lights in the room. I automatically notice that the book of the Undead is lying open in the middle of the big bed. Funny—I don't remember leaving it open. I walk slowly toward it, and the pages start to turn by themselves, before coming to a stop where a particular page is missing. Sitting down, I gently pick up the old book—the book that holds many fates and that people are going to war over. "What are you trying to tell me?" I whisper aloud.

I flip the book over, starting from the back, but I quickly notice that the rest of the pages are blank. All blank. It looks like the prophecy ends with the missing page. But why would the rest of the pages be blank? It is as if the pages are just waiting to be written on.

I know that there is a bloodline of Conveyers. The Conveyers are the writers of the book of the Undead. It is said that the book chooses the Conveyer as if both are drawn toward each other. What happened with the last of the prophecy that is now missing? Closing the book, I toss it on the floor, watching as it opens to a blank page, taunting me.

Walking away from the book, I take off the shirt that Scarlett recently bought me and toss it to the floor. I walk over to the window and look out into the dark sky. The moon is stained red again, just like the previous night, when the war had begun.

Death is coming. I close my eyes against the harsh reality, leaning my forehead against the window's cold glass. Death is always just coming. Fuck!

I made a vow to protect Scarlett, and I'll see that promise upheld whether death awaits me or not.

"Scarlett..."

I wake to the sound of my name being called out softly, beckoning me to open my eyes from the deep sleep I am in.

"Scarlett..." the soft voice calls out to me again.

Rubbing my eyes, I sit up from my bed. I'm not in the hotel, though. Where the hell am I? My body is wrapped in silky red sheets, and the beautiful suite I fell asleep in is the total opposite of this room. Where the suite was white, crisp, and clean, this room is red and dark. Is this a vision? I don't remember focusing on one. Are my visions becoming erratic again?

"Scarlett..."

I hear my name again, and I slowly slide out of the bed, my feet touching the plush black carpet on the floor. I look down at myself. I'm in the same clothes I fell asleep in: blue shorts and a white tank. The hairs on the back of my neck stand, sensing danger. I go to the door; it opens into a long hallway of a home. It's quiet, the air standing deadly still.

My name is said again: "Scarlett." The taunting voice leads me to a doorway that's faintly lit along the bottom. Swallowing hard, I turn the knob. The door silently opens.

The woman stands by a window with her back turned away from me, looking out into the dark sky. She wears a fitted, red peplum dress with a pair of gold heels with the famous red sole. Her lustrous red hair falls in soft waves down her back. Queen Ezarbet. Swallowing down the rage building up deep within me, I wait to see what my vision brings next.

"Close that door behind you. You're bringing in a draft," she says.

Blinking, I turn around to see who's behind me. There's no one. Who the hell is she talking to? Moving a little farther into the room, I start to look around and realize that this is the same bedroom as in my first vision with her and Ian. I instantly cringe at just the thought of him. *Don't think of him,* I yell at myself.

"Didn't you hear me?" she says, turning toward me, her haunting black eyes focused on me.

My eyes widen and my body freezes, the blood draining from my face. My fists clench at my sides. She smiles at me, noticing the effect she has on me. She crosses her arms together, staring at me with open amusement.

"Scarlett…oh, how I have longed to finally meet you."

"That's a shame, because I am pretty sure you're going to regret it," I whisper to her.

She shakes her head as if talking to a child. "Such bravery. You humans have this incredible way of showing that, but once you are tamed, that spirit can be easily broken."

I say nothing, walking farther into the room. I am ready to launch myself at her.

"I have to say, you really did cause quite a stir in my world. Ian becoming enthralled with you…" She stops once she sees my expression. "Oh dear, I am wrong, aren't I? He is not enthralled with you. He has already gotten what he wants, hasn't he? Did he get tired of you already?" She starts to laugh. "I wouldn't be surprised if he begs me to take him back—and knowing what we shared in this bedroom, I would probably let him."

I swallow hard. She's clearly baiting me for a reaction. I won't let her see me sweat. This is what she wants. I am going to strike, but on my terms.

Then, ever so slowly, she lifts her hand to smooth away her hair, and sitting on her ring finger is a gold ring with a diamond solitaire, ruby gemstones surrounding the band. My mother's ring! My heart stops, and I let out a loud scream, hurling myself at her with full force. She disappears before I can reach her, my arms flailing, catching air. I turn and she's right behind me, grabbing me by the throat and lifting my body up, my feet lifting from the floor.

"Don't let the pretty dress fool you, human," she growls, her beautiful face twisting. She slams my body to the floor. I instantly try to get up, but she moves her hands and I fly to the wall, my body held by magic.

She smiles, satisfied, as she watches me try to struggle out of the hold she has me under. Smoothing her dress and fixing her hair, she walks over to me. She leans her body close to mine, her mouth inches from my face. Her nostrils flair; I can see her getting hungry from the scent of my blood.

"I can see now why Ian wanted you so badly," she whispers, her teeth grazing my neck.

"And I can see why he didn't want you," I say through clenched teeth.

She looks up at the exact moment I want her to, her fangs long and ready to strike. Bringing my head forward, I head butt her right to the face, catching her by surprise. She falls to the floor stunned, holding her nose. Her magic momentarily weakens and releases me. I launch myself at her.

Throwing my body on top of her, I grab her by her precious hair and knot it in my hands as I slam her head against the floor. Her nose gets bloodied from it; just looking at it brings me satisfaction. *The devil in red bleeds.* I slam her head to the floor again as hard as I can, and she lets out a scream of pain; I let out the scream of a warrior. That sound is music to my ears.

She brings her hand up to my head, and a sharp shooting pain makes me release her instantly. I feel as if my whole body is being electrocuted. I fall back, holding my head in my hands, my whole body cringing in pain. I faintly hear her moving to get up. After what seems like forever, the pain stops, but my body is too weak to get up. I feel a sharp kick to my ribs. I hold myself but won't give her the pleasure of having me cry out in pain.

"You fucking bitch!" she screams at me. She leans down and grabs me by my hair, making me look up toward her. She has blood running down her nose; I think I may have broken it. I smile.

"Oh, you find this funny, do you, human? Everyone's blood will spill, and it will be upon your hands. Give a message to your followers and that warlock of yours. Nobody is safe." She roughly lets go of my head, grabs me by the hand instead, twists it over to my wrist, and bites down hard.

5

I wake with a wrenching scream of pain. I sit up in bed and quickly inspect my wrist. It's bleeding from the imprint of her fang marks. Clenching my teeth, I close my eyes, willing myself not to let out a scream of rage. *I had her. Well, almost—if it wasn't for her stupid magic, anyway.* Hugo and Big Red burst into my room like protective brothers.

"What happened?" Hugo asks, his eyes wide and bloodshot, as if I had woken him from sleep. Big Red is the exact opposite. His eyes are hungry, and he has the knife he'd been polishing earlier, ready to take on any battle that presents itself.

"I had a visit from the queen." I lift my wrist, showing my bite marks.

"How the fuck is that possible, pretty boy?" Big Red says, heading over to me. The sight of my blood makes him pause, and I watch for a moment as he struggles. It's his nature. "Yeah, well, maybe you better get cleaned up. Then we can talk," he says stiffly, walking out the door.

Hugo walks over to where I'm sitting on the bed. He's wearing one of the shirts I bought him and washboard jeans. He looks good even with bed hair.

"What happened?" he asks.

I tell him everything. How she came to me in a vision—the message she sent and how for just for the briefest of moments I'd had her ass.

"She has my mother's ring," I whisper, looking away. He stays silent, listening to me. "What if she comes again in my vision?"

"I promise you, she won't. I will figure out a way," he says, grabbing my wrist to examine it. It's almost healed now.

"OK," I say, trusting him fully. In the short amount of time I've known him, I have come to know his word is his bond.

"Hugo, why don't you want to find Flora?"

He looks up at me, startled by a question so out of the blue.

"Who says I don't want to find her?"

"Well," I say, "you're not exactly thrilled to try to save her."

He nods his head in agreement.

"No…I am not. We don't know if we can trust her. Yes, her sister has her imprisoned, but at the end of all of this, it's still her sister. I question whether she will have the guts to go against her in the end. That is what this will all boil down to. Making a choice and choosing a side. Will that side be ours? I can't say or see that for her."

"I trust her," I say simply.

"Time will tell, but make no mistake, Scarlett. If she strikes against you, I will not hesitate to kill her," he promises. His soft brown eyes darken, and his mouth sets in a grim line.

Before I can say anything else, my cell phone starts ringing. Scrambling from the bed in search of it, I find it in my jacket. The number is unknown. Maybe it is one of the Xs.

"Hello," I say, putting it to my ear.

"Hello, Scarlett, it's Michael Pearson."

I look at Hugo and mouth Michael's name.

"Oh, hello, Michael. It's funny, I was just thinking of you," I say, putting a purr into my voice as I plop myself on the bed. Hugo rolls his eyes. Michael lets out a laugh.

"All good things, I hope."

"Of course," I say flirtatiously. Hugo puts his finger in his mouth, pretending to gag himself. I stifle a giggle.

"The bank is doing our annual New Year's Eve party, and I wanted to know if you wanted to accompany me."

"Oh…I don't know…is this a date?"

"No, no…" he stammers. "Just business, of course."

"Oh, OK, well…I guess I'll go…" I say, trying my best to sound disappointed.

"Great, I will pick you up at ten o'clock. You can text me where you are staying."

"Sounds great. And Michael…I was hoping you would've said date," I say, hanging up, smiling as I do so. This is fun.

Hugo, watching me, lets out a laugh.

"You're enjoying this, aren't you?" he asks.

"Toying with a sentinel? Yes I do, but you know what I would enjoy more?" I say, standing up from the bed.

"Let me take a wild guess." He closes his eyes, pretending that he is thinking hard. "Shopping," he says with a girlish squeal, making me laugh. I walk to my bathroom and shut the door. *I do need a dress, after all.*

Turning to the mirror, I look myself over. My hair is getting longer, and I'm beginning to look a lot more like the person in my visions. *My visions.* I wouldn't really call them a power, but more of a curse. So much is going to come, but I don't know when. *Ian.* His name floats through me as if it has a will of its own. I don't want to think of him. I know on New Year's Eve our paths will cross again. Will I be ready to see him?

Swallowing a lump that forms in my throat, I notice my glowing eyes. Putting each of my hands on the sink, I hold it in a death grip. I close my eyes and will my body to calm down. I remember Hugo's words: that my glowing eyes are my vampire side, the glow being held by my emotions. Trying to control myself, I take a deep breath. Opening my eyes, I can still see a faint hue of a green glow. Closing my eyes again, I will my body to relax. *Think good thoughts, think good thoughts,* I chant over and over. Again I open my eyes, and they're still glowing. *Dammit!*

Closing my eyes and taking a deep breath, I think of my parents, the scene when they got married. How perfect they looked together. Remembering my father waving to me in a vision, I smile softy at the thought. I feel my body become overwhelmed with calm, my hands loosening the ironclad grip on the sink. I exhale. Opening my eyes slowly, I see that the glow is gone. Maybe that's it. Focusing on my parents is the key to controlling my emotions. They will keep me centered. Turning on the shower, I remove my clothes. I think I like this new person I have become.

I come out of my vision in a rush, gasping for breath, drenched in sweat. I look around to see that I'm no longer where my vision led me. We're in a house that we rented in upstate New York. We are safe, at least for now.

"Con, what is it?" Zayah reaches for me, her beautiful eyes wide with worry.

I swallow, finding it hard to speak. I push away from her and sit up from the bed, putting my head in my hands. I feel her come to me from behind, her soft naked body against my back as she wraps her arms around me, resting her head on my shoulder.

"You said you would always tell me, no matter how bad your visions were," she whispers softly.

I close my eyes at hearing the sound of her beautiful, silky voice. I'll always remember our first encounter. Several of us were selected to become soldiers for the king. We were all training for fencing, wearing white jackets and fie masks. I was to go up against a very tall and slender opponent. I'd thought it would be easy enough. I was much bigger than the guy, but I was wrong. Oh so wrong.

I'd lunged forward, and my opponent easily sidestepped me, flipping out of the way of the saber. I'd clumsily lost my footing and tripped over myself, my big body falling to the mat. My opponent was over me in a second and pointed the saber at my heart. The instructor had clapped his hands in praise. I'd watched as my opponent lifted his mask and realized it was not a *he* but a *she.*

She'd smiled down at me, gloating. "Big muscles won't let you win everything," she'd said, pulling her mask back down and walking away. I was instantly enthralled. Watching her every move, I saw she was a woman of grace and strength.

She'd finally come around, after my unrelenting persistence. She balances me in a way no other can. She's my everything. My blood mate.

Her soft hand touches my naked chest, bringing me back to reality. "What is it?" she whispers.

"I had a vision about Big Red," I confess, not telling her the full version.

Her body stiffens beside mine. Unwrapping herself, she turns my head to look at her, looking deeply into my eyes. Can she tell I'm telling her a half-truth? Saying nothing further, she wraps her arms around me, holding me tight.

"Does he die?"

Holding her tighter, I bring my face to her hair. She smells of sweet vanilla, her skin silky smooth. The last thought in my vision was a pink lotus flower. It came to me quickly, just before I was brought out of the scene. It was beautiful. It was a bright light in the otherwise dark vision. What did it mean? I don't want to talk or think further. I move my face, and my lips seek hers hungrily. She responds with a soft moan, her nipples hardening against my chest. I lay her back gently on the bed, my growing need for her all I can think of. She can make me forget. If only for a short time. Only she can make me forget.

Fresh out of the shower, I don my skinny jeans and black-knitted sweater. Smoothing out my hair, I apply my makeup quickly. Once satisfied, I put on my now-favorite knee-high boots. Hugo is sitting and waiting patiently for me in the main room. I smile as I see him. He is wearing a white V-neck shirt, black washed-out jeans, and his leather jacket with the rosary

I purchased for him. He has that sexy bed hair again. He's come a long way from that dreaded trench coat.

"OK, so we're we off to…?" he asks, getting up from the couch.

"We are going to have the time of our lives," I say, grinning from ear to ear.

"Let me guess? Chanel?"

Walking over and putting on my jacket, I nod my head excitedly. *A kid in a candy store.*

"Yes, we can definitely start there first…Oh, and don't let me forget I have to find Big Red a suit," I say as we walk out the door.

"I don't do suits," I hear Big Red yell out.

Smiling, I close the door.

It is freezing cold outside, but of course this is New York—the streets are packed no matter the weather. Our hotel is the hub. We're in the center of all the best shops, and Hugo is right, Chanel is indeed first. We walk in, and I swear I hear church bells ringing. My eyes go everywhere. I point to this; I point to that. I'm a woman crazed for fashion. I'd always come to this store with Jewels and we'd always just browse, never really going in with any intention of buying, just dreaming.

"Um…how many shoes do you actually need?" Hugo asks me.

"Hugo, a girl can never have too many shoes," I say, rolling my eyes as I hand him another box to hold.

We go to the cashier, and she begins to ring up each item—from purses and shoes, to items of clothing and scarves, all being boxed by her assistant.

"Oh no, how are we going to get this all to the hotel?" I say, looking at Hugo as I hand her my card. She gives me the grand total with a big smile on her face.

She hands me my card back, but Hugo grabs the card from her hands, making contact with her skin. She looks up, startled, meeting him in the eyes.

"You're going to get someone to deliver this to our hotel. We are staying at the Plaza. They may leave the packages with the front desk for Scarlett Dellarentis. Do you understand me?" he whispers softly to her.

"Yes, I understand. I will do this for you," she says, blinking her eyes rapidly.

"Great. Thank you so much," he says, giving her a side grin.

As we head out I look over at him, smiling.

"That was pretty awesome."

"Yes, I suppose it was," he says, grinning.

We walk a little farther, almost passing a dress boutique, but I pause slightly once I spot what's in its window. The mannequin is dressed in the same dress from my vision. The one that I wear for New Year's Eve. I stop and admire it for a second. It's sexy, but it gives off a look of elegance.

"I need that dress," I whisper, half to myself and half to Hugo, walking in without waiting for him.

The older salesclerk greets me right away. "Hello, welcome," she says, smiling at me.

"Hi, I'm looking for that dress in the window."

"Well, I am afraid that is our last piece. I only have that one size, I'm afraid."

"It's OK. I'll take it."

"Oh. OK, great. Just give me a second to get it out from the window and get it boxed for you," she says, walking toward the window.

"How do you know it will fit you?" Hugo whispers.

"I was wearing that same exact dress in my vision for the New Year's Eve party."

Hugo nods, and we both wait for the woman to box up the item. We walk out of the store and head over to Barneys to order Big Red a custom suit. As I give the measurements, the tailor looks a bit surprised.

"Are you sure you need the arms that wide?" he asks, lifting his glasses.

"Yes, I'm quite sure. Athletes and their steroids," I say, shrugging my shoulders and shaking my head sadly.

Hugo lets out a laugh that turns into a cough. The tailor turns to look at him, and Hugo stops immediately. The tailor eyes us both suspiciously.

"Fine, you can pick these up tomorrow," he says after a minute.

"Great. Thank you for your help," I say, smiling as he walks away mumbling something about young people.

As we head out, I hail a cab. We both slide into the backseat as I give the driver an address.

"What's in Manhattan?" Hugo asks.

"Red," I say, smirking and looking out the window.

"Red," Hugo says. "Why do I get the feeling that this is not going to be a good idea?"

Upon arriving, we see the beautiful neon yellow sign that says Ferrari.

"You've got to be kidding me," Hugo says as we step out of the cab.

I purposely ignore him. There's an array of exotic cars. From Enzos to Berlinettas, all lined up perfectly, looking like a rainbow with their bright colors. I am greeted by a salesman wearing a sleek suit with graying hair parted on the side. He instantly reminds me of Mr. W. Every hair is perfectly placed, and his clothes are wrinkle-free.

"Welcome to Ferrari. Can I assist you with anything?" He smiles at me and fixes his tie. He has a Italian accent and looks at Hugo's clothes distastefully. *Hey, I picked those clothes.*

I quickly glance at his name tag and then say, "I'm just looking right now, Jack."

"We have a large variety of models."

I nod, agreeing with him, but I still don't see Red.

"Let me bring you to the back. We have the newer cars that were just brought in yesterday," he says, leading the way.

Hugo and I follow him in silence. I take a quick sideways look at Hugo and see his mouth set in a straight line. He's not happy. *Tough!* As we walk through the showroom, I see her—Red, my perfect car—and she is perfection. She's parked sideways, showcasing her beauty. She's every bit as magnificent as she was in my vision. Ironically, she's blood-red in color, with tinted black windows, chrome rims, and black leather interior. If I thought Ian's car screamed sex, this car screams orgasm.

"You like her, eh? We just got this beauty in. A 458 Italia," he says, opening the door and beckoning me to get in.

Trying to hold in my excitement, I bite my lower lip, sliding in. The smell of the new leather hits me first. The inside is better than the outside. With its high-tech gadgets, I feel as if I'm in an airplane rather than a car.

"You wanna take her for a test run?" Jack asks me.

"No, I'll take her," I say, putting my hands on the steering wheel.

"Great! Let me fetch the paperwork," he says, rushing off before I can change my mind.

The passenger door opens and Hugo slides in. He says nothing, but he still has that same look of disapproval.

"What?" I ask, looking over to see him leaning back in the seat. I fold my arms across my chest, ready to do a verbal battle with him.

"Nothing. It's just that we are supposed to be in hiding, and here you go buying a standout, 'look at me, look at me' car," he says, shaking his head.

"I'm not hiding anymore. I refuse to live like that."

"It's about keeping you safe," Hugo half yells at me.

"I don't need protection," I yell back. Now I'm seething. I didn't ask for this. Any of it.

"Um…so I have your paperwork." Jack interrupts us, his eyes wide, standing there holding the papers awkwardly.

Without looking back at Hugo, I smile at Jack brightly.

"Where do I sign?"

We drive back in silence with the radio playing "Royals" by Lorde. It would have been awesome to hear a song like this if Hugo wasn't in such a pissy mood. I know why he's upset, but frankly I don't care. Ultimately, this is my life. I will no longer be held by fear. I feel nothing. Is that so bad?

I pull up to the front of the hotel, and Hugo is right—there are people just gawking at us, looking at Red with open envy. I hand the valet the keys, and we walk in. I keep my head lowered the whole time. I refuse to see Hugo's gloating face.

After my walk of shame, I get inside my room, plopping down on my bed. Closing my eyes, I know I need to escape. Going into the future and seeing who I want to see is becoming easy for me. I zoom in on the person I want to focus on. I know exactly who I want to see. Chayton. I want to know more about this mystery man to whom I'm so drawn to.

I look around and realize I'm standing inside someone's home—a living room. It's modern in decor with black and white furnishings. Walking across the room, I sense him right away, as if I'm connected with him in some way I can't describe. He's in his bedroom, standing with his back to the doorway, facing the window. He has on a black, fitted T-shirt and washboard jeans. Walking farther into the bedroom, I look around, thinking this is definitely a guy's bedroom. His headboard is covered in black leather, and his sheets are brown with a brown fur thrown across the bed. It's a modern look, like what I've seen in fancy home magazines. Coming to stand beside him, I realize he's wearing black Ray-Ban Wayfarer sunglasses, shielding his eyes from my view. His hair is dark, bordering on black, and his skin is pale. His muscular arms are folded across his chest. He's beautiful.

I want to see your eyes, I think. Why does he seem so familiar to me? The sun's heat is on my face and, judging by the street attire of the pedestrians outside, it's summer. Chayton's staring off into the distance, his mouth set in a straight line. He looks lonely and sad. I want so badly to talk to him, but I know he can't see or hear me. So I just stand there, side-by-side with this stranger, feeling as lonely as he looks.

6

Waking up, I am left with the images of Chayton. He's perfectly etched in my head. I had an instant connection with this man that I barely knew. What is it, though? I don't know.

My stomach is turning in knots. Today is the day. New Year's Eve. While most people are already raiding the streets of New York, waiting in the freezing cold for the big ball to drop, I have other plans. Of course, I try to tell myself that I'm just nervous because of the whole plan to get the information from Michael Pearson to get to Flora, but I know deep down it has to do with Ian.

Just thinking his name makes my stomach roll with tension. I will see him for the first time in what seems like a long time, when really it's only been a few days. My mind flashes back to me crying for him to stay with me, seeing his reaction. His words haunt me. *Never again,* I promise myself. Never will he catch me so weak, so…human. Rolling out of bed, feeling angry now, I start to feel the knots in my stomach subside. I go to the bathroom and brush my teeth, heading straight into the living room afterward. Hugo is sitting in front of the fireplace with his legs crossed and eyes closed. He looks as though he is meditating, but his lips are moving. In front of him I notice a small jar filled with a clear liquid. It seems as if every time he speaks it bubbles up.

"Sleep…sleep so deeply that when you wake you will have no recognition of the night before. Sleep deeply, as you never have before," he chants softly over and over again.

I watch him, quietly fascinated by him and his power. He stops chanting, and after what seems like forever he opens his eyes.

"What are you doing?" I ask him, sitting on the couch.

He grabs the small bottle and seals it shut.

"This is a sleeping spell. It will come in handy with Michael when you get him to his apartment. You're going to need him to sleep soundly as you and Big Red search his place," he says, getting up.

"I thought we would just knock him out the old-fashioned way," Big Red says, strutting into the living room.

"That would just get messy, and we wouldn't want him alerting the queen—especially since there is a great possibility he is already spelled by her."

I nod in agreement. He's once again right. The queen will always have a backup plan. I rub my wrist, thinking of her bite.

"Well, I guess I should try to get things done now," I say, walking over to my room to shower.

"Yeah, a bunch of boxes came for you, and I got my suit this morning," Big Red says to me.

"Did you try it on?" I ask, turning around.

"Yeah. I think I'll be the best-looking bloodsucker there," he says, pretending he's blowing on his nails.

I let out a laugh, covering my mouth.

"Yeah, pretty boy. I think I am even going to give you a run for your money."

Hugo rolls his eyes heavenward.

"Here—you're going to need this." Hugo hands Big Red a ticket.

"Nice." Big Red takes it, putting it into his pocket. "Con called me. They found another location not too far from here. He just needs a few more days to wrap some things up."

"Great," Hugo and I say in unison. We smile at each other, our argument yesterday clearly forgotten.

Looking at the clock hanging on the wall, I rush toward my room.

"Time to get ready. I texted Michael the address, and he'll be arriving here at nine."

"What will you be doing until then?" Hugo asks.

"Well, they have a spa and salon here, so I plan to take full advantage of that," I say, turning and smirking at them both before entering my room.

"Thanks for asking me if I wanted to get pampered," Big Red calls out before I close the door.

"Opal, look at what this bitch did to me," Queen Ezarbet yells, blood draining from her nose. She rushes to her bathroom and grabs a towel, putting it over her nose. Her black eyes flash accusingly at me.

"I told you not to underestimate her. She is a problem that you must get rid of," I say, shaking my head. I go over to help her wipe the blood from her beautiful face. A face that was wicked in youth and now evil as an adult. What a pair we make.

"Her taste," she pauses, and for the first time I see her weakness and something else.

"What is it?" I ask curiously.

She says nothing. She turns from me and goes to her closet, purposely trying to busy herself.

"You saw something in her blood, didn't you?" I say, moving closer to her.

"It's nothing," she snaps.

I cross my arms over myself, knowing her well enough not to bait her. Something is not right. I feel it wash over me like the plague.

"I think it's time you pay Flora a visit. Her days here are numbered."

I smile behind her as she starts to undress, taking my cue. I walk away, knowing I've been silently dismissed. I have wished for Flora's death since the moment I laid my eyes on her and have hated her every moment since. She was powerful even at a young age. She was everything I was not. She was the light, while I was the dark. *Just like her mother.* Even when taking her powers, I still saw her flesh glow with light. The spirits are on her side. The only way to end this light is with her death.

I walk with a new surge of purpose. I make my way to the cages where Flora is kept. It is dark and moldy, but I find my way around easily. There she lies on the dirty, cold ground with her eyes closed, a damn white glow cast protectively around her. I smile. Soon the spirits won't have a say. Her eyes open as if sensing me and my dark thoughts. She sits up hesitantly, either from fear of the sight of me or from sheer weakness.

"Opal…" she says softly, her eyes moving left to right, eyeing me cautiously.

"Greetings," I say, moving closer to the steel bars that imprison her.

She says nothing. Even smeared with dirt, her emerald green eyes stand out brightly against her face as she regards me intently. She is skin and bones, wearing a dress that was once yellow in color and is now ripped in several places and hanging very loosely on her body. It's quite a shame to look at her like this. When I imagined taking her life, it was after a fierce battle. But nonetheless, I will gladly take her soul just as I have taken her mother's.

"I have come to tell you that your sister has made her decision regarding what to do with you."

She sits up a little straighter.

"Her decision," she says, but it's not a question.

"Yes," I whisper, relishing in this power I have longed to have for what seems like forever.

"When?" she whispers, her shoulders slumping in defeat and head going down. I can't see the look of fear that has surely come across her hollow features.

I turn away from her and start my walk back, loving the fact that I'm leaving her in limbo. *Let her suffer just a bit longer.*

I look up as I hear her walking away. So my sister has finally made a decision. I can't help but wonder why it has taken her so long.

I get up slowly; my muscles don't ache as much as they have been. I have been trying to eat as much as I can, but with food brought to me less frequently, it has been hard. Striding over to the bars that cage me, I wrap my fingers around them, trying to get my last glimpse of her. In a flash, Alexander is in front of me, making me gasp in fear. I immediately step back and in my haste I fall on my backside, my hands breaking my fall. They get scraped in the process, making me grind my teeth in agony. He smiles at me sinisterly, his beautiful face looking at me as a lion would his prey.

"I couldn't help but overhear your predicament," he says, folding his arms over his chest.

I say nothing.

"I won't let her have you—you know that, don't you?" he says quietly, looking at my hands. I watch as his nostrils flare and fangs start to protrude from his mouth.

I close my eyes and damn myself. Not only do I have my sister to deal with, but now this. As if my luck couldn't get any worse. I nod in understanding, not knowing what to say. I fear that if I deny him, I will face his wrath.

"You are mine," he says.

I am no one's! I want to yell at him, but I nod again instead.

"I will take you from here tomorrow night, and you will be my blood slave. Do you understand?"

I look up at him, surprised. Whatever happened to him wanting to drink his fill of me? *Be his blood slave? Never!* I nod again, swallowing down the revulsion that creeps up at just the thought. *I will never be your slave. I would rather die a thousand deaths than be yet again another prisoner,* my mind is yelling at him.

"Good," he says, seeming pleased that I have not spoken or disagreed with him.

He walks away from the doorway, and I let out the whimper that I have been holding back. I cover my mouth, fearful that he might hear me. I get up from the cold ground and start to scramble for the key that is to be my salvation. I dig with my shaking fingers at a brick that is held loosely in the wall, constantly looking behind me to be sure I'm not being watched. I dug the key in there, keeping it securely in place. Finding the key, I pull it out, wincing as I scrape my bloodied hand. Grasping the key, I hold it to my mouth, kissing it, tears running down my face. Looks like I'll be making my escape sooner than I thought.

Do I have it in me? What choice do I have at this point? It's either find death from my sister with the assistance of Opal or live my life as a blood slave. I grip the key to my chest, knowing what the answer must be. I will escape tomorrow morning, come hell or high water. My sister has always gotten what she wanted. Tomorrow I will succeed in proving her wrong.

Gently putting in my mother's chandelier earrings, I complete my look. I sit back in the chair, looking myself over. My hair is swept to the side, soft curls giving me an old Hollywood look. It reminds me of Marilyn Monroe in *Gentlemen Prefer Blondes.* My makeup, which was done at the same salon downstairs, is beautiful, with light smoky eye shadow that complements my eyes and, of course, red lips to match the same exact color of my dress.

And the dress! It hugs my curves in all the right places. The sweetheart neckline plunges exceedingly low, which makes me feel even sexier. I have a part to play and, boy, will I play it. I get up and smooth out my dress, which has a daring spilt exposing my left leg and the most fabulous shoes I have ever worn. They're in this sheer fabric, clear jewels sprinkled from the back to the front, my sole showing the recognizable red of a Louboutin shoe that matches my dress perfectly. I grab my matching clutch and take one last look at myself, smiling. I walk out of my bedroom just in time to see Hugo trying to adjust Big Red's tie.

"I'm telling you, she got the wrong size," he's saying, his neck raised as he slouches down so Hugo can help him.

"No, she didn't. You're just not gentleman enough for a tie. There." Hugo steps back, proud of his work. I have to say Big Red looks amazing. The black suit fits him to a T, and the black-on-black undershirt and tie makes his flaming red hair stand out.

I let out a cough to get their attention. They both look at me with eyes wide and mouths gaping. I smile shyly at them.

"Well, what do you think?" I say, spinning for them.

"Oh my fuck!" Big Red says, smiling.

"I take that as good," I say, rolling my eyes as I walk over to him and place my hand on his arm.

"You know you look ravishing, love," he says, flashing me his most charming smile.

"OK, so here is what you will need to knock him out in his apartment," Hugo says all businesslike, holding out the small glass of clear liquid that he spelled earlier.

"I'll be fine," I say to him, quietly reassuring, as I grab the glass and put it into my clutch.

He nods his head, but I can still see the hint of doubt in his eyes.

"You look breathtaking," he says instead.

"Thank you," I say, smiling, knowing he's trying hard not to chastise me.

Big Red and I head toward the door.

"OK, so this is the plan. Michael is going to meet me downstairs, so you can take the stairs. I'll see you around the gala and communicate with you," I say, pressing the elevator button. I peek a glance over at him; he's adjusting his tie, looking uncomfortable.

"As soon as I sense any danger, we are out of there, and so is this fucking tie."

"OK," I say, letting out a laugh.

The elevator door opens, and I smile at the operator. Looking back over to Big Red to say my good-byes, I see he's gone already, heading for the stairs. I step into the elevator and anxiously wait for it to reach the bottom floor. I look at my reflection in the mirror, barely recognizing myself. I look like a woman of confidence, and that is exactly how I feel. I ooze with confidence.

Smiling again as I get out of the elevator, I get many stares from everyone around me. An elderly man at the reception desk stops midconversation with the same receptionist that checked Hugo and me in when we got here. I smile smugly at her and wink at the old man, causing him to fumble with his credit card.

Walking over to the bar, I spot Michael. He's dressed in a fitted tuxedo with a black bow tie, and his dark hair is combed neatly to the side. I would have thought he looked great if I didn't know he was a rat sentinel. He has a drink in his hand and is about to bring it to his lips, but he stops as he sees me. He sets the glass down fast and comes toward me, smiling.

"A woman on time—how can a man get so lucky?" he says, his eyes roaming over my body.

"I hate being late," I say flirtatiously, trying hard not to cringe as he places his hand at the small of my back, his hand grazing the skin that's exposed.

"I think I will have every man in there dying with jealousy. You don't have a coat?" he says, escorting me out of the bar, taking my hand, and putting it on his arm.

"The cold doesn't bother me." I shift so my body is closer to his, purposely letting my breast touch his arm.

He looks at me before helping me get into the limo, his blue eyes looking deeply into mine.

"Tonight is going to be a great night," he whispers and breaks his stare, his hand pulling me forward to get into the limo.

I'm counting on it, douche bag. We take the rest of the ride quietly. He asks me a few questions about my day and so on. I peer out the window, feeling my nerves creep up on me. I try to distract myself by fiddling with my clutch. I'm going to see Ian. This is it. God, I'm not ready—or am I? *Shit!* This is no time for self-doubt. Closing my eyes, I don't even realize the limo has stopped until I feel Michael's warm hand on my arm. My stomach does a big flip-flop.

"Hey, there. Are you nervous?" he asks, smiling a little at me, lifting my chin so I can look at him.

"I guess I am a little. I'm not used to being around so many accomplished folks; I guess I'm just a bit intimidated," I say, looking down shyly, biting my lower lip again and playing my part very well as I slightly tell the truth.

"Hey, don't be. You'll knock 'em dead," he says. *Let's hope so.* Gripping my hand, he turns. The driver is already opening the door. I follow behind him, inhaling deeply, the cold air making me feel as if I can let out the breath I was holding in. Pushing my shoulders back and holding my head high, I grip Michael's arm tighter, pushing my body flush to his side, smiling up at him confidently. *It's showtime.*

I really don't know what hit me first. The flash of her big blue eyes full of life or the scent of the sweetest blood I have ever smelled in my lifetime. I can't help but overhear her conversation with her friend, who is hanging on her every word. *Women!*

"I mean, can you believe this guy or what? He's just too romantic. What guy buys you flowers *and* cooks you dinner?" she says dreamily, her blue eyes going glassy. A strand of blond hair that has escaped from the tight bun that sits perfectly on top of her head, as though it were a crown, tickles her cheek, and she tucks it behind her ear. Her fitted white shirt hugs her curves, nicely showing off her ample breasts, and her pencil skirt makes her legs look as if they go on forever.

"You're so lucky! You always get the good ones," her friend says to her. They are about to walk past me as I wait in line.

She tilts her head back and laughs, showing me the paleness of her throat. Her laugh…it's the most beautiful sound I have ever heard. As though sensing me, she looks my way and stares, her blue eyes going wide. I hear her swallow hard. I cockily smile at her, blocking her and her friend from going any farther.

"Hello," I say, looking more closely at her, looking for any imperfection. I can't find any. She's flawless.

She says nothing—just narrows her pretty blues at me.

"Hi," her friend says too eagerly, nudging her to respond.

"I'm Bastian, but some of my friends call me Big Red. Are you here for the gala?"

I hear her let out an annoyed breath and see her roll her eyes. I hear her mutter under her breath, *Yeah, I bet you say that to all the ladies.* I pretend not to hear her, just cast an amused look at her.

"Big Red…I like that," says the girl beside her. "My name is Kiley. No, we aren't here for the gala; we're actually working for one of the shows that will be airing live. Playing dress-up for the celebrities. We were just heading there."

I shift my attention to her friend. She is pretty enough, with big brown eyes that match her hair and porcelain skin, but she pales in comparison to her friend, who still refuses to acknowledge me. My eyes drift back to the blonde. I smile at her. I never had a woman play hard to get. *Challenge accepted.*

"And what's your name?" I ask softly.

"Late. Come on, Kiley. We have to get back," she says, urging her friend forward. Before she can walk away from me, I grab her by her arm, pulling her toward me—not with enough force to scare her, though I feel her body stiffen. I get very close to her ear, so she alone can hear me.

"I wouldn't have just bought you flowers. I would've laid you over them and fucked that sweet body of yours till you were so sore that every time you moved you would think of just me. Now that's what I call romantic." I hear her gasp, pulling her arm away from me, and I feel as if she's holding herself back from slapping off the smug look I'm throwing her.

"Dream on, asshole! As if that would ever happen." She walks away from me as her friend stands there wondering what the hell happened.

“Sooner rather than later,” I shoot at her retreating back.

“Oh my God, Jewels! What happened?” I hear her friend say in the distance.

“Cocky bastard is what happened. He must think that any girl would just drop her panties with his one-liners.”

“I would’ve…Oh, come on! He’s hot—and that red hair… I’ll be thinking about him for days.”

“Oh God, Kiley, you’re such a mess,” she says, laughing at her and shaking her head.

“Excuse me, sir. Do you have your invitation?” The old doorman forces me to break my stare. He’s looking up at me, his eyes showing a worrisome look as he takes in my size.

Digging into my pocket, I produce the ticket that was craftily supplied by Hugo. Handing it to the man, I adjust my tie. *Damn Scarlett and this fucking tie!* He hands me the ticket back and I glide in, taking in the place. It’s filled with people of the wealthiest of classes. A server passes by me, offering me a glass of champagne. I shake my head politely. Taking my place at the bar, I order a scotch and start scanning the crowd. I see Scarlett right away. She stands out against all the rest in her flaming red dress. We make eye contact, and I give her a wink in acknowledgment. She smiles softly before looking up at Michael adoringly as he whispers in her ear.

“Sir, your drink,” the bartender says, placing the amber liquid before me. I lift it up to my lips, letting the taste linger in my mouth for a moment as I fall deep into thought.

I watch as Michael hands Scarlett a champagne glass and she seductively brings it to her lips. I have to wonder how far she will take this with Michael. Will she do all that is necessary to get the information on the queen? Even sleep with him if she has to? Hell, I am not one to judge. If she wants a rebound lay, she should get it. God knows I've had my share of the female population. Thinking back to the blonde with the eyes full of life, I smile.

Turning, I put my glass down, and I notice a woman staring at me. She's older but still very beautiful. Her hair is dirty blond and swept up partially in an updo. Her dress is cut down, exposing her shoulders and dipping low enough to still be considered modest. She smiles at me as she lifts her glass of champagne to her lips, and I can't help noticing a huge diamond on her ring finger. It's all the same for these rich housewives. They're bored with their everyday life of shopping. They're lonely as their husbands go away for travel or out to the country club to play golf. It's the same time and time again. *Humans!* But of course, who am I to judge? I raise my glass to my lips, smiling at her as I smell her arousal drift toward me, beckoning me to ease the ache her own husband can't possibly satisfy.

Her husband comes then, breaking her stare from me, gently placing his old wrinkled hand on her shoulder. No wonder she's bored. The guy is practically her father. She peeks a glance back at me, and I lift my drink to her, giving her my silent promise of satisfaction.

"Can you get your head outta your pants?" Scarlett's voice whispers in my head.

I let out a chuckle, my eyes searching the crowd for her.

"What? I'm bored. You're not the only one who'll be sucking face tonight."

"Agh, don't be such a pig. Just don't want you to get caught with your pants down when shit goes down."

"Wouldn't be the first time," I say, shrugging as I catch sight of her. She rolls her beautiful eyes heavenward. I am beginning

to enjoy our banter. I signal the bartender for another drink. He right away hands me another. Taking my drink, I absently touch the rim with my finger, deep in thought again. I have to admit, when I first heard of the human female prophet, I was not a believer; I hated her and all she represented. I only resentfully went along with Con and the others on this wild goose chase. I thought it was a load of bullshit, frankly. How can one human—and a female at that—save a world that is so bent on destroying itself? I took one look at her after her change, saw her big eyes full of fear, and thought we were all done for.

That was until I saw her in battle with Abel, when she fully gained my respect. She is everything Con said she was. I'm now a believer. I knew after that I would die for her just like I would for Con, my ally, my brother. We go way back—and when I say way back, I don't mean years, I mean centuries. He saved me from myself.

I can still remember when we first met. I was this young, untrained vampire who was reckless in everything I did. So reckless that I was summoned by the king for death. In our world, you remain hidden. It's the law. I, of course, thought I was above the law. Con talked to the king, saying I would be useful. With my fighting talents, I proved to be an asset. I owe Con my life.

Turning, I lean back so my body is against the bar. I begin to scan the crowd, which is starting to thicken. The air changes, and my nostrils flare in recognition. I quickly start to move through the crowd, scanning again for Scarlett and Michael. I spot her and she looks up, her face a little pale, before she quickly adjusts herself so she looks indifferent. She makes eye contact with me and nods.

There is another vampire here.

7

So this is definitely not your average "balloons everywhere, whistles blowing" kind of New Year's Eve celebration. This is a party of sophistication. The men wear black suits and ties, and the women wear beautiful, lavish ball gowns. Just like in my vision, there are butlers serving trays of caviar and champagne in flute glasses. Michael keeps me close at his side, introducing me to his colleagues, showing me off. I smile graciously and shake their hands. These are high rollers for sure, from doctors to people in the political world. I can't help but feel out of place.

I look around as Michael converses; he keeps stealing glances at me to make sure I'm OK, and I can see every time his eyes dip lower to glance at my cleavage. Smiling at him reassuringly, I start to look around again. Big Red is leaning against the bar, looking a bit lost in thought. If I feel out of place, he sure looks it.

The hairs on the back of my neck stand. I stiffen for an instant. My eyes meet Big Red's briefly.

"Are you OK?" Michael asks me as he feels my body tense.

Swallowing hard, I look at him and plaster on a fake smile. "Yes, sorry."

The band in the background begins to play a beautiful jazz melody. His eyes light up, and he moves closer to me to whisper in my ear.

"Come on." He places his hand at the small of my back and guides me to the dance floor. As we reach the center of the floor, his hands go around my waist, bringing me closer to his warm body, and I wrap my arms around his neck. We start to move to the sound of the music. I look over to Big Red again, who has also sensed that there is danger close by. But it isn't the kind of danger he is thinking of. It is worse. I'd felt him before I'd even seen him. I'd zinged with awareness, my treacherous body betraying me.

"It's Ian. Let me take care of him," I whisper to Big Red's mind.

"This should be interesting," Big Red says back to me, nodding.

"OK. We have five minutes before the countdown, ladies and gentlemen," a small man with a microphone announces, breaking me from my conversation with Big Red. "Thank you all for attending New York Bank's Annual Celebration. It is great to celebrate with our VIP customers. To all the new clients, we welcome you. Please grab a champagne glass, and let's toast in the new year together."

Michael leans in to whisper in my ear, his chin stubble tickling my skin.

"Would you think I was too forward if I said you are the sexiest woman here tonight?"

I can't stop myself from throwing my head back and laughing. He whisks me away from the dance floor, stopping at a butler with a tray. He grabs two champagne glasses, handing me one. I bring the glass to my lips, taking a sip of the sweet liquid—and I freeze. I know I should have expected this—hell, I should have been prepared for this—but still his presence alone has stunned me. Ian.

He looks every bit as great as he did in my vision. His black suit, with a matching bow tie, fits him to perfection. His pale blond hair is slicked to the side perfectly. *James Bond, eat your heart out and bury your body!* I put up my wall, deciding that his presence does nothing to me, and my heart turns to ice.

Just then, like in my vision, the small man comes back on the mic again and begins the countdown. Michael smiles down at me, and I return his smile seductively as he wraps his arm around my waist. I look over at Ian and he meets my stare, looking between Michael and me. His stare is icy; he's clearly not happy.

"Five...four...three...two...one...Happy New Year!" everyone screams in unison.

I look over to where Ian stands, arching my eyebrow. I lick my lips, taunting him.

"Happy new year," my mind whispers to him.

He jerks back a little, looking surprised. He's stoic, as if he knows what I am about to do.

I turn to look up at Michael. He starts to lower his head as he looks at me, desire clear in his eyes. I slide my hand up the front of his suit, wrapping my hands around his neck and bringing his head down to mine as I kiss him...while Ian stands there and watches. I pour everything I have into this one kiss—the hurt, the anger, and most of all the hate I have for him.

Michael seems a bit startled by my aggressiveness, but he holds me tightly, entwining his tongue with mine. He tastes of champagne and mint. I can feel his want for me as he pulls me in closer. I pull away from him hesitantly, biting my lower lip as I look up at him shyly.

"I'm sorry. I don't know what came over me, but I can't seem to help myself when I'm with you. I just don't want this night to end," I say, looking away.

Michael grasps my chin gently so we're once again meeting eye to eye. His eyes are dark with desire as he smiles down at me. *Sucker.*

"Don't be sorry. I don't want this night to end either. I don't live too far from here..." He stops, his request undeniable.

"Just give me a moment to freshen up. I'll be right back." I reach and place a soft kiss on his lips, promising him a night to remember. Unfortunately, he won't remember.

I walk away, heading for the ladies' room, smiling at several people as I gulp the last of the champagne before handing the flute to a server, walking more confidently than ever. I know Ian is following me. This was inevitable. He grasps my arm, forcing me to turn before I head into the ladies' room. His touch sends a jolt of recognition through my body. I automatically feel hot, though hot isn't really the word. I sizzle.

"What the fuck do you think you're doing?" he whispers to me, his cold, steel-blue eyes shooting daggers my way.

"Get your hands off me," I say, yanking my arm from him, looking around, not wanting to cause a scene.

"I asked you a fucking question." His hand tightens as he starts to pull me from the bathroom door.

"I believe she said to let her go," Big Red says near the doorway where the party is taking place, still holding his scotch in his hands. His stare is fixed on Ian's hand on me. He and Ian have unfinished business. Looks like he is ready for round two. Ian laughs at him.

"You're going to have to kill me first, Bastian. I suggest you leave now," he says menacingly. I look at Ian again. He looks like a man who is not going to stand down. *Goddamn it!* I don't need this right now. Michael could come at any minute and become suspicious. It would ruin everything.

"Big Red, it's OK. Ian just wants to talk, and then he'll be leaving." Ian snickers. I ignore him, trying to pacify Big Red.

"You sure? 'Cause I would be more than glad to *talk* to Ian," he says, slowly bringing his drink to his lips. He's trying very hard to contain himself; I can tell by his whitening fingers on his drink. I think the glass could shatter in his hand at any moment.

"Yes, I'm sure," I say, smiling at him. He grudgingly nods and gives Ian a silent warning before retreating.

"What is it that you want?" I ask, my voice low and angry as I turn back to Ian. He looks down at me, his eyes darkening as they roam all over me. I feel my body begin to heat up again as I suddenly feel naked.

"I think you know exactly what I want." He pulls me into the bathroom before I have a chance to come back with a smart remark.

Being dragged inside makes it clear what he wants. It's what I want too. *Fuck, this is not going according to plan!* But it's as if my body has a mind of its own. Breathing heavily, my mind is made up.

"Excuse me! You cannot be here, mister," an older lady yells, her puffy cheeks going red with anger. She eyes me and Ian, apparently knowing we're up to no good. I would laugh if it were different circumstances, but now I just want her to get the hell out. Ian lets me go and grabs ahold of her, looking deeply into her eyes.

"You will leave here and won't remember us. This bathroom is out of order."

"Yes, it's out of order," she says in a daze.

"Now leave," he commands.

She obeys, saying nothing more. He locks the door, leaving us alone.

"Why are you here?" I have to ask, even though at this very moment it doesn't matter.

"I came back for what is mine," he says simply.

"Yours?" I ask sarcastically.

Before I can say anything else, his lips come crashing down on mine. His kiss is so very different from Michael's. This kiss is fire. It burns every part of me. Michael's body is warm, yes, and Ian's is cold—but it's a burning cold that lights me up like a fever. My hands are in his hair instantly, bringing him closer as my breasts crush against his chest. I moan softy as he leaves my lips and starts to trail kisses to my neck.

"Does he kiss better than me? Can he make your pussy wet like I can?"

I swallow as I hear his crude words.

"I guess you're just going to have to find out," I resort to taunting him back, trying to bait him.

He looks up at me, his mouth clenched in anger. *Hook, line, and sinker.* He roughly turns me so I'm facing the sink, my back toward him. Our eyes meet in the mirror. I look wanton, my face flushed, my breasts nearly spilling out of my dress. He looks dead set on proving a point.

He starts on my shoulders, licking and kissing, making me shiver with response. My thighs are quivering with need. He kneels down on the floor, lifting my dress, slowly revealing my backside to him. I've never felt so wickedly exposed.

"Grip the counter and spread your legs," he commands, his voice alluring but still holding a hint of his anger. I do what he wants; at this point, I can no longer think.

His hands caress my ass, going between my legs, briefly making me moan loudly. Just when I feel the gentleness of his touch, the palm of his hand crashes down, slapping me on my ass, making my eyes open widely. *Oh God!* This is so hot; I think if he did that again I'd be ready to come apart right here.

I feel his lips on my flesh where he'd hit, kissing almost tenderly. Then another slap follows. I grip the counter tighter. Now I realize why he wanted me to hold on. Again he kisses me where he hit. Then, when I think I can't take anymore, I feel his teeth sink into me. I gasp from the sting on my tender flesh but quickly feel as if I'm floating. I'm going to lose myself. I grasp his head, pulling him closer to me as he drinks. Looking back in the mirror, I can't help but think that this is the most erotic thing I have ever seen.

And as if things couldn't get any more erotic, he moves from drinking me to moving my thong to the side, placing his lips at the center of me and plunging his tongue deep inside. I put my hand over my mouth, screaming as I explode on his devious tongue. He takes his time licking my release, holding me up because I'm absolutely sure I'm going to fall.

He stands up. I don't even realize he's unzipped his pants until he drives into me with one forceful thrust. I gasp again, holding onto the counter for dear life as he starts to fuck me hard. My body begins to feel on edge again from the pleasure. I look into the mirror, and his eyes meet mine. I quickly close them. He can have my body, but not my mind. Never again.

"Open your eyes. I want you to see it's me fucking you and not him." He yanks my hair, forcing me to look at him as he drives harder inside me. The sound of our flesh slapping is echoing around us. I push back against him urgently as I feel myself on the verge of climax. He lets go of my hair and slaps my ass again, growling, and that is my undoing. I scream from the force of it, my body shaking as I lean over the sink, my face up against the mirror. With the force of my orgasm tightening around him, he places his hand on my shoulder, holding me in place as he comes, groaning his pleasure.

Both catching our breaths, we say nothing. He pulls out of me, and I hear the sink turn on. A warm cloth is put between my legs as he cleanses me. His gentleness startles me. *This is a first.* I pull away from him, starting to fix my dress and hair, still not looking at him. I look the same as I did coming into the bathroom, though my cheeks are still flushed and my heart is still racing. I turn to leave, not wanting to look at him.

"Where do you think you're going? We are not finished here," Ian says, his hand shooting out, stopping me from leaving. He looks perfect, seeming unfazed by what just happened.

"Yes, we are. What's the problem? We both got what we wanted, right? It's just fucking, remember?" I yank my arm from him, and he lets me go. As I exit, I swear I see him flinch with surprise.

She'd taken me by surprise, her eyes glowing as she'd flung my words back at me. My body instantly hardens again, and I have to stop myself from yanking her back and taking her again.

I wait a few more moments after she leaves before exiting the ladies' room. I watch her go back to this Michael Pearson, this man who is Queen Ezarbet's sentinel. She smiles at him, and he puts his hand at the small of her back, leading her outside to a waiting car. I clench my teeth in anger, keeping myself from ripping his filthy hands off her. *Mine!*

I turn and meet Big Red's eyes across the room and smile at him, purposefully zipping up my pants, letting him know what just took place between Scarlett and me. Big Red just smiles, but the tick in his jaw gives him away as he starts to leave as well. I start to follow, maintaining a good distance. I know where Michael lives.

Since leaving Scarlett, I decided it was best this way; the real problem was I couldn't seem to stay away. I could think of nothing but her since the moment I'd left. My mind kept reflecting back on the look of hurt on her face. It haunted me. Seeing her tonight had just added fuel to the fire. She'd looked stunning walking into the gala—not as the young lady I'd first met, but as a woman. She was confident and sure of herself. Seeing her with Michael only finalized my decision. I am a heartless, selfish bastard who takes what he wants. Putting my hands in my pockets, I walk out into the cold, watching drunken fools sing "Auld Lang Syne." I still can't get her out of my head. Her voice in my head—was it imagined? No. I'm sure it's a new power. I'd like to find out, but knowing Scarlett, she's going to make me work for it.

Feeling a smirk cross my face, I stop walking as I see their limo come to a stop. The driver opens their door, and Michael gets out first, leaning down to grasp her hand. She gets out and my breath catches. She is still the most desirable woman I have ever seen. She's different, though. I noticed it when I first saw her standing there proudly in her red dress, looking like a Greek goddess; there is something different about her eyes.

I watch as Michael leads her to the doorway of his luxury apartment building. Of course I already know there is a doorman and they have the ultimate security. Why does one human need so much security? Michael Pearson is not a dumb man. Big Red approaches, walking past the building as though an innocent pedestrian, looking briefly inside the glass windows as he watches Scarlett being led inside an elevator by Michael. I watch as Big Red takes out his cell phone and starts to text, most likely Scarlett. Of course Big Red can't get inside without being noticed. Did they not plan ahead? Is it her intention to spend the night? *Like fuck she will!* Clenching my jaw, I approach him. As he sees me, his green eyes darken.

"What kind of shit-show operation is this?" I say, barely holding my anger in check as I try not to punch the smug look off his face.

"You have a lot of nerve just showing up here," Big Red says, not answering my question. His phone beeps in response; he grabs it, looking down at the text.

"Well, what does it say?" I ask furiously.

Big Red just smirks at me. "You have no part of this anymore," he says, walking away from me.

"Yeah…We'll see about that. There's a back entrance you can get in. You can meet her that way. His apartment number is 9B."

"I'm not going in. That was never the plan," he says, still walking away.

"What do you mean that isn't the fucking plan?" I yell after him.

"She can take care of herself. Duty calls," he says, walking back over to the gala.

I run a hand through my hair furiously; it takes everything I have not to drag him back and make him go up there and protect her. I've never felt so out of control in my life; this feeling is foreign to me. I felt it once before, when I saw her being held by Abel and I was powerless to help her. I didn't like it then either. I don't like the feelings she evokes in me.

I didn't like the words of anger I threw at her. I didn't like the look she gave me when I did. But most of all, I didn't like the feeling of leaving her.

Going to the back of the building, I find a guard standing there.

"Hello, sir. I will let all the staff know that you have arrived," an African American man says. He is wearing a suit and has an earpiece.

"You already know what the plan is. Turn off the cameras when I give the OK. Got that?" I say, looking deeply into his eyes.

"Yes, the cameras will shut down," he says, opening the door for me.

"Thank you. Make sure no one goes to the ninth floor. I will be securing that area," I demand, walking forward with purposeful strides.

"Yes, sir," the man says, walking to the control room in the opposite direction.

What Scarlett and Big Red don't know is that I already have the guards entranced. To play in this game, you have to play dirty. If Scarlett thinks she is going to do this alone, she'd better think again. Getting out of the elevator, I walk to Michael's door. I've already scanned the apartment and found the information Scarlett needs. I smile as I picture her face full of anger and shock. I can hear her soft voice through the doorway and Michael's laugh in response. Trying to contain a growl, I wait patiently.

Thinking back to that moment when I first saw her at the gala, I know now what was so different about her eyes: they looked as cold as mine.

Laughing, I stare at the beautiful woman in red before me. I've wanted her from the moment she walked into my bank with her annoying dog. With her long dark hair and exotic eyes, she's had me wrapped around her finger ever since. And the fact that she has money helps immensely. She leans forward and removes my jacket, smiling up at me, biting her lip shyly. I feel myself get hard just by her looking at me like that.

"Let's get you more comfortable," she says softly.

I say nothing, just letting her take over. She removes my bow tie, letting it drop to the carpeted floor while still maintaining eye contact with me. She pushes me back so I fall softly onto my couch.

"I'm thirsty; do you want a drink?"

How can she possibly think of a drink now? I am ready to explode.

"No, but you can help yourself to the bar," I say, pointing behind her.

She turns around and walks gracefully to the bar, making herself a drink. *God, she looks sexy, even when she concentrated.*

"So how long have you worked at the bank?" she says, breaking me from my stare.

"A couple of years. You know I started off just like Greg's position as an investment coordinator."

"Really? And just a couple of years later you became the president?"

I grin at her. *Smart girl.*

"I landed a huge account. Guess I just got lucky." I let my eyes roam over her face. I look down and notice her clutch bag on the floor, open. I lean over and pick it up, shutting it closed. *Women and their purses.*

"Wow. Talk about being in the right place at the right time."

I smile in response. Indeed, I was in the right place at the right time. I can still remember meeting with Ezarbet. She'd responded only in e-mail to me that she was looking to invest in the United States. She'd heard about me, that I was a new up-and-coming investment coordinator. How she got my name or e-mail address is still a mystery, but I was intrigued. I was to meet with her at a location of her choosing, and when I recommended I bring a colleague, she refused. It was just me, or the deal was off.

A driver had picked me up and led me to a very secluded area in Greenwich, Connecticut. I tried to peer outside, but it had been dark as we headed into a heavily wooded area. Finally we stopped in front of a large black gate; it had creaked as it opened. The home had reeked of ambiance. With its stone finish, it resembled a small castle. There were guards everywhere. One of the men had opened the door for me. I instantly feared for my life. He had a hideous scar going down his face, and he was huge. He carried a sword by his side and told me to follow him; I kept my eyes on his back. I couldn't help but think to myself, "Who carries swords nowadays? Surely a gun would suffice?" But I remember thinking, staring at his back, that it looked like this man would want to kill you slowly if he had the chance. We stopped at a door and he knocked, waiting patiently to get the OK to enter.

"Come in," a sultry voice called.

We entered the hugest living room I'd ever seen, before or since. I don't know if "living room" is even the appropriate name for this room. It was grand. Besides the intricate details on the burning fireplace, the furnishings looked very royal, all reds and golds. *Who the fuck is this lady?*

"Queen Ezarbet. May I present Michael Pearson," the huge man said, bowing to her.

A queen! I was shocked, to say the least. I had just struck gold. I looked to see where she was and noticed she was sitting on a chair, slightly turned so she was facing the fire. Her profile was very beautiful. Her cascading red hair fell down her back, exposing her pale skin. I felt a stirring in my groin.

"You may leave us, Abel."

Abel had moved to leave, eyeing me in warning before he did so. I quickly looked away.

"Thank you for joining me, Mr. Pearson," she said, getting my attention quickly.

"I am sorry...I didn't know you are a queen. What country?"

She started to laugh, still not turning to acknowledge me. I cursed myself for speaking out.

"I am a queen to my people."

I breathed out. I wasn't qualified for this. Surely she would need someone with more experience.

"I think there's been some mistake. I don't think I'm the man you seek to help you. I can give you a few names of men that I think would better suit your needs." I reached into my briefcase, trying to find the business cards.

"I have watched you for a long time, Michael. Don't think I don't know what you crave." She turned to me then, and I saw her very dark eyes. She looked almost angelic, in a dark sort of way. I couldn't help but fall under her spell. "You crave success, money, power? I can get you all your hopes and dreams just like *that*." She snapped her fingers.

"How? What do you want me to do?" I asked. How did she know? That *was* what I craved the most. I didn't want to be a consultant all my life. I was drowning in debt.

"It's time for me to invest in the States. You move my money here and there. You work for me privately. I don't want my name on the books, do you understand?"

"I don't have access to the accounts like that. I am just a consultant." I shook my head.

"You let me worry about that." She came closer, and I found myself captivated by her. It was almost as if she'd been weaving me in her web, and I'd been too fascinated to be let go.

So we sealed our bond not with a handshake, but with a bite. That was the day I'd learned of vampires. True to her word, she came through. Everyone at the bank was under her spell. The president stepped down, and I was promoted. No one questioned it. I did exactly what she wanted me to. Kept her off the books. I invested her money all over the world, from real estate to bogus charities, making sure she invested in everything she could make money on. She also invested in blood banks; I guess it made it easier for her kind to buy the supply through her. It led her people to depend on her.

My thinking on the whole blood slave thing is this: eat or be eaten. I follow the rules. I enjoy the power, money, and success of it all. Who wouldn't? The queen does know me very well. I have been to places that I've only dreamed of and owned properties that you would see on television. I'm living the high life. Am I betraying my kind? Yes. Do I feel guilty? No. Not by one ounce. I don't owe anyone anything. I do what I have to do to survive. It's been survival of the fittest. And I have survived.

"Are you sure you don't want any?" Scarlett asks, coming back toward me, holding a pink drink that bubbles on top.

I look curiously at it. I have to keep my head about me; I'm planning for us to go at it all night long.

"No, thanks."

"That's too bad. I wanted to share," she pouts sexily. She sits very close to me on the love seat. I turn and her lips meet mine. I capture her face between my hands, and she leans over me to straddle my hips.

"I like to share. Open your mouth," she says, so alluringly that I can't help but comply.

She brings her drink to her mouth and goes back to my lips, pouring the sweet drink into my mouth. She smiles down at me, her eyes twinkling as she watches me drink. I feel ready to come right then and there.

"See? Don't you like to share?" she asks, bringing her mouth back to mine, kissing more forcefully. I feel my heart speed up even as I start to feel very groggy. *Fuck!* What's wrong with me? I pull away from her, shaking my head.

"What's wrong?" she asks, but she's still smiling.

"I, um…I have to use the bathroom." I pull her off me gently and begin to get up. I wobble as I start walking, and my vision begins to double.

"What the fuck is happening to me? Oh my God—am I dying?" I fall to my knees, my chest feeling as though it's ready to explode. I don't realize I've said the words out loud until she kneels beside me. Her beautiful eyes are glowing brightly.

"Not today," she says.

I try to lift my head and speak; the world around me is starting to fade out. She gets up, and all I can remember is watching her sexy shoes as she walks away from me.

8

Walking away from Michael's limp body on the floor, I stride to the doorway. Peeking through the peephole, I see Ian with his head down, shielding his eyes, his face contorted in anger. *Good! I hope he enjoyed the show.* As if I didn't know he was there the whole time—I feel as if my body is totally in tune with his. *Will that ever go away?* I unlock the door.

"What are you doing here?" As soon as I swing it open, he brushes past me and goes into the living room. His eyes look stark black. He walks in with purpose.

"What are you doing?" I ask again as I see him go over to Michael's limp body. My eyes widen as he roughly pulls Michael's head up by his hair. He grabs him by the neck as if to break it.

"Ian, stop—" I half scream.

"You think to toy with me? Is that the game we're now playing? Because, Scarlett, when you get to know me, you're going to realize *I* always win."

I shake my head in denial. *Get to know him?* He has a wild glint in his eyes I've never seen before.

"Don't do that. I need him alive, dammit. He knows where the queen is keeping Flora. We need Flora, Ian." I rush over, trying to pry his arms away from Michael. Michael is groaning now in pain.

He says nothing but still doesn't release Michael.

"Damn you…this is my…my…stakeout!" I have no idea what to call this thing with Michael. "I knew you were there the whole time," I admit softly.

He releases him then, Michael's head falling down with a thump.

I exhale in relief. We stare at each other for a long time. He starts to walk toward me, and I put my hand up, stopping him. "Stop," I say, suddenly feeling tired. Emotionally. He looks away from me briefly and has the audacity to look uncomfortable.

"I realize I hurt you—"

I let out a laugh, stopping him.

"Hurt? How can you speak words you can't possibly know about? I actually thank you. You taught me a few things." I pause, curling my lips suggestively. "I thank you for making me see the bigger picture. I can't get blinded by this bullshit." Shaking my head, I walk away from him and his demanding eyes and start looking through Michael's bedroom. It's a modern bedroom, elegantly decorated but giving off a masculine feel. I go through his walk-in closet, carefully looking through some boxes and placing them carefully back into place.

"I have a proposition for you," Ian says, leaning in the doorway, watching me.

My back stiffens. *Why don't I like the sound of that? What's he up to?* "I don't make deals with the devil. Unlike some people I know," I say sarcastically.

"Everyone does, and I think I have an offer that you are not going to refuse."

"I doubt it." I briskly walk past him, careful not to touch him.

I go into Michael's personal office. *Bingo!* I start to look through his cabinets, leafing through files, looking for anything that might give me a clue. I sit on his chair and start looking through drawers. As I go to close one of them, I notice it's caught on something. My curiosity spiking, I take the drawer out and notice a small remote. Picking it up, I see a neon green button on it. Pressing it, I'm amazed to see one of the paintings on the wall opening up to reveal a hidden safe. Getting up quickly, I walk toward it and open it, noticing a file. *Yes!* Backing up, I open it quickly—it's empty. *Why the hell would there be an empty file hidden behind a painting?* Letting out a frustrated breath, I slam the empty file on the desk.

"Do you want to hear my proposition now?" Ian says, walking into the small office.

"Listen, I'm not into your indecent proposal," I say, crossing my arms around myself but still curious. *Curiosity killed the cat.*

He arches his eyebrow, and I break my stare. I feel myself flush from our previous encounter. *Indecent proposal indeed!* He reaches inside the jacket of his suit and produces some papers neatly folded into four.

"What is that?" But I think I already know; I just want to hear him say it.

"The answers to your questions. The information needed to find Flora," he says simply.

"OK...Why do you have it? Or...let me guess. Here comes the proposition part, am I right?"

"I want to meet with you tomorrow night, after you send the witch out on this wild goose chase."

"He's a warlock! And no, I won't meet with you tomorrow night or any other night. You know I can easily take that from you." My fists clench at my sides.

He tilts his head to the side and actually looks at me admiringly.

"I would love nothing better than to get in a tussle with you, but we both know how that would end once we got our hands on each other."

I inwardly groan as my body begins to heat. God, he is right. Besides he just wants to meet tomorrow. What harm could that do? Flora's life is at stake.

"OK, fine, I'll meet with you tomorrow. You have my word. Then we cut ties." I hold out my hand, waiting for him to agree to the deal. His steel-blue eyes flash triumphantly as my will bends to his game. He hands me what I need in order to find Flora. Our hands touch briefly, and I feel a jolt of electricity go up my arm. *Will that ever change?*

"I think the *warlock* will be able to narrow down the location," he says, breaking my thoughts. I don't say anything; I just nod my head in agreement, walking past him. I'm now almost desperate to leave. Of course, I can tell myself it's to go straight to Hugo with the information on Flora's whereabouts. I can picture him pacing back and forth, impatiently waiting for my return. But it's really to get away from Ian. He's *snaking* his way back in my life. I don't like the way he's making me feel. There's the hate, but underlying that is something more. Something I don't even want to begin to broach. As I make my way out of the apartment, I pass through the living room first, grabbing my clutch and taking out my cell phone to text Big Red.

Got the info we needed. I'm leaving now.

That's good to hear, love. I'll make my way there; leaving now.

Where are you?

Duty called.

OMG. Really?

When I say duty calls, I'm never joking.

Rolling my eyes, I put my phone in my clutch along with the papers. Snapping it shut, I briefly look at Michael, still sleeping soundlessly on the floor. He doesn't even know it, but he's been close to death tonight. Next time he won't be so lucky.

When I'm almost at the door, Ian grabs me by the arm, turning me toward him. I instantly try to yank my arm away.

"You will meet me in my room right when the sun sets," he says quietly.

"Your room?" I ask. His hand tightens as I begin to pull.

"Yes. I think you are rather familiar with it. The Plaza. Room one one three zero." He smirks at my look of surprise.

"OK, fine. Let me go." He releases me. I practically race to the elevator. I press the buttons frantically, just wishing to be away from him. As soon as it dings open, I all but throw myself in there.

"Just know, Scarlett, this will be the last time you run away from me. I always get what's *mine,*" he promises me as the elevator door shuts on his beautiful, menacing face.

Pacing back and forth in front of the door, I wait impatiently for Scarlett to return. I should have gone with them. Big Red texted me that all was well and Scarlett made it into Michael's apartment. That was an hour ago. I'm about to take out my cell phone to text Big Red when the door opens. She looks tired, but her eyes light up when she sees I'm still awake.

"Happy new year, Hugo," she says.

Before I can reply she wraps her arms around me, bringing me in for a hug. She rests her head on my shoulder as if she needs some type of comfort.

"Happy new year, Scarlett," I say softly.

She pulls away, and for the briefest of moments I have the old Scarlett back. The one from before the war, before Ian.

"What's wrong? You can tell me."

"It's nothing." She shakes her head as if she's made a decision that she doesn't want to talk about it. "I have to get out of this dress. Give me a minute, OK?"

I nod my head and almost anxiously wait for her. Going over to the window, I look outside, deep in thought. I know Scarlett got the information needed to find Flora. I still don't know if it is wise to save Flora. It could very well be a trap.

"Hugo." Her soft voice causes me to turn from the window and away from my dark thoughts. Makeup-free and clad in pajama pants that look too big even for me, she still looks beautiful. She's pulled her hair up into a messy bun that sits atop her head; seeing her so natural and comfortable makes me smile. She sits crossed-legged on the floor in front of the fireplace. I snap my fingers to light the fireplace, which casts an amber glow that seems to almost magically fill the room.

"God, why can't I be a witch?" Scarlett shakes her head in amazement as I sit down across from her on the carpeted floor.

"Why? Don't you like saving the world?" I ask sarcastically. She scoffs at me.

"Speaking of saving the world..." She reaches behind her for her clutch. Opening it, she takes out some folded papers. She begins to tell me about what transpired between her and Michael. But she keeps looking away, as though there is more to say. There's definitely more to the story she isn't telling me, but that argument can be had another day. There are bigger issues ahead of us.

"Looks like queen bitch has properties all over the world. I don't know how we'll begin to narrow these down."

"Lay the papers on the floor in front of me." Doing as I say, she stays silent, watching me closely.

I close my eyes and being to chant, placing my hands over the papers.

"Follow the trail of blood. Follow the trail of blood," I whisper over and over again. The fire burns brighter than ever, and the windows begin to shake. I will the spirits to grant me access. After a moment of stilled silence, I open my eyes. I have my answer.

"What happened?" Scarlett asks. Her eyes are wide, looking down at the papers.

"Nothing happened." She looks back up at me, worried. I half smile at her.

"I think you should leave. You may not like this part."

"What? I'm not going anywhere. Why are you taking your dagger out?" she half screams at me.

"I have to follow the trail of blood." Before she can stop me, I cut my hand, causing her to gasp before putting her hand over her mouth.

The drops of blood stand suspended in the air, trailing just above the papers.

"Come on. Find her," I coax the blood softy.

As if my gentle coaxing is enough, the blood drops right next to the whereabouts of Flora.

Scarlett quickly picks up that sheet of paper.

"Malta…where the hell is that?"

"Europe," I say.

"Europe. Oh God, are you OK?" She drops the paper and examines my hand, which is already healed.

"So you guys can heal yourselves as well. What else can you do?"

"It's really limitless. We don't have to age if we don't want to," I say, picking up the paper.

"Really? Do you think I am going to age?" she asks me curiously.

"No. You stopped aging on your twenty-first birthday."

"So I'll live forever? Just like vampires?"

"Yes." I grab the paper from the floor. My finger touches the country where Flora is.

"Scarlett, if I don't come back—"

"Stop it! You will." Her eyes flash angrily, and she looks as though she wants to hit me.

"OK. Just promise me you won't do anything rash. I am your guardian. It is my responsibility to look after you. I promised your uncle, and your uncle promised your father."

She looks away for a moment, looking into the fire. "You know...you say you're my guardian, because I know that is what you are in the prophecy. But I feel like they got it totally wrong. You are my best friend, besides Jewels. I know you feel the same, so you can quit the whole guardian act."

"You're right," I agree. She is right. My need to protect her, comfort her, is something that comes very easily for me.

"Every girl needs a Hugo in her life," she says, beaming brightly.

"Well, I wouldn't know about that," I say, shaking my head.

She lets out a laugh, and I can't help but join her. We both stop after a moment, and I look down at the paper clutched in my hand. It can change the way this all plays out.

"So what now?" she asks softly, wrapping her arms around her stomach.

"I leave."

"When?"

"Now," I say, turning around to face the fire.

"Now?" She comes to stand in front of me. Her glowing eyes look at me sadly. She looks close to crying, but she holds herself back. "Promise me something, and I promise you that I won't do anything rash."

"What?"

"Promise me you won't be too harsh with Flora. Trust her."

"I have to go now," I say. Closing my eyes, I begin to chant again, thinking of the blue waters that surround the island.

I feel her arms wrap around me, holding me tightly. I hold her closely as I begin to fade. Before I leave to my known destination, I hear her whisper in my ear.

"But you never promised me..."

My eyes open as soon as I hear my gate being opened. It's the one person I could have done without seeing. Alexander. I quickly close my eyes, not wanting him to see that I'm awake. It's always best this way. I feel him crouch down, his fingers grazing my cheek, and I try hard not to squirm away from him and his touch.

"Soon we will leave this place. Tonight, I promise you. No one will have you but me," he promises, getting up and closing the gate behind him.

I wait until I hear him leave before sitting up. I dig into the wall for the key that I've kept hidden. It's now or never. Grasping the key in my hand, I get up and walk slowly over to the gates. Leaning against the bars, I try to peek through to see if there's anyone else present. No one. I put my arm through the bars with the key in my hand. I reach the keyhole and insert the key. Ever so slowly, I turn it. It unlatches the lock. It's the sweetest sound I've ever heard. Breathing heavily, I feel myself begin to sweat, not knowing if it's from fear or excitement. Opening the door slowly, so that it won't make much noise, I walk out. For the first time in ages, I'm walking out and not being put back in. It's an exhilarating moment.

I quickly start to run. I know that down at the farthest end of the basement there is a doorway leading to the outside. There will be no guards out there until the sun sets. Opening the door, I breathe in the fresh air. My eyes begin to water, as if trying to adjust themselves to the bright light. I forge ahead, not caring if I can't see. I run into a wooded area, trying not to grimace in pain as my bare feet are scratched by rocks and sticks, not bothering to look back. I run and I run. I gasp for breath, but I know I have to forge ahead.

I run for a few hours, until the sun starts to go down and it begins to get dark. I keep looking behind, swearing I'm being tracked. Am I beginning to hallucinate? It's hot outside, and I'm drenched in sweat. I'm hungry and tired, but I have to keep moving. I can hear water in the distance. With the darkness, it's getting difficult to see through the heavily wooded surroundings. I trip over a branch and fall to the ground, scraping my knees and hands. Gasping with pain, I quickly try to stand up, stumbling a few times before I catch my bearings.

Resting my hand on a tree trunk briefly, I lay my head against it, willing myself to gather as much strength as I can. I quickly begin to run again. Hearing the sound of waves crashing brings me renewed energy. I'm almost there; I can feel it. Finally seeing a path that leads out of the woods, I almost let out a cry of happiness. But just as easily, it's deflated when I see a stone wall at least ten feet tall preventing my escape. I let out a scream of frustration.

"*No!* No..." I hit the wall, a plain wall to most, but to me the barricade to my survival. "No, this cannot be..." I press my head against the stone wall and let my shoulders slump in failure, tears flowing freely down my dirty face. Feeling a hand on my shoulder, I turn my head to the left, expecting it to be my captors ready to take me in once more.

Instead...my vision is slightly blurred, but I make her out perfectly. She is an angel. She looks nothing like her mother, but her eyes remind me so much of her. She gives me hope. She looks worried; I can't really blame her.

"Help me, Scarlett," I whisper to her. I watch as her eyes widen in surprise. She starts to speak, but there's movement behind me. I let out a scream of horror as I see Alexander advance toward me. His face is sinister, and his eyes blacken as he nears me. I try to run, but he easily catches me by the waist, turning me so he's looking at me.

"How did you escape?" he snarls at me.

I snap my mouth shut defiantly, trying to struggle out of his hold. It's useless, though. He slaps me hard, causing me to gasp with pain. I taste the tang of blood in my mouth. Still I refuse to answer him, knowing it will anger him further. I'm at the point where I just don't care.

"Oh, you think you're so brave now, do you?" he yells in my face, slapping me even harder. He lets me go, and I fall to the floor. This time there's blood running down my nose. He yanks me up by my hair, causing me to stand.

"You still think you are brave?" he says, whispering it in my ear.

I turn so my face is close to his. "Yes," I answer, knowing this will most likely be the last thing I ever say. He growls, twisting my hair in his hands and twisting my head so hard I think surely my neck will break. I scream as he bites down hard on my exposed flesh and drinks his fill of me, as he once promised.

"Mommy, look what I found! A puppy." She holds me up, displaying me excitedly to her mother.

"Oh, darling. You know we can't have any pets," her mother scolds her. She's wearing servant clothing as she begins to stock the dishes away. "You must let the dog go. You know I wasn't allowed to bring you here, but with your father being away at the moment I was left with little choice. Run along before you get us both into trouble." She shoos her daughter out of the kitchen, all the way outside.

"Now let it go and come back inside. It's dark and cold out," she says to her daughter before walking back inside.

She sets me down with tears in her eyes.

"I'm sorry. My mommy is always so mean when she brings me here." She leans down, petting me gently.

"Samantha?" her mother calls after her.

"OK, Mommy," she yells. "I'm going to leave the door open for you, OK? This house is big enough for you to hide," she whispers to me, picking up a rock and putting it between the door and the jamb so it's just open enough to squeeze through.

Going through the kitchen, making sure I'm not seen by the girl's mother, I hurriedly exit, making my way through a huge hallway that leads to a grand staircase. Looking right and left, I watch for any sign of a doorway leading below. Scarlett told me Flora was trapped in the basement. I watch from the corner as an ancient comes charging through, speaking into an earpiece.

"Prisoner has escaped. Send all men into the wooded area. She can't have gone too far."

If I could have slapped my paw to my forehead, I would have. Out of all the days to escape, she *would* choose today. *Fuck!* I shake my head at my choice of words. Big Red and Scarlett are beginning to have a great influence on me.

Focusing on the task at hand, I see an ancient female vampire, jet-black hair and eyes cold as ice, emerge from a doorway that looks like it leads to the basement. She looks like a force to be reckoned with. Her expression holds no ounce of worry as she climbs the steps to let the queen know of the prisoner escaping. She leaves the door open.

As I begin to head toward the doorway, I hear the hiss of a cat behind me. The cat is black and long-haired, with a diamond necklace around its fat neck. It starts to come at me slowly, leaning back, taut and ready to strike, letting out another hiss in warning as its green eyes flash at me menacingly. *Fuck and shit!* I let out a growl of my own, hoping to scare the damn cat off, but instead it continues to come at me slowly. It quickly attacks, nails out, trying to scratch me and letting out another of its wild hisses. It misses me by inches.

I can't just transform now without blowing my cover. I chant quickly as the cat makes another go at me, this time scratching my side. I growl with pain and decide I'm going to take this cat on. I quickly rush over and get it by its tail, biting down hard as it howls with pain and tries to scurry away from me. This time I jump on its back before it can get away from me, biting hard enough not to break its skin, but enough to let it know who's boss. It lets out a cry of agony and I release it, watching it run up the staircase with its tail between its legs.

Running out the way I came in, I head toward the back of the castle, knowing that's where the wooded area is. Sniffing the ground, I see telltale marks of her trail; from the smell of it, she is bleeding. *Double shit!* The vampires would find her for sure. *How stupid can she be?* I think furiously. Not wanting to transform just yet, I begin to track her. Better I find her than those hungry ancients.

Hearing a piercing scream, I run toward it, shifting myself to man form. What I see before me sends me into a rage I have never known before. I see her limp body being held by an ancient vampire as he drinks from her savagely. I run toward him without a second thought, tackling him to the ground as he almost drinks the last life from her.

I take him by surprise, but he quickly recovers, rolling me onto my back, punching me in the groin. Feeling the air whoosh out of my body, I block his next punch with my arm, rolling so I'm now on top of him. I punch him once or twice; I lose count. Putting my hand on his head, I conjure up a quick chant. I watch him make a soundless scream, letting go of me as he grabs his head. He starts to cry blood as his body begins to convulse. No one will hear him as he dies a slow, painful death.

I step back from him and remember Flora. I'd almost forgotten about the witch. I walk over to her; if it weren't for hearing her faint breathing, I would think she was dead. I crouch down and turn her over, holding my breath as I see how badly she was beaten and bloodied. I quickly find the source of the bleeding and press my hand to it, healing the marks instantly. She moans lightly, thrashing her head and trying to get away from me.

"Stop moving, damn you. I am trying to save your life," I yell at her, trying to still her.

She opens her eyes, and my breath catches. Even with her dirty and bruised face, her eyes are captivating. The perfect shade of green that comes to life once spring comes. It's as if we both stop moving, riveted by each other. I feel a stirring in my groin, and I curse under my breath. *Fuck, I have been too long without a woman.*

"A warlock? Now I know I must have the worst luck ever," she whispers, closing her eyes and fading out.

The sound of someone clapping their hands together breaks me from my stare and hold of Flora as I lay her gently on the ground. Without turning I know who it is.

"Opal, I would say it's a pleasure to see you, but a gentleman never lies," I say, getting up to look at the sinister woman before me. She is the epitome of the childhood stories of the evil witch who preys upon children. She wears a long black cape, her long dark hair in knots falling past her shoulders. Her white eyes are just that: white, empty, with no soul.

"I have to say I am quite impressed with you. Hugo, is it? Very touching how your prophet chose to name her pet." She smiles, and her eyes roam over me, narrowing slightly as she catches a glimpse of Flora behind me. I silently chant, providing an invisible shield around us. She takes a step forward and stops smiling.

"Don't you know who I am? You think this force field can protect you? What makes you think that you can get away from here?" she snaps at me.

"No, I don't think it can protect me, but for the time being this will do." I turn, raising my palm so that it faces her as a blue beam shoots out. She quickly holds out her own palm, stopping the beam in midair to keep it from hitting her. Knowing she's distracted, I quickly turn and crouch down, clutching Flora to me as I begin to chant. I hear Opal laugh again.

"I'll let you go for now. This should prove to be most interesting. Give my friend a message for me. Watching her mother suffer was glorious, but it will be so much sweeter to watch this one do the same."

Her words and the wooded area begin to fade. Without realizing it, I've bought Flora back to the small cottage I was raised in. With the force of the transport, she begins to dry heave. Her small body coughs and shakes. She's beyond malnourished and in desperate need of a bath. I drop to the floor with her, gently rubbing her back as her stomach begins to settle. She flinches away from my touch.

"Where are we? Where is Scarlett? And the most important question of all: why would a warlock save a witch?" she whispers. At first I think she's lost consciousness again, but I watch as she opens her eyes and looks at me with a guarded expression.

"First answer to your questions. We are in my family home. Unfortunately, using all my power has weakened me momentarily. I need to replenish, and you need to rest. Second and third answers to your questions, Scarlett is in New York. She knew you would be in danger, so I retrieved you."

"Sounds like you didn't want to save me. Powers weakened? That would never happen to a witch," she says, having the nerve to scoff at me after saving her life.

"Yeah, well, last we checked you're not even a witch," I say, stung. I can't believe her nerve. I know my own reply will touch a sore spot, but she says nothing, and I realize she's fallen asleep. I pick her up easily, and she rests her head on my shoulder. I begin to feel bad. She weighs less than a child.

I enter my room and set her gently down on the bed. Her soiled clothing needs to be removed. Going into the bathroom, I grab a basin and fill it with warm water. I also grab a wash towel. Turning back into the bedroom, I set the basin down on the nightstand and begin to wonder how I should go about removing her clothes. *Shit!* There isn't much to remove anyhow. The dress is in tatters.

Sitting on the edge of the bed, I begin to unbutton her dress. I notice she has a gold chain around her neck with a locket. Curiously clasping the locket in my hand, I wonder if it opens at all. I see a little latch, and it opens for me. Inside is a picture of a man. He is young and handsome. I wonder if this is a former lover of hers. I ignore an annoying stab of jealousy at the thought. *Why would I be jealous?* Putting my thoughts aside, I wince when I notice all the bruises covering her body. There's not a place that is not marked. Her feet are badly scraped. I begin to gently bathe her, careful not to disturb her from her deep sleep. I try hard not to notice how beautifully pale her skin looks against her red hair. I definitely try not to notice how her nipples are a faint pink color, how they harden into tight rosebuds when I draw the towel over them. After I'm done, I rub my hands together and put my hand on her forehead. She moans and thrashes her body from my touch, but she settles back into the dream she's having. I begin to chant.

"The body that rests can begin to heal. Begin to heal… begin to heal…" I whisper over and over again.

The bruises begin to fade instantly. The cuts on her feet begin to close, leaving no trace of scars. Satisfied, I pull the blanket over her naked body. She just needs food in her now. Closing the door behind me, I take out my cell phone and call Scarlett.

"Hugo," she says, answering right away.

"Hey, I got her."

"Good. How is she?"

"Not good, but she will be. I will come to you in two days tops. I need to recover my strength, and she needs to rest before I can transport back to you."

"OK. Con's been in contact, and he's found another location for us."

"That's good to hear. I'll be in touch. Take care."

"You too, Hugo."

It sounds like she wants to say more to me, but I wait until she ends the call. I know that she's worried about my treatment of Flora. Hell, I even wondered what my treatment of her was going to be. Our first encounter had not been a good one. Right away she couldn't keep her dislike of me contained, even when she was on the verge of death, so I can't imagine what she'll be like when she's alive and well.

I smile to myself, knowing she'll wake up naked under the blankets, in a panic, because she'll know that I've seen every inch of her. I cross my arms over my chest and smile smugly as I picture the horrified look on her face.

9

Ending the call with dread, I sit on the bed, feeling very much alone. I wonder what Hugo would think of my predicament with Ian. *Maybe I just won't show up.* But I know I can't. I need to get my final fix of Ian. He's my drug, and I need to break free from my addiction. I ask myself over and over, "Why did he have to come back? What did his cryptic message mean?" *This will be the last time you will run from me.*

"Get out of my fucking head," I say aloud, getting up from the bed furiously. I'm dressed in my bathrobe with my make-up already applied and hair styled down in loose curls. Going into my walk-in closet, I see how many fabulous choices I have to choose from. Flipping through my new clothes, I choose a pale pink see-through blouse with black buttons that run down the back and a black pencil skirt. Opening some drawers, I take out my fancy underwear set with matching garter belt and stockings that I got at La Perla. It is black and lacy and makes me feel sexy as hell as I slip into it.

Putting on my clothes, I look at the time, smiling as I see that I'm running late. I take my time putting on my

Louboutins and my leather jacket, taking one final look in the mirror. I like what I see: a woman looking like she has a point to prove, not only to herself but to Ian. I mean business. Grabbing my handbag, I walk out of my room with a new sense of purpose. Of course, that's totally blown as I see Big Red sitting on the small couch, polishing his knife collection.

"Whoa…looks like somebody's heading out for a late-night rendezvous," he says, smiling at me knowingly.

"Don't you have anything better to do than polish your knives?" I say, crossing my arms over myself.

"Love, I am not judging you. You do what you have to do. God knows I do," he says, giving me a wink.

"Well, thank you for not judging me. You missed a spot," I say, laughing as I walk toward the door.

"Yeah, yeah," he says, going back to see what spot I was talking about.

"Got to go! Don't wait up for me. Duty calls." I close the door, hearing Big Red shout, "That's my line!"

Smiling and shaking my head, I go to the elevator, my hand extending to press the button—but before I do the elevator doors open abruptly, making me take a startled step back. My heart flutters as I see Ian filling the doorway, seemingly pissed off that he had to come and get me.

"I thought you weren't going to show," he says, his eyes roaming over me.

"So what? You thought you'd come get me? I gave you my word." I walk into the elevator, greeting the elevator operator, who is clearly entranced by Ian.

"I made reservations downstairs," he says, walking in behind me.

"Cancel them. I'm not hungry. Let's just get this over with—Eleventh floor, please," I say sweetly to the dazed man.

"As you wish," Ian says quietly.

I try not to look at him from the corner of my eye, but I can't help it. He's wearing a fitted black blazer with a white V-neck T-shirt underneath and stonewashed jeans. His hair is styled perfectly to the side. His smell is not of cologne, but of pure Ian. It intoxicatingly envelops me. I curse my body again for betraying me. When the elevator stops at his floor, he lets me out first. He follows closely behind me as we make our way to his room. His face is set in stone, and his eyes give nothing away. *What is he up to?* He inserts his card into the lock, and the door opens. He lets me into the room, and I cross my arms around myself, not sure how this is going to play out. His room is decorated very much like my own: white, crisp, and clean. I try very hard not to look at the bed.

"So what's your proposition?" I ask, wanting to cut to the chase.

He says nothing as he walks over to the bed and sits down with his elbows on his knees, regarding me intently. It reminds me of when he was in my apartment for the first time, the bed looking small compared to his big frame. It was one of my many firsts with him.

"I want in on whatever you're planning," Ian says easily.

"Sorry, not gonna to happen," I say.

"And what would you say if I told you you had no choice in the matter?" he says, smiling at me.

"I would call your bluff. I'm the leader here. Do you think the Xs would go against me for *you?* I doubt it. That's what happens when you have no friends," I say shortly, enjoying the hint of anger that flashes through his eyes.

"Don't test me, Scarlett. Trust me—you will not like the results," he says, this time standing up and stalking toward me slowly.

"Don't threaten me. Trust me—*you* will not like the results," I say, doubling down and refusing to cower as he comes closer to me, so close that if he leaned forward his lips would be mere inches from mine. He inhales deeply and smiles knowingly.

"Tell me, Scarlett. How does it feel to hate a man you are still dying to fuck? I can smell how much you want me," he says cruelly.

"Tell me, Ian, how does it feel to leave the woman you are dying to be with?" I say just as cruelly. He smiles again but doesn't deny it.

"Do you hate me?" he asks softly, his hand touching my face with a gentleness he's never shown me before.

"Yes," I say with no hesitation, my body beginning to warm from his closeness and touch.

"Show me how much you hate me," he whispers to me, his eyes going dark.

I launch myself at him, and he easily clutches me to him, our lips coming together in perfect unison. He takes my jacket off, and I push him back toward the bed roughly. I quickly slide on top of him, straddling his hips, my pencil skirt riding dangerously up. He rips my shirt off, the buttons flying everywhere. Breaking our kiss, I peel off his blazer, tossing it to the side as I rip open his shirt, desperate to feel my warm skin against his cold. He starts to kiss my neck as his hips buck upward, making me moan with want. I don't even notice he's taken off my bra until I feel his lips on my breast, my nipple in his eager mouth.

Throwing my head back, I let out a gasp of delight, feathering my fingers in his hair, gathering him closer to me. I hear the zipper on my skirt as he begins to lower it down. Smiling, I get off of him, turning over and shimmying the skirt down along with my panties. I bend over to give him a perfect view of my ass and my welcoming wetness. I hear him growl, and I revel in it.

"Leave those on," he says, looking at my stockings and garter belt. Before I can do anything else, he grabs me by the waist and sits me astride him. I unzip his pants as he begins to give me sweet kisses, starting from neck to my breasts.

"That's it…show me how fucking much you hate me," he encourages me, laying back as I guide his thick shaft into my opening. We both let out a shout of pleasure as he fills me completely, so completely. We stare at each other for a moment as I begin to set the pace, placing my hands on his chest, moving up and down as his hips jerk upward to meet me. I close my eyes from his intense stare, throwing my head back. *Just this one time. Let me get my fix of him and be done with it.*

"Look at me," he says, sitting up a little so his arm can reach for my neck. He grasps the side of my face as he forces me to open my eyes. I refuse to obey him. I feel my insides begin to tingle. I dig my nails into his flesh. Hearing him growl at my refusal, I feel his fangs graze by my neck before he bites me spitefully at the same time that he grips my ass roughly, thrusting into me at a hard pace. I come apart instantly. I scream from the pleasure of it. I hear him groan against my throat as my orgasm clenches around him tightly.

While still inside of me, he quickly turns so now I'm lying on my back as he keeps thrusting into me. *Surely I can't…can I?* I feel my body begin that sweet tightening again as another wave of release threatens to crash. My vision feels blurred, but I watch in total amazement as he bites down on his wrist while still ramming hard into me.

"What…what are you doing?" I ask, gasping.

"I play to win," he says. Before I can register his intention, he puts his bloody wrist to my mouth, making me swallow. I struggle under him, but as soon as his blood touches my tongue, I am consumed. The fight goes out of me as I clutch his wrist, drinking from him greedily. He closes his eyes in pleasure and continues to fuck me.

This is my undoing. I come again and again. He follows close behind me, growling his pleasure just above me, but I don't seem to notice that. I concentrate on what I am feeling at this very moment, and it's the taste of his blood. I'm hooked. I feel him gently touching my hair, saying words to me I can't quite understand. I close my eyes as I continue to drink from him. His blood consumes me. It awakens another half of me. I have never felt so alive, so in the moment, as I do right now.

"They have to die," I shout at both Opal and Matthias. I pace back and forth. I was stunned to hear the news from Maylina, my trusted soldier, that Flora had managed to escape, but then Opal delivered the news that it was with the assistance of that warlock, Hugo. Flora is now Team Scarlett.

"I don't care how you do it, but I want my sister dead. I want Scarlett dead," I say, thinking of the vision I'd had of her once I'd drunk her blood. "I want proof of her death by you delivering me her heart." I look at Matthias.

"Of course, my queen. I will begin to make the preparations now for my departure to the States," he says, going to the doorway, knowing my words were dismissing him.

I continue to pace back and forth as I feel Opal's penetrating stare. I feel like I'm going to pull my hair out.

"What?" I stop pacing and snap at her.

"Nothing, my queen. I'm just curious as to why you feel that now you want Scarlett dead when you were so eager to bring her here," she says, her white eyes looking at me curiously.

"Don't worry about it. Do we have everything we need for tomorrow?"

Her eyes drop from me momentarily as she sees that I've dismissed any further conversation on the subject.

"Yes, tomorrow is the start of the blood moon. You need to clear your mind of all this energy and remain calm."

"Remain calm? You just better make sure that Flora and that warlock end up dead! Opal, you know how I get when people disappoint me," I say, walking over to her.

She takes a step back, her eyes narrowing, perhaps in fear of what I might do next.

"Consider it done."

"Good. Now get out of my sight," I say, turning away from her. She closes the door behind her, leaving me alone. I still cannot believe that Flora made it out. Scarlett is a huge problem. The moment I tasted her blood I knew she had to die. Not that it wasn't my intention in the first place, but I'd wanted to toy with her first. But now, knowing what I know, I am certain she must be stopped. Before...I didn't want to think of it. I close my eyes in frustration. I want to curse, kick, scream. To kill someone.

There's a knock on my door, breaking me from my sadistic thoughts.

"Come in," I all but yell.

Damian enters in all his glory. Wearing a loose collar shirt and black pants, he is a symbol of sexy. No one has ever quite caught my attention as much as Ian has, but Damian has come the closest. With his long dark hair and dark eyes, he is a mystery. I am fascinated by him. My body begins to heat up. I've only slept with humans or vampires. Of course, I've heard stories of sleeping with beasts. They are ferocious. When they mate, it can be quite painful…something I am very much looking forward to.

"My queen." He smiles at me deviously, as though reading my thoughts.

"Damian," I whisper. I walk over to him until I'm standing before him. I touch his face, and he sways toward me as though he's seeking my touch. The juncture of my thighs begins to pool. I tell myself that it's because it's the blood moon that I'm getting so excited, but no. I want him. I want the beast.

"The preparations have been made for tomorrow," I say to him. Coming much closer to him, I can feel his erection pressing against my belly.

"Do we have to wait until tomorrow?" His hands caress my back, and I arch my body wantonly, rubbing my breasts against his shirt.

"No," I whisper.

This is apparently all he needs to hear. He growls and rips my dress from my body. His eyes gleam red as he steps away, looking at the body that is now his. I watch him in stunned fascination as if watching two people struggle for control. Man and beast. He all but tosses me on the bed, ripping off his clothes before pouncing on top of me. *Yes, I needed this.* He enters me roughly, and I welcome it with much rage of my own. He starts to pound into me roughly, pulling my hair. My last thoughts before I let the sweet pleasure take over are of Scarlett lying on cold concrete, surrounded by her precious Xs as they look upon her lifeless body.

I wake to the heat of the sun shining down on my face. I smile sleepily. Am I dreaming? If this is a dream, I don't want to wake up. *Strange, the floor doesn't seem so hard.* I snuggle deeper into the covers. *Wait, this isn't right!* My eyes fly open, and I sit up in a rush, seeing that I'm on a very comfortable bed. The room is beautifully decorated, giving off a country feel. Last night's events rush back to me. My escape, Alexander, and the warlock. He saved me. Even though I could tell he didn't want to, he saved me, regardless of his reasons. I remember him being arrogantly handsome and his soft brown eyes showing me gentleness. *Maybe all warlocks aren't so bad?*

Looking down at myself, I let out a scream loud enough to wake the dead, and it isn't because my skin is no longer marred by bruises; it's because I'm completely and utterly naked. *The pervert!* Quickly wrapping the blanket around myself, I get up and notice that I'm not wincing from pain. Apparently I was healed, thanks to that pervert warlock.

The door opens in a rush; the warlock's eyes are wide. He looks to be fresh from a shower. His hair is wet and he's shirtless, his black pants fitted to him like a second skin. My mouth gapes open as my eyes feast on him. He's cut perfectly. Dark hair lightly sprinkles his chest and makes a sweet trail down to his muscled stomach—and lower. I feel my face flame as I quickly look away, but not before I see his smug smile.

"Where are my clothes, Warlock?" I spit out *Warlock* as if I'm disgusted just by saying it.

"I had to remove them. You smelled. My name is Hugo, but only my friends call me that. You can call me Heneric," he says, folding his arms over his chest.

"There are a lot of things I could call you right now, and Heneric is not one of them," I say angrily. Once again my eyes drift to his chest. "I will not talk to you any further until you put a shirt on."

He has the nerve to laugh.

"You don't give orders around here, *Princess*."

Princess? I've just about had enough of him. I look at him, and he's still smiling smugly at me. I want so badly to slap his handsome face. *Handsome? OK, he's more than just handsome.*

"Where is Scarlett? I want to talk to Scarlett."

"You'll meet her when I decide it's OK for you to meet her. First, I want to figure you out."

I clutch the sheets tighter to my chest. He steps closer to me and I step back.

"What do you mean, figure me out?"

"I need to know if you can be trusted," he says quietly, shrugging his shoulders. His soft brown eyes look at me carefully, as if to capture some secret I am hiding.

"You can trust me," I say, just as softly. It's the truth. He can. It's *he* who can't be trusted. After all, it was his kind that did the betraying.

He steps closer to me, and my lips part. He's quite a beautiful man. I start to get goose bumps on my arms. I look away from him, hoping he can't sense my wild attraction toward him. He lets out an uncomfortable cough. "Time will tell. I'll get you some clothes." He walks out the door, slamming it shut.

I walk over to the bed and sit down, putting my head in my hands. Closing my eyes, I think, *Can things get any worse?*

10

I feel fingertips grazing my face, gently smoothing my hair away from my face. Sighing with pleasure, I lean into the touch. Then I remember who I'm with. My eyes flutter open, and Ian is above me, looking down at me, his eyes darkening. He's so beautiful; he takes my breath away. *Will that ever change?* I sit up from the bed, bringing the covers up to my naked chest.

"I've never shared a bed with a woman before," he admits to me quietly.

I don't say anything but simply get up, not bothering to cover myself. I notice he must have taken off my garter belt and my stockings while I was sleeping. I pick up my underwear, putting them on, refusing to look at him.

"Where are you going?" he asks quietly.

I still don't answer him. I put on my pencil skirt and notice my blouse is seriously beyond repair. So I just put on my jacket, zipping it up.

"I asked you a question." he says roughly.

"Leaving. This *fucking* has been great and all, but I think I've just about had my fill of you. Thanks. You've taught me so much," I say, putting my hand over my heart. He leaps off the bed, but before he can get to me I open the curtains so the sunlight burrows into the room. He hisses and flies into the corner of the space before he can get burned. His eyes are dark and fangs protrude from his mouth viciously as he stands there in his naked glory.

"You see, Ian. I'm not the same girl you decided to leave behind. *I* play to win," I say, heading toward the doorway, the sun casting a perfect trail in my wake. I watch as he straightens, his erection standing out proudly, his eyes showing me a promise that this is not over.

I leave the room and smile. He is going to be standing there for a while. I take the steps instead of the elevator, feeling this amazing energy that I haven't felt in a while. When I open the door to my suite, Big Red is, of course, still sitting on the couch watching TV. *Maury* is on.

"Hey," I say. I walk over to the small dining area. Looking at the array of assorted croissants and muffins, I feel my mouth begin to water. I pour myself a cup of coffee, and Big Red walks in with a weird expression on his face.

"What?" I ask, taking a bite of a buttered croissant.

"Um…nothing," he says, raking a hand through his hair with a bewildered expression. He opens his mouth to say something but quickly shuts it.

"I got a text from Con. Did you hear from him?" I ask, getting uncomfortable. Big Red is still looking at me weird. *What the hell is his problem? Didn't he say he wouldn't judge me?*

"Yes, we'll meet with him tonight. He found another location. Not too far from the city. Which is good because I'm becoming restless here with all this fruitiness," he says, waving his big arm around our surroundings.

I let out a laugh. OK, he is back.

"I have to say, I do miss the others. Do you?" I ask him.

"Con is my brother," he says, shrugging his shoulders. I guess he wants that to be his answer.

Taking a last sip of coffee, I head out of the dining room. "I'm going to go to sleep. I guess I'll just check us out later," I call out to him.

"OK, love. Goddamn it! I knew he wasn't the father," he says as he continues watching TV.

Smiling I close the door to my bedroom, taking off my shoes and loving the feel of the plush carpet on my feet. I peel off my jacket, dropping it to the floor. The skirt follows. I go straight to the bathroom and turn on the bathtub. *My little sanctuary.* Taking off my underwear and bra, I sink into the water. I let out a gasp of pleasure as the heat of the water touches my overly sensitive skin.

Even though I'd promised myself I wouldn't think of him, it's hard not to. Every time I close my eyes, there he is. I don't know why he let me drink from him. I don't know what it means. *He was purely mindfucking me.* But just thinking about his blood was enough to turn me on. I mean, what sane person would want to drink blood? I wasn't a vampire, I was human—but why did it feel so right? Everything about what we did last night felt so right.

Stop it! I shout at myself. Stop questioning why Ian did what he did. He didn't like to lose. That was it. Plain and simple. Closing my eyes, I feel my body begin to relax, and I begin to doze. Still thinking of the way Ian had looked at me when I woke up…

The same memory was with me as I was thrust into the past. A little boy who was at least five years of age with pale blond hair and steel-blue eyes was hiding under a table. I was as captivated by him then as I was now. Ian…I watched as he flinched in fear, as I heard a man yelling at the top of his lungs. A glass smashed to the floor very close to him.

"Pick up this mess, you fucking whore," the man yelled again at a woman who was cowering in fear. I realized she was in front of the table, perhaps to shield Ian from the man's wrath. She had a bloodied lip and the shadow of a black eye, her pale blond hair very much like Ian's falling in her face, shielding the tears that cascaded down. The man slammed out of the house. She bent down, crying and shaking as she picked up the pieces of the glass that he had thrown on the floor.

"Mother," the boy said, gently placing his small hand on her back.

"Ian, darling. Get out from under there. Careful, I don't want you to get hurt," she said, trying to wipe the tears from her face as she pushed him gently away.

"Mother, let's leave. I hate him," he said quietly. Even at a young age, he was too prideful to show emotion.

"Darling, do not say that. He's your father. He is just under a lot of stress. He doesn't mean to get angry," she said, shaking her head as she began to pick up the pieces again. He let out a huff and picked up the remaining glass with her. She stood, wincing a little as she combed his hair back, kissing him before she walked toward the kitchen. I looked at the little boy that was Ian, and I just wanted to wrap my arms around him. No one should witness abuse like this. I watched as he went outside and the other kids made fun of him for his drunken dad and the clothes he wore. They called him a commoner and a farmer's boy. He was a loner, even at a young age. His beautiful eyes told a sad story.

As it began to get dark, he was in his room sleeping deeply but quickly came awake at his mother's screams. He opened his door, slowly peeking through, his small fist balled up as he watched his drunken father stagger over to his mother, slapping her yet again before taking his plate of food and slamming it to the floor, the food scattering everywhere.

"You fucking whore, you call this a cooked meal?" he slurred, pulling her hair, making her go down on her knees before pushing her face into the food that he'd dropped. He laughed as he heard her scream, begging him to stop.

Ian rushed forward, swinging at his father with all his might, his small fist doing nothing.

"Stop it! Stop it!" he yelled at him over and over again.

His father released his hold on his mother and backslapped Ian. His small body hit the floor, and I let out a scream. My hand fisted into my mouth as I watch in horror.

"No!" his mother screamed.

"Oh, you want to protect your whore of a mother. Come here." He walked over to Ian, grabbing him by the hair and smearing his small face into the food on the floor. "Look at you both, both garbage…"

Then I was taken away from this horrific memory to another. Ian was much older now—not the young boy he had been but now a young man. His mother was sitting with him, her hair grayed and her eyes looking tired. Once a beautiful woman, she was now a product of her own circumstance. We were in the same cabin as in the vision of his youth. It looked exactly the same. They were sitting at the same table Ian had hidden under when he had heard his parents argue. He was pleading with his mother.

"Come away with me. I have some things lined up for work. We can leave right now, while he is still at work."

His mother placed her hand on his cheek, smiling at him lovingly with tears in her eyes. She shook her head sadly.

"No, I can't. You leave. What would an old lady like me do? This is all I know. Make something of yourself. Be happy, Ian," she said.

He shook his head, standing up away from her, his hands on his hips.

"How can you stay? How can you want to be with him? He is a monster," he yelled at her.

"I don't expect you to understand. For all of his faults, he was once a good man. I love him."

"Fuck love," he shouted.

"Ian..." she trailed off, getting up to try to hug him, to possibly make him understand, but he pulled away from her.

"I am leaving," he said.

"Ian...I love you. I really love you. Please don't leave here angry. I am just a woman that is scared, but I love you..." she begged him, tears flowing down her face.

"You're just a woman who is weak," he said, shoving her hands away from him. I winced at his choice of words, but I saw he instantly regretted them. His mother put her hand over her mouth as she cried even harder, watching him walk out of the house. She fell to her knees like a woman in pain. Even when her husband beat her, I had never seen her cry as hard. She was losing not just Ian, but a piece of herself.

I slowly wake from my vision, feeling very overwhelmed. Was that a vision? It felt more like dream. I don't recall summoning a vision. If I had, it surely wouldn't be of Ian's past. And what a horrible past it was. Were those the last words he'd spoken to his mother? I get up from the tub; the water is now cold. I wrap a towel around myself; finding my terrycloth robe, I put it on before walking over to the bed. I pull the covers back and slide in. I thought I was done with Ian, but it looks like a part of me doesn't want to let go. *Will that ever change?* I don't want to feel sorry for him. I let out a huff of frustration. Closing my eyes, I start to drift again into a troubled sleep in which I dream of a little boy with steel-blue eyes.

❧

Hours later I am at the checkout desk with Big Red. He's still looking at me strangely but saying nothing, just keeping a watchful eye. I hand over the keys. The bellhop has our luggage ready, and the valet has my car waiting for us out front. I keep looking over my shoulder to make sure Ian isn't going to make an appearance, but he doesn't. I'm sure he was super pissed, having to sit in a corner all day, waiting impatiently for the sun to go down. The thought makes me smile.

Walking out with Big Red, I can tell that everyone's eyes are on us. We're quite a pair. He has on a gray zip-up with a hood and stonewashed jeans. He is massive in size, so of course his presence by my side is impressive. And the hair! Don't get me started on the sexy red hair. I have on my leather jacket zipped up to the top, black tights, and my six-inch-heel knee-high boots. My thick hair is messily braided to the side, and my two-carat studs flash brightly every time I move my head, courtesy of Cartier. It's cold outside, the air smelling of the rain that hasn't yet come.

"Holy shit, love. This is yours?" Big Red asks as he looks at my car in awe. I smile. *Men and cars.*

"Yup. Big Red, meet Red. Red, meet Big Red," I say, getting in.

He gets in beside me, though he can hardly fit. His massive legs hit the dashboard. He puts his seat back as far as it will go, but he still looks quite uncomfortable.

"I like how you named your car after me. Makes me think you fancy me," he says, grinning wolfishly at me.

"Please don't flatter yourself," I say, laughing and rolling my eyes. I pull out quickly into traffic, and he nervously clutches the dashboard.

"Woman, where did you learn to drive?" he says, buckling his seat belt.

"What? I drive perfectly safe," I say, cutting into the lane before another driver can block me from turning. I eye Big Red and smile at him deviously.

"My foster dad's side job was working on cars. He used to take me with him on his runs, when Jennifer wanted to be alone. Jennifer was my foster mother," I say quietly, reminiscing.

"I don't get it. They took you in but wanted to be alone," he says, looking angry just at the thought.

"Yeah, well. As they say, not everyone is meant to be a parent," I say, shrugging my shoulders. At the word *parent,* I feel an ache in my heart as I think of my parents. I wonder if they were normal…if my father was human. What would my life have been like with them? I pull up to a stoplight and glance at Big Red.

"Did you know my parents?"

"I knew of Edrick. Con saved my life just before all this prophecy shit went down. So I went along with this not knowing what I was getting myself into. Tell you the truth, I didn't believe in this 'girl saves the world' crap. From what Con told me, your father was admired by many. From the stories, I have to say I see much of him in you," he admits seriously.

I swallow, grateful that he is being so open with me. If I wasn't driving, I would probably hug him.

"Thank you," I say instead.

During the drive, I get to know him much better. I figure out how he turned. He'd been the age of twenty-eight when he died. He was visiting a whorehouse in New London when he was attacked by a group of vampires. One of the leaders of the group liked that he put up a fight and thought he would make a great protégé. He'd bitten his wrist, and before he could take his last breath, he made him drink. Unfortunately, the leader of the group underestimated him, and he killed all of them the next day.

"Does it hurt?" I ask.

"Does what hurt?"

"Turning. Does it hurt?" I ask curiously.

"I don't remember," he says honestly.

I pull into the gates of the new center. Looks like there is an alarm system in place. I press in the four-digit number Con gave me. The gate opens after a second, and it leads to a long trail. Big Red lets out a whistle as we both take in our new surroundings. After driving some more, we finally reach our new home. Strange, the words *our home.* It is pristine—nothing at all like the grungy warehouse. This is a mansion. It is painted white and covered with vines and greenery. I spot Ian's Maserati right away—it's kind of hard to miss…as if he purposely parked up front. I stiffen. *What is he doing here?*

"Um…" I say, pulling into the massive driveway.

"Looks like Con outdid himself. He did say he wanted something more secure. It's a pretty big trail, so no one can get to us without us having enough time to be ready," he says, swinging his big body out of the car, totally oblivious to my tension.

I reach into the backseat and get my bags out, grinding my teeth together. *He has some nerve just showing up here! And why the hell would Con let him?* I walk in, and Zayah greets me. She looks at me oddly, and her smile wavers a little. My stomach turns.

"Zayah," I say, giving her a hug. She looks beautiful as always, wearing, of course, all black. She's wearing her signature ruby red lips that complement her dark skin beautifully.

"Scarlett," she says, hugging me back. "Just leave your bags here. Come, the others are waiting."

It feels so great to be around another female. I look around as I follow behind her. The house is huge and gives off a feeling of home. *Who would have thought? Vampires that are normal.* As I get to the doorway, my stomach turns again, and I get a really bad feeling—a feeling circled all around by a steel-blue-eyed snake. Ian has to go. He is not part of the Xs. He is not part of me. Stiffening my shoulders, I walk into the room ready to do battle. All the Xs are in discussion, but they stop talking as soon as I enter. Ian has his back to me, talking to Con, but—as if he senses me—he turns, smiling at me mockingly, his eyes narrowing. I just want to rip that smug smile off his face.

"What's he doing here?" I say, looking at Con accusingly.

Con comes forward, looking uncomfortable.

"Scarlett…" He breaks off as if he doesn't have the words to tell me.

"What? I want him gone," I say furiously. I feel a bit guilty for yelling at Con, but I'm on the verge of hitting someone.

"Well, it's not that easy," Con says, looking now at Zayah for some help.

"What are you talking about? Big Red, get Ian the fuck out of here," I say, looking at Big Red for some backup.

Big Red looks at me a bit sadly but says nothing and doesn't move. His eyes show me that even though he would gladly do it, it's out of his hands.

"You see, *wife,* I am not going anywhere," Ian says to me, folding his arms across his chest, regarding me coolly.

I ignore him.

"What the fuck is going on?" I yell at the Xs, who now all look away from me. I feel like I'm hyperventilating. *Wait, what did he just call me?* My breath hitches, and my heart freezes.

"What did you just say?" I look at Ian and advance toward him slowly.

Zayah jumps in front of me, grabbing me by the shoulders, forcing me to break my stare from Ian.

"Scarlett, do you remember when I said that it was very sacred for our kind to drink from each other?" she asks me.

"Yes," I say, still not sure where she is going with this.

"Even before you walked through that doorway, I knew you were marked. Ian's scent is all over you," she says softly, as if she were talking to a child.

Swallowing hard, I think, *Marked?* Before she says what she has to say, I have a flashback of Hugo and me having a conversation about vampire drinking. I know that whatever Zayah is about to say will once again change the course of my life as I know it. My stomach drops to the floor with dread. Ian has once again played to win, and I am the prize.

"You and Ian are blood mated."

11

Putting my head under the shower, I raise my face against the beating heat of the water. Who would have thought I would miss simple luxuries like this so terribly?

I must have spent a whole hour under the steaming water, smiling with delight. Shutting off the water, I wrap a towel around myself and head to the bedroom, gathering the clothes the warlock left for me. I put on the underwear and bra, wondering how he would know my measurements. *Pervert!* He has left me a pair of jeans and a white cotton sweater. The clothes fit me a little loosely, but they will do. I look into the mirror and begin to comb my hair. I haven't looked in a mirror for twenty-one years. I have no bruises, but with the loss of weight I look pale, my eyes looking too big for my face. I quickly try to pinch my cheeks to give myself color. I braid my hair and step back. *Do I look OK? Wait, why should I care anyway?*

I turn away from the mirror and step out of the room nervously. The warlock is in the kitchen, his back turned as he reads something in his hand. *At least he has a shirt on.* I study him as he studies the book he is reading. He's deep in thought, his eyebrows coming together in a frown. He places an apple in his mouth, taking a hearty bite. My cheeks begin to warm as I find myself jealous of that damn apple. *Flora, get ahold of yourself!* I let out a cough, and he turns toward me silently, looking at me from head to toe. I once again feel naked under his scrutiny.

"There's food in the fridge, Princess. You can help yourself," he says, biting into his apple again.

I swear the man has no manners. I know, of course, that I'm not a welcome guest in his home, but he can at least try not to be so rude.

"Thank you," I say. I head over to the fridge and open it. Looks like there's leftover chicken and potatoes. My mouth waters at the sight. I quickly grab the food and put it into a microwave, waiting impatiently for the alarm to beep. Before it can go off, I open it frantically. My hands sting from the heat of the plate, but I barely notice. Sitting beside him, I dig in. Stuffing my face, I keep my head down, eating quickly. I keep feeling like someone is going to steal the plate right out from under me. *Stop it; you're not a prisoner anymore.*

I only slowly become aware of the warlock staring at me with wide eyes. And then I realize that I've been eating with my hands. I close my eyes as they begin to water, and my face reddens from embarrassment. I hear him begin to chant softly and another plate full of the same food is set in front of me. This time with napkins, utensils, and something to drink.

"Thank you," I say softly, still not looking up from the food.

"You don't have to be ashamed, Princess," he says.

I look up at him, suddenly liking his term of endearment. He looks away from me again, his soft brown eyes narrowing in anger. *What have I done?* The smell of the hot food in front of me causes my mouth to salivate, and I opt to ignore him. This time I try to eat with calmness, feeling his eyes on me from time to time. Drinking the last of the tea he gave me, I study him from the rim of the cup. He's wearing a fitted white V-neck shirt and black jeans. His hair is messy, but in a sexy way. I wonder if it's as soft as it looks. My fingers itch to touch it. *Flora, get ahold of yourself!* He's once again concentrating on that book. I notice when he is in deep thought he likes to play with his bottom lip.

"What is that?" I ask curiously, trying hard not to look at his lips.

He looks up briefly and then goes back to flipping the pages gently. At first I think he isn't going to answer me.

"The book of the Undead," he says, shutting the book and narrowing his eyes, trying to gauge my response.

"Really?" I say, my eyes opening wide in fascination. "Can I see?"

He looks hesitant at first but slides the book over to me. I notice his hands look gentle and long. I can't help but wonder what they felt like over my skin as he healed me. *Flora, contain yourself.* Moving my plate to the side, I slide the book so it is in front of me. I've heard so many stories of this book, and here it is in front of my face. It is brown, the clasp in gold. A simple book to others, but to us mythical creatures it means so much more. It is a look into what is yet to come. A moment that would catapult a change. Whether it be good or bad, this book conveys what is to happen. No magic involved, just plain ol' destiny. I open it gently to the page the warlock had folded over. It reads, in Latin:

A child will be born, a miracle, from two species, from a male vampire and a human female. This child will come of age and with this age will have amazing strength and power. A new era is coming, a coming of evil and coming of war. A queen will rise. Rivers of blood will spill; death is inevitable. The prophet will have the aid of her guardian, a man with a marking of the moon. The man marked with the moon will meet his full potential when he comes together with a woman marked with a star. Together they will be one. Lost brothers will be in a crossroad of a point of no return. Sides will be taken; rules will be broken. The prophet will lead in the war of the undead, and anyone against her will be defeated.

I sit back as I finish reading. *The man marked with the moon and a woman marked with a star will come together as one.* I stand, raising my sweater absently, looking for the mark I was born with. It's on the side of my rib cage, small, but I can still make out the shape of a star. I feel the hairs go up on my arm, not realizing I still have my shirt raised until I feel the warlock's eyes looking at my pale flesh. I quickly lower my shirt, sitting back down. I turn the page and notice it is missing. Strange. I place my hand over it. Closing my eyes I see flashes, almost like snapshots, coming to me quickly. Opal has her hand on the missing piece; another flash comes of Ezarbet and Damian, a dark presence around them. Black magic. And just as quickly it fades to an image of red, gleaming eyes and fangs. Gasping at the terrifying image, I open my eyes quickly. *What was that?* I haven't had visions in so long. It was a bit startling.

"What happened?" the warlock asks me.

"I don't know. I saw flashes of images. The other half of the prophecy." I put my hand on my forehead, feeling the dull pain of a headache coming on. Are my powers coming back?"

"I thought you lost your powers to Opal," he says, his eyes regarding me distrustfully.

"I did, but even as powerful as she is, she can't take some things. I was born a natural witch. No black magic can take that, but I haven't had a vision for a very long time," I explain, rubbing my temples.

He nods, letting me continue.

"We must get that other half of that prophecy back. Ezarbet and Opal have something really bad planned. Don't ask me what, because I am still trying to figure that out. Whatever it is, Scarlett is in very much danger now," I say, getting up from the table.

He is quiet for a moment, assessing everything I just said.

"Where are you going?" he asks me as he watches me head out of the house.

"We can't return to Scarlett until I have at least some of my powers back. I'll be completely useless to you if I don't have them."

He stands up with his hands on his hips.

"Oh yes, and how to do you expect to accomplish that, Princess?"

"You are named in the prophecy with me. Whether you like me or not," I say softly, walking out of the house with that, not wanting to hear his smug remark.

He stubbornly stays inside. I close my eyes against the sunlight. The cool breeze hits my face gently. It's quite beautiful where he lives. It's secluded, with green meadows, like a picture in a storybook. The scenery is breathtaking. I sit on the grass. I feel tears sting my eyes as I place my hands on the earth, silently thanking the spirits for my release. The wind again picks up, blowing some loose hair on my face as if they've received my message of thanks.

I close my eyes against the sun, against the images of the beast with the red eyes and fangs. I wonder what it all means. I'm scared. What if I don't get my powers back? What if I can't stop Opal? Again I bring my fingers up to my temples.

"You're overthinking it," the warlock's voice says from behind me.

"Overthinking what?" I say, opening my eyes and looking back at him.

He says nothing, just comes to sit in front of me on the plush grass. His knees graze mine, causing me to move back a bit and blush a little.

"You're overthinking your magic," he says simply.

"Will you help me?" I ask. I know the answer. He'll do anything to save the life of Scarlett, even if it means helping the likes of my kind. I wonder what his relationship to Scarlett is. Does he love her?

"You just need to relax. You're too uptight. Here, give me your hands." He holds out his hands. I hesitantly place my hands in his. I feel a bolt of energy as soon as our hands meet. I look up at him, startled by what I feel. His eyes widen, and I know he feels it too.

"Close your eyes," he says softly.

Swallowing hard, I obey.

"Now I want you to show me what you can do," he says.

"What do you mean? I can't," I say, opening my eyes, trying to pull my hands back.

He tightens his grip, his eyes narrowing.

"You can. Now close your eyes and focus," he says sternly.

Closing my eyes again, I try to focus. Thinking of my childhood, I begin by first summoning nature to ask its permission to spell. I chant softly. The breeze blows again around us. I shiver from the chill and clutch his warm hands tighter. I open my eyes, and there are white butterflies surrounding us. I laugh when one lands on my nose.

"I used to do this spell with my mother. I can't believe that I can still do it," I say, smiling at him.

He smiles back, but he is looking at me weirdly.

"What is it?" I ask.

"I expected you to be so much different," he says honestly.

"You mean like my sister?"

He nods, looking away briefly. "Yes."

I can't really blame him, can I? I don't answer him. What am I supposed to say to that? *No, no, I am nothing like my sister.* What would that prove? He wouldn't believe me anyway. I have two things against me. I am a witch who just happens to be the identical twin sister of his worst enemy. Nothing will ever change that or the opinion he already had of me before even meeting me. *Why does that thought seem to bother me?*

"Who's the man in the locket?" he asks, breaking me from my thoughts.

"I don't know what you're talking about," I say, shaking my head in confusion.

"Is he your former lover? The man in your locket." He leans over, grasping my locket in his hand, causing me to tilt forward toward him—which in turn causes me to look at his lips.

"What are you talking about? This locket doesn't open," I mumble, wishing he would look down at me. I tentatively lick my lips.

"What game are you playing, Princess? Look, it clearly opens," he says angrily.

All in one moment, I go from wanting to kiss him to wanting to kill him. It all happens in slow motion. I watch in stunned disbelief as he grabs the clasp, and it easily opens for him. I wrench myself from him quickly, standing up furiously.

"What did you do?" I scream at him.

"Settle down! I didn't do anything," he says, standing up and dusting his hands off.

"This has never opened before! What spell did you use to open it?" I yell at him accusingly, clutching my locket.

He holds up his hands in innocence. "What, you're afraid your boyfriend will find out? Tell me, do you think he waited for you? Something tells me no," he says, smiling smugly.

Before I have a chance to stop myself, the palm of my hand cracks his cheek hard, making his head turn. I gasp, feeling automatically sorry for hitting him. Before I can apologize, he roughly grabs me by the arms, pulling my body flush to his, his brown eyes looking down at me in anger. I open my mouth to shout at him to let me go, but his mouth crashes down on mine. And just like that…I am addicted.

His lips are exactly as I imagined. They're soft but hold strength. Sighing, I allow myself to be consumed by him. He lets go of my arms and brings his hands up, cradling my face gently as his tongue begins to explore my mouth. He tastes of apples…so sweet. I breathe him in, savoring every taste. My body melts into his. My nipples harden when they graze his chest, and a sweet throbbing begins to pulse between my legs. He groans, pressing himself to me so I can feel his hardening length. He breaks our kiss gently, and we stand silent, both of us spellbound by one another.

"I would have waited for you," he whispers to me, his eyes penetrating me deeply.

I am instantly brought back to the present. *My mother's locket.* This is not supposed to have happened, and especially not with a warlock. I pull away from him.

"I…I think I better go inside," I say, not waiting to hear his reply. I rush inside and go into the bedroom I'd slept in, closing the door behind me. Leaning against the door, I feel tears go down my face. I slide down to the floor and grab the locket, holding it up. Opening it, I see it is a picture of a man with dark hair and a mustache. He was very handsome. *My grandfather.* I let out a hysterical giggle as I think of how the warlock thought he was my lover. God, he couldn't be more wrong. I wonder what his reaction would be if I told him the legend surrounding the necklace. *Only your true love will be able to open the locket.*

Remembering my mother's words, I feel my tears begin to pool again. I wish she were here. What would she think of my warlock? *Wait,* my *warlock?* He is not mine. As soon as the war is over, we'll part. End of story. But why doesn't it feel right to just think that? I remember my sister's young voice in my head, replaying a taunt over and over again. *I bet Flora will fall in love with a warlock.*

The room has darkened just to my liking, the faint amber of the candles setting a glow to the room. I'm standing in the center of the room, surrounded by six candles that form a circle. The black paint on the hard wooden floors paint a hexagram. It consists of six sides, six points, and six triangles. *666.* I know exactly how to summon the blackest of magic, the darkest of evil. It is the blood moon. Raising my hands,

I begin to conjure. The candles begin to flicker as I invoke each spell.

"The eyes of two species become one. Let there be one... let there be one." I take my dagger out of my caped dress and cut my hand, offering penitence.

"Have the strength of two halves. Have eyes as red as my blood. Have a soul as black as mine." The drops of blood fall to the floor, beginning to sizzle as the floor grows hot.

I smile as I see it begin to work.

Hearing the sound of a whimper, I turn toward a young girl tied at the hands. She cowers against the wall, sobbing.

"Come here, child." I beckon her, holding out my hand toward her.

She is no more than fifteen years of age. She has light brown hair that has been cut short, and her big hazel eyes look at me with horror. My haunted appearance often receives that response.

"Come here, child. Do not make me ask you again," I say, this time with authority.

She gets up slowly, her small body trembling. It looks like the ancient stole her in her sleep. She has an ivory sleeping gown on. *How becoming...how virginal...*

"Who...who...are you? Please...please...I just want to leave," she begs me as she stands in front of me.

"I am Opal. You are better off in here than you are out there. Trust me. The death I will give you will be quick compared to what those animals would do to you." I grab her by her neck, gently bringing her closer to my face.

"Please...I don't want to die...I don't want to die." Her eyes are frantic, and she tries to claw her nails into my hands. I wrap them even tighter around her delicate neck.

"But I need you. Would you rather I take your baby brother instead ?" She halts her struggles, her teary eyes going wide. I knew everything there was to know about this girl the moment I touched her flesh. I knew she had a loving family. I knew she was sweet and had many friends. She had a crush on a boy named David, who did not seem to notice her yet. She was an innocent. Not even kissed yet. In order to complete the spell, I need to take a soul that is pure.

"Don't hurt him…I'll do anything you want me to do, please."

"I know." I nod. Using my fingertip, I open her mouth. I close my eyes and begin to chant.

"The breath of innocence is what I offer. The death of an innocent is the birth of evil." I lean my head forward, my lips inches from hers. Opening my mouth, I begin to suck the life out of her. *Ironic.* She begins to struggle again, but I hold her easily. Her small face begins to turn gray, and her eyes roll back. Consuming her life, I let her small body fall to the floor. I kneel down with my hands raised again. I feel slightly dazed.

Leaning down over my spilled blood, I exhale the innocent life that I've taken. I fall over from the impact of releasing the soul. The candles blow out, and the floors begin to shake beneath me. I may have passed out; I'm not sure. The magic is taking over me. I feel my body begin to rise, and I am suspended in the air. Every time I try to open my eyes, I see flashes of red eyes piercing my soul. It is a soul as blackened as mine. As blackened as the queen's. As blackened as Damian's. It is strangely a part of me. It is my creation. This creature that I have envisioned over and over. It calls to me.

I begin to lower as the spell reaches its completion, the candles lit once again. It is done. I step over the lifeless body of the girl without a second thought and leave the room. I enter my room and sit down, thinking of the warlock and Flora. He's put a shield over them so I can't find their location, but of course there are always loopholes. He will drop that shield once he needs to use his magic. It will be just a matter of time before I catch up with them.

The preparations are made for me to travel with Matthias to New York. Walking over to the bathroom, I put my hands over my eyes, changing them from white to hazel. Something will have to done about my appearance. Thinking of a great solution, I put my palms against the mirror and began to chant. The lights begin to flicker. Opening my eyes slowly, I am happy with what I see. I fix my newly short hairstyle. I don't want to stand out; I have to blend in perfectly for this to work. Smiling at myself, I leave the bathroom, taking off my cape and putting on ordinary clothes. *There! No one will suspect anything from a sweet fifteen-year-old girl, now will they?*

12

"You and Ian are blood mated."

I hear her words but I can't seem to grasp their meaning. Again I look over to Big Red, but he looks away.

"Scarlett, do you know what that means?" Zayah asks me gently.

I can't talk. I wrap my arms around myself, slowly shaking my head.

"In our world, you and Ian are married," she says, now looking at me nervously.

The blow of her words hits me hard. *Married?* I look over at Ian, and again he smiles at me.

"You fucking asshole." I push Zayah out of the way, roughly knocking her against Con. I launch myself at Ian, ready to claw his eyes out and wipe that smile off his face. Big Red grabs me before I can, his massive hands going around my waist.

"Love, calm down," Big Red whispers to me.

"Get your fucking hands off of her," Ian yells, coming toward Big Red, who is still trying to hold me back. Con blocks him.

"Everyone settle down," Con says forcefully.

"I want him out of here, Con. I mean it," I yell at him.

He lets a breath out, putting his hands on his hips.

"Scarlett, it's so much more complicated than that. Once you are blood mated, we have to respect that. Your side is with your husband. It is the way of our people," he says, trying to reason with me.

"Husband! Con, can't you see what he is trying to do? I thought you were smarter than that." My voice is starting to sound hoarse from screaming.

"It is the way of our people," he says again.

"I am *not* your people." I shove off Big Red hard. I watch Con's eyes widen at my words, but I couldn't care less. I run out of the room as fast as I can. It begins to rain heavily now, drenching my hair and clothes as I run to my car. Opening the driver door, I feel the overwhelming need to escape. Putting the keys into the ignition, I speed out of the driveway. Going as fast as I can, I see the gates are still locked. Pressing into the gas, I hope those gates are going to open because I am more than ready to drive through them. But they open at the last possible second.

My hands are freezing, and I grind my teeth so they won't chatter. *Married?* It can't be. I grab the front of my shirt, smelling it. I do smell different. The essence of Ian is all over me. There has been something different about me altogether since drinking his blood.

"Dammit," I say aloud, slamming my hand on the steering wheel.

I pass several cars, shifting gears as I do, driving a bit recklessly. Drivers begin to get annoyed with me for cutting them off, begin to honk their horns. I don't really know where I am going; I just know I need to go.

In my rearview mirror I see someone's car flashing its lights behind me. It's hard to see with all the rain, but I speed up faster. The car easily catches up with me. The silver-blue Aston Martin swings over to the left, pulling up beside me. Ian. We make eye contact, and there's a jolt of electricity between us. Pulling off into an abandoned alley, I quickly get out of the car. It starts to rain even harder. He gets out of his car, slicking his already-wet hair back.

"What were you thinking?" I yell at him.

"I didn't think. I warned you—I play to win," he says, putting his hands in his pockets.

"I'm not some game. Everything that has happened in my life has been dictated, and now this? You're just a selfish asshole. You don't think about anyone but yourself. You don't care about anything," I say, turning my back on him. I can't bear to look at him.

"I *care* more than you think," he shouts at me.

"What do you want from me? You want me to save you? Is that it? Well, I can't. How can I save you when I can't even save myself?" I scream, turning around to face him again. I hate him.

He says nothing, just stares at me intently. His cold eyes darken further.

"If you thought I hated you before, nothing compares to what I feel for you now," I say softly.

"You loved me once..." he trails off. I don't know what stuns me more: the fact that he would even think of me loving him again or the way he sounds almost hopeful.

He shrugs his shoulders, seemingly angry with himself for showing me a glimpse of what he tries to hide with everyone else. It confuses me more than I want. I don't need to see this side of him now. I needed it before, but he turned his back on me.

"It doesn't matter. Give me your anger. Give me your hate, because I will take you any way I can have you," he says instead, once again turning off that light.

I shake my head at his craziness. This is just all crazy. This can't be happening. Just when I thought I had the upper hand, he blindsides me once again. "So, what, are you now admitting you're enthralled?" I say, goading him.

He comes to me quickly, so he's standing inches from me. He raises his hand and starts to gently caress my cheek, wiping away the wetness from the rain. It takes everything in me not to lean into his touch.

"Let me be the man you want me to be," he says softly, his eyes looking so very different than before. He's given me this look before. When?

"Oh yeah. And what *man* is that?" I ask, moving away from his devious touch.

"The man from your vision," he whispers to me, jerking me back to him, his hands on either side of my face.

I feel a landslide of emotions all at once…things that I don't want to feel; my precious feelings that I gave to him freely. The ones he all but held in the palm of his hand, which he dropped to the floor before carelessly walking away without a second glance back. I can't possibly show him that he was close to breaking the wall I built against him. Looking into his eyes now, I begin to get lost. His head slowly descends on mine, his eyes now focusing on my lips.

"Well, well, look what we got here," an ancient vampire says from behind us.

Ian's hands tighten briefly on my face as he slowly turns. There are three ancients, all looking mean and vicious. The one who spoke seems like the leader of the group. He has long, dark blond hair, and his nose seems too big for his thin face. He spoke with what seems like a Russian accent. He reminds me of the big Russian from that Rocky movie. The other two are just as hideous-looking. Big and mean. They keep looking between Ian and me. Their nostrils flare as they catch the scent of Ian on me.

Great, not only was I marked for being the prophet, but now I'm marked as Ian's blood mate? Wife? I swallow hard just thinking that word. *I haven't even been on a date with this guy, but now I'm his wife?* I grind my teeth as I think of this, feeling my anger once again building up. I wrap my arms around myself, thinking this is going to be a show I will enjoy.

Ian strikes first, like a rattlesnake, going for the first ancient, punching him in the groin before kicking out at the other ancient. He quickly snaps the neck of one, turning him into ash. The Russian, surprised by this, grabs Ian from behind, but Ian is quick, bringing his head back and smashing the guy's nose. He screams out in pain, holding his nose before falling to the ground. The other ancient takes advantage of Ian's brief distraction by punching him and tackling him to the ground. I have to say, I do feel a bit of satisfaction seeing the ancient hit Ian. I actually smile.

Ian quickly rolls on top so that the ancient is on his belly and grabs him by the hair, yanking his neck back and breaking it. Ian looks up at me and smiles a wicked smile. He turns just in time to see the Russian come charging at him with a small dagger. When the Russian goes in to stab him, Ian quickly blocks his arm, twisting it roughly. The Russian screams, and I hear the bones break in his arm. Ian grabs the knife before it falls to the ground and stabs him in the heart, turning him to ash.

All the ancients are dead. Ian was amazing. He fought so viciously and with such ease. *The grace of a killer.*

"Where did you learn to fight?" I ask.

"A man taught me," he says after a moment's thought.

Nodding, I go and open Red's door. Pausing before I get in, I look at him.

"You're too late," I say to him.

"Too late for what?" he asks, his eyes trying to peer into my soul. *Do I even have one anymore?*

"I no longer want the man from my vision. He doesn't exist," I say softly. Getting into my car, I shift it into drive without bothering to look back.

❧

The sound of movement around the house jolts me awake. Sitting up, I comb my hand through my hair in frustration. I've only been with her one day, and she's already gotten under my skin; my constant hard-on whenever she's around is a reminder that doesn't help matters. The feel of her lips, her soft body flush to mine…I let out a groan.

Shifting myself in my pants, I get up from the bed, going into the bathroom. My eyes are slightly bloodshot, but my face is regaining its lost color. Using my powers for the shield and transporting us took most of my energy, but I know today we will be heading back to Scarlett. I wash my face of the sleep that I didn't really get.

I start to think of the moment I held Flora's hand when she began to chant. She didn't know it, but I had my eyes open the whole time. She was enchanting. Her soft voice was alluring. She did nothing extravagant—just a chant we all learned as children when first being taught to spell. Nonetheless, I was spellbound by her beauty. When she opened her eyes, I saw a twinkle I had not seen since being with her, and it made me want to laugh as I saw her playful enjoyment. Then I had to go ahead and ask her about the man in her locket. She got upset. I hated to admit it, but I got upset as well. I lashed out, and I deserved her anger. But that still made me wonder: *who the hell was he?* Then I had to do something even more stupid and kiss her. I feel the lower half of me stir at the memory. *I've been too long without a woman. That's all this is.*

Shaking my head in denial, I head out of the bathroom in search of her. Walking to the room where she is staying, I knock softly. When no answer comes after the third knock, I open the door and see that she isn't there. In fact, the bed is made up as if she was never here at all. Feeling my palms begin to sweat, I walk out and go to the kitchen—still no sign of her. *What the fuck?* I head out the door in a rush, cursing under my breath, thinking she's fooled me. Once I find her, there will be hell to pay—

Outside, I stop in my tracks, my stomach falling to the floor at the sight that I'm now witnessing. Flora is standing there, her beautiful red hair blowing in the wind. She has on the same outfit as yesterday. But she is not alone. Standing before her is a black bear. She seems not at all fazed by this deadly creature. I do not share her calmness. I inch myself forward. The bear turns its head toward me and growls viciously.

I gear myself up with a quick chant, raising my palm toward the animal.

"Don't you dare," she yells at me, turning toward me and stepping in front of the creature.

"Are you crazy?" I half yell at her, trying not to cause any more movement. One swipe of this bear's claw, and she is a goner.

"Please, don't," she says more quietly and turns back to the creature. She smiles. *She actually smiles!* "I am sorry, my friend. Come." She holds out her hand, and the bear turns back to her slowly and hesitantly, walking on all fours toward her. She looks so small against the animal's bulk. My breath stills as I watch as its head meets her hand. She pets it gently, her fingers brushing into its fur, cooing to it softly. The bear lets out a sound of pleasure at being touched by her.

"I am getting my powers back," she says softly. At first I think she isn't talking to me; I am too busy admiring her beauty.

"How do you know?" I ask after a minute.

"Can't you sense it? There is a different current in the air. Ever since..." she trails off shyly, biting her lower lip. I want so badly to bite that lip.

"Ever since what?" I come closer, but the bear lets out a growl in warning. I take a step back. *Damn bear—she's mine! Wait...what?* I shake my head at my thoughts. I need a woman now, and quick.

"Shhh...there now..." she says, smiling at the bear. "Thank you," she whispers to it. It walks away but looks back at me, it's big black eyes looking at me in warning before letting out another of its annoying growls.

"How did you do that?" I ask.

"I could always summon animals as a child. It's one of the first things I knew how to do. I can talk to them, and sometimes they can talk back, but only if they want to."

"Really? What did that bear say?" I ask curiously.

"He didn't trust you," she says, shrugging her shoulders, looking away.

"Really now? Did you tell that damn thing I saved your life?" I say, folding my arms across my chest.

"I did. He agreed I could trust you with my life—" She cut off, looking uncomfortable again.

"But...?" I ask, coming closer to her. I can't help it. I'm drawn to her like no other. Did she spell me? Is that what I'm feeling?

"It's nothing," she says, her green eyes going wide nervously as I near. I smile knowingly; she feels the same way.

"So as I was saying," she continues, "my powers are coming back slowly. It must be some loophole in Opal's spell. I think what must have triggered it was you. What? Don't you think it's a bit strange that all of a sudden my powers are coming back?" she asks.

"A loophole in Opal's spell. No. She would never have that. As far as me? Well, we are named in the prophecy together. It would only make sense, I guess," I say, looking at her as she begins to pace back and forth.

"I think that may be it, but I just get this feeling that it's more than that. What if Opal *wants* me to have my power back?" she stops and looks at me.

Interesting. I hadn't thought of that.

"Why would she do that?"

"You don't know her like I do. She hates me. Hate may be too soft of a word for what she feels about me, actually. And she loves to toy with her prey."

I am silent, thinking of the message she left for Flora as I transported us back to my family cottage.

"Watching her mother suffer was glorious, but it will be so much sweeter to watch this one do the same."

Did she kill Flora's mother? And, better question, did Flora know? My guess is no. I watch her pace back and forth again. She stops as she sees my expression. She pauses, her eyes wide. "What? What is it?"

"Nothing. Just thinking." I shake my head sadly. I don't want to be the one to tell her. I don't need that kind of responsibility. My responsibility is with Scarlett.

"OK, we need to find Liam," she says, looking at me suspiciously but changing the subject.

"How do you know of Liam?"

"Well, I wasn't the only one locked in a cage. His, though, was by choice. Damian was in the cell with me, plotting with Ezarbet." As my eyes widen, she continues, "He not only wants to help Ezarbet rule, but he wants to rule with her. He plans to take down his brother's pack and start a pack of his very own. And thus, as in the prophecy, *brothers will be at a crossroads.*"

I am stunned by her words. It shocks me that she knows so much. But I guess when you're locked in a cell, there is not much else to do but listen. I can't imagine what she has gone through. But even as she says, "Let's go find Liam," I know it's easier said than done.

"It's impossible to find him. The pack is just not out in the open. They hide, and they are a very watchful pack. It could be dangerous," I say.

"Nothing is impossible. Besides, their pack is much closer than you think," she says, flashing one of those dazzling smiles.

"How close?"

"The bear says maybe a mile from here."

"What? That's impossible," I say, shaking my head.

"Can you stop saying that? And yes. They have been right under your nose the whole time, Warlock." She starts to walk toward the area where she pointed. Turning back to me, she calls out, "Well, are you coming? Or are you just going to stand there all day? Scarlett is waiting for us, so let's get this done quickly."

Letting out a frustrated breath, I follow behind her. There is a forest just ahead, as the trail begins to fade. We walk in silence, my arm grazing hers as we walk side-by-side. She stumbles a few times, making me reach automatically for her. As our skin makes contact, there is this sense of awareness that is undeniable between us. Every so often I feel her stare and know she is feeling the same thing. She keeps tucking her long red hair behind her ear and biting her lower lip.

The more I get to know her, the more I become accustomed to her emotions. When she desires or becomes nervous, she bites her lower lip. When she's angered, her green eyes flash brightly, and when sad, they darken into a shadow. I saw that look when she talked about her mother. And when she chanted, her face glowed beautifully. She looked so alive and serene. It was almost breathtaking. She's right; there is a different current in the air. It oozes all around her, pulling everything in—especially me. She is getting her powers back, slowly, but surely. But would she use that power against her sister? I honestly don't know. If she went against Scarlett,

I would kill her without hesitation. *Why do I feel so sickened at the thought?* She stumbles again, and I quickly grab her by the arm, preventing her fall.

"Can you watch where you're walking?" I say angrily as I feel my body begin to once again heat from touching her.

"Sorry, Warlock. I didn't ask you to catch me," she snaps back, shoving her arm back, her green eyes flashing angrily.

"I would catch you," a voice says from behind us. I instantly put Flora's body behind me as I spot a man with long, dirty blond hair pulled back into a ponytail. He wears jeans and nothing else. His eyes give him away as they gleam red. *Beast.*

"We are looking for a man named Liam. We came here just to talk," I say to him, holding my hands up.

"Well, in order to get to Liam, you get through me first," he says, folding his massive arms across his chest.

"Well, who might you be?" I ask, trying to mask my annoyance.

"Adam. And who might the lady in red be…Eve?" he trails off.

"She is none of your concern," I say through clenched teeth.

"My name is Flora. We must speak to Liam," she says, stepping out from behind me.

Adam's eyes roam over her, gleaming lustfully. I feel that familiar and annoying sense of jealousy form from the pit of my stomach. I'm about to yank her back behind me, but she steps out of my reach.

"This is about Damian," she says softly.

"Damian! What about him?" he growls.

"He has sided with Queen Ezarbet and plans to take down your pack."

He is silent for a moment, seeming to take in her words. Does he believe her? He turns around, starting to walk away.

"Come on, follow me," he says simply.

We follow him in silence. Looking around, I gradually notice that we are actually surrounded by his pack. There are red eyes everywhere. *Shit!* Things could get tricky if they decide we are the enemy. The smell of smoke engulfs me as we near what seems to be a huge fire pit. Sitting down nonchalantly is a man that I know right away is Liam. He is a man who looks to hold power with just the grace of a stare. Unlike his friend Adam, he is actually very clean cut. His haircut is short, and he wears a flannel shirt and jeans. He is silent as we approach. Looking between Flora and me, he gives no emotion away as we stand before him.

"So Adam here tells me you have news of my brother," he says, his voice rough.

I pause for a moment, forgetting that these beasts have the power to communicate with one another without speaking.

"Yes. The prophecy has begun—" I begin, but he quickly cuts me off.

"I could give two shits about the fucking prophecy. If those bloodsuckers want to go to war, that's their problem. Not ours."

Before I can speak, Flora cuts me off. She's beginning to make a habit out of this.

"Oh, but it is very much your problem. Your brother has formed an alliance with Queen Ezarbet—who, by the way, is going to come after your pack."

For the first time, I see emotion waver over his face as his mouth clenches tight at the mention of his brother. "He wouldn't do that. He was once part of this pack." He stands up, his red eyes gleaming menacingly as he focuses on her. I grab Flora by the arm, bringing her close to me.

"Believe what you want. Your brother is an enemy now. We need you as an ally," I say to him.

"You want an alliance? What kind of joke is this?" He lets out a harsh laugh. "My alliance is held with my pack and my brother."

"Suit yourself. We're outta here." I look pointedly at Flora, grabbing her by the arm and hauling our asses out of there.

"Wait." Flora looks up at me. I let her go but stand close to her as she walks back to Liam, who still looks like he is about to boil over.

"Your brother's alliance is not with you. Just as my sister, Queen Ezarbet, is not allied with me. He has chosen a side. You care for him, but he thinks nothing of you. The time will come when you will have no choice but to stand against him," she says to him sadly. She walks over to me with her head bent down. As she grabs me by the hand, we begin to walk out of the forest. After we are safely away from the pack, I turn to her.

"That was very brave of you," I say softly to her.

"He had to know the truth." She shrugs her shoulders.

I notice we are still holding hands. *Why does this feel so right?* As we near the cottage, the sun is beginning to go down. It's time to go to Scarlett and the others.

"Are you ready?" I ask, looking down at her as I stop.

"Yes," she says softly.

"Close your eyes," I whisper. As she does so, I bring my hands to her waist, pulling her body flush to mine. I can't take my eyes off of her. The wind picks up, blowing her long hair around us as we begin to fade. I can't stop thinking to myself how badly I want to kiss her again.

13

I found myself in a room with a little girl no more than five years of age. She was a tiny thing with long, dark curls running down her back. Her eyes were closed as she cried. Her little face was turned against the window, the sunshine casting a glow on her. I felt myself squint against the bright light that I had not seen in what seemed like forever. When was the last time I had felt the sun graze my face? Hearing the child whimper, I turned back to her. I wondered why she was crying. I felt for whatever reason protective of her. Why?

"I promise I will be a good girl, Mrs. Lang. Please don't make me go," she said in a very sweet little voice, her bottom lip pouting prettily.

I turned to the woman who was seated next to the girl, ready to strike the person who would make her cry. She was an elderly African American woman with graying hair and glasses too big for her face. Her pantsuit, once navy blue in color, now looked old and faded. She put her hands on her glasses as she adjusted them. Her eyes held sadness, but it looked as if she had no choice in the matter.

"Scarlett, you are a very good girl. This has nothing to do with your behavior. Don't you want to be with a loving family?"

I jerked back, stunned. I turned around, staring out the window at the sun. What was this? Was I dreaming? I had heard stories that once becoming blood mated you shared the memories of your blood mate. Was this it?

"I don't want to go." I turned back to the soft voice of Scarlett as a youth. My wife.

"Oh, honey, you will be fine. Just wait and see, OK? Let me bring in the Andersons." Mrs. Lang got up and left Scarlett alone with me.

I sat down hesitantly beside her. She looked so vulnerable. Even as a youth, her future beauty was unmistakable. Her cheeks were reddened from crying, and her mismatched eyes welled up with renewed tears as she watched Mrs. Lang go to get what I assumed were her new parents. Her small hand was within my reach; I wanted so badly to show her comfort. Did I even know how to do that?

Wiping her eyes, she got up slowly and walked over to the old wooden bookcase that sat in the corner of the room. She picked up a book and clutched it tightly to her chest as she went under a table to hide. I briefly thought back to my own childhood, the one I usually willed myself to forget. It all came back to me. The smell of the alcohol on his breath. Hiding under the table as a child as he would beat my mother repeatedly. I felt my chest tighten with anxiety.

Without realizing what I was doing, I felt myself crawling in with her, sitting beside her as she opened the book that she took from the shelf. It was called Aria's Everafter. *It was a bright and colorful book, full of pictures of enchanting forests and magic. In the end, a prince saved the princess from her dreadful fate, and they lived out their happily ever after. Fairy tales.*

Swallowing hard against the lump that formed in my throat, I looked away from her as she began to read. Her soft voice calmed me when I started to think about my dark past. Even now, her voice alone can bring me out into the light even though all I have known is darkness. I studied her as she read, wanting to ease her fear, wanting to save the young girl that was Scarlett. Did she see my memories? I closed my eyes, briefly wondering if she thought the same thing I was thinking at this very moment. We were more alike than I ever thought.

Walking back into our new training center, drenched from the rain, I can't help but feel like I am home. The staircase is huge and inviting. I wonder if my bedroom is upstairs. I realize then how tired I am.

"Scarlett." I turn toward Zayah's voice. She looks a bit worried, regarding me hesitantly. "Are you OK?" she asks me.

"I will be," I say. I don't really know what I mean by that comment. Driving back here, I was contemplating a thousand ways to kill Ian. I can only assume blood mate divorce is out of the question. "Can you give me the grand tour?"

"Sure," she says, smiling.

The home is big, and *big* is an understatement. It has a basketball court and indoor and outdoor pools. The kitchen is decorated in a modern fashion, with white cabinets, stainless steel appliances, and a beautiful gray granite-top island.

"Con wanted you to feel like this was home," Zayah says from behind me.

"Is he upset with me?" I say, turning back to her. I feel guilty for what I said. I don't mean to take my anger out on him or Zayah, thinking of how I roughly pushed her.

"No, don't worry. He has a lot on his mind; actually he has been quite distant lately," she says, looking away, her brow furrowed deep in thought. Concern shadows her face.

"What do you mean by 'a lot on his mind'?" I ask.

"I don't know..." she says sadly.

I walk over to touch her arm lightly, trying to reassure her.

"Come on, let me show you your room," she says, shaking her head and smiling once more, seeming to want to change the subject.

"OK," I say cheerfully.

She leads me up the grand staircase and brings me to the first door on the left. The huge bedroom is everything I wanted, if I ever had that type of money to have it. The room is the size of my whole apartment. A huge, canopied California king bed is the focal point of the room. It is covered with white bedding and a comforter, with an array of pillows on top that make me want to just dive in. The woodwork is impressive. A crystal chandelier hangs from the ceiling. The walls are painted a soft lavender color, giving off a romantic feel. The fireplace is just as romantic. A lavender fabric settee sits in front of it. If I were a reader, this would be the perfect spot to curl up with a good book. Speaking of which, there is a built-in bookshelf...with no books. Odd. I start thinking to myself, *When was the last time I picked up a book? Face it; you don't have time to read. You're saving the world, remember?*

"Do you like the color? I picked it out. Thought it was definitely better than black," Zayah says teasingly.

I let out a laugh. "Yes, any color but black," I say. I walk over to where I see another doorway. And I swear I can almost hear church bells chiming in the distance. It is my perfect sanctuary. The en suite bathroom is even better than the Plaza's. The walls are painted a soft pink color. A French-style bathtub big enough for two stands in the center, and there is a separate shower. The tiles and granite top are white with gold flecks.

There are his and hers sinks. If this bathroom could get any better…and then it does. I see a vanity table with a beautiful gold chair, a pink fabric cushion that matches the walls sitting lightly atop it. This is the ultimate girl's bathroom. I notice, sitting by the bathtub, the bath salts that I use all the time. I pick up the jar to check the scent: chamomile lavender. *How did they know?*

"Ian said that you loved that scent," Zayah says, answering my unspoken question.

"So…was he a part of this process?" I say quietly, gesturing to my surroundings.

"Yes. He has been in contact with Con since the moment after the battle. Give or take a day or two."

"Zayah, don't you see how fucked up this whole thing is? He tricked me," I say, putting down the salts. My heart surges just a little, knowing he thought of me after he decided to leave me. But I quickly douse it. It doesn't matter anymore. *Liar.*

"He made a mistake, Scarlett. We all do. People change," she says.

"People don't change. Situations do. He'll always be a selfish asshole," I say, shaking my head.

"A selfish asshole who is in love with you," Zayah counters back.

I swallow hard. Whose side is she on, anyway? Ian isn't in love with me; he is in lust with me. Huge difference. Before I can tell her this, the lights begin to flicker, and the house seems to shake a little. *Hugo.* I rush out of the room in a hurry, practically flying down the stairs, Zayah right behind me. All the Xs are downstairs in the dining room as Hugo appears with Flora in his arms.

I smile with a surge of relief. Hugo is back. I feel tears sting my eyes briefly. He lets go of Flora, and she smiles up at him shyly. She is more beautiful in person than I thought. So different from her sister. I can't help but feel a bit weird as I see Hugo looking down at her adoringly. *So my visions were right.* He turns then, making eye contact with me, smiling wider.

"Scarlett," he says, and I walk into his waiting arms. We hug, and I lay my head gently on his shoulder. I didn't realize how much I needed this. I'm so happy to see him. When I raise my head, I see Flora's face, and she seems a bit caught off guard by the affection between Hugo and me.

"Flora," I say, going over to her, not knowing what to say. "Welcome" doesn't sound right, and "Hey there" sounds downright crazy.

She smiles shyly, and before I can say anything else, she hugs me. I stagger back briefly, slightly shocked. For one so small, she holds strength.

"It is an honor to finally meet you. I am forever indebted to you," she whispers in my ear.

She pulls away, and I find myself smiling. I go to introduce the Xs. They all seem OK with her being there, but I can still feel their tension.

"Looks like I may have some competition. Scarlett, will you name her Little Red?" Big Red says, grabbing Flora by the hand and bringing it to his lips, kissing it. Flora blushes shyly, and Hugo looks extremely pissed off.

"No, I like Flora just fine," I say, rolling my eyes as he flashes a charming smile at her. I wonder if he knew his action would get a rise out of Hugo. Knowing Big Red like I know him now...yes, he did.

"Now, that's a shame," he says, looking at Hugo, grinning from cheek to cheek. *He knew.*

"OK, so now that the introductions are done, let's go see you to your room." I start to lead her out.

"You forgot about me." Ian's voice shoots from the doorway, stopping me in my tracks. The silence in the room is beyond thick. If my eyes could shoot daggers at him, they would kill him in an instant. His hair is still wet from the rain, and he looks sexy as hell. Feeling my body stir for him, I second that thought. *Yeah, I would kill him slowly. Let him suffer.*

"What is he doing here?" Hugo breaks the silence and my sadistic thoughts. I didn't even feel him come to stand beside me. Swallowing hard, I can't even form the words.

"This is going to be fucking good. Come on, love. Let's get you out of the way," Big Red says as he pulls Flora out of harm's way.

"Scarlett, what is going on?" Hugo asks me again.

I look over to him nervously. I know in breaking the news to him I'll see the look of disappointment on his face. He warned me not to do anything rash. This was way beyond rash. But wait—did this really count? I was tricked. Ian is in front of us before I can get the right words out.

"She didn't tell you yet, Warlock? She and I have become blood mated. She is now my wife. I think congratulations are in order, wouldn't you say, Scarlett?" he says cruelly.

God, he is such an asshole. He couldn't just let me explain.

"Scarlett, is this true?" Hugo asks softly. His face is contorted in a quiet anger I have never seen before.

"Yes," I say softly, looking away momentarily. I look at Big Red for help as he silently shrugs his shoulders.

"You son of bitch," Hugo shouts.

"Hugo," I scream.

He moves so fast I don't have time to stop him. He swings his left hand, punching Ian so hard that Ian staggers back. Flora lets out a scream. Some of the Xs try to hold Hugo back as he charges forward to hit Ian again. Big Red lets out a shout of laughter. Con grabs ahold of Ian as he menacingly wipes the blood from his mouth, stalking over to Hugo. It all happens in slow motion, and I can't help but watch as all hell breaks loose around me.

"So what you're telling me is you have no idea where you've been for the past day and a half? Come on, Jessica. Your family has been worried sick about you. Your tests have come back clean. No drugs involved. You have to give me something," I say, staring at the young girl.

"I really don't know, Officer..." she says, seeming to forget my name. She's hooked up to IVs. She was brought in by a cab driver who'd seen her sitting down on the sidewalk. He'd seen her picture on the news and called the police right away.

"Alvarez. Officer Alvarez."

I was the first one to respond to the call. She needed a blood transfusion, but the doctors couldn't seem to figure out where the blood loss was coming from. They assumed it was internal, but all tests cleared her. It was just like many of the other cases being reported lately. Memory and blood loss. Of course I won't voice these opinions to my superiors. If I want to keep my job, it is best to keep this to myself. I know I am walking down a dark path, but fuck it. I have to know what the hell is going on. It is my duty, after all, to keep my city safe.

"I just remember being at this club," she says, breaking me from my thoughts.

"OK, what club?" I ask, taking out my notepad and pen.

"It's called…God, what is it called?" She closes her eyes, thinking hard.

"Did you go with anyone? Were you meeting someone there?"

"No, I was supposed to hang out with my girlfriend, and she bailed on me last minute. I was already dressed, so I thought, 'screw it,' and I went by myself." She shrugs her shoulders.

"OK," I say, writing this down. Next to my notes I write "dumbass."

"I can't think of the name, but I keep seeing images of an eye," she says after a minute.

"Of an eye?" I ask curiously.

"Yes, a red eye," she says, nodding her head confidently.

"OK. I'll look into this." I get up, folding my pad closed and putting it into my back pocket. "If you remember anything at all, I want you to call me, OK?" I hand her my card.

"OK, I will," she promises as I walk out.

I head straight to the station, wanting to do some digging. It's a quiet night. I get a few hellos from the guys as I head straight to my desk, not wanting to make small talk with anyone. I am known for this. Gathering all the information on Jessica, I start to build my report. I also Google all the clubs in New York City—and there are many—looking for anything that might catch my eye.

After searching for over an hour, I see a nightclub called After the Sun. Curious, I move the cursor, double-clicking on it. The logo of a red eye is the first thing I see. *Interesting.* The club is dark and gothic-looking, with red and black furnishings. It has a distinctly medieval look. Why would a young girl like Jessica go into such a place, and how the hell did she manage to get in since she was underage? Looking into her wallet earlier, I'd seen that she had no fake ID on her. *Looks like I'll be making a trip to the club.*

Turning off the computer, I rub my hand over my eyes. Looking at the time, I see that it's one in the morning. The club will still be open. Getting up, I make my way out. The club is approximately thirty minutes from here. Hightailing it as fast as I can, I make it there in record time. *Sometimes it just pays to be a cop.*

I see the red eye first, outlined in bold red neon lighting above the After the Sun sign. There's still a line. Curious onlookers gawk at me, because the uniform always either puts people at ease or makes them nervous. The big beefy guard folds his arms as he sees me approaching. He wears a tight, short-sleeved turtleneck with matching tight pants. Why he is wearing sunglasses too small for his face, I don't know.

"No cops," he says to me.

"Really now? Here I was just going to say hello to the owner. Either you let me in nicely, or you're going to regret not letting me in. I will have this place closed for good. Before the sun—no pun intended, of course," I say cockily to him.

He studies me a moment more. He grabs his walkie-talkie, speaking into it.

"We got company," he growls.

I wait patiently for the reply.

"Let him in," the voice replies nervously.

"Go in. All the way down, first door, take a right," he says, moving out of the way.

Smiling, I enter. The music is too loud, and the place is overcrowded. I could give them a citation right here if I wanted. The place is filled with weirdos. It looks more like a fetish club than anything else. There are cages that hang from the ceiling with dancers in them wearing tight leather shorts and matching bras. Looks like everyone here has a thing for leather. I cautiously open the door the bouncer directed me to, stepping inside.

"Hello, Officer, may I help you?" the man seated behind the desk says. He's dressed like his club-goers, wearing a red collared shirt and leather pants. He extends his hand to me in greeting. I don't take it.

"Are you the owner of this place?" I ask. I watch as he begins to sweat nervously.

"Um…no, I am the manager," he stutters.

"Well, I am looking for the owner. Recently, a girl went missing, and then she was found. This is the last place she remembers before suffering memory loss."

"I can assure you that no funny business goes on here—"

I cut him off. "I want access to your security cameras."

"I don't have access to the cameras," he says, his eyes looking away from me briefly.

Lie. I can always sense when someone is lying to me. Police 101. When a man sweats and keeps shifting his eyes, he has something to hide. *What exactly is going on in this club?*

"I want to know who the owner is. I have questions for him."

"OK, fine, I'll call him," he says, reaching for his phone.

"No, tell him I'll be back tomorrow. I want to see him in person, and I'll have a warrant in hand." Reaching into my back pocket, I get my notepad and pen out, wanting to have the upper hand on whoever I was dealing with.

"What's his name?" I ask.

Writing down his name, I snap my pad closed, walking out of the room without saying anything more. I make it out of the club and back to the patrol car, and then I take out my cell phone.

"Officer Reed," the voice snaps.

"Rita, pulling in a favor. I'm going to I need info on a guy, and when I say info, I mean I want to know what time he wakes up in the morning to take a piss."

"You act as if I have nothing better to do. I'm swamped in paperwork over here," she complains.

Rita and I go way back. We met at the police academy. Coming from a family with a strong police background, it was in her blood to follow suit. We became friends right away—more like family. She married one of our other friends, Tom, who of course is also a policeman, recently promoted to detective. They are two of my best friends.

"Come on, I'm working a case, and you're the only one I know quick enough to get me what I need," I say, starting the car. I know, with the right amount of compliments, I will get my way.

"Agh, fine. Give me an hour, and let me see what I can find," she huffs after a minute.

"I'll give you thirty minutes, and coffee is on me," I say, snapping my phone shut and starting the car.

Back at the station, Captain Horace sees me and waves for my attention. *Shit.*

"Officer Alvarez, please come in. I've been meaning to talk to you." I step into his office and have a seat.

He follows me in, closing the door behind him. Captain Horace has been my captain for five years now. He's one of the most respected men on the force. His age is catching up with him, but he's still tough as shit. When he speaks, we listen.

"OK, so I think you may have an idea why I brought you in here," he says, crossing his arms over his chest.

"No, I actually don't," I say, shaking my head.

"Well, we're getting new recruits. You have shown great work as a patrol officer. You assisted with that hostage situation and were also there to help that family from a fire in their home."

"I was just at the right place at the right time," I say nonchalantly.

"You show promise, son."

I don't reply. What was I supposed to say to that? I'm not a man who is comfortable with compliments.

"With that being said, you're being promoted to detective," he says proudly.

My mouth gapes open. I'm stunned. I was not expecting this. Sure, I knew the day would come that I would get recognized for my good deeds, but I'm better off staying in the background. I'm comfortable there. I don't need a promotion to protect my city.

"So no more uniform after tomorrow," he says to me, not noticing the battle brewing in my head.

"OK," I say, getting up from the chair, shaking his hand. I turn toward the door and pause, turning back to him. "With all due respect, Captain, I've been working on the Jessica Moore case. I would like to finish it myself," I say.

"Yes, of course, you do what you need to do, and I will set you up on other assignments," he says.

Nodding, I walk out. No longer Officer Alvarez, but Detective Alvarez. *Nice ring to it.* Everyone seems to know that I got promoted; I start getting handshakes and congratulations from everyone in my department. I walk back over to my desk to fix my paperwork when my phone starts ringing.

"Officer Alvarez."

"Don't you mean Detective Alvarez?" Rita says, laughing. "Tom told me the good news. Congratulations, Bud," she says, stopping me from asking her how she knew.

"Thanks," I say.

"OK, so who is your best girl?" she asks.

"You know you are," I say, smiling and leaning back in my chair.

"Yeah, I know, just wanted to hear you say it. Well, it looks like I have some info on your guy."

"Spill."

After getting off the phone, I stare at the notes I took on the owner. It doesn't make sense why a successful guy like him would own a club like After the Sun. Part of an investment deal? I'm curious about this, and usually my curiosity is spot-on. Something's not right about this picture. I can't seem to put my finger on it, but I am going to get to the bottom of it. *Michael Pearson is not going to be happy once he gets a load of me.*

14

"Everyone needs to calm down," Con cries out, his thunderous voice causing everyone to shut up.

"I let you have the first one, Warlock. Next one, you won't be so lucky," Ian snarls quietly behind Con, who still has his hand up against his chest, forcing him back.

"Come on, I am dying to punch you again," I snarl. Skull is holding me back. I put in a quick chant, holding him immobile as I move away from him to get to Ian. I see red. I put the same spell on Con as well. Ian and I charge at each other like raging bulls.

"Bastian, do something; I can't move, for fuck's sake," Con says, calling out to his brother.

"No, let them have at it. This is just too enjoyable to stop," Big Red says.

I hear a scream in the distance as I tackle Ian into a French doorway. The door breaks, glass shattering everywhere. I begin to aim punches anywhere I can.

"Stop it." I hear Flora's voice reaching me, and I momentarily look up. I see her face go pale, and her eyes well up with tears. Of fear? Taking advantage of my distraction, like a snake, Ian punches me. Rolling on top of me, he raises his fist to strike me, but someone grabs ahold of his hand in a viselike grip.

"Don't," Scarlett says softly to him.

He looks at her and then back at me, seeming conflicted, as if he's waging a personal war with himself. *Strange.* He gets up slowly, away from me, still staring at Scarlett, before walking out of the room. I get up, grunting, waving Scarlett off as she tries to help me up.

"Warlock, release this fucking spell," Skull snaps at me.

"Sorry," I say, releasing them of my casting.

I look over to Flora, and she looks away from me. I feel suddenly guilty. Why did I have to act like such a violent ass? *Way to welcome her.*

"Are you OK?" Scarlett asks me, breaking me from my thoughts.

"Agh, yeah. I've been dying to do that for a while now. Scarlett, I am sorry. I should have been here to protect you," I say, looking down.

"There is nothing to be sorry about. I got myself into this mess. You're not always going to be here to protect me." Then she adds quietly, so I am the only one who can hear, "Besides, it looks like you have someone else to protect as well."

I don't deny it. What's the point? I feel things for Flora. My need to protect her is growing stronger by the day. My need to be with her in the physical sense is even stronger. I yearn for her like no other. I let out an uncomfortable cough.

"So I was just telling Flora that I would show her to her room," Big Red says, smiling charmingly again at Flora, who still looks scared as shit but gives a small smile of thanks.

"I don't think that will be necessary. I will show Flora to her room," I practically growl.

Hearing my angered reply, Flora looks at me, confused. *What is she thinking?*

"My, my...pretty boy came back from his trip feisty. What did you do to him?" Big Red holds up his hands, innocently looking at Flora.

Flora says nothing as I put my hand at the small of her back; she slightly stiffens from my touch. Zayah tells me what room it is, and we go up the grand staircase, going all the way down the hall to the left. I open her door. It's quite a refreshing room, with pink walls and white furnishings. A white comforter and white pillows of all sizes are on the bed. I find myself wondering how her red hair would look against the white sheets as she sleeps.

"You're bleeding," she says softly.

"What?" I ask, looking back at her.

"I said you're bleeding," she repeats, coming over to me, gently touching the cut that is above my eye. I wince slightly from the sting.

I guess I deserved that. It was stupid of me to lose my cool. I hardly ever do. But seeing Scarlett's face looking so hopeless and lost, I felt a surge of loathing I'd never felt before, and it was aimed at Ian. And rightfully so. I know Ian to be a snake, but this? What game is he playing? I will figure this out one way or another.

"It doesn't hurt much," I say, looking down at her, loving the feel of her touch.

"Are you in love with her?" she asks, so softly it's almost hard to hear her.

"With who?" I ask, confused.

"Scarlett," she says, looking at me as if I should know who she is talking about.

In love with Scarlett? What?

"You're not answering me, so I guess I can take that as a yes." She turns away from me, her green eyes flashing angrily.

"No, I am not in love with Scarlett," I say quietly.

I move closer to her, turning her around gently so she faces me. She bites her lower lip, shyly looking away.

"Would it bother you if I was?" I ask.

"Yes. Yes, it would," she answers me honestly.

I feel myself harden as I think of her jealousy. *What are you doing to me?*

"Why? Why would it bother you?" I reach out, softly caressing her face. She leans into my touch, her lips parting slightly as her eyes close, denying me the look of desire that is there. *What is going on in that beautiful mind of yours?* I grasp her chin gently, forcing her to meet me in the eyes.

"Look at me and tell me," I say, a gentle command in my voice.

"Because even though you may not want it or you may not realize it yet, you are mine," she says to me, her voice so alluring. Her proclamation sends a jolt in me. I've wanted to tell her I was hers the moment she claimed a warlock saved her. I lean my head down, and she meets me halfway, going on her tiptoes for a kiss. The candles in the room all light simultaneously as the energy between us flares, undeniable. I don't know if the spell came from me or her. Her arms go around my neck as I pull her closer to me. She gasps as I bite her bottom lip; her mouth opens as my tongue makes its way in. Tasting her is becoming an addiction for me.

I pick her up without breaking our kiss and lay her on the bed, resting my body gently on top of her. She parts her legs trustingly, making me settle down against her heated core. Her welcoming warmth envelops me. She is soft in all the right places. My hand creeps up into her shirt and touches her breast. It fits perfectly into my palm. She moans loudly into my mouth as my fingertips graze her nipple. Breaking our kiss, I take her sweater off. The white bra she's wearing does nothing to conceal her pink nipples, which harden as they anxiously await my mouth, the gold necklace lying beautifully against her pale skin.

"You're perfect," I say softly to her. I look down at her in awe. Just as I imagined, her red hair looks beautiful against the white sheets.

She looks away shyly, her face flushing as she tries to cover herself.

"No, don't. You're perfect. Made just for me." She smiles, raising her arms to bring my head down again. Our lips meet more softly this time. I take my time peeling the rest of her clothes off. She helps me with my shirt, her fingertips grazing my chest gently. I let out a groan of pleasure as her soft hand dips lower, coming to settle on my hardened erection. Her green eyes darken with desire, and her mouth forms an O. I want to learn everything there is to know about her. I want to know what it would take to make her shiver in pleasure. I want to know what would make her scream in ecstasy. I will know everything about her before this night is done.

She was right. I am hers in every way that's possible. She is everything I thought I didn't want. She is a witch. She is Queen Ezarbet's sister. But none of that matters. She is Flora. She is mine. She is my beloved.

Closing my door softly, I lean my head back against it, closing my eyes. *How could things go so crazy in such a short amount of time? Damn and fuck Ian.* Walking away from the door, I go into my bathroom, peeling my clothes off. I turn on the bathwater. Letting it heat up, I pour my bath salts in. Dipping my toes in to test the water, I settle in a moment later, letting the heat of the water envelop me. Sighing with pleasure, I close my eyes and feel myself drift not into a vision, but into a memory of Ian's.

"Catch 'im before he gets away," a man yelled as he and five others ran after Ian. The hairs on the back of my neck stood. Vampires. They caught up with him easily enough, grabbing him by the neck, holding him down as he tried to fight them off.

"You dare to try to steal from us, young vampire? You picked the wrong people," the ancient snarled at him.

I could tell they were warriors from the gear they wore and the looks on their faces, hungry for a fight. Ian's hair was longer; he seemed younger somehow, even though he was a vampire. They each started to beat him individually. He tried to attack, but they were too smart, outweighing him with their strength. One of the men kicked him in the mouth, causing him to spit out blood. I inwardly winced. Shit! This was not the Ian I saw today. That Ian would take these assholes down with no hesitation. The same ancient grabbed him by the hair, yanking his head back and making him meet him in the eyes.

"Have you had a enough?" the man spat at him.

"Fuck you," Ian whispered, spitting blood at the ancient's face.

"I think you want more." He punched him in the face, knocking Ian once more to the floor.

Wiping the spit from his face, the man ordered the others to lift Ian up. They complied. I saw his face and closed my eyes. It was bloodied and bruised. The ancient took a sharp knife from his pocket.

"I am going to carve my name on you with this silver, so every time you think of stealing, you will think of me." He came over to him, menacing, almost taunting Ian. If he was hoping to see fear in Ian's eyes, he was disappointed.

"That's enough, Landan," a voice commanded from behind the shadows—a voice that was so recognizable my heart stilled, and my body froze.

"Stay out of this, Edrick. He stole from me; he deserves to be punished."

"Come now, Landan. He is a young vampire, as you once were. He was reckless; leave him be." He stepped out from the shadows, making his presence known. All the ancients took a step back, and the ones holding Ian let him go. He dropped to his knees on the floor. Edrick was one man alone, but when he spoke he commanded either respect or fear. These men gave him both.

"Edrick, always the savior," Landan said, angrily turning away, back toward Ian. He gave him one final kick to the groin. Ian winced, holding himself as Landon and the others left.

It was quiet for a moment as Ian began to stand, thinking he was alone. He looked up; seeing Edrick, he shifted his eyes distrustfully toward him. What were the odds? My father knew Ian. Two totally different men. My father was honorable. Ian was a snake. My father was loyal. Ian was only loyal to himself. How could this be? How could their paths have crossed?

"Why? Why would you help me?" Ian asked him.

"It doesn't matter why I helped you. If you're going to steal from ancients, at least be good at it and don't get caught," Edrick said sternly to him.

"Who says I wasn't trying to get caught? I don't need your help. I can take care of myself!" Ian yelled, turning to walk away.

"I can teach you to protect yourself," Edrick called to him, causing Ian to stop in his tracks. "How did I know that would get your attention?" Edrick said smiling.

So began their relationship. I knew one of the answers to my question. Why hadn't I noticed it before? Ian's fighting style was very similar to that of my father. I watched as Ian met Edrick every night just before the sun went down. Edrick trained him on everything, from one-on-one combat to entrancing humans. Ian, in this memory, was new to the vampire world. It was strange seeing him that way. He was so domineering in my present.

Edrick took him in, but they never spoke as friends would. They both seemed to have a purpose, whatever that was. The only real interaction was of Edrick explaining something and Ian giving the occasional nod. Still, I could tell that Ian hung on every word my father said to him. He seemed to admire him. I closed my eyes briefly from the sting of tears I felt coming to my eyes.

"What pushes you?" Edrick asked him. It was the first time they had ever spoken of something personal.

"Nothing. I feel nothing," Ian said softly, looking away from him.

Edrick was quiet for a moment, seeming to contemplate what Ian had just said. "Don't try to figure him out, Dad. It's a waste of time," I said aloud.

"You'll feel one day, and when you do, it will knock you on your ass. Your training is done. You're on your own now," Edrick said, walking away from him.

"Wait. You never really said why you helped me," Ian said.

"I have my reasons. You are exactly what I need you to be...for now."

"To be what exactly?" Ian's piercing blue eyes shone fiercely as he demanded an answer to his question.

"Ruthless," Edrick said, walking away from him forever.

Opening my eyes from the memory, my heart aches. *You knew, didn't you? You knew what Ian was going to be for me.* I wonder if Ian knows. Does he know Edrick was my father? Something tells me that he doesn't. Getting out of the water, which is now cold, I wrap a towel around myself. I walk into my bedroom, and Ian is lying on the bed waiting for me.

"What are you doing here?" I practically yell. All the things I had started to feel for him through the memory quickly dissipate as he smiles smugly. *That stupid, sexy smile.*

"Doesn't a husband usually sleep in the same bed as his wife?" he asks, leaning back with one of his arms behind his head and making himself comfortable against the plush pillows. A little too comfortable. Gone is his leather jacket; instead he's wearing a newly dried white T-shirt and stone-washed jeans. He's also barefoot. I've never seen him so comfortable before, and it unnerves me.

"That's a load of bull. Vampires don't sleep. And you're not my husband, so get out!" I yell, crossing my arms across my chest.

"I am your *husband,* and I am not going anywhere," he says, staring up at the ceiling and choosing to ignore me as I huff and puff.

Oh yeah? You want to ignore me? OK, two can play this game. I let the towel drop from my still-wet body. Before it hits the floor, he turns his head, his eyes now focused on me and gleaming darkly with desire. *Gotcha!* Turning around I reach into one of the drawers, taking out a pair of underwear and an oversized Mets T-shirt.

Sorry, Yankees! Pulling it over my body, I glance at him watching me. He tries his best to look unaffected by me, but from the tick of his jaw and the clenching of his hands behind his head, he looks as if he's restraining himself from leaping at me.

"I would fight you on this, but right now I'm just too tired to fight. Besides, it looks like you got enough of a beating from Hugo." I turn off the lights, but the room glows from the fireplace. I start to pull off the pillows one by one before pulling back the covers. I slide in between the sheets, loving the feel of the soft cotton on my legs. I keep a cool distance away from him, staring at the ceiling. I can't believe he's lying on the bed with me. It just seems so…so normal. I turn toward him, wanting to hear him talk.

"Why did you goad Hugo?" I whisper.

He turns slowly to me so he is lying on his side, his steel-blue eyes regarding me intently.

"Because he had his hands on you," he says in a low voice.

"Will you ever give me an appropriate answer?" I ask him sleepily. I feel my eyes beginning to droop. I guess I am more tired than I thought.

"I didn't like seeing his hands on you," he whispers as he gently takes my left hand in his, caressing it softly.

"Why?" I press. I try to pull my hand away, but he only tightens his hold. Sighing, I give up, settling more deeply into the pillows.

"Because you're my wife," he says quietly, looking away. I feel his finger absently rub my ring finger.

"Liar," I say softly. My eyes are feeling heavier by the second.

"I was jealous," he says, and I feel his cold fingertips graze my face. Some people would flinch from the coldness of that touch, but I find it soothing…as soothing as his voice.

"Careful, Ian, your emotions are starting to show. Some would call that a weakness," I say as I feel myself begin to doze off.

"You are my weakness," I think I hear him say as I drift off into a deep sleep.

I don't bother to knock, since I was already summoned by one of the guards to meet with her. Walking into the dark bedroom, lit by only the fireplace, I walk over to Queen Ezarbet. She has a silk sheet wrapped around her body, her back turned to me as she stares at the fire where she lies on the carpeted floor. I have come to learn that this is a thing she does when she is deep in thought. *What is she thinking of now?* I wonder. I can't wait to see her expression when she sees my new appearance, but mainly I want to see if the spell has been cast correctly, even though I know without a doubt it has.

"How do you feel?" I ask softly, fixing my new short hair. My new voice takes some getting used to.

She turns, clearly startled by the childlike voice. She lets out a laugh as she sees me.

"I must say, I am quite impressed by this new appearance, Opal. Who would have thought?"

I laugh with her. I can't wait to see the look of surprise on Flora's face, or Hugo's. I just need to get close enough to Scarlett, and of course I know playing the damsel in distress will bring her right to me. Right where I want her. *Dead.*

"We have to kill her, Opal," she says, getting my attention.

"We will," I reassure her. "Do you feel any different?"

"Yes. Yes, I do. That beast has given me a run for my money. They are just as rough as they look." She smiles sadistically. She holds out her hands, silently asking me to sit on the floor with her. I take her perfectly manicured, cold hands into mine, closing my eyes. I see the images I want to see. The images of the red eyes and fangs come to me like flashes of a picture. Yes, it did indeed work. I wonder how long it will be before I meet this fascinating being. Opening my eyes and smiling, I gently let go of her hands, placing them back on her lap. "It worked. The arrangements have been made. Matthias and I will be heading to New York, just as you wanted," I say quietly, getting up from the floor and walking over to the door to exit.

"Opal," the queen calls out to me softly. She looks so innocent sitting there in the glow of the fireplace. Her black eyes darken further, and her beautiful, lustrous red hair looks vibrant against the white sheets she holds. Only she isn't innocent in the least.

"Yes, my queen," I say, pausing by the doorway.

"I want you to kill Flora, just like you killed my mother. I want her to suffer," she says, smiling.

"As you wish," I say, closing the door behind me, smiling all the while. *I thought you'd never ask.*

15

"*I love you...*"

The sound of my ringing cell phone wakes me up with a start. I'm lying with my head on Ian's chest, my naked legs curled up around his waist. Somehow Ian managed to get under the covers with me. I quickly untangle myself from him and look for my cell phone.

"Shit," I say as soon as I find it. One missed call from Michael Pearson. "Shit," I say again, quickly dialing his number, rubbing my eyes.

"Who was that?" Ian says, sitting up and looking at me curiously. He has bed hair and looks yummy. Looks almost... human.

"Michael," I say simply, turning away from him as soon as I hear Michael's voice.

"Scarlett. Why did you leave? I was dying to call you, but I didn't want to seem overzealous," he breathes.

"I didn't want to make things awkward. I was planning on visiting soon," I say, rolling my eyes. I hear the bed shift and turn around as Ian gets up, towering over me.

"How about we meet tomorrow? You can meet me here, and we can go to lunch together," Michael says.

"Yes, tomorrow would be great," I say, looking at Ian as he begins to scowl.

"Great—and Scarlett, I am looking forward to seeing you again," he says flirtatiously before hanging up.

"You're not going anywhere near him again," Ian practically shouts at me before I can bring the phone down from my ear.

"You have no say about what I can and can't do." I hold up my hand before he can speak, cutting him off. "And before you say 'because I am your husband,' just save it. We both know that's a load of *bullshit*," I say angrily, back-stepping away from him.

Before I can make it to the bathroom, he's behind me, spinning me into his arms, his mouth crashing down on mine hungrily. My hot body melts into his cold. *Will that ever change?*

My fingers feather into his hair, bringing him closer to me, moaning as my nipples graze his chest. "You are mine in every sense of the word," he whispers against my mouth.

Grinding my teeth, I push myself away from him, angered not at him but at myself. "If this is going to work, we have to start with the queen's investments. Michael is the key to all of that. And you acting like a caveman is not going to stop me from seeing him," I say, folding my arms around myself.

"Fine, I'll go with you then," he says, as if it's a done deal.

"No. I'll go alone. Besides, we're going out in daylight. We wouldn't want you to get sunburned, now, would we?" I smile at just the thought.

He walks over to the bed, sits down, and runs his hand through his hair. Then he smiles back at me, seeming to drop into a good mood. It's a look I am becoming only too familiar with. *Oh God, what's he up to now?*

"Scarlett, you're going to have a lot of explaining to do when he sees you wearing that," he says, pointing to my left hand.

"What are you talking..." My voice trails off as I lift my hand, letting out a gasp of surprise. On my ring finger is an emerald-cut diamond solitaire, shining in its brilliance. It has to be eight carats of pure perfection. I have never seen anything like it. The matching platinum band is just as perfect. The row of diamonds going all the way around indicates forever. *Eternity.*

"I purchased this right after I left you," he says quietly. I look up, my lips parting, once again surprised by his confession. His eyes seem to burrow into me.

"Where's your ring?" I ask, not knowing what to say, looking away from his intense gaze. "Con wears one."

"Do you want me to wear one?"

"No. I don't care what you do. Purchasing this after you left just shows how fucked up you are. You left me. Do you think that all of this is going to get me to bend to your way? It doesn't work that way. Whatever happened to asking a girl on a date? At least buy her dinner before tricking her into a vampire marriage. God, you have to be the most frustrating..." On the verge of tears, I turn my back on him. I will never let him see me cry again.

"Do you think it was easy for me to leave you? But that's what I do. I leave people, Scarlett. Do you have any idea what I felt when I saw Abel with his hands around you, knowing I couldn't protect you?" he says softly from behind me. He was closer. Turning around, I notice that his eyes look so different…so familiar. I have seen him look at me this way before. *But when?*

"How did that make you feel, Ian?" I ask breathlessly, curiously.

"I felt…I felt fear," he says softly.

Swallowing hard, I look down for a moment. His dark confessions are slowly but surely breaking down this protective wall I built against him.

"I can't do this right now. I have to get ready," I whisper. I move toward the bathroom, and he doesn't stop me. Closing the door quietly behind me, I lean against the door. Exhaling a breath out, I close my eyes in frustration, rubbing my temples. A dull headache is beginning to form. Looking down at my left hand, I hear him saying, *"I purchased this as soon as I left you."* How the hell am I supposed to meet with Michael wearing this rock? I know I should take it off, but something is keeping me from doing it. It feels right on my finger, fitting me perfectly.

I feel a sharp pain in my head. It's time for me to get a vision. It's like my head is overloaded and needs release. Just like when my body tells me vampires are near, it also lets me know when I need to expel a vision. Sliding down to the floor, I close my eyes and start to feel myself drift. Before I do, I think back to why I feel Ian looks so different, yet so familiar.

He's starting to look a lot like the man from my vision.

I walked into Michael's apartment. I had a letter in my hand. I saw myself look at the letter hesitantly before walking into his building. The Xs were with me; I sensed them, even though I couldn't see them. I wasn't dressed for a dinner date—I was dressed to kill. With my leather jacket, black leggings, and boots, I looked as if I was ready to do battle with whoever was in the building.

There were no security guards, which was strange on its own. The hairs on the back of my neck stood. Instead of taking the elevator, I took the steps slowly, cautiously. I opened the door that led down the long hallway to Michael's door. There was an eerie calmness in the air. Before I opened the door, I watched myself close my eyes. I was talking to my Xs, I was sure of it. Licking my lips, I opened the door.

The apartment was cold, as if the windows were open. The lights were flickering. The smell of blood enveloped me. Walking into the living room, I saw a man tied to a chair. His hands were bound behind his back, and his head was bent down toward his chest. Hearing his strong heartbeat, I rushed over to him, taking out my dagger and cutting the tape around his wrists. Groaning, he came to, lifting his head slowly. My eyes widened in recognition. The cop! What the fuck was he doing here?

"Shit, what did I tell you about getting involved, Bronx?" I whispered to him, ripping off the tape from his mouth, making him wince.

"It's too late; I'm already involved," he grunted as I helped him up.

"Well, lucky for you, I am in a saving kind of mood," I said to him, putting his arm around my shoulder.

"I find it fascinating that you think you could save him," Michael's voice said from behind him.

My body stiffened. I put Bronx back in the chair. Leaning forward, I whispered in his ear, loud enough so Michael could hear me, "I'll be right back. Try not to get into too much trouble." I turned back to Michael.

He looked at me cockily, adjusting his tie. He was as tailored as ever in his sleek black suit and cuff links. Too bad, because in about ten minutes he was not going to look perfect anymore. I moved to step toward him, and he held out his hand, stopping me.

"Wait a second. Come on, Scarlett. You are in my home, and I didn't introduce you to my friend. How rude of me," he said, smiling as if he had the upper hand, his eyes raking me from head to toe.

From behind him out stepped a young girl, a teenager maybe, with short hair that was perfectly cut. Something was not right with this picture. I knew when vampires were near that the hairs on the back of my neck stood, and I also knew my head ached when I needed to get a vision out, but this was so different. The smell around me reeked of black death.

She covered her mouth as she let out a girlish giggle. As she did, her face screwed up, giving her a demonic expression as she lifted her palm, hissing out a chant. My body rose in midair before I could react. I hung suspended for a brief moment. She chanted again and brought her palm down roughly, slamming my body to the floor. My body let out a whoosh. Before I could even try to stand, she was over me, putting her foot down on my chest, holding me down effortlessly. Her eyes turned white, giving away who she truly was.

"It's so nice to finally meet you, Scarlett," she said, staring down at me, her eyes widening with open wonder.

"Opal," I said in greeting.

"You know who I am. Very impressive."

"I know a lot more than you think," I said.

"Come now, don't leave me in suspense. What could you know that I don't already?" she asked sarcastically.

"I know that karma is a bitch. You chose the wrong people to fuck with. You will die exactly how you should."

"Oh yeah? How is that, prophet? How will you kill me?" she asked, savagely ramming her foot harder into my chest.

"Not me. Flora," I croaked.

Looking behind her, the images of Flora and Hugo came flashing before my vision began to fade, but not before I saw the look of fear on Opal's face as she turned to meet her adversary.

I wake feeling deliciously achy in all the right places. Opening my eyes, I find Hugo's soft brown eyes gazing down at me lovingly. Smiling shyly, I feel myself begin to redden as I think of all that took place last night.

"Are you in pain?" he asks me, gently brushing the hair away from my face.

"No," I say, blushing even more. Having been my sister's shadow for as long as I can remember, there was never any room for romance, and being locked away in a cage for twenty-one years sealed my fate when it came to men. Of course, watching Ezarbet being fawned over by men always left me not with jealousy, but a yearning. A yearning to be held, touched in a way that was not in kindness, but with want. I wanted a man to look at me as though I was the most desirable woman he had ever laid eyes on. I wanted a man to kiss me until I was left breathless. So yes, I am achy, but it is a good kind of ache…an ache that wants to be fixed by him and him alone.

"Red is very becoming on you. I love that you can blush that easily and knowing that I caused it…well…you know," he says teasingly.

I let out a laugh as he begins to tickle me. He leans over and kisses me slowly, softly. I didn't think I could ever be kissed like this by someone else. It moves me beyond what words can ever explain. We are more than just a man and woman; we are one. He gently breaks our kiss, looking deeply into my eyes, moving my unruly hair from my forehead again.

"I have to go downstairs and meet with the Xs," he says gently, pulling away from me and putting on his pants.

I automatically feel cold. Of course I know we can't stay in bed all day; however, the thought is very appealing.

"I'll go with you. We have to strategize about Opal and Ezarbet. Like I said before, they are planning something big," I say, sitting up, bringing the sheets up over my naked chest.

"No, you should stay here. Get some rest," he says gently, pulling his shirt over his head.

"I don't want to rest. I have done enough resting. My sister has to be stopped."

He turns toward me, and the loving look in his soft brown eyes is gone; he now regards me with a look of suspicion, and I don't have to be a witch to know what that means. "You still don't trust me," I say incredulously, shaking my head.

"Of course I trust you. I just think that when it comes to your sister—"

I cut him off. "What? When it comes to my sister, what? I am weak? Let me tell you something, Warlock, you don't know a damn thing about me," I hurl at him, standing up from the bed, wrapping the sheets around me tightly. On the verge of tears, I suddenly wonder how I could have given myself so freely to a man who thinks so little of me.

"Oh, so now we're back to *Warlock*, Princess," he says sarcastically.

Without answering him, I head over to my door, opening it.

"Get out," I say with as much venom as I can muster.

His eyes are shadowed in anger he is trying to conceal. He looks as if he wants to say more, but he thinks better of it. Striding over to the door, he pauses in front of me, grasping my chin when I won't meet his eyes. Swallowing hard from his intense stare, I feel my body once again begin to warm from his touch.

"This is not over," he whispers against my mouth. He leaves with that, and I slam the door shut, leaning against it, closing my eyes in frustration. He says he trusts me, but yet he doesn't believe I can follow through with Ezarbet. How can he *know* me but not know me? Does he not know that his lack of faith in me cuts me more deeply than the daily whippings I received when I was caged? I head over to the bathroom and shower, wanting to forget how he made me feel moments ago and how he ruined it just as easily.

The more I keep thinking about it, the angrier I get. Stepping out, I dry my body as best as I can. I put on the clothes that were purchased by the female vampire Zayah—a white silk blouse and black tights. With my hair wrapped in a towel, I sit in front of the fireplace. It is turned off. It was on previously, during my lovemaking with Hugo. *All the lights were on during that,* I thought, blushing. *Concentrate, Flora.* Opening my palms toward the fireplace, I begin to chant.

"Fire…fire…into the night…fire into the night to make it bright," I chant over and over again, watching as the wood catches fire. Smiling, I snap my fingers, turning it off. *Yes, it's coming back.* Going to stand in front of the window, I push aside the thick curtain that shields the room from the bright sun. I've never tried this. Only the most powerful of witches can do this. I remember my mother talking about being able to invoke nature. Closing my eyes, I let my body relax. Taking a deep breath, I begin to chant softly.

"The sun that shines so brightly can be trained; I want to dance in the rain."

Opening my eyes I see the sun beginning to get clouded over. The bright sky darkens and begins to rain. At first a few drops here and there. More of a drizzle.

"Harder," I whisper.

It pours. Covering my mouth in surprise, I let out a laugh. I can't believe I can do this. Biting my lower lip, I clap my hands. The dark skies boom with thunder, scattering several birds from the oak tree that sits next to my window. Afraid to harm anyone, I snap my fingers. The rain automatically stops and the clouds begin to pull back, showing the sun once again. My powers are back, stronger than ever, and it's all thanks to Hugo. *Hugo.*

I am in love with him. That's why his look of distrust cuts me so deep.

I begin to daydream for I don't know how long. I stand there, just staring out the window, feeling lost…so lost in this new world where I am now free. Hearing a soft knock on my door, I break away from the window, going over to open it. I am greeted by Scarlett. She is more beautiful than I envisioned her. Was that even a vision I had of her? Her dark hair is swept back in soft curls, and she wears a long, white, knitted sweater with skinny jeans and the longest pair of booted heels I have ever seen. We are about the same height, but with those boots on she towers over me. She looks fierce, like a beautiful warrior goddess. But she is so much more than that. She is a savior—of myself and of so many others.

"Can I come in?" she asks me.

It takes me a moment to understand her words. I am awestruck.

"Of course," I say rather quickly. "You have to excuse me. I have been waiting a long time to finally meet you."

"Well, I've been waiting a long time to meet you too," she says, smiling. She walks farther into the room, taking a seat on my bed.

"Where's Hugo?" she asks, looking around.

"Um..." I trail off uncomfortably, tucking my hair behind my ear and looking away.

"Flora, I know he came in here last night. What happened?"

"He doesn't trust me," I say, tears welling up in my eyes.

She looks at me sadly, and just seeing that I begin to cry. She gets up and puts her arms around me. I go willingly into her arms. It has been so long since I had any female companionship.

"OK, OK...Tell me what happened," she says, pulling away, her arm going around my shoulder as she leads me to the bed to have a seat.

I tell her everything. About how Hugo and I first met. Our growing attraction to each other. His distrust of me, and how he will probably always distrust me when it comes to Ezarbet.

"You have to understand something about Hugo. He's a worrier. He doesn't trust easily. That's who he is. Would he intentionally hurt you? No," she says, quick to defend her best friend.

"Yes, but he can at least explain his fears to me. Is that so difficult?" I ask.

Asking her this makes her seem to think of something. Her face pulls into a frown, and then it is quickly gone. She looks at me expectantly.

"You're in love with Hugo," she states.

"Yes," I whisper, looking down at my hands.

She's quiet for a moment, seeming to consider what I've admitted to her.

"You're in love too," I say to her.

She looks taken aback for a moment and shakes her head in denial.

"No. I thought I was once, but I was a fool," she says.

I don't bother to argue with her. I know love when I see it. There is no mistaking the powerful connection between that frightening vampire and Scarlett. There is so much energy between the two of them it was overwhelming. I also notice the big ring that's sitting on her ring finger. Even a blind person could see that.

"I have an idea. It's something I do that always makes me feel better," Scarlett says.

"Oh yes? What is that?" I ask curiously, wiping my eyes.

"Shopping! Let's go; my treat," she says, grabbing my hands.

As soon as she grabs my hands, I have a flash into her future. Once again, it's like a flash of pictures being seen. I stand frozen as I see bits and pieces of what is to come. Everything that is to be. I gasp, pulling away from her.

"What? What did you see?" She grabs me by the shoulders, slightly shaking me out of the trance I was in.

"You're hurting me," I finally gasp, coming out of it.

"Oh, sorry." She quickly lets me go. "What happened?" she asks me, her beautiful eyes going wide.

"I don't really know. I had a vision earlier. I have to piece everything together. Scarlett, you are in more danger than I ever thought," I say, getting up to pace.

"Tell me something I didn't know," she says, rolling her eyes.

"Who is Chayton?" I ask.

"Chayton! You know who Chayton is?" she says, her eyes widening with excitement.

"No, I don't. But you do," I say, waiting for her to answer.

"Well. Where do I begin? He is half-vampire, half-human. He can go into sunlight. I've been having visions of him."

"Did you see his eyes, Scarlett?" I ask her worriedly.

"No, I never got to look at his eyes. He had sunglasses on."

I don't say anything further. What could I say? I don't know what to say. This is huge.

"Why are you asking me if I have seen his eyes?" she asks me.

"I don't know. I have to piece everything together. My powers are coming back to me, and it can be overwhelming."

"Yeah, of course," she says, believing me, but not really. Letting out a breath, she walks over to the doorway and opens the door. "OK, enough of this serious talk. Let's go shopping."

"Are you sure it's safe? Won't the others get mad?" I ask, following her out, thinking of the frightening vampire with the cold eyes I'm certain she loves.

"You can be my protection. And the others getting mad? Flora, let me let you in on a secret. The best revenge you can get on someone is not doing what you're supposed to do," she says, smirking deviously and nudging my shoulder.

As we make our way downstairs, I see all the men gathered around the table. I spot Hugo right away; his eyes bore into mine. I quickly break my stare from him.

"We are going out," Scarlett announces as she walks away, not waiting to hear anyone try to stop her. The frightening vampire with the cold eyes stares at Scarlett as she walks away.

His cold eyes don't look so cold when he looks at her. They almost seem to soften, if that were possible. He's in love with her—deeply, the love you would stop breathing for. Stop living for. He catches my stare, his cold glare shooting daggers at me, and I quickly look away, almost running after Scarlett. Once outside, Scarlett is about to get in her fancy red car, and I open the door to follow.

"Flora." Hugo's voice stops me.

I turn slightly before getting in. Looking at him takes my breath away. He's beautiful, his soft, kind eyes telling me he's sorry. But is just saying sorry enough? Is he sorry enough to trust me?

"Word of advice a good friend once told me. Give him hell," Scarlett's voice whispers in my head.

I turn my widening eyes toward her, thinking I must have imagined her talking to me. She winks at me before putting on designer sunglasses that almost cover her whole face.

"Good-bye, *Warlock,*" I say nonchalantly, turning back to him, lifting my chin proudly even as I know he will hate how I addressed him. His mouth tightens, and he looks thoroughly pissed. I get in the car and fasten my seat belt nervously as Scarlett speeds off. She's right, of course. I have to stop this pattern of people not believing in me. I am a force to be reckoned with. I am my own person. My own woman. For the first time in a long time, I feel validated. I am going to give *everyone* hell.

The car speeds off before I have a chance to say anything further, even though I don't know exactly what to say to make things right. *"You're an idiot..."* I hear Scarlett's voice whisper in my mind. Placing my hands on my hips, I look heavenward, closing my eyes. Shit! She is right. Of course I trust Flora, but subconsciously I was being guarded. Hell, why can't she understand that? Not only do I have to protect Scarlett, but now her. Just the thought of her looking like she did when I rescued her makes my stomach drop with fear. Sighing, I head back inside. The Xs are all huddled together, coming up with the next phase in the war.

"Hugo, what do you think of this Michael Pearson? Do you think we can gain more info from him?" Con asks me, his massive body getting up from the chair he'd been sitting on.

Since first meeting him, I have come to know that Con is the leader of the Xs, even though Scarlett is the prophet. All the Xs look to him for guidance. He is the most honorable and noble of them all. Even that asshole Ian seems to respect the elder vampire. Con's aura is somewhat hazy, though, as if something is on his mind and weighs heavily upon his shoulders. It seems as if I'm not the only one with issues.

"I think we are going to have bigger problems than Michael Pearson," I say, looking at each of the Xs.

"What problems?" Zayah asks, coming to stand beside Con.

"A witch by the name of Opal. She is one of the most powerful witches." I begin to tell them the story of Opal. How Flora has no idea that Opal killed Flora's mother with the help of her sister Ezarbet. They sit in stunned silence as I reveal all the events that took place, surprising even Big Red.

"Can she be stopped?" Con asks me.

"I don't know," I say honestly.

"We'll find a way," Con says, placing his hand on my shoulder. His words are reassuring, but his aura is telling me something else. *He's hiding something.* I feel it in my core. He must see the look of questioning in my eyes, for he looks quickly away from me, grabbing Zayah's hand and leading her out of the room. Swallowing hard, I grab a seat, feeling my body deflate from dread. Can Opal be stopped? I truly don't know. She is strong, stronger than any power I have ever encountered. I am so unsure of a lot of things—Flora, Opal, and myself.

The Xs quietly disburse, leaving me and my dark thoughts alone. Running my hand over my tired face, feeling the shadow of a beard, I exhale, deeply tired. Before I can even blink, Ian grabs a seat across from me, his cold eyes boring into me. He has a bottle of scotch in his hands and two empty glasses. It takes all I have in me not to hurl myself across the table and bash his face in. He sets them down side-by-side, opening up the amber liquid and pouring it into the glasses.

"I think we need to set a few things straight, Warlock," he says, sliding a drink toward me.

"Please, enlighten me," I say sarcastically, grabbing the drink and taking a sip. It goes down with a burn, but my next sip goes down more smoothly. Leaning back in my chair, I regard him curiously.

"That first punch was a freebie. It won't be happening again," he says casually, also taking on my relaxed stance, leaning his big body against the chair and taking a gulp of his drink.

"That punch was fair game and you know it. As far as punching you again? Just give me another reason to." I put my glass down, grabbing the scotch and pouring myself another drink.

After another minute, I ask him, "I really don't want to know why you felt the need to do what you did, but are your intentions ever clear?"

"I don't have to prove anything to you, Warlock," he says, his eyes darkening in anger.

"Yeah, why do I get the feeling you have everything to prove?" Looking at him above the rim of my glass, I observe him looking for the first time uncomfortable. He shifts in his seat—I don't know if it's because he's restraining himself from throwing himself at me to rip out my throat or because I'd hit a soft spot. My guess is soft spot.

"Why don't you worry about your little witch and leave Scarlett to me?" he says, shifting gears. I pause. He clearly knows he just hit *my* soft spot. *Touché.*

"Leave Flora out of this," I say, setting down my glass more forcefully than I intended. This got Ian to smile once again. *God, I would do anything to punch that smile off his face.*

"Flora, is it? You think she would turn against her sister? Don't you wonder?" Ian says, picking up his drink and taking a sip, regarding me coolly.

"Of course she would. She is on our side," I say, angrily refusing to take his bait.

"Why do I get the impression you don't believe what you say, Warlock?" he says, leaning back in his seat.

"You don't know what you're talking about. What would you know?" I seethe.

"That's the thing, Warlock. I know more than you think. She wouldn't betray Scarlett. Too bad her lover doubts her, though. Looks like I'm not the only one with something to prove." He finishes his drink and sets the glass down, standing, leaving me alone.

What the fuck just happened? What the fuck does he know? Pouring myself another drink, I gulp it down quickly before pouring myself another. *Fuck Ian.*

Running my hand over my face, my mind begins to turn hazy from the drink. I don't know how long I sit there. But this feeling of dread is overwhelming me. I feel like I can't breathe. I look down at my hands, and they're filled with blood. I can't decipher if it's my blood or someone else's. I get up quickly, my drink spilling to the floor as I rush out of the room. Opening the door to go outside, I feel as if I can finally breathe, away from the poisonous air I was just in, the air of death.

It had been all around, suffocating me. There is nothing I can do to stop the inevitable. Not even Scarlett can stop it. It is already written in stone. One of us will fall upon death. The big question is who?

16

"Wait a second. You mean to tell me you've never had pizza before?" I stare at her dumbfounded. How is it possible to meet another person in this "vampire apocalypse" who has never eaten pizza?

"Um...I just never have," she says, staring at me sadly, looking down.

I automatically feel bad. Of course she's never eaten pizza; she was locked up as a prisoner. After a day's worth of shopping, we are literally surrounded by shopping bags. We stop to grab a bite to eat, sitting at a small pizzeria called Angelo's in the town square. Grabbing a seat in view of both doorways to see who is coming in and out, I take a seat across from Flora, her back facing the door.

"Sorry. Just wait until you try this. I promise, you'll love it." As soon as I say this, the waitress, Maria, sets the warm pizza down in front of us. I pick up a slice for Flora, placing it on the plate for her.

"It does smells delicious," she says, smiling up at me as she picks up her fork and knife to cut into it.

"No, no. This is the way you eat it." I grab a slice of pie, folding it at the crust and placing the narrow end into my mouth. "No utensils needed," I say, smiling as I chew.

She mimics me, taking a small, ladylike bite. Her eyes widen from the taste, and she breaks out into an infectious smile.

"Told you," I say, grinning and taking another bite, making her laugh as the cheese pulls from the pizza, refusing to break.

"That's a beautiful ring," she says after a minute.

I am about to ask her what ring when I realize what she is talking about. I mean, seriously, how can I forget the ring? It stands out like a sore thumb. But why do I get a feeling of pride instead of dread when I look at it? *God, maybe I am just as fucked in the head as Ian is.*

"Thanks," I say softly, looking away.

"The frightening vampire is your husband?" she asks curiously.

"Frightening vampire?" I ask, laughing. "Yeah, I guess he is a bit frightening. He *thinks* he's my husband."

"But if he isn't, why are you wearing a ring? I know I have been out of touch with the world, but I think that qualifies as being married."

"He tricked me. He made me drink his blood after he drank from me and—boom—out of nowhere, we're blood mated," I say angrily.

"I have heard of this. Did he put a spell on you to drink his blood?" she asks me.

"Um…no," I say. My body stiffens, thinking about Ian's blood. I feel myself begin to get hot; I take off my jacket. *Is the heat on in here?*

"Did he entrance you?"

"No, I can't be entranced," I say, licking my lips. I'm thirsty; grabbing my cup of water, I gulp the whole thing down, still not feeling right. I signal Maria for another drink.

"So you weren't entranced and you were not spelled. You know, Scarlett, maybe you wanted to be blood mated."

"What?" I say, confused. I can't seem to focus on her words. *What the fuck is wrong with me?*

"Are you OK?" she asks, concerned. Maria comes over then, handing me another tall glass of water. I quickly grab it, drinking it down. Something is wrong. I feel jittery.

"I'm not feeling so good. We...we have to go," I quickly get up and toss money on the table, grabbing the bags and exiting the pizzeria as Flora trails behind me. We get to the car and I get in, putting my head down on the steering wheel, breathing heavily. I feel a hand on my back, remembering Flora is with me.

"What is going on?" she asks me.

"I don't know..." I trail off as I feel my stomach clench with hunger, with thirst, for blood. *Ian's blood.*

Flora grabs my hands. I lift my face from the steering wheel, looking at her as she closes her eyes. She's reading me. She opens her eyes in a gasp. She's looking at me in awe and something else I can't quite catch.

"You really need to stop doing that," I say, trying to laugh, but I groan when my stomach clenches again.

"Sorry...I am sorry...Scarlett..." She stops as she sees me groaning again.

"I don't think I can drive like this," I mutter.

"OK, I am a bit rusty at this, but we'll give it a try," she says.

I lean back in the seat slightly weak, wondering what she has planned. She places her small hand on the steering wheel; closing her eyes, she begins to chant. The car starts. She smiles and, with a snap of her fingers, the car shifts into drive and begins to move out of the parking space and onto the street, driving us back home.

"Agh, why couldn't I be a witch?" I say, shaking my head.

"But who would save the world?" she says, smiling.

"You and Hugo are so perfect for each other," I say, shaking my head as I think back to the words Hugo had shot at me. I feel her stiffen beside me.

"Like you and the frightening vampire?" she asks me.

I let out a deep sigh, closing my eyes, mulling over her words. We drive the rest of the way home in silence. She gets out of the car, opening my door as I will my body to work.

"Thanks," I say as she grabs all the bags.

"Of course," she says as she opens the front door for me.

I go right up the steps, wanting the privacy of my room. *I can't want blood—can I?* Why doesn't my stomach turn at the thought? Instead it clenches as if starved. I feel dehydrated. Opening the door to my bedroom, I close the door, flopping down on the bed, burying my face in the pillows as I smell Ian's scent. My body begins to curl up in a ball from the pain in my stomach. My door opens and my nostrils flare in recognition. *Oh God.* "Go away," I say through clenched teeth, burrowing my face into the pillows.

"You're hungry. Come here," he says softly to me.

I lift my head slowly. He is beautiful. I don't think I could ever want someone as much as I want him. Maybe it's my thirst for him fucking with my mind, but I want him fiercely. And no, I don't think that will ever go away. He sits down on the seat by the fireplace.

"You knew this would happen." I didn't pose it as a question.

"Yes. Once you are blood mated, you need your other half for nourishment," he says, shrugging his shoulders. His muscles bunch against his white T-shirt.

"Oh God, I don't think I can do this," I say, panicking.

He says nothing, but brings his wrist to his mouth, his fangs biting down on his wrist. I gasp as I see his blood beginning to spill. My mouth begins to salivate. His black eyes gleam as he looks on, tempting me more than he could ever know.

I somehow manage to get off the bed, staggering to the floor clumsily. *This ought to be a sight to see.* I'm just too weak to walk, so I manage to crawl to him. By the time I reach him, I'm breathing heavily. He slicks my hair from my face, but I'm too consumed with hunger to be embarrassed. *Red is now my favorite color.* I bring his wrist up to my mouth, looking up at him before I take my first drink. I really wish he would stop looking at me like the man from my vision. We both know it's a facade. He's not the person I made up in my head. He can never be that person.

"Another reason to hate you," I say, my eyes lowering, sticking out my tongue tentatively to lick the blood that was starting to dry. He chuckles but then lets out a groan of pleasure, putting his hand in my hair, encouraging me to drink from him. With my eyes rolling back in my head, I began to take great pulls of his sweet taste. I moan from the pleasure of it as it begins to settle into my stomach. His taste is of him and more. It soothes everything I crave and everything I didn't know I wanted. All my worries and issues don't seem so bad now. The queen, Ian, the war. *What war?* Nothing matters at this moment. It can wait. Tomorrow...yeah, I'll think about it tomorrow.

Watching her clumsily fall to the floor, I almost shoot up to help her. But the look of determination in her eyes gives me pause. She crawls to me, her eyes focused on my bleeding wrist. I know exactly how she feels. She yearns for me as I for her. She's a gorgeous creature as she slithers toward me, making my body harden for her. She's panting heavily as she finally reaches me. Reaching out, I smooth the hair out of her face, thinking she is the most magnificent sight to behold. Her face softens for the briefest of moments, and then she puts up a wall, shielding me from her emotions. Her eyes become cold, very much like my own.

"Another reason to hate you," she whispers to me, lowering her head as she begins to lick the blood that's started to dry on my arm. I let out a chuckle at her words, but as soon as I feel her soft, warm tongue on my skin, it turns into a groan of pleasure. As she suckles from me, I run my fingers through her hair, silently encouraging her. She moans, from either my touch or my blood, and she grasps my arms, sliding her body between my legs and purring like a cat. I lean my head back, closing my eyes. It takes all that's in me to remain restrained, to not pull her up, rip off her pants, take her. But I settle on her closeness, her warmth, her scent. I feel myself begin to fade, going into one of her memories.

"Come on, Scarlett. Let's go already," her foster mother yelled from the other room.

"OK, I'm coming," a young Scarlett called back, hiding her book under her small pillow. She'd been reading. She seemed to treasure the book.

Her pale cheeks were a rosy pink color, and her hair was pulled into two ponytails. She had on a light pink sweater and jeans. She ran from the room hastily, not wanting her new mother to get upset. I couldn't help myself; I looked under the pillow at the book she was so infatuated with. It was the same book she had taken with her before, Aria's Everafter. *Why did she feel the need to hide this book?*

I hurried after her, entering a dining room to watch as the woman scolded her. She was rail thin with gray streaks in her brown hair. She had plates in her hand and was setting the table for dinner. She looked down at Scarlett in disappointment.

"Now young lady, you know you have chores around this house—one of them being setting the table. What have I told you about all that silly reading?" she said to her.

"I wasn't reading." Scarlett shook her head, lying.

I stood next to her, even though I knew I couldn't prevent the woman from striking her. With my fucked-up childhood, it was sad to think this was my automatic reaction to a parent's anger.

"Scarlett, we don't tolerate lying in this house," she said sternly to her.

"No, I'm not lying," she mumbled, looking down at her pink tennis shoes.

"Lookee what I found here." A man I assumed was her foster father came out, holding Scarlett's book in his dirty hand. He had on a flannel shirt, unbuttoned because of his pot belly, and he was wearing jeans with holes at the knees. He smelled of car oil, and by the look of his hands I could guess he worked on cars. Scarlett looked down in fear, and her beautiful eyes pooled with unshed tears.

"Do you wanna to know what happens to little girls who lie in this house?" he said roughly.

She didn't say anything, just looked to the woman, her eyes silently pleading with her, but the woman looked away from her. She simply went back to what she was doing.

"Come here. Let me show you." He grabbed her by her small arm, all but dragging her into the living room. Her unshed tears began to fall freely down her small face. He turned on the fireplace and began to rip the pages from her precious book.

"No...no...don't, please!" she screamed at him, stunning him when she grabbed the book from his tight grip and tried to run with it. He quickly grabbed her before she made it to the door. I all but growled as I watched her whimper in pain as he pinched her arm. She let go of the book, her small body falling to her knees as she cried. He walked back over to the fireplace and tossed the rest of the book into the burning fire.

"Now you know what happens when you lie," he taunted, walking away from her.

I break away from her memory...feeling...feeling something I have not felt in centuries. What was that emotion that I buried so deep within me? I look down at her, noticing that she has stopped feeding and has instead curled up against me, still on the floor, her head resting on my knee as she sleeps. I reach down, touching her silky hair. *What are you doing to me?*

She sighs in her sleep, a smile coming to her beautiful face from my touch. I cannot get enough of looking at her while she sleeps. I look at her wonderingly as I try to imagine what she dreams about. *Does she dream of me?* I gently pick her up, curling my arms under her legs; she automatically wraps her arm around my neck, nestling into me. In her sleep, she seems to trust me.

Lying her down on her back, I take her pants off, trying not to notice the black lacy underwear she's wearing or how creamy her skin looks against the sheer fabric. I go over to the drawers and take out one of my T-shirts. I smirk, thinking how pissed she'll be, knowing that I have made a drawer for myself.

Walking over to her, I raise her shirt and gently lift it over her head, removing it. I contain myself from growling as I look at the sight before me. Of course she had to wear the lacy bra that matched the underwear.

Letting out a breath, I put my T-shirt on her. Seeing her in my clothes, I feel an overwhelming sense of possessiveness. I like her in my clothes. Grabbing the covers, I pull them over her. I turn off the lights, taking off my pants and T-shirt. I get into the bed with her, sliding under the cool sheets. As though sensing me, she turns toward me, her smooth legs going around my waist. I wince when she knees my growing hard-on.

I bring her closer to me, enjoying this closeness, her scent—but most of all her. Just her. I feel like in her sleep I can say things to her. In my head, of course. I go back to that foreign emotion I felt earlier. I am sure I've felt it before. Maybe as a youth? I remember feeling that way when my mother would cry for my bastard of a father. I remember feeling it when my mother passed away. I remember it when I left Scarlett. I begin to stroke her hair gently, coming to grips with everything she was starting to make me feel.

Yes. I know that emotion. It's sadness.

Sitting down in front of Michael Pearson, I know right away he is lying by the nervous tic in his hand as he plays with his pen and by the way he will not meet me in the eyes as I speak. *Police 101, fucker.* We are in the office of the club. Adjusting my tie, I bite back a curse. Not wearing a uniform is going to take some getting used to.

"So you mean to tell me that your cameras just happened to be out of service the night this young lady went inside your club?" I ask, holding up the picture of Jessica.

Again his eyes lower before pretending to glance at the picture.

"I'll explain to you again, Officer Alvarez; we do routine maintenance monthly. You can check our records. We document everything," he says.

Maintenance? How fucking convenient.

"Detective Alvarez. And yes, I want to see a full copy of your records."

"Great, I have a copy already here for you," he says, smiling at me sarcastically.

I don't like this guy. I can't put a finger on it, but something about him is not right.

"I have to ask you a personal question. What is a guy like you, the president of a big bank, doing owning a club like this?"

"I am a wise man, *Detective* Alvarez. I invest my money where it's profitable," he says, leaning back in his chair, lowering his eyes again.

Fucking liar.

I look through the paperwork he's given me. It looks perfect. Too perfect. I slam the papers on his desk, getting up from my chair. "You wanna know what I love most about my job?" I ask him. Not waiting for his reply, I continue, "I love catching fucking liars."

"*Detective* Alvarez, if you have no witnesses seeing the young woman come into my club, then I think we have nothing further to say to each other," he says cockily.

Of course he has a point, but I don't let him know that. I say nothing to him as I walk out, slamming his door shut. Music blasts as the club starts to get crowded. Everyone sneaks glances at me as if they know I don't belong here. *Just one of the downsides of being in my profession.* Deciding to have a drink, I head over to the bar.

"Yeah, let me get a Corona," I say to the bartender. She's a gothic-looking chick with an earring on her left eyebrow and makeup that's too dark for her pale face. Her black tank and skirt go with the look she's going for. I can't help but begin to profile her. *Another downside of being a cop.* Young girl, probably decided to run away from her rich parents because she wanted to discover herself. She's desperately trying too hard to fit into this lifestyle. She's in way over her head; she doesn't belong here. As she hands me my drink, I notice her wrist has a bandage on it.

"What happened?" I say, pointing to her wound before raising my beer to my mouth.

She startles, seemingly surprised that I am talking to her. Her brown eyes go wide. I bet she'd look pretty if it weren't for all that horrible makeup.

"Um. Nothing, just an accident," she says, looking away.

Lie.

"Too bad. Hope all is well. What's your name?"

Again she looks away. She seems to fidget. At first I think she isn't going to answer me.

"Angel. My name is Angel," she says.

"Pretty name. Listen, Angel, I need your help. Have you seen this girl here?" I ask, holding up her picture.

She peers at the picture. Her eyes widen in recognition. *Bingo.*

"Um...no. No, I haven't. Are you a cop?" she asks, looking fearful as her eyes look over me.

"Yeah, I am. Angel, this girl was badly hurt. We think this was the last place she was at before she went missing," I say roughly.

"I'm sorry. I can't help you," she says, lowering her eyes, pretending she's busy cleaning the counter.

"That's a shame." I toss my money on the counter, getting up.

"Cop, wait." I pause, waiting for her to speak. When she does, she looks me in the eyes and whispers to me.

"If you know what's good for you, you won't come back here."

Truth.

The cameras show a clear view of Detective Alvarez talking to the female bartender. I watch as he drops some money on the counter. She stops him from walking away, muttering a few more words. He says something back to her. *Stupid move, girl. Why can't you keep your fucking mouth shut?* Rubbing my hand over my face, I watch as the cop turns and leaves. *Fuck!* Something tells me this isn't the last time I'll be seeing him.

"Mr. Pearson, what do you want to do about the cop?" the manager of my club asks me.

"Let me worry about it." I turn away from the cameras and head over to my office.

The cop had asked me why I decided to own a club like this—of course it was for profit, but mostly it was a haven for vampires. This is where they can lure their victims in. They can drink freely here. Of course, no victims are ever killed. Those are the rules. Entrance them and send them on their way. The queen couldn't give a shit if there were rules or not, but with the risk of getting caught we came to an agreement, since my name was on the property. When the war began, the sentinels would live normally, unlike the human blood slaves. *It pays to be on the bad team.*

Sitting in my leather chair, I lean back and pick up the detective's business card, running my fingers over the embossed lettering. I look him up. He has an excellent service record with the force. Twenty-eight-year-old male, single, no living relatives, and his credit score is decent. Every case that he's been on has been solved. The only flaw I can find is when he was about eight his mother was murdered, and, due to post-traumatic stress, he was held in a psychiatric ward where he told doctors his mother was attacked by a fanged monster. I have to wonder: Does he still believe that? Or does he think he was cured? The doctors had ruled out psychosis but instead decided it was just a boy coming to grips with the gruesome death of his mother.

I remember receiving the call from my manager saying a cop had come by regarding a missing girl case. We'd scanned the cameras and gotten rid of the evidence. Of course the paperwork I gave the detective was botched. He knew it too. I knew he could tell I was full of shit. Getting up from the chair, I reach into my back pocket, getting out my cell phone before going into our camera room. The detective is outside, leaning up against the building as if waiting for someone. *Fuck.* Dialing a number quickly, I wait impatiently until it's answered.

"We have a problem," I say, still looking at the cameras.

"It seems we have more than one problem, Mr. Pearson. What do you know of our friend Scarlett?"

17

I don't know what woke me first: the sound of a woman screaming in agony or the sound of running steps as they chased down the halls hurriedly. My room was dark, and the hairs on the back of my neck stood up proudly, my constant reminder that vampires were near. The sound of a scream again echoed through the halls.

Swallowing hard, I got up from the bed, slowly looking between the bed and the doorway. Was this a dream or a vision? Or was this one of the queen's games? This was definitely not my bedroom. Where my bedroom was romantic, this was dark and gloomy. Slowly creeping toward the door, I heard more running down the hall; it sounded like pure chaos. Putting my hand on the knob, I slowly opened the door. The hall was long, and people were running up and down it. The sound of more screaming was coming from the open doorway five doors down from where I was.

There were two huge men standing by the door. I walked toward it. For whatever reason, my heart was racing. I felt it in the pit of my stomach, that something behind this doorway was going to change everything. Reaching the big men, I sensed that these men were not ancients, but they were not human either. Another scream sounded, and as I was about to step in a woman came out of the room, holding bloody clothes. What the fuck was going on? The men looked at each other and grunted in appreciation, their eyes gleaming red. Beasts.

I walked into the room, my body stilling at the sight before me. I seriously couldn't make it up even if I wanted to. Lying on a grand bed was none other than Queen Ezarbet—drenched in sweat, withering in pain, and swollen with child. My hand went over my mouth. How could this be? What the fuck was going on? She screamed again in pain as another contraction rocketed her body. There was a woman, a human, wiping the sweat from her forehead. Damian was in the room with her, standing over the bed with his arms crossed across his lean body. He showed her no comfort, no empathy. But there was a red gleam to his eyes that looked like pride. Wait a second…looking between Ezarbet and Damian, I felt my eyes begin to water with dread. Half-vampire, half-beast…

Her scream once again tore me from my own agonized thoughts. Her lush red hair was stuck to her face as her face contorted in another wave of pain. Blood was beginning to drench the bottom of her white silk gown.

"It needs to come out," she screamed, spreading her legs wider as she began to push.

I had to look away. This was nothing like the birth I had witnessed with my mother. This was gruesome and dark. I heard her growl and scream a high shriek.

"The head is out, my queen. One more push, and you will meet your son."

She pushed down again, letting out another of her screams, her body sagging with relief as the baby came free from her body. I couldn't stop myself from coming forward as I heard the baby let out a wail. The woman wrapped a white blanket around the baby, handing it down to

Queen Ezarbet. She took it as she sat up, smiling down at it—not as a mother would, with love, but with an agenda.

"He is perfect," Damian said, his eyes bright red as he looked down at the baby.

"Just like his father." She looked up at Damian.

So I had guessed right. Damian was the father.

"What will you name him?" he asked.

"I haven't really thought much of it, but I do have one in mind," she said, pursing her lips.

The baby let out a cry, his hand going into his mouth, sucking on his small fingers.

"He's hungry," Damian said.

"Mildred, get me an empty bottle," she demanded.

Mildred hurriedly brought over a bottle, handing it to Queen Ezarbet. She took the empty bottle, handing it as well as their baby to Damian.

"Sit," she commanded Mildred, and she obediently sat down on the bed next to the queen. I could almost see her heart begin to race as she looked fearfully between Queen Ezarbet and Damian.

"Wrist," she commanded Mildred.

Mildred raised her wrist, and Ezarbet roughly grabbed it and bit down hard, making Mildred gasp in pain. She drank from her roughly, as if starved. Mildred began to go pale, and her body began to sway. Queen Ezarbet stopped drinking, red blood smeared around her lips, as she smiled sinisterly. Mildred tried to stand but was stopped by Queen Ezarbet.

"Wait; my baby needs to feed too," she said, smiling at Mildred. "Give me your other wrist."

She hesitated a minute too long—Queen Ezarbet hissed, grabbing her by the throat, her long nails cutting into her jugular. Mildred couldn't let out a scream even if she'd wanted to. Ezarbet grabbed the bottle from Damian quickly and began to pour the blood into the bottle. Once the bleeding stopped, she pushed Mildred's lifeless body to the floor as if she were nothing. Grabbing hold of the hungry baby, she began to feed him. He hungrily began to suckle, making little noises of being satisfied.

I walked forward, feeling completely hopeless as I watched the baby open its eyes. Little red gleaming eyes stared back at me—staring at me as if it knew me.

Coming out of the vision, I sit up from the bed hurriedly. My stomach turns in all kinds of ways. I run to the bathroom as fast as I can, barely making it to the toilet. I throw up like I've never thrown up before. I feel sweaty and clammy. Trying to raise my head, I think back to my vision and feel my stomach tighten again. I vomit until my body is retching with dry heaves. My arms clutch the toilet as if it were a lifeline. Oh God. That baby is Chayton. That's what Flora saw in her vision. That's why she asked me if I saw his eyes. It makes so much sense now. How can this have happened? There is only one answer to that, and that is Opal.

"You're sick?" Ian asks from behind me.

"Blood hangover," I say, flushing the toilet. I don't want him to see me like this.

"No such thing," he says, leaning down.

"I had a really bad vision," I admit.

He says nothing, waiting for me to continue. It's then that I notice that he's shirtless, wearing white boxer briefs, and I can outline his—

"If you continue staring at me like that, I am not going to let you tell me about your vision; I'll just haul you over to our bed," he teases me.

I know without looking at myself that I'm flushing with embarrassment from his suggestion and at myself for being caught staring. I don't know how I feel about this playful Ian. I slowly get up from the cold granite floor and walk toward the bedroom.

"Queen Ezarbet has a baby," I blurt out, turning so I can see his reaction.

"Come again?" he asks, his eyes widening.

"She does. I know this sounds batshit crazy, but it's true. She and Damian have a baby. I'm assuming with the help of Opal. His name is Chayton. He's going to come into our group as a decoy or something. He's going to gain my trust," I whisper the last part. Why do I feel so hurt by this?

Ian is quiet for a moment, seeming to take in everything I've said.

"When the time comes, and it will, I will kill this Chayton," he says.

My stomach turns at his words. I feel like I'm going to throw up again. I put my hand over my mouth and run to the bathroom again. This time nothing comes up but me gagging air. I feel Ian behind me, and I close my eyes as I try to stop the tears from running down my face.

"Tell me what to do," he says softly.

"What?" I whisper, not really understanding what he's asking.

"Tell me what you need me to do to comfort you," he says.

I slowly stand up, looking at him as I wipe my eyes and mouth.

"I don't think you can ever be the person to comfort me. You're just not that person for me," I say forcefully.

His eyes darken at my words. I know I am being a bitch, but I can't care less. I walk back over to the bed and sit. I notice that I have on one of his T-shirts. He comes back in and bites his wrist. I let out a hiss but stop myself when I realize what I am doing. Oh God. The smell of his blood is intoxicating me.

"What are you doing?" I ask, licking my lips greedily.

"You're hungry and sick. This will help," he says, shrugging his shoulders.

"Am I going to need to feed on others?" I ask, feeling sickened by the thought.

He lets out a growl at my question. My eyes widen when he comes forward.

"You will never have to feed from another. Just me. Only me," he says.

"Oh yeah? What about you? Will you feed from just me?" I counter back.

"The moment I tasted you, no other would do. Just you."

My mouth slightly opens at his confession. Why does this make my heart skip a beat? I shouldn't care where he feeds from. But just the thought of him feeding from another makes me want to go apeshit on someone. Bringing his wrist to my mouth, not breaking eye contact, I drink. His taste explodes in my mouth. I can't stop the moan of pleasure that erupts from my chest. After a few pulls, I stop, satisfied. My stomach seems to settle happily. Swallowing, I move my hair to the side, exposing my neck. His eyes darken into hungry slits as he views my exposed pale flesh.

"I figure I can at least return the favor," I whisper, my body tensing in anticipation.

He moves closer to me, putting his hands on my hips, bringing my body flush to his. His lips graze my neck, making me quiver slightly and sound out a whimper of pleasure. Jesus, I'm so turned on. I squeeze my legs together, trying to alleviate the tension that's building inside me. He bites down softly, drinking from me gently. I let out a moan of pleasure as I feel like my body molds into his perfectly. I grab onto his arms, my hands sliding up onto his naked shoulders, my fingers finding their way into his hair. He growls at my touch, and I can't help my womanly smile. He is affected as much as me.

He stops drinking and pulls his head up, looking down at me. Slowly he lowers his head, kissing me tenderly. My body screams with want. I moan with pleasure as my breasts crush against his chest. I deepen the kiss. I'm tempted to jump on him and wrap my legs around his waist, but he pulls away, leaving me with my eyes still closed. I drop my head down, not wanting him to see how disappointed I am from the loss of his touch.

"Seems I found one way to comfort you," he says softly, turning away to go into the bathroom.

Letting out a huff, I refuse to answer him. Going into my closet, I take out a white blouse with little black buttons down the front and some black jeans that have leather down the sides. I put the jeans on quickly. The more I think about my vision and Chayton, the angrier I become. The queen wants to trick me. To use my human side of "trust" against me. Little does she know that I'm beginning to lose that side of myself. Yanking off Ian's T-shirt and dropping it to the floor, I angrily put my arm through the sleeves of the white blouse.

As I begin to button, Ian walks out into the bedroom, looking hotter than ever. I glance back down to continue buttoning, happy for the distraction. I can hear him sitting on the bed, watching my every move. Slipping on my black pumps, I turn to face him.

"I am meeting with Michael today," I say, preparing myself for battle.

His body is lying against the headboard, and he regards me coolly. Too coolly.

"I know," he says simply, smiling slightly.

"What? That's it? You *know*? No 'Scarlett, you are *mine*'?" I attempt to look like a monkey, pounding on my chest.

Then he does the most unexpected thing ever. Something that catches me completely off guard, making me question everything I thought about him. He laughs. Not your *ha ha* laugh. He throws back his head and laughs heartedly. It is one of the most beautiful sights I have ever seen. He seems so natural…so human. Either the look I throw his way makes him stop, or he's just as stunned as I am. His beautiful eyes narrow briefly as if he's trying to figure out what to do next with this newfound discovery.

I let out an uncomfortable cough, turning to grab my jacket. He's behind me before I can turn.

"When the sun goes down, we are going out. Just me and you," he says softly.

"Are you asking me out on a date?" I ask him, folding my arms across my chest.

"A date?" He pauses, seeming to ponder this. "Yes. I guess I am asking you on a date."

"Well, I don't know. I just may be a bit busy. Girl's gotta save the world, ya know." I move away from him as he lets out another of his infectious laughs. Closing the door to my bedroom, I lean back against the door before heading down the stairs. I shake my head at myself as I begin to enter this danger zone with Ian. *What the fuck are you doing? Get your head back in the game!* Nodding, I shoot down the stairs in search of Hugo, only to find him in the sitting room with Big Red watching Maury. Big Red is beginning to become a huge fan.

"I bet he's not the father," Big Red says aloud.

Looking at Hugo, I know something's off. He looks tired and completely out of it. His hair is tousled, which isn't a bad look for him. But his eyes tell a story of their own. They're bloodshot, and he stares at me with a worried expression.

"Come on, I have to go meet Michael," I say to him.

"Yeah, please take him. I can't have someone brooding over me when I watch my shows," Big Red says.

Hugo gets up and follows me out, his tall body seeming to slouch as if he has a big weight upon his shoulders. The bright, sunny skies greet us as soon as we open the door. It's still cold out but very manageable. Lifting my face toward the sky, I inhale deeply. I love the smell of winter. Since my change, things are very different for me. My sense of touch and smell. Everything is amplified. My hate, my anger, my love. *Love?* No, not love. My thirst for vengeance is bigger than any of these feelings.

I look at Hugo again as I watch him brood over his own thoughts, knowing exactly how he feels. My own thoughts are eating away at me. What the hell am I going to do about Chayton? Why do I feel this attachment to him? Is this all part of his plot with the queen? I do know something, though. There is no way I'm going to allow Ian to kill him. I can't. Just the thought makes my stomach clench with nausea. There's one way to find out what is going on, and that's with Michael Pearson.

Watching Hugo walk out with Scarlett leaves me feeling all sorts of ways. I want so badly to run after him and hold him. Something is bothering him, and it isn't just our argument earlier. He seems withdrawn. He's off somewhere else, and I don't think anyone can reach him, not even me.

So here I am practicing with my spells, trying to prepare myself for the battle that is going to come whether I want it or not. I have to do whatever is in my power to help Scarlett. If that means putting aside my feelings for Hugo, I will. *Liar.* OK, maybe not put aside my feelings, but put them on hold. Scarlett needs me. She needs *us.*

Raising my hand so it's palm up, I begin to chant. I'm on the other side of the huge mansion. There's an indoor pool. Why there's a pool inside, I don't know. When I posed this question to Big Red, his response was, "That's how we roll," whatever that means. He's massive in size—some would find him intimidating, but I don't. With his dark sense of humor, I can never really tell if he's joking or telling the truth. But I do know one thing: he's quite charming and a devious flirt. He can make the most modest of women blush. He left me here sitting by the pool to practice.

I wave my hand, and the water begins to move, mimicking my hand movements. I am beginning to get used to having my powers back. Since Hugo came into my life, my powers have only seemed to strengthen. I don't remember being this powerful before.

"I think we are going to need more than water tricks to take down your sister," a hard voice comes from behind me, making me jump with fright.

Looking behind me, I see Scarlett's frightening vampire. Even his voice is frightening. When I say *frightening,* I don't mean in a grotesque way. I mean in a cold, unfeeling way. He lacks emotion, except when it comes to Scarlett. But someone who lacks emotion is the most frightening kind of person of all. He's just that. A beautiful male specimen with a dark soul. *Does he have a dark soul, or is it just tainted?* What makes him what he is?

"Stop trying to read me. It won't get you anywhere, Witch," he says.

"Um…I am sorry. I…" I can't finish. Turning around, I begin to fiddle my hands. He makes me nervous.

He says nothing but comes to sit next to me. I take a quick peek at him; he's staring at the water. He's wearing stonewashed jeans and a gray V-neck T-shirt. His hair's nicely slicked. I can see why Scarlett's so attracted to him. He's beautiful.

"Are you making any process with your magic?" he asks.

"Yes, a little," I say, nodding my head, tucking my hair behind my ear, looking away nervously.

"You need anger. Try to train your anger," he says, looking at me directly now.

"Anger? What good can come out of anger?" I say, turning my body so it's facing his.

"You'd be surprised what anger can do. Are you going to have what it takes to take down Opal? Your sister?"

"Let me worry about that," I whisper.

"I don't worry," he says.

Looking at him, I again wonder what happened to him. I know he plays a big part in Scarlett's future. But who's the man behind the cold exterior? Who's the man who would do something great, even if he doesn't think he's capable of doing it? Who's the man who thinks he's incapable of feeling but feels so deeply for Scarlett?

I reach out; I can't stop myself from touching his cold hand. He doesn't stop me. Closing my eyes, I get my first glimpse of his life. The beatings, the hate, the need for vengeance. He got all of those things, but still he remains closed off to the world. I get glimpses of his encounter with Edrick, Scarlett's father. His first sight of Scarlett, becoming enthralled once he set his eyes on her. Their relationship. Their instant attraction. They couldn't keep their hands off each other. I blush when I begin to see just how much they couldn't seem to keep their hands to themselves. I see Scarlett confessing her love to him as he freezes. I feel his fear when he sees Scarlett in the hands of Abel. I feel his sadness when he leaves her. Then I feel his love when he makes her his blood mate.

I see other things that I will hold onto in secret. Time will reveal itself. Opening my eyes, I smile softly at him. "He chose you for her," I say softly.

"Chose who?" he asks.

"Edrick, the man who trained you to fight. He knew."

"Edrick? Where is he?" he says, grabbing onto my arms.

"Edrick was Scarlett's father," I tell him. He loosens his grip on me. The stunned look on his face tells me he had no idea.

"Edrick was Scarlett's father? Why? Why would he pick me?" he says, shaking his head in denial.

"Because even if you don't know it yet, you're a good man," I say.

He laughs harshly, getting up. I get up with him, not liking the look I see in his eyes. "I am not a good man. Just ask Scarlett," he says harshly.

"I don't have to ask Scarlett. I read you."

"Oh yeah? Didn't you see something more important?"

"What would that be?" I say, seeing the cold seep into his eyes.

"Did you not see Opal and your sister killing your mother?"

My world stops as soon as the words leave his mouth. I feel like someone just punched me in the stomach. I can't breathe.

"What?" I ask him, shaking, as soon as the words can leave my lips. I want to hear him say it again.

"Your sister plotted with Opal to kill your mother. They killed your mother," he repeats.

I cry. I fall down to my knees, sobbing uncontrollably. I know his words ring true. My mother did not die by natural causes—she was murdered. *Murdered by my sister and Opal.* I feel him lean down toward me. For a moment I think he will comfort me, but instead he leans in and whispers in my ear.

"You see, Witch, I am not such a good man after all. I'm a cold and calculating asshole. So before you go thinking we just became friends, just know that I don't play well with others. Don't ever forget that. Now, are you angry yet?"

I stop crying, looking up at him, feeling my hands beginning to curl into fists. Even though my lips still tremble, I feel anger begin to pour from me. Fury makes me grind my teeth together.

"Yes," I say.

His cold blue eyes darken, and his fangs protrude from his mouth.

"Say it like you fucking mean it," he hisses at me.

"Yes! Yes, I am fucking *angry*," I yell at the top of my lungs.

"Good. Now use it."

18

I don't know what's more depressing: hearing Miley Cyrus's "Wrecking Ball" blasting through the speakers of my car or watching Hugo sulk.

"Oh shut up, Miley," I say, switching stations. I take a sharp right, making Hugo clutch the dashboard. "Listen, do you want to hear my advice about Flora?" I ask him, looking at him when we're stopped at a light.

"If I say no, why do I have a feeling you are going to tell me anyway?" he says quietly.

"You're right. I think you should just go talk to her. Tell her how you feel. That it was a misunderstanding," I say, pulling into a private parking lot. I quickly find one that is free and away from cameras. I turn off the car and turn toward him. He seems so conflicted, but at least there's a look of agreement in his eyes as he nods his head.

"Also, whatever happens in the bank, I just want you to go with it," I say this time, getting his attention as he looks at me.

"What do you mean 'whatever happens in the bank'?" he asks.

I get out of the car not really wanting to explain. He turns into the pup I fell in love with as I open his door, putting him in my arms. "Come on, just go with the flow and follow my lead."

I walk into the bank fully aware of all of my attentions. Michael Pearson knows who I am—or if he doesn't, he's about to find out.

I notice right away the bank seems empty. That's odd; it's a Monday. There's no one to greet me.

"Scarlett." Michael's voice makes me turn my head. He looks nicely tailored, his suit fitting him just right. He smiles at me cockily. I smile back just as much.

"We are doing some renovations, so we are down for today," he says, coming to stand next to me, putting his hand on the small of my back and leading me to his office. "I thought we could eat in. Do you like sushi?"

"Yes, I love it." I feel Hugo begin to quietly growl. He knows something's up. The hairs on the back of my neck stand up. *Great!*

I place Hugo on the floor and have a seat across from Michael as he takes out the trays of the different assortments of sushi. Grabbing the chopsticks, I study him.

"I didn't know which you liked, so I got them all," he says.

"Looks great," I say, waiting for him to sit.

"So what did you do all day?" he asks me innocently, grabbing chopsticks and making a plate for himself. He takes a seat, and I watch him eat.

"Aren't you going to eat?" he asks me in between bites.

"I didn't come here to eat."

He regards me as he would any woman, I suppose. He has no care whatsoever. He would step on anyone who got in his way. I look around his office. For what? For money?

"How do you do it?" I ask him.

He wipes his mouth, regarding me coolly.

"What are you talking about?" he says, leaning back in his chair with a cocky gleam in his eye, seeming to know exactly what I am talking about.

"How do you sleep at night?"

"Sleep at night? They get what they want, I get what I want. It's really a win-win situation," he says, shrugging his shoulders. "I mean, look at this. Look around you, sweetheart. I get the money and the power. So going back to your question, I sleep quite easily. Like a baby, in fact."

"You think you're so smart, don't you?" I say, leaning closer to him.

He leans in closer, putting his hands flat on the desk, just where I want them.

"I think I am fucking brilliant," he whispers.

"So when are your two vampires going to come join us? Are they waiting for your call?"

Again he smiles at me as if he has me cornered. *He really has no idea.*

"Yes," he says.

"That's exactly what I thought you would say." I smile back. Before he can move, I grip my chopsticks roughly, swinging them and stabbing him in the hand, holding him to the desk. He lets out a scream of pain, shooting up from the chair and trying to get his hand free. The door bursts open, and one ancient comes charging through, briefly distracted by Michael screaming like a baby and his blood. I use this to my advantage, slamming the door against the ancient's face and kicking him in the groin. He falls down to the floor with a grunt, and I get behind him, breaking his neck quickly. I feel a hand spinning me around, but before I can get a piece of him, Hugo transforms, grabbing the ancient from behind and placing his hand on his temples, letting out a chant. The ancient falls down onto his knees, convulsing before turning into ash.

"You fucking bitch. You're going to fucking pay," Michael spits out. He no longer looks so tailored. His hand's bleeding profusely, and his perfectly slicked hair's drenched in sweat.

I tsk. "Michael, I think you're in no position to make any threats," I say.

"So what now? Am I going to die?"

I am quiet for a moment, making him think I am pondering it.

"Not today. I want you to deliver a message to your queen. I want you to tell her I know all about Chayton. Tell her she can go fuck herself. She doesn't have to send anyone to do her dirty work. Tell her, 'Come get me yourself; I'm waiting.'" I turn and leave with Hugo behind me.

"Well, that was exciting," Hugo says.

"Told you," I say, leading us out of the bank and hearing Michael's scream for help.

As we head back to the car, I get the feeling we're being followed.

"Hugo, head back to the car. I'll be just a minute," I say, handing him the keys. He looks at me questioningly. I just shake my head. I turn and head in the opposite direction.

In the thick crowd of New York streets, I bump into people here and there. Once I find an alley, I turn with my hands on my hips, waiting for him. He's not wearing his cop uniform, but a suit this time. He's more good looking than I remembered.

"So I found you," he says.

"So I let you *find* me," I counter back.

He slowly walks deeper into the alley. His eyes keep looking behind me, cautiously.

"What are you doing with Michael Pearson?"

"If I told you, you wouldn't believe me."

"Try me," he says.

Before he can move, I am in front of him, shoving him up against a wall, my hand at his throat. He raises his hands, and the look in his eyes tells me he means me no harm.

"Listen, Bronx. You don't want to know. Just stay away from Michael. Forget you ever met me. It's dangerous," I whisper in his ear.

"Are you one of them?" he asks, completely ignoring my threat.

I don't need to ask what "one of them" means. He knows about this world that is now mine. I wonder how he knows.

"Are you a vampire?" he asks me, confirming that he does indeed know.

"I'm half," I say, letting go of his throat.

"How is that even possible?"

"Well, I've asked myself that question a couple of times, Bronx. It's all part of this grand mystery called destiny," I say, shaking my head and backing away from him. "You really need to stay away from Michael Pearson. He's bad news," I tell him.

"I can't. He's part of my investigation."

I nod in understanding, beginning to exit the alley.

"Wait," he says from behind me. I turn around to face him.

"Will I see you again?" he asks.

"Yeah, you'll be seeing a lot more of me, I think."

"What's your name?"

"Scarlett," I say, beginning to turn around again.

"Hey, don't you want to know my name?" he asks.

"I don't need to know your name. You're Bronx," I say, going back into the thick crowd and this time going fast enough so he won't follow.

I get back into the car where Hugo's waiting impatiently for me.

"What happened?" he asks as soon as I sit down.

"A cop. He knows about vampires. He's too curious for his own good."

"Did you warn him to stay away?"

I turn on the car, pulling out of the parking spot fast and making Hugo buckle his seat belt a little too quickly. *Geez, why does everyone get nervous when I am behind the wheel?*

"Yeah, I did. But he's not going to listen. I had a vision of him."

"Great, that's just what we need. A human to get involved in the mix," he says.

I purposely leave out the vision I had of the queen and her giving birth to Chayton. My stomach rolls at the thought, and I swallow hard as my mouth begins to salivate. *God, why do I feel so bothered by this?*

"What's wrong? You look like you're going to be sick." He puts his hand over my forehead.

"Great, thanks for telling me I look like crap. I haven't been feeling good. I must be coming down with something," I say, fearing that's the truth.

"That's weird. You're not supposed to get sick," he says, looking puzzled. Finally, my Hugo the worrier is back.

"Why? Does it say that in the prophecy?"

"Well, no. But once you have that vampire gene, you are supposed to be free from infections and viruses."

"Well, guess I'm just not that lucky."

"That's a beautiful ring," he says, switching gears.

"Yeah…thanks. And no, I don't want to talk about it. Once you patch things up with Flora, then will I let you hear all about my vampire-husband problems."

He laughs, holding up his hands.

"Fair enough."

Heading back the rest of the way in silence, I think back anxiously to Ian and our first date. Finally making it back home, Hugo goes in first in search of Flora. Smiling, I go up the steps to my room. I shower and dress in a black long-sleeve wrap dress. I don't know what to do with my hair, so I just leave it loose. I put on mascara and a light pink lipstick. There is a knock on the door. My breath halts. Ian is standing there, looking completely delicious. He's wearing a black blazer, a white V-neck T-shirt, and black dress pants.

"Whoa, he knocks," I say, remembering there was a time he never knocked.

He cocks his head, smiling that smile that makes me either want to hit him or melt. This time I melt.

"You look stunning," he whispers.

"Thank you," I say, blushing. "OK, so where are we off to?" I grab my jacket, quickly moving out into the hallway before we never make it to dinner. I have to admit I am famished.

"I made reservations in the city. Nice restaurant, or so I hear." We walk outside together, and I get into his car. He gets in, looking at me before starting the car. It's so crazy, because we've known each other for such a short amount of time, but I feel like we have such a huge history together. He's so many of my firsts. My first in sexuality, my first in love, and my first in heartbreak. My heartbreak stands out the strongest. Will I ever let him have that chance again? My mind's already made up. No.

༄

Standing in front of the window, I am in awe of the sight before me. New York's a magical place indeed; with its bright lights and tall buildings, it makes one feel so small. Never having traveled before, I look at everything around me in wonder.

Having been here for two days now, I can feel Flora. She's not too far from me, but with Hugo's spell all I can do is sense her. But of course, there are always loopholes. Turning away from the window, I sit before the fireplace, snapping my fingers to turn it on. I usually like to work in the darkness, but with this new spell I need everything to be perfect. Grabbing an object wrapped in a black cloth, I gently set it down and unfold it. It's a pure silver dagger with a handle engraved with the dark angel of death. I take out a vial from my pocket and uncap it gently. Picking up the dagger, I dip the tip of it into the clear liquid in the vial. I place the dagger back down. Raising my palms up, I begin to chant. My body rocks back and forth, the fire begins to flare, and the windows begin to shake. Then all at once, it's quiet again.

"What did you just do?" Matthias asks from behind me.

Picking up the dagger, I hold it in my hand, pointing it up so that the tip's touching my palm.

"This is our weapon," I say, looking at him.

"It looks like just a dagger to me," he says, shrugging his massive shoulders.

"Yes. But what you don't see is that there is beast venom in this. One touch into a vampire's flesh, and they will die a slow, painful death. Would you like to try?" I ask, laughing, when he rears back from me.

He's a big man in size, with looks that could kill. Queen Ezarbet hired him to see a job done, and now it is time for his actual test. Let's see if he can live up to all the stories that have been told about him—and there are many. The queen told me he loved to punish his mate, which is one of the reasons why the queen was interested in him. But the truth is he has not only an appetite for blood, but a need to see someone bleed. He is a cruel, dark lover who gets off on pain. He was like this before turning, and with his new power it has only become worse. He likes his girls young, blond, and human. What he does after he's done with them, only he knows—or so he thinks. I know too. He burns them, after he skins them to the bone.

"That man, Michael Pearson, called me. Seems like he just had a run-in with our prophet. She did some damage and killed two of my men. She also left a sweet message for our queen," he says, repeating Scarlett's message.

I sit in stunned silence. So she already knows of the queen's plan. Placing the dagger back down, I stare briefly into the lit fire.

"So are you planning on using that against Scarlett?" he asks me after a moment.

I let out a deep sigh, nodding. I can't wait to get started. If Scarlett thinks she's going to ruin my plans with the queen and this precious baby, she better think again. This baby who, in my own wicked way, I've come to love. He's my creation, after all. He's part of me, just as he's part of the queen and Damian. Scarlett's a dead woman walking. She just doesn't know it yet.

I take Scarlett's advice and go search for Flora. I'm an idiot for not doing this sooner, but with my own thoughts consuming me and thinking she needed her space, I honestly thought I was doing the right thing. But with knowing what I know, life is short. I don't want to waste a moment more with her not knowing what I feel for her. I am in love with her. I think I might have been in love with her from the moment she first insulted me. I smile at the thought.

I go into the living area and find Big Red sitting front and center watching television. Does the man do nothing all day but watch TV?

"Have you seen Flora?" I ask him.

He breaks his stare from the screen and gives me a sideways glance.

"She left," he says, growling.

My body stiffens in fear.

"What do you mean, 'she left'?" I say urgently. "Why didn't you stop her?"

"Don't you think I fucking tried? She put some chant on me, and now I can't fucking move from this seat."

I stare at him and notice that he really can't move. His hands are lying on his knees, and his back looks stiff. I raise my palms to his shoulders and begin to chant. The spell she has him under is a strong one, taking me a few minutes to undo. Finally his shoulders begin to relax, and he lets out a sigh of relief.

"Why did she leave?" I ask him.

"I don't know. She looked like she was crying and seemed really pissed off—two things I love about a woman, by the way. And I watched her as she went to the door. I instantly blocked her from going and asked her what was up. And she told me to move or she'd move me herself. Of course, I laughed, and that seemed to piss her off even more. Then she went all witchy on me, and I was floating in the air, sitting in front of the TV, and watching Lifetime," he says sadly, shaking his head.

I don't know what to make of her sudden change of mood. All I know is that I have to find her. I leave the living room and go out into the entryway, toward the door. It's nightfall now and beginning to snow.

"Hey, do you want me to go with you?" Big Red says behind me.

"No, I'll find her on my own. Thank you," I say, a bit surprised he even offered to help. I begin to walk urgently, my senses telling me she's not too far from here. What is she thinking? Does she think I would just let her leave? She's mine. I know she feels the same about me. One thing's for sure: I will find her and she will listen to what I have to say. Standing still, I raise my palms and close my eyes. The air stands still for the briefest of moments as I am brought to her. She is walking with steady purpose but stills as soon as she senses me. I know she's cold, wearing just a sweater and jeans, but she's not shivering.

"Did you know?" she asks me without turning around.

"Know what?" I ask, treading carefully. Her voice seems withdrawn and angry. I need to get her inside where it's safe and warm.

"Did you know she killed my mother?" She turns around then, the snow beginning to stick in her hair. She looks pale, her eyes full of anger. So much anger, I see there.

"Yes…yes, I did know," I say softly to her.

"Why didn't you tell me?" she says accusingly, wrapping her arms around herself. I step toward her with every intention of holding her, but she takes a step back.

"I wanted to. You wouldn't believe how I wanted to. I didn't want to see you anymore hurt than you already were," I say honestly.

"I am not some glass doll that will shatter! I am not as weak as I look," she yells at me, tears running down her face as her anger redirects toward me.

"Shit, I didn't mean it that way. All I meant was—" I don't get to finish as the air around us begins to change, going deadly still. Opal has sensed us. Vampires are on their way. *Fuck!*

"We need to go, now." I step toward her, and by the way her eyes narrow I can tell she's sensed what I've sensed. But her expression isn't one of fear—it's vengeance. I grab her by the arm before she can get any ideas, pushing her forward in a fast walk with me. From what I can sense, there are at least five ancients on their way. Their anticipation for blood is their main thought as they descend upon us. Running faster, we go into a public park, heading toward the trees.

"Come on. We can try to lose them, and I can transport us back," I whisper to Flora.

I tug on her arm earnestly but pause once I feel her resistance.

"Hugo, wait. My locket is missing," she hisses, touching her neck.

Fuck! I know what the locket means to her. There's no way in hell she's leaving without her locket, and there's no way in hell I can let her stay here. Grabbing her face between my hands, I lock eyes with her.

"I am going to go find it. Whatever happens I want you to run. Don't come looking for me."

"Hugo..." she trails off, shaking her head.

"I love you, Flora," I whisper against her lips before I kiss her roughly, and then I'm running back in the direction we came from.

The ancients begin to close in on me as I look frantically about, searching the grounds. Slicking back my hair, wet from the snow, I close my eyes and try to focus. As if hearing a voice, I snap my eyes open and focus on something that isn't far from where I am. It's shining beautifully against the snow. I pick it up gently in my hands but soon tighten my grip, shoving it into my pocket. I turn just as one of the ancients approaches me. Hissing, he plunges out of the darkness, his fangs looking rabid. Wasting no time, I lift my palm and whisper a chant. A white beam of light catches the ancient in midair, turning him into ash. Another ancient appears too quickly, tackling me to the cold, wet ground. He punches me in the face, making me taste my own blood. I see stars briefly as he gets me up. I hear the other ancients as they near.

"Quick! Cover his mouth and tie his hands!" the long-haired vampire yells at the ancient who's still towering over me. "He is just human without them."

The ancient grabs the bottom of my shirt and rips it, using one half as a gag for my mouth and the other half of the fabric to tie up my hands.

"Not so fucking tough now without your magic, Warlock," the ancient hisses at me, kicking me in the stomach. Letting out a grunt of pain, I try to bring my knees up to lessen the blows, but they get a few good shots in.

They soon bring me up to my knees, and I raise my head. I notice that all four are surrounding me with hunger in their eyes. I guess the vision I had of someone dying was of me. *Out of all the ways to die,* I think helplessly. I close my eyes, my thoughts of Flora. I just told her I love her, but I never got to hear the words returned to me. A warlock's mind-set is always to stay away from a witch and her trickery. She really did a number on me. She stole my heart with her looks and took my love with her words. No spells needed. She captivated me. She left me spellbound. And for that I will die a happy man.

"I want to drink from him before we kill him," the long-haired vampire says, pulling me up to my feet.

"Yes. Let's drink him dry," the other says excitedly, licking his lips greedily.

That's when something amazing happens. The air around us becomes still, eerily so. From the darkness comes the loud scream of a woman in fury. The long-haired vampire lets me go as I fall to my knees, looking into the thick darkness the sound came from. All four ancients scurry away from me, but not quickly enough to escape what unfolds. A huge, bright light comes forth from the shadows in slow motion, making it hard to see. I close my eyes as the screams of pain engulf me, and just like that, it's quiet. Opening my eyes wide, I look at the black ash around me. *Holy shit! What the fuck just happened?* Coming out of the darkness is Flora. My heart catches at her beauty. I know she's something great, but this? She's a phenomenon. She smiles shyly at me as she kneels to remove my gag and untie me.

"I thought I told you to not come for me," I say softly to her.

"I can't let you die without me telling you that I love you too. I am in love with you, Hugo," she proclaims, her emerald green eyes darkening as she looks upon mine.

I grab her by the waist, bringing her closer to me as I lean forward, kissing her deeply. I promise myself that from this day forward, I will never let her go.

19

If you would have told me a couple of weeks ago that I would be sitting across from Ian at a swank New York restaurant on a date, I think I would have called you batshit crazy. But yes, here he is, sitting across from me. I look at him when he's not watching me. He sits there, pretending to look at the menu—or maybe he is. He catches me watching him, and I quickly send my eyes back to the menu. I notice it's all types of food that are either too pretty to eat or too hard to pronounce. *Fancy food.* My eyes gravitate toward their prime steak burger. My stomach clenches in hunger.

"So I take it you found something you wanted," Ian says.

I raise my head, not even realizing how greedily I am smiling. *Geez, relax, Scarlett, it's just a burger!*

"Yes, I did. Did you?" I ask teasingly.

"Yes. Yes, I did," he says seductively, his eyes darkening as he stares pointedly at me.

The girl of a few weeks ago would have blushed and looked away shyly, but I am no longer her. I just smile at him and begin to look around the restaurant to distract myself from his flirtation. It's a small restaurant with black bejeweled chandeliers hanging from the ceiling. The decor's red and black, giving it a sexy look. Candles are lit everywhere, setting off an amber glow around the room. I noticed that there were no other customers as soon as we sat down and wondered if Ian had planned it just that way. We sit in the middle of the restaurant with my back facing the doorway. I know he purposely sat me that way so he could view who's coming in and out. I stare at him as he glances behind me. I glance behind him, looking at the exit. The thing I miss the most since being thrown into this world is my sense of security. Something most people don't really think about. I guess I am one of those people who didn't think much of my safety. Never again will I feel truly safe. I wonder if that will come to an end one day. Will I ever be able to live a normal life? What would I be doing right now if I'd never met the Xs, Hugo, Ian?

"What are you thinking?" he asks me softly, making me look at him.

"I am thinking of my life before any of this," I say honestly.

"Do you miss it?"

"Yes. Life was so simple then. What about you? Don't you miss your life before you turned?" I ask. I inwardly wince, knowing what his answer will be.

"I don't really remember my life before my change. I remember the bad. If there are any good memories, they died with me the day I turned. I got turned by a woman named Natasha," he says, leaning back in his chair and looking relaxed. At the mention of another woman's name, I feel a sting of jealousy, but I continue to listen without interrupting for fear that he might stop.

"She has an insatiable appetite for blood. Eventually she was caught by the king's men and ordered to death by the sun."

"The queen's husband," I state.

"Yes, the queen's husband," he agrees.

Just then the waiter comes, and we place our orders. Ian smiles at me with a twinkle in his eyes.

"What?" I ask him, smiling with him.

"I bring you to a five-star restaurant, and you order a burger and fries."

I laugh.

"Hey, the menu says they're fancy-cut French fries. If you could eat, what would you order?"

He seems to think about it for a moment.

"I think I would have ordered the duck."

"Nice. Tell me more, please," I say softly.

He looks away for a moment. At first I think he won't answer, but he looks back at me, sighing slightly.

"Once I was turned, I found out my mother died. The rage that I felt blinded me. I felt it toward her, my father, but most of all myself. I'd left her. I left her just like I left you," he admits. He looks away from me, seeming uncomfortable. I reach over and gently place my hand over his. He looks at our hands, and just when I think he will pull away he grips mine back. "My father was an alcoholic who would put his hands on the first thing he set his eyes on—which would usually be my mother, before he eventually moved on to me. So to answer your first question, no, I don't miss my life, because the day I turned was the day I died and was reborn."

Taking in everything he's telling me, I am surprised that he is actually willing to share all of this. As much as I tell myself I want—no, need—to hear all of this, the bottom line is I am not ready to hear his dark confessions. *Don't let him in.*

"Reborn into what you are now," I say sarcastically, removing my hand from his.

He smiles that snarky smile at my dig.

"A great man once told me to be exactly what I needed to be, and that's ruthless. If that is what it takes to protect you, yes, I will be ruthless."

He knows. He knows Edrick is my father.

"Even great men can be mistaken," I counter.

The food comes before he can respond, and I am thankful for the reprieve. I happily dig in, eating with much gusto. It's delicious. Even my fancy-cut fries. Ian looks at me with wide eyes, smiling and seeming to enjoy watching me eat. I am not embarrassed in the least; I am just enjoying this too much. Plus I have never been one of those girls who is afraid to eat in front of a guy. After I am done, I lean back in my chair, sighing with contentment. The waiter comes by to clear the dishes; I politely decline dessert.

"That was great. Thank you," I say.

"I have something for you," he says. Reaching under the table, he takes out a white box that's prettily packaged with a silver bow.

My mouth drops open. Again he looks away uneasily. Swallowing hard, I take the box from him. It's a bit heavy, and I just hold it for a moment, wondering what it can possibly be. Nervously untying the bow, I lift the lid, placing it gently on the table. Removing the tissue paper, I realize it's a book. A children's book called *Aria's Everafter.* I gently touch the cover as my childhood memories begin to sink in. This was my all-time favorite childhood book. I'd forgotten this. I remember staring out the window, just like the princess in the story, with the hopes of my prince coming to my rescue. But I'd learned. The day that Steve threw my book in the fire, I'd learned that my prince was never coming to my rescue. All my childhood idolizations died that day, and just when I had a glimmer of hope, Ian had crushed it the day he'd left me. Fairy tales do not exist. I quickly put the lid back over the package, pushing it away from me.

"I saw your memories. I wanted to get your book back for you," he says. His eyes look conflicted as he tries to gauge my reaction.

I clench my teeth. *Who does he think he is? What, he's seen parts of my past, and now he thinks he has me all figured out?* "I don't read books like this. I was a stupid little girl," I say angrily.

"No. You wanted your knight in shining armor to come rescue you."

"You know nothing about me! What, because you saw a few of my memories, you think I'm some helpless girl with abandonment issues? Who needs a knight in shining armor when I can rescue myself?"

"I know you…" he says quietly as he clenches his hands, his mouth forming a thin line.

I shake my head. "I can't do this with you." I jump up from my chair and grab my jacket.

He stays seated, watching me intently. "Now, who is running from whom, Scarlett?"

"Fuck you," I hiss, walking quickly out into the cold, snowy night. The streets are somewhat crowded, with bars running up and down the strip. I feel his presence suddenly blocking me from walking farther. He grabs my face between his hands, his face close to my own. I refuse to look at him, so I close my eyes.

"Scarlett, look at me," he says.

I of course refuse to.

"I know I don't deserve your forgiveness. I know I don't deserve you. Hell, any man would just apologize, but I am not built that way. Have you ever asked yourself what if this was all supposed to happen? What if my turning had nothing at all to do with my greed for power or revenge? What if it had to do with you all along, and I just didn't know it?"

I open my eyes and he continues.

"Your father knew. He knew, Scarlett. I was born for you, just as you were born to be the prophet. Yes, I am a cold, ruthless person. Yes, I am the bad guy, but you make me want..." He trails off, seeming to not want to finish as he looks away from me.

"What? Want what, Ian?" I say, putting my hands on his forearms.

He looks back at me, looking exactly like the man from my vision, his steel-blue eyes shining brighter than ever.

"You make me want to be the good guy. You make me wish...you make me wish I was human," he whispers, now looking at my lips. He leans down, and with one soft kiss he conquers me. I wrap my arms around him as he deepens his kiss, as we both become totally oblivious to everyone around us. I cling hungrily to him as his fingers go into my hair. It's just Ian and me.

"Oh my God, Scarlett, is that you?" I hear a very familiar voice just behind Ian. I break our kiss, and my breath catches as I look behind him and see Jewels. Her eyes are wide as she looks between Ian and me...more so Ian. She is openly checking him out and smiling back at me with approval. *That's my Jewels.*

I try to step out of his arms; he tightens them briefly around my waist as if he doesn't want to let me go but sighs as he walks very closely next to me. I practically throw myself at Jewels, hugging her tightly. I thought I would never see her again. I didn't realize how much I missed her.

"Whoa," she exclaims as she hugs me back.

"I missed you so much! What are you doing here?" I ask, pulling away from her.

"I missed you too! I got a little side gig going here for the winter, styling the rich and fabulous. Speaking of fabulous, you look amazing. And who might this be?" she asks now, looking back at Ian.

Leave it to Jewels to get right to the point.

"Um…this is…this is…" I start nervously, hiding my left hand in my pocket. *What was Ian? I can't introduce him as my vampire husband.*

"I am her boyfriend, Ian. Jewels, I have heard so many wonderful things about you. It is a pleasure to finally meet you." He holds out his hand, grasping Jewels's hand, bringing it up to his lips.

Jewels stares at him in shock, practically swooning at his charm, just like I am. *Boyfriend? Did I just hear him right? Since when is he the gentleman?* There are so many layers to Ian that I am only beginning to discover.

"Boyfriend, Scarlett? It seems to me we have a lot of catching up to do," she says, looking at me and smirking.

Boy, is she right. But what role does she fill in my life? There's no way I can go back to my life without endangering the people I care for the most.

"I'd like that," I lie to her.

"Great, I will be at the W again starting tomorrow. We can catch up then," she says, looking at me earnestly.

I feel my heartstrings pull by her look. I've never ever lied to Jewels. She's my best friend, and she can tell with one look when I'm lying. But this new person that I have become, she can't see. I am not the same girl.

"OK," I agree, lying again.

"OK, I get out at six. We can go out for some much-needed drinks," she says, her eyes seeming to cloud over. It looks like I'm not the only one having guy issues.

"All right, it's a date," I say, hugging her good-bye. I hug her back a little longer. I guess it's my way of silently apologizing to her. I can't be her friend. It's just too dangerous. She walks away, and I watch her. If I could cry right now, I probably would. But I can't. I can't seem to conjure that emotion anymore.

"She'll thank you in the long run that you are not in her life," Ian says quietly from behind me.

"Yeah...it's better this way. Just stay away from everyone," I say, turning around and staring at him.

He comes forward again, but this time there is a sound coming from behind him. Looking over his shoulder, he sees three men coming forward, all wearing black leather jackets and black pants. The one in the middle stands out, with his long hair and red gleaming eyes that stare straight at me. *Beast.* He growls as Ian spins around quickly, shielding his body in front of mine. All three are beasts. I know Damian's forming his own pack, but this was quick. I look around; there are many people outside, either waiting to get into the bar or smoking. There is no way they would reveal themselves in public, I think, but I am wrong. Letting out howls, they begin to tear off their clothing, all at once taking on their painful transformations.

"Run," Ian whispers.

I set off at a fast pace, hearing the howls behind me and the screams of people as they witness the horror that's supposed to be kept in secret. *All bets are off.* Everyone begins running as the beasts crash and claw their way toward us. We make it to Ian's car, and I go to the driver's side.

"Let me drive," I yell at Ian. He doesn't question me as he tosses me the keys. Catching them with one hand, I settle into the driver's side quickly, turning on the car. Ian gets in, opens his glove department, and takes out two guns with clips. I back out quickly, the tires screeching as I do. One beast flies on top of the back window, breaking the glass with his fist and making it shatter everywhere. Ian aims the gun and shoots, hitting the beast square in his chest. The beast flies back, hitting the ground, his body twitching from the poisonous silver. I slam on the gas as we fly out of the parking lot. I look to my left, and I can see one of the beasts clawing his way up the buildings. I zigzag my way through traffic, almost hitting several cars in the process.

"Move!" I scream at the cars, honking my horn.

Ian jumps in the backseat, shooting at the beast that's on my left. I notice the other beast's on my right.

"Ian, give me a gun," I say, lowering my window.

He hands me one. I take aim, holding the steering wheel with one hand and shooting at the beast with the other. I shoot several times, missing. As I am out of bullets, the beast takes advantage by jumping onto the roof of the car.

"Oh, you're going to wish you never did that," I whisper. "Ian, hold on." I press on the brakes hard, stopping the car suddenly. The beast flies back over the car, crashing down onto the street. As he slowly gets up I press hard on the gas, causing the tires to shriek, and without hesitation I run him over. I get out quickly, reloading the gun as I do so. The beast is twitching and groaning in pain, but as I look, his body's starting to put itself back together. The broken bones are slowly arranging themselves. Even though it looks painful, it's quite a fascinating thing to see. I step my Louboutin foot on his chest, holding him down, and point the gun at his heart.

"How many of you are there?" I ask.

The man, no longer a beast, stares back at me. He transformed right before my eyes. His red eyes turn green. He stares back at me with pain and sorrow. So much sorrow.

"Hundreds. He captured a lot of us and turned us all," he whispers.

"Are you all here in New York?"

"No, Damian wanted thirty of us to go," he admits freely.

"Great. Is Damian here?"

"No. Please show me mercy and kill me," he begs me.

I wait for the guilt to come. Maybe even hesitation, but none comes.

"Gladly," I say instead, pointing the gun to his head and shooting.

Hearing police sirens, Ian and I head back to the car. He drives us back in silence. I look out the window as we head out of the city, closing my eyes briefly. If I didn't feel another wave of nausea hit me, I would have thought I was completely numb. I feel as if I am made of stone. Gone is the feeling of the girl I once was. What's becoming of me? And the big question is, do I really like this new person?

I stand outside, watching the night sky as snow slowly begins to descend on the cold ground. It's peaceful out here, which is one of the reasons I decided to buy the property. Besides the intent of having it as a training facility, it's home—a home I thought would be exactly what we needed.

"What are you doing out here, brother?" Big Red's voice makes me turn.

Brothers we indeed are. He's one of the most egotistical, stubborn SOBs I know, but he has a heart of gold. I can still remember the day I met him, which was the day I saved his life. After convincing the king that I thought he would be an asset to us, I took him under my wing. He was so reckless—maybe still is a little—but with the right guidance he made a great warrior.

"Enjoying the view," I lie. He comes to stand next to me, seeming to look at the view as if bored.

"Do you think about the future?" I ask him.

He scoffs predictably at me.

"The future? Yeah, sure, I think about when all is said and done I'd like to take a vacation to one of those tropical islands," he jokes.

"No, Bastian. The future. Don't you think it's time to find the woman, the one who you can call your own?"

"Whoa, whoa, stop right there, Con. No one thinks that way anymore. We're in new times. You and I both know that's never going to happen for me. Just the thought makes me want to run out into the sun. Besides, there is plenty of me to share," he says, smirking.

"You will find your lotus flower before you know it," I say to him.

He looks at me as if I have lost my mind, and maybe he is right. Maybe I have. The war has barely started, and I am consumed. Ian's car comes speeding into the driveway, and I notice that the back window's smashed.

"What the fuck happened?" Big Red asks, opening the door for Scarlett. She comes out looking pale and her eyes looking distant. Ian comes to stand by her side; she moves away a little, and I watch Ian clench his jaw in frustration.

"We were attacked by beasts. It seems that our friend Damian has started creating his own pack."

Big Red growls beside me. This is unexpected. Why start a pack now? Something big is going down, I can feel it.

"Something is not right," I voice my concern.

Scarlett remains quiet but seems to go paler by the minute.

"I'll be right back," she says, practically running into the house.

We all stare after her. I look to Ian, whose eyes have darkened. It reminds me of the way I stare after Zayah.

"I know you're not one to take advice from another, and I respect that. Trust me, I do, but don't wait a moment longer to tell her how you feel. Before it's too late." I walk away to go into the house after Scarlett. She seemed lost. I knock gently at her door, waiting patiently for her to open it.

"Just a second." I hear her gargled voice come from her room.

She opens the door hurriedly, changed out of her dress for a sweater and sweats, her hair up in a ponytail.

"May I come in?" I ask.

"Sure, of course," she says, opening the door wide for me. I sit down on the seat by the fire.

"Con, I wanted to apologize for how I came off the other day. I didn't mean it. I'm just so angry with Ian..." she trails off, looking into the fire.

"I didn't come here for an apology. I came here to see what is wrong with you."

"I think I'm getting the flu," she says, looking at me.

I get up and stand in front of her. She looks at me, and I swear she reminds me so much of her father. So brave. Just like Big Red, he was my brother. Our loyalty to each other was what bonded us.

"I am not talking about that. I am talking about this." I point to her head.

"Nothing is wrong; I'm just fine," she says, her eyes shadowing. She steps away from me.

"You know, I used to know when your father was lying to me. He would do this thing with his eyes, just like you're doing."

She says nothing, but I see the hint of sadness there. *Good, she's not lost yet.*

"He was such a bad liar. He could never lie, so that's why he barely ever did it. He was a great man, Scarlett. You remind me so much of him," I say sadly, thinking of my friend. "Whatever it is you're feeling, let it out, Scarlett. Let all that anger, fear, hate, out."

"It's better not to feel," she whispers.

"No. No, it's not. You want vengeance for your father? For your mother? Be the person you are meant to be. Not a cold-hearted vampire, but our human prophet."

She looks at me, seeming to take in all that I have said. Only she can save herself. My job's simple—lead her in the right direction. All I can hope for is I am doing right by Edrick.

"The queen is expecting," she finally says.

"Excuse me?" I say, arching my eyebrow. I didn't hear her right.

"She's having a baby. Damian is the father."

"That's impossible." Shaking my head, I take my seat again. Talk about upsetting the balance. This is an abomination. I put my head in my hands, rubbing my bald head. I swear if I had hair I would be pulling it out. *What the fuck is going on?*

"They're making their own breed. I saw him in my vision. His name is Chayton," she whispers.

My head snaps up. What did she say? "What did you say?" I ask.

"My vision. I had a vision of a man named Chayton. He's the queen's son."

Is this just a coincidence? What is this game the queen is playing? She fights dirty, but this? No one knows Edrick's family but me. How would she get this name that meant so much to Edrick?

"What?" Scarlett asks.

I swallow hard, looking at her gently. Maybe this is one of the queen's tricks.

"I remember the name Chayton, because that's Edrick's father's, your grandfather's, name, Scarlett."

21

I blink several times, staring at Con, most likely with my mouth open.

"How can that be?" I ask, shocked, feeling again like I am going to throw up. Chayton's my grandfather's name. *What does this all mean?*

"I don't know how she would have gotten the name. No one knew of Edrick's past but me. Your father's a bad liar, but he is good at keeping secrets."

"Yeah, I am starting to see that. Did you know he knew about Ian? He trained him to fight."

"No, I didn't know." He shakes his head.

"Secrets," I whisper.

"Your father always went against the grain. He saw something in Ian."

"Well, he's probably one in a few," I say angrily.

He's quiet as he looks at the fire, seemingly lost in his own thoughts. Yes, I am the prophet, but he is the leader. The real leader. All of us look to him for guidance, as I am sure my father did. As far as letting my emotions free, it feels safer to just stay closed off. Looking at Con makes me like the way I am handling my emotions, because his are running all across his face. He is a fierce warrior who looks just as conflicted as I feel. I'm not the only one who lost someone that night. He lost his brother.

"Do you miss my father?" I ask him.

He smiles softly, looking at me with so much conviction.

"Yes. Yes, I miss your father. I am his maker. I think, when he died, a little of me died. There is not a day that goes by that I don't think of him."

"If you could go back, would you change any of this? Would you have tried to change his mind about my mother? Me? If you could have your friend back?"

"No. I would not change a thing. Trust me, I wanted so badly to stop him that day, but he made his choice. Everyone has the right to choose. He chose you," he says with no hesitation.

"Yeah," I say sadly.

We both sit quietly after that, looking into the fire, lost in our thoughts. I am glad he came to talk to me. Maybe through him I can learn more about my father.

Suddenly, a commotion downstairs has us both looking at each other and flying to my door to get downstairs. I can hear Hugo's voice yelling angrily, "What the fuck were you thinking? What gave you the right to think you can tell her something like that?"

I am halfway down the stairs, watching their exchange. Ian is just smirking at Hugo. Shaking my head at him, I, with the rest, wait for his snarky reply.

"Someone has to do it, Warlock."

Knew it. Whether I wish it or not, I am coming to know him too well. My heart swells with feeling at the thought, and

I abruptly wish it away. I watch Hugo cock his arm back, ready to hit Ian, but Flora puts a gentle hand on his arm, stopping him. He stills, looking down at her, his face softening. Hugo is in love, I think, smiling softly. Flora breaks her hold on Hugo and turns to Ian, stepping closer to him.

"Thank you," she whispers.

I am shocked, but even more shocked when she wraps her arms around Ian's neck, hugging him. He looks as shocked as I am. He doesn't hug her back, seeming very uncomfortable. I smirk as he lets out a cough.

"Thank me for what?" he says as she pulls away from him.

"Thank you for setting me free." She leans forward and whispers something for just him to hear, and I swear I see a hint of a smile appear on his face as he turns away, leaving the room. *What did she say to him?*

"Wait a second. You mean to tell me that asshole gets a hug? You went all witchy on me because you were in emotional turmoil, but he gets a hug," Big Red says.

"Emotional turmoil?" Con asks, laughing and slapping him on the back.

"Yeah, learned that shit on Lifetime," he says.

"I am sorry, so sorry, for that," Flora says.

"Yeah, you're lucky you're hot," Big Red says, wiggling his eyebrows suggestively.

"She's taken, asshole," Hugo says, pulling Flora close to his side.

We all laugh but Hugo. *What's with all of these alpha males?* Flora breaks away from Hugo and walks over to me.

"You don't look so good," she says to me.

"Thanks. That's the polite way of saying I look like shit," I say jokingly, thinking that Hugo voiced the same thing to me.

"Sorry. Come on, I can help you," she says, taking my hand. We head up the steps as Hugo and Big Red continue to argue. We go to my room, and she asks me to lie on my bed. I do, lying on Ian's side, comforted by his scent.

"I think I am getting the flu," I say, swallowing hard as saliva begins to build in my mouth and another wave of nausea hits me.

She doesn't say anything, but she has a knowing smile. She rubs her hands together and places one hand on my forehead and one on my stomach. Her touch is gentle as she begins to chant. I close my eyes, hoping that this will work. I slowly feel my nausea begin to dissipate. I feel myself begin to relax, my body absorbing this lightness that I need so badly. Darkness has surrounded me at all turns.

"How do you feel now?" she asks me in a soothing voice.

I give an incoherent reply. *God, I didn't realize I was this tired,* I think, as I begin to drift into more memories of Ian.

Looking at the time on my watch again, I patiently wait outside of the club for Angel, just as she suggested before her shift ended for the night. I'm waiting across the street from the club in the side of an apartment complex. The snow's beginning to thicken. I rub my hands together, hoping the friction will warm them. I can't seem to get Scarlett out of my head. She's beautiful. *She's also half-vampire, asshole,* my mind shouts at me. But for whatever reason, call it me thinking with my other head, I feel like she's not one of the bad guys. She warned me in a not-so-subtle way. I read her, and whatever she's telling me is the truth. Will I listen to her warning? Fuck no. This is my city, and I will do whatever I have to do to protect it. After she left me in the alley, I headed back to the bank, and Michael Pearson was nowhere to be seen; a sign on the bank said it was closed for renovations. *Yeah, renovations, my ass.* Just what is she doing with Michael Pearson? Do the vampires have to do with the missing people in the city? *Vampires? Christ, am I even really thinking this?*

"Cop." Angel interrupts my thoughts.

She is wearing the same ridiculous clothes, but this time she wears a long coat that's not zipped, a short skirt with a pattern, fishnet stockings, and a shirt barely covering her stomach. Makeup that's heavily done still can't hide the fact that she's young, too young to be around this place.

"We can't talk long," she says, nervously fidgeting with her hands.

I follow closely behind her. She looks scared, her eyes wandering behind my back.

"Relax; you're safe with me. I'll protect you."

"You don't get it, Cop. These…these…they're bad people. I'm not fucking safe in there, and I'm sure as hell not safe with you out here." She goes to move past me, but I grab her by the arm, spinning her toward me.

"Listen, I understand you're scared. But there are lives endangered. People are going missing, Angel. Good people. People with families."

She looks away for a moment, and I know I have her.

"You wouldn't believe me even if I told you," she whispers, her eyes watering and lips trembling.

"Try me," I whisper back, remembering Scarlett's exact words.

"Do you believe in monsters?" she asks me.

"Yes," I answer honestly.

"They bring them in the back."

"Bring who to the back?" OK, now we're getting somewhere. Cop mode's back on.

"The people who have gone missing. They bring them in the back of the club. It's hard to say if they're drugged or not. I don't really know. Sometimes they keep them around for a few days and then release them, but the others..." She trails off again, looking around as if she is waiting for someone to come out of the shadows.

"What are they bringing them there for? And what happens to the others?" I ask.

"The...the monsters...they...they feed. The others get shipped off."

Feed? So the feeling I had was right. Vampires are in that club, and they have to do with the missing people. Is Michael Pearson a vampire? Wait, but he is out in daylight, so that can't be right. Right?

"Where do the others get shipped to? Michael Pearson, is he the one in charge?" I ask.

Again her eyes flick behind me.

"No...he's not in charge. I've only seen her once from behind. She's the one in charge. She's one of them." She wraps her arms around herself, beginning to shake from the cold.

"Who? Who is she?"

Before she can answer me, a figure appears behind her as if he just flew down from the sky. I take my gun from my holster as I feel someone behind me. I turn, pointing my gun, but he's too quick, knocking the gun out of my hands. His left arm comes swinging, and I quickly block him, swinging with my right. I clock him real good, but it does absolutely nothing to him. His head turns to the side from the impact of my punch, and he slowly turns back to me with a menacing smile. *Fuck.* He grabs me by the collar of my shirt and flings me, my body smacking into the wall. Grunting, I try to get up, but I am kicked in the ribs, my body once again smacking into the wall. I hear her scream as I raise my head to try to see where she is. My vision is blurred, but I hear her whimpering in pain. I look up, and the vampire that's behind me has its mouth latched onto her neck, feeding from her. I crawl for my gun, but the other vampire's too quick, kicking it out of my reach.

"Keep him alive." I hear a childlike voice.

The vampire easily picks me up, putting me on my knees to watch as the vampire sucks Angel dry. I close my eyes but feel them snap open against my will.

"You will watch, Detective Alvarez." Kneeling next to me is a young girl with short hair; she looks innocent, but there's something cruel in her voice. I watch helplessly as Angel's body begins to twitch in the vampire's arms. "Look at what you have done. You shouldn't have gone snooping around, wouldn't you say?"

I break my stare from Angel briefly and look at this girl. I so badly want to put my hands around her neck. Her brown eyes shift in color, almost turning white.

"What…what are you? Are you one of them?"

"No, I am so much better than them." She stands, leaving me to witness the rest of Angel's death. I again try to close my eyes, but I can't. The vampire drops her lifeless body to the ground as if she's nothing but trash. Her skin is pale and her eyes are open. I said I would protect her, and I can't. I try to crawl over to her, but I get held down as I begin to fight earnestly. My efforts are nothing compared to their strength. I get clocked real good in the head, and I fall to the ground, seeing stars. I am now lying on the concrete with a perfect view of Angel, her lifeless eyes staring at me. *You failed her* is my last thought before everything goes black.

The sound of someone moving around wakes me. My eyes feel heavy as I try to open them. *Why can't I move?* My head pounds something fierce.

"Come on…There you go. Wake up," someone tells me, snapping fingers in my face.

Again I try to move, to no avail. I get my eyes to open, and I slowly lift my head, the bright lights hurting my eyes. My arms and feet are tied tightly as I sit in the chair looking at Michael Pearson's smug face.

"About time. I was starting to get worried," he says to me.

"Where am I?" I croak out. My mouth has gone dry, and my lips feel chapped. Again I try to move, causing the rope to rub against my skin.

"You really shouldn't worry about where you are. What you should be worried about is where you're going." He tsks, straightening his tie. I notice his hand is bandaged. I look around; we're in some kind of fancy apartment. I can see the exit behind him. From the looks of it, we're alone. But why bring me here? Why not just kill me and be done with it?

"I have a proposition for you, Detective Alvarez," he says, cutting off my thoughts.

"Proposition?" I ask incredulously.

"Yes. It's quite simple really. You work for them."

"Work for them? You want me to work for vampires?"

"Yes. You do whatever it is they tell you to. You can become a great asset, with you working on the force and all. They can move you up in title and rank, and you can help them by hiding their indiscretions. It's really a win-win situation, if you ask me. They are willing to overlook your curiosity." He pushes out a chair and swings it forward to sit in front of me. He seriously looks so sure of himself, it's sickening. He places his elbows on his knees, leaning forward. "I also want to know what you know about Scarlett. Where is she?"

My breath catches at the mention of her name. If anyone has a good poker face, it's me.

"I don't know who that is," I say, attempting to shrug my shoulders but finding it hard with my arms tied to my back.

Michael shakes his head, getting up from the chair. He walks over to his doorway and opens it, letting in a huge man. He is tall and lean, with long hair that is tied up in a ponytail, and his eyes blacken. All my instincts tell me he's a vampire. Well, that and the fact that fangs protrude from his mouth when he smiles at me. Behind him comes that little girl from the alleyway, wearing the same clothes she was wearing then.

"I was afraid you were going to say that, Detective Alvarez. I want you to meet some of the people I work for. This is Opal and Matthias."

"Detective Alvarez, so nice to see you again. I was hoping we wouldn't have to do this the hard way," Opal says with feigned regret.

"You don't have to do this," I try to reason with her. She's mixed up with bad people; maybe I can get through to her. She comes to sit in the chair Michael vacated.

"Oh, but I do," she says softly.

"Why are you working for them?" I ask.

"Who says I am working for them? How do you know Scarlett? Do you know where she and the Xs are hiding?"

"I don't know a Scarlett."

"Lie," she whispers.

I try not to swallow hard as I look at her head on.

"You're not the only one who can read people, Detective Alvarez," she says, leaning forward and touching my knee. I flinch from her touch, but she holds tighter, her nails digging into my knee. As she blinks, her eyes turn white.

What the fuck is she doing? Better yet, what is she if she isn't a vampire? She releases me, and her eyes are back to its original color.

"To answer your first question, I read you. Your second question: you are right, I am no vampire. I am a witch. And you lied to me," she hisses, grabbing me by the throat. Her fingernails dig into my jugular, keeping me from breathing.

"You know who Scarlett is. But unfortunately for you, you are no good to us. He doesn't know of her location. Kill him," she snarls at Matthias, who is more than eager to jump forward and finish the business. She releases my neck, and I let out a cough. Then I begin to laugh. I laugh hysterically. She looks at me like I have gone mad. Hell, maybe I have.

"What do you find so funny?" she says darkly, her face coming close to mine.

"What I find funny is, if you're a witch, how come you can't just find her instead of asking me? I'm thinking maybe you're not that strong after all."

She flinches back from me as my insult strikes a nerve. *Bingo. I got you, you witch bitch.*

"I'm right, aren't I? I hope Scarlett finds you and fucking kills you. All of you disgusting fucks!" I yell.

Matthias steps in front of Opal and grabs me by the hair, twisting it so that my neck's jerked to the side. He bares his fangs, his face contorted in rage. Shit, this is it. I am going to die. I wonder at this moment if there's a heaven or hell. Who will meet me on the other side? My mother? Out of all the bad things I saw in the world, I always questioned if there's a god. Why do bad things happen to good people? Looking at the evil before me, I have to think yes. Yes, there is. Because with evil, there is good. Because if bad things didn't happen to good people, how would we ever learn? I relax my body and succumb to my fate.

"Wait!" Opal yells as Matthias's mouth hangs inches from my neck. Matthias growls in anger, his face shifting back to look at her.

"Wait," she says again, more forcefully. "Let's let him live," she says.

"Let him live? Are you sure?" he asks, his dark eyes widening in surprise.

"Yes," she answers.

He drops my head roughly, shifting away from me. She comes forward, leans toward me, and whispers. "I am going to make you wish you were dead," she promises, turning away from me.

"Make him suffer," she tells Matthias.

"Hang on a minute. This guy just can't stay in my apartment. What are we going to do with him?" Michael asks.

She goes over to the doorway, opening it and pausing before she heads out.

"We can't find Scarlett. We will make *her* find us. Alvarez is another person we can use as bait." And with that, she turns away and walks out of the apartment.

Another person? Who else is being held? My thoughts quickly shift as I watch the man named Matthias begin to crack his knuckles and approach me once more.

22

I love you…

The sound of those words wake me. Did I dream it? I sit up from my bed and look around, seeing that I am alone. I feel better. So much better. The nausea's gone. *Thank you, Flora!* Sitting on the pillow right next to me is the book Ian gifted me. *So he was here.* I remember so long ago taking the book with me when I went to live with my foster parents. I pick it up and gently rest it on my lap, opening it up to read. I wait for my tears to come, but none do. This part of my life's over. I am not that little girl who's afraid…not anymore. I jump up from the bed with renewed energy. Yes, I feel great. Going into the bathroom, I brush my teeth and clean my face. Looking into the mirror, I notice that not only do I feel refreshed, but I look it too. My face has a soft glow, and my cheeks are tinged with pinkness. My ring sparkles at me as if saying, "Look at me! Look at me!" Holding my hand away from it, I gently slip off the ring and put it onto the granite countertop. Grabbing a brush for my hair, I pull it back away from my face, gathering it into a ponytail. I head out and put on a pair of black shorts and a black tank top. Finding an old pair of Nikes in the closet, I slide them on and head downstairs. I make a beeline into the kitchen. In the center of the island is a glass bowl full of assorted fruit. I curiously open the fridge and am surprised to see it full of food. *No one would think this is a vampire home,* I think to myself, laughing quietly. Settling on a banana, I lean over the island, thankful for the quietness.

"Nice shorts." I hear Big Red's voice from behind me.

I'm wrong.

God, I am sure half my ass is hanging out, so I quickly stand up straight. He takes up the kitchen with his huge frame. Looking like he had the same idea as me, he is in workout clothes—a gray muscle shirt and black jogging pants. His red hair's messily done but looks great.

"Who cuts your hair?" I ask.

"I do. Why?" he says, going to the fridge and opening it as if he's going to eat.

I wonder if he does this out of habit.

"Whoa. Really? It looks good," I say, biting into my banana.

"Of course it does. You know all women dig men with red hair, right? And I am red everywhere," he says, winking at me.

I let out a shout of laughter. Only he can get away with saying something so crude and make it funny. I like him.

"There you go," he says, looking at me seriously.

"What?"

"Got you to laugh. OK, you can stop ogling me. Let's work out," he says.

"Agh. Get over yourself," I say, going over to the trash to dump my banana peel. "Come on, let's go train."

I follow him as we go over to the training area of our home. *Our home.* That so easily falls from my lips. Coming to stand at the doorway, I take it all in. It's a huge gym that's aligned with floor mats from top to bottom. In one corner there is gym equipment. Climbing ropes hang from the ceilings. It even has a sparring ring, the exact kind you would see if you were watching an MMA fight.

"Race you to the top," Big Red challenges, looking at the ropes.

I was never athletic at all, but since my change, I feel like I can do almost anything.

"Bring it on."

We both run to the ropes, and I get a firm grip, curling my leg on the bottom and lifting my body up and quickly. I look to my left, and Big Red has started climbing up already. *Fuck. You can do this.* I quickly haul myself up, and before I know it, I am practically gliding up. I reach the top before Big Red.

"Yes," I squeal out, laughing as I watch his facial expression following being beaten by a girl.

"Yeah, yeah," Big Red grumbles as we begin to slide down.

We go over to the punching bag, and I put on some gloves. He holds the bag for me as I begin to take some jabs; his big body moves to the force of my punches.

"You're getting stronger," he muses as his arms strain to steady the bag.

"Yeah, I feel stronger." I shift my feet and begin jabbing with my other hand. "So…question for you."

"Shoot."

"Since I became vampire married and I can drink Ian's blood, do you think I'll be able to entrance someone?"

"I don't see why not. Who do you want to entrance?" he asks curiously.

"Well, I saw my best friend, Jewels. I am supposed to meet her today. I just think it's in her best interest if I can just entrance her so she'll forget all about me," I say, stopping hitting the bag to look at him. I feel something like sadness at the thought of doing it, but to keep Jewels safe I would have to. What if she hadn't left at the nick of time when those beasts arrived?

"I don't blame you. If it will make you feel better, I can always do it for you," he says, looking at me sincerely.

"Really? You would do it?" I ask, hopeful.

"Sure, why not? Is she as hot as you?" He goes into being playful again.

"She is gorgeous, but don't get any ideas. Not everyone is swooning at your charm. In fact, she is like the girl version of you. She'll eat you alive."

He seems to ponder that as if thinking back at a memory. Then he smiles his charming smile.

"Doubt it," he says.

I feel someone behind me, and by the way I see Big Red stiffen I know it's Ian. He's wearing black shorts and a white T-shirt. I ignore the dull ache I get when I see him. He smiles slightly at me and nods his head at Big Red.

"You should be doing hand-to-hand combat," he says.

Just his voice alone sends a shiver up my spine, and my body responds automatically. He silently walks over to the gated ring, opening it, and waits. Is he challenging me? I must have questioned it in my head, for he smiles that smile I find so utterly annoying and so utterly sexy. Taking off my gloves, I hand them to Big Red. *Game on.*

I take off my sneakers and socks as I enter the octagon. The ring's so much bigger than it looks on TV. It's wide open with just Ian and me. Xs begin forming a group around the octagon. I circle my head around, trying to loosen my muscles. My heart beats fast in anticipation.

"Do you need to do stretches?" Ian has the nerve to ask me, his eyes twinkling. *He's trying to bait me.*

"I don't. Maybe you do since you're the old vampire. What are you pushing—three hundred?" I ask.

The guys start laughing. He laughs as well as he begins to circle me.

"If you win, I will tell you how old I am," he says.

I begin to circle too. It's like cat and mouse. Weeks ago, I would have most certainly said I was the mouse. Things have changed.

"What do you get if you win? Though I doubt you will," I add in quickly.

"A kiss," he states.

Like the snake that he is, he takes my moment of slight distraction, and in lightning speed he is behind me with his arms wrapped around my neck and head in a choke hold. His body is pressed up tightly to my bottom.

"You shouldn't get distracted," he whispers in my ear.

I wiggle my bottom, making him hiss a breath in arousal as I bend over, lifting his body up over me and slamming him to the floor hard. I quickly grab his arm, putting it into an armlock bar. I hear the guys begin cheering for me.

"You shouldn't get distracted," I whisper to Ian.

His steel-blue eyes shine brightly as he stares at me, smiling. I don't think his current situation warrants a smile. But he places his feet against the bars, lifting the lower half of his body and flipping over, making me release my firm grip on his arm.

"Did my father teach you that?" I ask, grabbing his arm again, this time curling my legs tightly around it so he can't get out of it.

"Yes," he grunts.

Grinding my teeth, I twist—not enough to break his arm, but just enough to let him know I am about to win this little bet. He is on his knees, and he begins to lift, my bottom lifting from the mat. I hiss in a breath of surprise as he does it again, this time lifting me a little further. He looks down at me and smiles. *Shit!* I hold on for dear life as he lifts his knees again; this time my whole body lifts from the floor mat, still clutching his arm. For whatever reason, I know he isn't going to slam me down to the floor; he holds me suspended in the air. I close my eyes, waiting for the impact, but none comes. He has his hands at the small of my back and begins to bring me down gently. I uncurl my legs and jump down, feeling confused and angry about why he didn't just do it. *You know why.* I must have a puzzled expression, because once again he stares at me with an intensity that boils my blood and casts an ache of arousal between my legs. I feel my nipples harden to the point that they hurt. Ian's eyes drift downward as he notices, his lips curling into a smug smile. I feel my cheeks flame as I wrap my arms around myself, covering my breasts.

Con's voice breaks us both from our silent war. "Looks like a draw to me."

I get out of the cage and say nothing as Big Red hands me a towel. My body feels sticky and flush. I need to get out of here before I jump his bones. Maybe it's the adrenaline that's making me so turned on. I feel like my body's on fire. I head out without one word to the guys. Going into what I know is the pool room, I am thankful no one's here. It's a long pool that's five feet deep. I sit down on the edge and dip my feet in, loving the coldness that welcomes my hot flesh. Out of all the shopping I've done, I realize regrettably that I didn't buy a swimsuit. I would die for a swim right now.

"Two hundred ninety-three," Ian says softly from behind me.

I turn around, surprised to see him. "What?" I ask, soaking in the man's sexiness.

"My age. You wanted to know my age."

My mouth gapes open. So I wasn't as far off as I thought. I turn back and continue to look at the water longingly.

"So when is your birthday?" I ask curiously.

"November twenty-fifth."

I smile slightly, thinking of him celebrating a birthday. Like me, he probably never celebrates a birthday—well, that was until I turned twenty-one. There was never a balloon-hat wearing celebration with my foster parents. I am sure it was the same for him. We are different but yet not. I hear him moving around behind me; he is taking off his shirt, revealing his pale skin, muscled chest, and six-pack stomach. I suck in a breath as I see his perfection. He's just that. Perfection. My eyes roam over him. The girl I used to be would have probably looked away shyly, but this girl…this girl looks on, appreciating his body. *Mine.*

"What are you doing?" I ask him huskily.

"Going for a swim," he says.

"But you don't have any swim trunks on…" I don't finish as he lowers his pants, revealing his nudity to me without a moment's thought. I realize he must always go commando. And boy, am I not complaining. He smiles smugly as my eyes travel down his body to his very erect cock. I almost moan out loud as I feel my panties begin to dampen. His eyes darken as I know he catches the scent of my arousal. He steps forward next to me and dives in; his muscular buttocks are an image I can't get out of my mind now. His head pops up, and he swims rather expertly to me.

"Come in."

"No," I say, shaking my head.

"Are you afraid?" he asks, taunting me. He begins to swim backward.

"Why would I be afraid?" I ask, standing up and turning to leave. The ache between my legs is beyond intense.

"You're running again," he says softly.

That gets me to stop. I turn around and lift my tank top over my head, my sports bra next. Removing my shorts, I don't hesitate to remove my panties as well. I stand there in all my glory, letting his eyes feast on me, my nipples hardening under his gaze. I take my hair out of its ponytail, letting my hair fall freely down my back. I run toward the water, diving in. The feel of the cold water against my hot body is wondrous. I realize that's what Ian feels like. His coldness settles me. As much as I don't want to admit it, it's true. My head breaks out of the water, slicking my hair back. He is inches from me. *God, I want him. I want him helplessly.* There's no point in denying that. But I can't give him more than that. I can't feel anything else. My sense of self is lost, and I don't think I want to be found.

"What are you thinking?" he asks me.

"I don't know," I lie.

"Your eyes. They look different," he says, pushing me into the wall of the pool. My breasts are crushed into his chest. His hand skims up my waist; he palms me, his finger grazing my achy nipple. I hiss from the pleasure and pain.

"Yeah? How so?" I ask, trying to remain focused. He puts his knee between my legs, pushing up so that I can grind myself on him. I let out a whimper, closing my eyes.

"They look like mine. Cold," he whispers against my lips.

I open my eyes. I don't meet his stare as I begin to explore his body. I run my hands over his wet shoulders, kissing his neck. He growls as I playfully bite him. I run my other hand down his muscled stomach, grabbing his cock. It's so hard as I begin to move my hand up and down his thick shaft.

"Then we shouldn't have a problem. Why complicate things? It's just fucking, right?" I whisper in his ear.

I feel his body stiffen at my words. He yanks my hair back—not roughly, but enough to cause a slight sting. My body heats from it. He brings his lips very close to mine, but instead of kissing me, he drags his lips to my ear.

"Fucking, is it? Is that what you think this is? Because the next time we fuck, you're going to beg me for it."

He pulls away from me with those words, and my body already begs for his.

"Is this another of your games?" I ask angrily as I begin to swim away from him.

"Not a game. A promise." He stays in the water, watching me intently as I climb out of the pool and hurriedly put on my clothes. Pissed and horny, I grind my teeth in frustration. I turn around. I am starting to feel the telltale signs of a headache coming on. A vision wants to push itself through. I will it away. I want to argue, goddamn it!

I spin around, yelling at him, "What is it exactly that you want from me?"

With lightning speed, he is in front of me. I blink at his intensity, so much so that I back up a step.

"I want everything," he says.

I swallow. I close my eyes, thinking back to the girl who just a few weeks ago had wanted so badly to hear that. *You still do.* I shake my head, more to myself than to his words. My headache's beginning to make me see white. I feel my legs begin to give out; Ian's arms wrap around me before I hit the floor. I begin to fade into my vision. I have no power over what I see; it's as if the vision will reveal a secret it wants me to see.

I opened my eyes. I was sitting on a wooden bench at the end of an aisle in a church. Looking straight ahead, I felt Jesus's eyes piercing through me as he hung from his cross. The church was small but made up beautifully. The ceiling was made of glass mosaics showing the scriptures of the Bible.

I felt a bit sinful sitting there in a church where I knew I had no right to be. The number of sins I'd committed over the past few weeks were my one-way ticket to hell...if there was a hell. I got up and wandered to the front of the aisle, wondering what I could possibly be doing there. I heard the voices of two women whispering urgently to each other. I walked toward the back, where I saw the women talking; to my surprise, they were nuns. They were elderly, and both seemed very close to death.

It was strange that I could sense these things now. It was something I didn't really want to sense, but I could smell it in their blood. The one with the blue eyes and soft voice had some sort of blood disorder and Type 1 diabetes. Her hair, once blond, was now brittle and gray. I could tell she had once been beautiful; the wrinkles around her mouth told me she smiled often. The other nun was a different story. Her voice was raspy—too raspy. She was once a smoker. Every time she began to talk, she fell into coughing spells. She had lung cancer. She would be the first to die between the two of them.

"We must come up with a plan for Violet, Sister Abigail," the soft-speaking nun said, clasping her hands together worriedly.

Sister Abigail looked away briefly, looking saddened by the prospect. Before she could speak, she began to cough into a napkin. The soft-speaking nun went over to her and patted her back gently. They had to have been taking care of each other for a long time. They were not just sisters of the church but friends. Once the coughing spell stopped, she looked up, closing her eyes as tears began to fall. I could hear her silent prayer to God. She grabbed her friend's hand.

"We will take her to a family that I know of. It's not the best of homes, but it will have to do. If they found out what she is, they would use her. We cannot let that happen."

My ears perked up at this. Who was this Violet, and who would use her?

"She is the first of her kind in generations. I know we have been in denial for this long, but I know the church cannot protect her any longer. If those monsters get their hands on her—" She breaks off, tears beginning to run down her face.

"We have done all that we can. We must leave it in God's hands now."

I left their chatter as I began walking, without realizing it, toward a doorway. It was if my vision was trying to tell me something. I opened the door, and I saw a young girl sitting on the floor with a bunch of art supplies surrounding her small frame. The room didn't look like a child's room. It had plain white walls and a simple twin bed. If it weren't for the crayons on the floor, I would never have thought a child lived there. She had long, strawberry-blond hair. Her back was to me as she continued to draw. She seemed to be in deep concentration as she drew furiously in fast strokes.

Puzzled, I walked slowly over to her so that I was facing her. My heart felt like it dropped to my stomach, and my hand flew over my mouth as I let out a gasp. Her eyes were completely white as she drew; she wasn't even looking at the paper. Her drawing was perfect. The shading was just right as she began to capture a man with red eyes. This was not Chayton—looked nothing like him, in fact. He was very good-looking, in a dark sort of way. Who was this? Under the drawing, the girl wrote a single word: Dominic. Why did that name sound familiar to me?

"Darling," the sister with the soft voice called from the doorway.

As if pulled from her trance, the girl's eyes faded from being white to a unique color between dark blue and gray. She was a very beautiful little girl who was both extremely gifted and cursed. I knew without a doubt she was a Conveyer.

"Sister Catherine," she said, her voice full of fright. She held up the picture. Sister Catherine took the picture from her small hands and ripped the picture in two.

"Why can't he leave me alone? He's all that I see," Violet shook her head and began to cry.

"Oh my darling." She hugged Violet and consoled her, rocking her gently back and forth.

"I am scared, Sister Catherine. I'm so scared."

Sister Catherine sighed softly and continued to comfort her, not by words, but by touch.

I wished there was a way to comfort her. But I knew as well as Sister Catherine that she had every reason to be scared.

"Do you think Chayton will protect me?" she asked after a minute.

My ears perked up and my body stiffened.

"I hope he does, my child," Sister Catherine said above her head. Her eyes reflected that she wasn't sure at all.

My vision began to blur as it began to take me elsewhere. It was dark outside, and the feel of heat made my throat dry. It definitely wasn't the city I was used to.

There were crowds of people waiting to go into a club called the Crazy Eight. I could hear the sound of loud music as I began to make my way through. My eyes widened as I realized the women who worked there were scantily dressed. I'm all about showing cleavage, but these women were practically spilling out. At least their "girls" looked like they didn't move an inch. Plastics! I smiled at the memory of Jewels comparing New York women to LA women.

Going into the center of the club, I realized this was not just any nightclub. This was a strip club. There were eight sections to the club, each with a small stage that held a golden stripper pole that went up into the ceiling. The center stage was the biggest, and no one was dancing on it. Each of the girls who were on stage had their tops off. I seriously tried not to look, I really did. But with their balloon-sized breasts, it was kind of hard not to. Each wore black wigs and crystal-bejeweled thongs. The men were practically drooling over them, shouting obscene remarks and whistling.

"Gentlemen, take your seats. Our main event is about to begin. You know you've all been waiting for her. She's the reason why you came. Give it up for the one, the only…Violet!" the balding host said, dragging out her name theatrically as he disappeared off the stage.

My body stilled at the mention of the name. No fucking way! I scanned the room quickly, trying to find any hint that would give me a clue to my whereabouts. Just then, the lights went out and the club went quiet in anticipation of the main event. The sound of slow, tantalizing music broke the silence. The center stage lit up and there she was: Violet, wearing a shoulder-length white wig with bangs and a barely there crystal bra top and thong. Her makeup was applied heavily, and if it weren't for the sad look in her eyes, I probably wouldn't have recognized her. She was a long way from the church.

I wrapped my arms around myself as she began to move to the music. I felt protective toward her; if this hadn't been a vision, I would have hauled her crystal-encrusted ass off the stage. She was still very young. I wondered how old you had to be to work at a place like this. It wasn't that the place was sleazy. It actually looked like a very high-end strip club. She just didn't belong there, even though her moves up there said otherwise.

She commanded the stage. Everyone's eyes were glued to her. No man was hooting or hollering. They sat perfectly still in their seats, riveted by her beauty and, of course, her ass. I scanned the crowd once again as I felt the hairs at the back of my neck begin to stand. I began to move around as I watched a dark figure standing against the wall and staring intently at Violet.

Just then, she dropped her top to reveal her breasts, and the crowd went crazy. The men all stood, and once again I was overwhelmed by their shouts. I lost sight of the man who was against the wall. Fuck!

"There you have it, gentlemen. Let's hear one more round of applause for our main attraction, Violet!" the host said as she strutted off the stage, still topless.

I followed her backstage to the dressing room. She took a seat, still a little breathless, and removed her wig, revealing her luscious strawberry-blond hair.

"Girl, if I had your hair, I wouldn't be wearin' this wig," one of the strippers said with a country accent. She looked older than the rest of the girls.

Violet just smiled softly at her and began to touch up her makeup.

The host came into the dressing room, looking expectantly at Violet. "Violet, you have a customer," he said.

"Customer? You know I don't do private dances," she said, putting down her lipstick and looking at the host in the mirror.

"Oh, honey—you're going to want to do this one. He's offering a lot of moola we are not going to pass up."

"The answer is no. Tell him I don't do private dances," she said sternly.

"The man is offering five grand for one dance with you."

"Shit, if she don't want it, I'll do it," the stripper with the country accent said, sitting up eagerly.

"Great, problem solved. Honey will do it," Violet said, going back to doing her makeup.

"No, no. This man specially asked for you. He knew you would refuse, so he told me to tell you ten grand!"

"You gotta be shittin' me," Honey said, now staring at Violet as if she had two heads.

Violet looked too stunned to speak, but after a minute her shoulders slumped. "OK, fine, but just let him know one lap dance—and that's it."

"OK, OK. I'll have Rock stand out by the doorway," he said, shuffling out. I could tell he was already trying to figure out what his cut of the cost of the lap dance was going to be.

"Shit, girl, you're lucky," Honey said.

"Yeah, thanks for thinking so." I watched as Violet took out a small glass mirror. Reaching into a drawer, she took out a small bag of white powder and poured a pile of it onto the glass. With a razor blade, she made it into a perfect white line. With a rolled-up dollar bill, she leaned her head forward and snorted up the white substance. Her eyes rolled to the back of her head as she leaned her head back, letting out a sigh of bliss. I felt at a total loss. First the strip club, and now this? An overwhelming feeling of sadness overtook me as I remembered the scared little girl being cradled by Sister Catherine. What had happened between then and now? What had brought her to this life?

"Girl, I don't know why you do that stuff," Honey said disapprovingly as she began to light up a cigarette.

I didn't think Violet was going to respond as she put on her white wig and fixed the bangs. Wiping her nose, she grabbed another bejeweled top, this one with all-black crystal, and answered, "It keeps the voices out of my head." She stood up, sauntering out of the room with glazed eyes.

Violet walked down the long, dark hallway, with me trailing right behind her. The sound of music blasting away was so loud that the walls seemed to vibrate. Putting her hand against the wall to steady her steps, she leaned against it for a moment. She was beginning to get messy. She shook her head as if to clear it, sweat dampening her forehead. She took a deep breath, plastered on a fake smile, and walked on, this time a little straighter. A big black man was standing at the doorway; I could only assume he was Rock. He was wearing all black, his muscle T-shirt bulging at the seams. Big Red was huge, but this guy? His veins were popping out of his skin. I could tell he was chemically enhanced.

"Hey Violet, you let me know if you need me," he said, opening the door.

Either she was too high to get scared or she just wasn't nervous. I was nervous for her, instead; every hair on my body told me that whoever was behind that door was a vampire. She walked in, and we both saw a man sitting down on a chair. I couldn't get a look at his face because of the lighting in the room. All I could see were his legs and hands. His silhouette was of a man with confidence. He reeked with it. The music began, and Violet slowly began to move, her hips moving sensually to the rhythm of the music.

"Take off your wig," the male voice said.

The voice sounded familiar. It was nice and deep. It made Violet shiver.

"No," she said and continued to dance. She walked over to him with her eyes closed. Her heart was beating faster. I didn't know if it

was from the drugs or if it was from nerves. She turned around, showing him her ass, bending over as her hands glided down her legs and touched her ankles. I looked away, slightly uncomfortable. The man growled and touched her ass. She swatted his hand, turning.

"No touching," she whispered, and then smiled, stumbling a little.

"You're mine, and you don't even know it yet," he said, the words thick with meaning.

Why did his voice sound so familiar? I walked over to him and noticed right away the sunglasses and dark hair. Holy shit. It was Chayton. Violet let out a giggle.

"What do you look like? Your voice..." She trailed off.

"Are you sure you're ready to see me?"

"Why wouldn't I be?" she said, taking a step back.

"Because you're not sure if I'm here to kill you or save you, Violet," he said, leaning forward so that the light revealed his face.

Her eyes widened in terror as she tried to run toward the door, but she tripped in the process. He was off his chair in a second, grabbing her before her body hit the floor. She let out a scream as she began to twist and turn out of his arms. The door swung open so fast I was sure it was broken at the hinges. Rock came through the doorway, meaning business. Chayton turned toward the doorway as he let go of Violet. She ran. He stared after her, but she stopped behind Rock, looking over her shoulder in horror at him. Wait...did he just do what I think he just did? Did he have my power? He smiled smugly at her. That smile...I know that smile.

"Kill him," she whispered to Rock.

"This is going to be fun," he said, cracking his knuckles as he approached Chayton.

23

"Hey, can I get another martini?" I ask the female bartender that I now know as Shannon. I again look at my watch, waiting for Scarlett to show. It isn't like her to be late. But then there's so much about my best friend I don't know. Like, for instance, where she's staying now. When she gave her notice to Mr. W, I was curious, so I went to her apartment. When a stranger answered the door, I was shocked, to say the least. *Where did she go?*

I ended up talking to the super. His answer to me was "Scarlett who?" He had no idea who I was talking about. It was strange. Then, the world being as small as it is, I saw her. And not just her. I saw her with this gorgeous male specimen who is apparently her boyfriend. I've known Scarlett a long time, and she's never, ever had a boyfriend. This man watched her every move, and his stare was for her and her only. I could tell he is intensely in love with her.

To be loved like that…I sigh, thinking of Jake. Jake is… safe. I mean, don't get me wrong, he loves me and cares for me. But…is that enough? I am so used to being the one wearing the pants in the relationship. To being the one in charge. I must say, I get that trait from my father. But for once, maybe I want to be the one dominated. Maybe I want to be in love intensely and get that back just as much.

"Here you go, doll," Shannon hands me another green apple martini—my favorite.

"Thanks." I take a sip, scanning the crowd, looking for Scarlett. She's thirty minutes late.

"Hello, may I join you?" a man asks. He's a good-looking man, probably in his late thirties with olive skin and dark hair that's sprinkled with white, which I always find rather sexy. He's wearing a suit and tie; it looks like he's just come from work. Never one to pass up a good-looking man's company, I smile and gesture for him to sit. There's nothing wrong with harmless flirting.

"Hi, I'm Bradley. Pleased to meet you," he says, offering me his hand.

I shake his hand. "Likewise. Jewels."

He smiles, his blue eyes twinkling as he tries to keep them only on my face. I can't blame him; I know I look great. My cream-colored short romper gives my skin a luminous glow. It's long-sleeved, but it exposes my legs. My hair is down, with loose curls. Not that I'm conceited, or maybe I am, but I know I can get most men's attention. I am a woman of confidence... that trait I got from my mother.

"So are you meeting someone?" he asks me after a minute, sipping the drink Shannon got him.

"Yes. My best friend. But from the looks of it, she's not showing up," I say, picking up my drink and taking a sip.

"Now that's a shame." He sets his drink down, looking at me.

"Yeah. We have been out of touch for a while now."

"Well, it looks like it's time to make a new friend," he says, his eyes suggesting something far different from just friends.

"I have too many friends to make new ones," I crack back. I wave at Shannon, silently asking her to give me my final check.

I can't give up on Scarlett. She's my best friend. I know without a doubt that she wouldn't give up on me, I think stubbornly. I'll be damned if I let her push me away. She looks different, and I want to know what the hell's going on. If she knew me like I knew her, she would know I'm the most stubborn person ever…a trait from both of my parents, unfortunately.

As I begin to pay my bill, I look up across the bar. I can't explain why I do, but as I do I see that red-headed man. What's his name? Something Red? Big Red. My breath catches, and before he can see me I quickly turn around. I didn't like him one bit. *Liar. You got so worked up over him, you went home to finish what he started by yourself.* I cringe at the thought. Sadly, it's true. I felt so guilty afterward. I felt like I had cheated on Jake. I know if this guy gets me alone it's going to be trouble. I quickly make my way to the bathroom without even saying one more word to Brad…Bradley…whatever his name is. I go inside and take a look in the mirror. My cheeks are blushed pink, and it feels like every nerve in my body is alive. Am I nervous? I'm never nervous around men. What makes him so different? *Because he knows exactly what you really need!* Shit! Hoping he doesn't see me, I exit the bathroom with my head down, about to walk out into safety.

"Jewels, is it?" a very sexy Irish voice says from behind me.

A wave of arousal goes through me just from the sound of his voice. I get angry at myself and then in turn get angry at him. He's leaning against the wall with his hands in his pockets next to the ladies' bathroom. It's almost like he was waiting for me. He's big and muscular, wearing a black sweater that makes his red hair stand out and a dark pair of jeans. He looks like such a bad boy. I bet he's used to women falling at his feet.

"I'm sorry. Do I know you from somewhere?" I ask, knowing saying that would probably bruise his already-big ego.

"Come on, love. You know me," he says, smiling conceitedly.

"Sorry, I don't. You might not have left a good impression on me." With that, I give him a wink and walk out of the bar with my head held high. I love the look of surprise hinted at in his beautiful green eyes. I walk out into the cold air to hail a cab.

Before I can even try, I'm swung into an alley without even a chance to let out a protest or scream. He crashes my back into the wall, not roughly enough to hurt me but enough to get my attention. Before I can ask him what the hell he's doing, his lips crash down on mine, and he's kissing me thoroughly. I've been kissed by plenty of men…and even a few girlfriends during some drunken college nights…but this… this is being kissed. This is being fucked without getting fucked. I moan helplessly as his big hands trail up from my waist, to my breasts, to my face, clutching me tightly to him. I flinch from the coldness of his hands but that doesn't stop me from getting closer. His big body overwhelms me; I'm pretty tall, and I'm almost standing on my tiptoes to meet him. Our tongues battle with each other as his hand skims back down to my breast, his fingers grazing my nipple. Breaking away from his intoxicating lips, I turn slightly, opening my eyes as his hands tighten around me. His eyes look dark, almost black. I don't know if it's because of the lighting or maybe my one-too-many martinis. *Yeah, blame it on the alcohol, slut.*

"Wait, stop it," I say, shoving at his chest.

His hand goes into my hair, pulling it back roughly. Again, my body zings with pleasure. My lips part, waiting for the kiss that I know is coming. Softly his lips descend on mine. This time he takes his time, and his tongue teases me, licking and lapping at my bottom lip. My eyes are still closed as his lips leave mine.

"Open your eyes," he whispers.

I don't usually take orders from anyone, but him…I know at this moment I would do just about anything for him. Opening my eyes, I see his eyes staring directly into mine. They *are* black. They're black, lifeless eyes. I try to let out a scream, but he silences me with a hand over my mouth.

"Listen to me, love. You have a friend named Scarlett?"

I begin to tremble in his arms in fear. What the fuck is wrong with his eyes? I feel my eyes begin to pool with tears. What did he want with Scarlett? I shake my head at him, denying that I know Scarlett. He lets out a sigh at my denial, and his thumb catches the tear that falls down my cheek.

"So brave," he whispers.

My eyes widen at him. *Brave? I'm ready to piss my pants.*

His eyes begin to shift, and I feel hypnotized in a sense. My body begins to go lax, and I don't fear him as I know I should.

"You're going to forget about your friend Scarlett. You've never met her," he whispers to me, brushing my hair from my forehead, releasing my mouth.

"Scarlett. Who's Scarlett?" I whisper back.

"Nobody. She is nobody to you."

"She is nobody to me," I repeat back to him. "What about you? What are you to me?" I ask after a minute.

"Nobody. You're going to forget all about me. You never met me," he says after a minute.

"I never met you," I repeat softly.

He turns to leave, and I automatically feel a sense of loss. I look around aimlessly, wondering how I got here. Then he comes rushing back to me with a look of frustration. He grabs me and kisses me again. I helplessly moan, putting my arms around his neck. He breaks away from me, growling.

"I am such a fucking asshole." He pauses after a minute, his thumb grazing my bottom lip and making me sigh with pleasure. "Every time you kiss someone, you're going to be reminded of my kiss. Remember that. No kiss will make you feel the way I make you feel when I kiss you. That's how you will remember me again."

"It won't be enough. I'll remember you again," I repeat softly, looking deeply into his eyes and wishing he would kiss me again.

Then he is gone. Wait, where the hell am I? I touch my lips, closing my eyes and trying to remember why the hell I'm here. My body feels warm, even though it's cold outside. I step out of the alley and hail a passing cab. OK, I remember going to the bar to meet someone. Who the hell was I supposed to meet? I quickly get into the cab and give the driver my address, looking out the window. Why do I feel like I'm forgetting something?

I look out the window, and I see a gorgeous man with red hair standing outside the bar with his hands in his pockets, staring at me and giving me a smug smirk. Swallowing hard, I look away. Do I know that guy? I think if I'd ever run into someone like him, I would definitely remember him.

Once the driver gets me to my apartment, I pay the fare and head inside. The doorman greets me, opening the door and smiling. It's great to live in a secure building in the city. Of course, with my parents' help I can afford such luxuries. Once they found out that their little girl was going to be working in the city most of the time, they decided to get me an apartment here. I am the apple of my parents' eye, and unfortunately that comes with consequences. One: do as I'm told (which does not work so well for me). Two: do as they do. Marry, have kids, all by the age of thirty-five. They think the world of Jake. He's what my mother so annoyingly points out as...safe. I don't want safe. What do I want? I don't know.

Opening the door to my apartment, I'm greeted by darkness. I always leave the light on because I hate coming home to a dark, lonely apartment. I flick on the light in my hallway, hanging up my coat and purse. Taking off my heels, I sigh in relief as I head over to my bedroom. My phone begins ringing as soon as I attempt to lie down. The alcohol must be leaving me, because a major headache's coming on.

"Hello," I grit out.

"Hey, hon. I tried reaching you on your cell," Jake says on the other end.

"Sorry. I must've had it on silent," I say, pinching the bridge of my nose.

"OK. So what are you doing now?" he asks, totally ignoring my apology.

"About to take a shower and go to bed," I say, hoping he takes the hint.

"Are you drunk?"

"No. Why would you ask me that?" I say, sitting down now, bracing myself for a fight.

"Because you don't sound like yourself. You know I don't like it when you drink," he says.

I take a deep breath, gripping the phone hard to my ear. This is why I'm starting to become irritated with him. He acts way too much like a parent and not a boyfriend. Sure, he's romantic. Sure, he's responsible. But I don't need another parent. I have two of those, thank you very fucking much.

"I'm not a child, Jake."

"I'm not saying you're a child. I just think that maybe you should curb the going out."

"Curb the going out"? Is he serious right now? What am I, pushing fifty? I am twenty-two years old, for Christ's sake.

"Jake, I think we should talk. Like, have a serious conversation," I say.

"Jewels, I don't want to argue. I'm just trying to look out for you. I love you, and I'm sorry."

I close my eyes, feeling the guilt rush to me. Maybe I'm just being a bitch because I am indeed drunk. I mean, I did end up in a bar, and I have no idea who the hell I was supposed to meet.

"I…I love you too," I respond back. Saying it now, it feels like it's lost its validity.

"OK. Let me come over and make it up to you. We can order takeout."

"OK," I say hesitantly. I know I'm stalling, but my mind's made up. It just isn't going to work between Jake and me. I'm sorry I didn't realize it sooner. I'll tell him tonight, and hopefully we can end things as friends. Even though I know there's no way we can be friends. *Word of advice: you can never be friends with your ex.*

"OK, great, be there soon." He hangs up.

Taking the phone away from my ear, I hear a sound coming from my living room. I walk halfway there and pause in fear as I see a tall, frightening man, his hair slicked back into a ponytail, his back toward me. Putting my hand over my mouth to hold in my scream, I take a step back, hoping he hasn't heard me.

"The smell of you is intoxicating." His voice makes me go still. My heart drops down into my stomach, and I am paralyzed with fear.

"My boyfriend is coming…" I am inching toward my doorway.

"Running would make this so much funnier, don't you think, Jewels?" he says.

I don't know how he knows my name, and at this point I'm not going to ask. I turn and begin to run, screaming. He's at me in a flash, grabbing me by the hair and smashing my body hard against the wall. The pictures hanging on the walls crash to the floor, glass shattering everywhere. My body sinks to the floor, and I whimper when my hands get cut by the shards of glass. I try to crawl away, tears running down my face. He's behind me. I feel sick thinking that he may be enjoying this.

"Someone help me!" I scream.

He laughs.

"They can't hear you." He lifts me, and I feel pieces of glass dig into my soles. I scream in pain. As I try to shove him away from me, he laughs again at my efforts. He stares directly into my eyes. I feel like I'm being sucked into whatever dark place he's sending me to.

"You will not move," he commands me.

I stand still. Why can't I move?

I watch as he brings my bloody hand up. Finding my wound, he takes it to his mouth and drinks. I am having a panic attack. I am imagining this. This can't be real. I will my hand to move, but it won't. I am under his control. I must have let out a sound of distress, because he drops my hand roughly and leans forward toward my face. His nostrils begin to flare, and his eyes blacken in anger.

"Who are you with?" he demands, grabbing me roughly by the arms.

"I don't..." I trail off when he slaps me.

It's hard enough that I see stars. I lick my lips, tasting blood.

"You are with one of the Xs! Which one?" He stares deeply into my eyes.

"I don't know what you're talking about," I plead with him.

"I smell him all over you. I'll find him though. Where is Scarlett?"

"Scarlett?" I ask, shaking my head.

Again a slap to the face. If it wasn't for the voodoo power he has over me, my body would've sagged to the floor.

"Don't fucking lie to me," he says roughly. Reaching down, he shows me a picture of me and a girl with dark hair. My arm is around her, and we're making silly kissy faces at the camera. For the life of me, I can't remember who she is.

"He fucking entranced you," he says as he clearly sees the confusion in my eyes.

He touches my face almost gently. He licks my bottom lip, sucking at the blood that's there.

"You have such beautiful skin. Has anyone told you that? It's already bruising. So beautiful."

I swallow hard as he grips my throat, roughly cutting off my air. As my world begins to fade, I notice his fangs.

"You don't know Scarlett right now. But once I am done with you, my sweet, I promise you, you're going to wish you'd never even heard her name."

I stare numbly at the fire for what seems like forever. Its heated blaze does nothing to calm the coldness I'm beginning to feel. A part of me feels gone. How did this come to be? If my parents were alive, what would they say? Would this have even happened? My guess is yes. I am the youngest after my brother, Damian. My mother died shortly after I was born, and my dad took us both under his wing. It was easy for my father, having a pack full of women who nurtured us. We could always tell he was still heartbroken over the loss of my mother. Whenever he would speak of her, he would get this sadness in his eyes. Even when he would look at me sometimes, he would get sad, because I looked so much like her. She was the love of his life, and he never took another after her.

We have a long bloodline of royalty. Being the first of our kind, we are not made but born. As the first born, my brother, Damian, naturally took reign. Our sworn enemies were the ancients, vampires. My father often told stories about how that war began. The war began with a man by the name of Draken, who sought to wipe out our race. It ended up with a lot of lives lost. The fathers before my father struck a deal with Draken. The deal was for us to live freely and not to involve ourselves in vampire business. I asked my father if anyone knew what had happened to the man known as Draken. My father said he vanished. No one knew of his whereabouts, not even the men who had fought by his side. I told my father that maybe he had died. My father shook his head vigorously, saying a man as evil as him never dies.

Damian would often ask my father why we wouldn't just take over the vampires now that their leader was gone. He believed we were strong enough to do so; I thought so as well. My father would just say there was a need for balance. We never attacked unless there was a threat to us. We had given our word. The vampires would stay on their side of the world, and we would stay on ours. Damian always had a wicked gleam in his eyes that I didn't notice, but my father did. Damian's need for power was almost as powerful as a vampire's craving for blood. *Ironic, right?* This, I know, must have been hard for my father. As a parent, you don't want to see the bad things in your child, only the good.

Damian always went against the pack, always traveling outside of our guarded parameters—which was not allowed unless you were with others in the pack. It was mainly for protection. He rebelled against our ways. I should have seen it then, but I was the adoring younger brother. In my eyes, he could do no wrong. He set his own fate in defying my father.

One day it all caught up with him when a group of vamps attacked our pack because he decided to pick a fight with one of them. It cost him gravely. Lots of our men were hurt, my father especially so. That was the beginning of Damian's demise. He was dethroned. My father cast me as the new leader of the pack. That was when our relationship changed. Gone was the look I would receive from Damian as his smaller brother; now he saw me instead as his adversary. My father died shortly after the attack. The pack and I sat with him, with Damian quietly looking on, as he croaked his final wishes. That was when Damian really began to rebel. He fought with me tooth and nail. Everything I said, he questioned. He thought I had no right to be the leader, and he even had the members of the pack try to go against me. But their loyalty to me was as great as the loyalty to my father. I can still remember the last conversation I had with Damian. I remember the dark look in his eyes and the venom of hate he spilled in his words.

It was a full moon that night. I remember gazing up at the sky after my father's death, remembering his last words to me, which he had whispered so that no one but me would hear. The fire was beginning to burn out as the rest of the pack wandered off to sleep.

"It's time we take our revenge." Damian said from behind me.

I turned around, feeling annoyed. I was losing so much respect for him. How dare he talk about revenge when he was the one to bring trouble to us?

"Revenge? We took revenge, do you not remember? The ones that attacked us got what they deserved."

Damian shook his head at me, coming so close that we were standing man to man. I remembered wrestling with him when we were younger. He'd always been stronger, quicker. We were no longer little boys.

"We can wipe them all out. You and I, we can take over the world, little brother," he said. He had always used that as a term of endearment; it soon lost its value.

I said nothing, so he continued. "Just think of it. We would take over the vamps and the humans. We would no longer have to go into hiding. There would be no need for protection, because we would be free."

I felt my anger begin to build. I clenched my fists at my side, refraining from launching myself at him. It didn't go unnoticed as he smiled at me. Who was this person? How could he say these things to me after our father had just died? He just didn't get it and probably never would.

"That is not our way. We protect what is ours."

"Ours? Look around you, dear brother," he said, waving his hand around our home. "This is mine! I was meant to rule and be the leader of this pack," he hissed.

"Things have changed, and not by my doing, brother, but your own. If you want to be in this pack, you will have to obey or leave. The decision is up to you," I said calmly, my stare unbreakable.

"You will regret this, Liam. I promise you. You will regret this," he stated angrily, giving me one final look and walking away from not only me but our pack.

I remember hanging my head in disappointment then, as I am right now. I know, no matter how hard I try to deny it, it's there as clear as day. I lost my brother that night…either to the temptation of the outside world or to the power that would surely consume him. Or hell, maybe it was both. Is the red-headed witch right? Did he really side with the queen?

"She's right, you know," Adam says, sitting down next to me, staring at the fire.

"Who?" I ask, even though I already know who he's talking about.

Adam's like another brother. We are a few months apart in age, and he witnessed everything that went down with Damian. He stood by me and was loyal to a fault. In fact, he's the one who told me Damian was trying to round up the pack to turn against me. He's not only my brother, but my ears.

"The witch. She was right. Damian is in cahoots with the queen. He's turning humans. Making a big army of them, too. Something big is going down, Liam. I can sense it."

"The prophecy," I say, getting up, picking up my backpack in the process. I begin to walk out, away from the protection of the pack.

"Wait a minute; you can't possibly believe the prophecy is true! We don't even know what the Goddamn thing says," he yells, right on my heels. I know he will try to talk me out of it, but my mind's made up. I know what I have to do.

"A war is coming. I have to find that girl the witch was talking about."

"The prophet? You don't even know where the hell to look."

"I am going to leave you in charge," I say, not bothering to answer his question. I turn toward him. It's best not to let him know where I am going.

"Be safe, brother," he says, lowering his head in defeat, knowing this conversation's over. He turns and walks away.

I make it out of our safety zone. I am now on the man's land. I didn't tell Adam that the red-headed witch had already been in contact with me, but she had. Whatever witchery she's using is strong. Her soft voice is in my head constantly. She tells me of the future. If it is true, we are all endangered. She gave me a plane ticket with the location of the training site the Xs use. I take the ticket out of my backpack. New York City. I have never been out of our safety zone. It's time I meet the human girl named Scarlett, and it's also time I face not the man I called my brother, but the man called Damian. My enemy.

24

After Scarlett fell into my arms, I brought her to our room and set her on the bed as she sighed, tossing and turning on the cool sheets. I watched her for a moment, her expression showing that she was troubled by what she was seeing. I wanted to care for her, but how?

I have had many visions of her taking a warm bath. It always seems to calm her, and I know it's something she enjoys. I go into the bathroom, turning on the water and grabbing the lavender bath salts that seem to be her favorite. *Hell, they're my favorite.* I go back into the bedroom and see that she's now turned on her side, facing me. Her face has gone pale, and her wet hair's stuck to her face, but she's still just as beautiful. I remove her clothes gently, ignoring my growing hard-on as I get her good and naked. Her pink nipples tighten unbearably, almost taunting me.

Sighing a little, I contain myself, not allowing myself to just rip off my clothes and sink myself so deeply into her welcoming wetness. Instead I pick her up and place her gently into the warm water, watching the bubbles rise at an alarming rate. I quickly turn off the water and wait. I lean against the sink, folding my arms across my chest as I watch her. I could watch her forever, I realize. Her cheeks begin to go rosy, and she begins to sigh in bliss.

I think back to the last memory I have with her. I have to say it affected me uncomfortably.

I saw the array of emotions float on her face as she watched her parents get married. It was strange to watch the man I knew as Edrick and nothing more. He never discussed his life with me and then again, I never asked, but I always did wonder why he was helping me. Why did he feel the need to train me on how to survive? And most of all, what would he think now that I had hurt her?

As I'd watched that memory of hers, I saw how much Scarlett resembled him. She looked nothing at all like her mother. I remembered her from the picture I held when I found the location of her whereabouts. I sat beside her on the grass as they both begin to recite their vows. My parents never showed any affection toward each other. The only time my father would put his hands on my mother was to harm her. What would it be like to have parents like this, who loved and doted on each other?

I'd looked across at Scarlett as she fought the tears that pooled in her eyes and knew she felt the same. So unlike her and me, but yet not.

Scarlett begins to stir, which quickly snaps me from my thoughts. Her eyes begin to flutter open and she moves a little, making the water overflow and spill onto the cold marble floor.

"What happened?" she whispers raising her hand and placing it on her forehead.

"You fainted."

"Fainted," she repeats.

She moves again, and her rosy pink nipples peek above the bubbles, which are beginning to dissipate. I clench my teeth.

"How did you know I liked hot baths?" she asks me.

"Your memories. Did it comfort you?" I ask curiously.

"Yes. The *water* did comfort me," she says sarcastically. I know she's hinting at the moment when she told me I can never be that person to comfort her. It…what was that feeling I'd felt when she'd said that? It stung. I know I deserved it. Because the truth is I don't know if I *can* ever be that person. I don't even know how.

"Are you just going to stare at me?" she says as she gets up in all her glory, the bubbles sliding down her luscious body. I swallow hard as she gets out of the tub, standing before me with a knowing smile as her eyes lower toward my raging hard-on. I don't try to conceal it—she knows how she affects me. I know I said I wouldn't fuck her until she begged for it, but hell, I'm ready to go down on my knees and worship her. I want to lick every last drop of wetness dripping from her body. She makes me feel so many things all at once. It's overwhelming. If she were a witch, I would say she'd cast a spell on me. I'd felt dead and lifeless for so many years, but she makes me feel…she makes me feel alive.

Standing completely naked before him should have made me nervous, but it doesn't. If anything, it made me feel sexy, liberated. I feel the heat of his gaze as if he's touching my skin. My breasts feel heavy, and my thighs begin to pool. After my vision of Violet and Chayton, I need an escape. Opening my eyes, it was almost like a sign that Ian stood across from me shirtless and in shorts. Yes. He can help me escape.

But wait, what had he said? He would make me beg before he fucked me again. I am close to it. What the hell's going on with me? I am one big raging hormone. As if to confirm this, Ian palms my breast, making me wince in pain as his thumb grazes my nipple, but God, it feels good. His eyes darken, and he softly smiles. He must think I flinched from his coldness, but my nipples are so achy. I lean into his touch, pressing my lips to his chest. He hisses between his teeth.

"I don't have fangs," I murmur against his neck as I watch his vein pop.

"Are you hungry?" He doesn't let me answer. He pulls away from me slightly, lifting his wrist to his mouth.

"No. I don't need that," I say, grabbing his wrist, stopping him.

"What do you want, Scarlett? Do you want me to fuck you?" he whispers, touching my hair, his mouth barely touching mine.

I smile, remembering the similar words he spoke at my birthday party.

"Yes," I whisper as he grabs my ass, bringing me flush to his naked chest.

"You're going to have to beg me first," he whispers in my ear, causing my body to shiver.

I pull away from him roughly, pushing him back, but he quickly grabs me by the face, crashing his mouth over mine before I can tell him what he can do with his begging. His tongue invades my mouth as all my thoughts are swept away. That's what he does to me. Just one kiss and everything is gone. I need him. *There, I said it.* I need him as much as I need air. I need him. It's that simple.

I latch onto him for dear life. He hoists me up by the waist, making me gasp with excitement as he sets me down on top of the bathroom countertop. He presses himself between my legs as he begins to leave wet kisses trailing down my neck to my aching breast. I let out a whimper as he takes one of my nipples in his mouth, his tongue twirling around my extended tip. I almost scream from the pleasure of it. I grasp his head tightly to me as I begin to grind myself against his hardened length.

"Are you ready to beg yet?" he says, looking up at me.

"Not even close," I say, lying, starting to like this game we're playing.

"Then I guess I have my work cut out for me," he says, sinking to his knees, opening my legs wide, his eyes darkening as he gazes at my wet, aching flesh. I lick my lips in anticipation. He brings each of my legs over his shoulders, sliding me now so that my ass is hanging off the counter and my head is resting back against the mirror. But he does nothing else.

"Tell me," he says, looking up at me.

"Tell you what?" I bite my bottom lip.

"Tell me what you want me to do," he says, smiling, his eyes twinkling with amusement.

I arch my eyebrow. *Two can play this game.*

"I want to feel your lips on me. I want you to taste how wet you make me, and I want you to lick every last drop." I bravely lower my hand. I touch my swollen clit, and without blushing, I bring my fingers to my mouth, tasting myself.

He releases a growl and brings his head down, doing exactly what I'd asked. I let out a moan of pleasure.

"Ian...oh, God..." I say, over and over again.

I am so close. He licks me from top to bottom, even stopping over my puckered flesh. I still briefly, weirded out by this unexpected pleasure. *Whoa. Hang on a minute?*

He stops, lifting his head as his finger grazes my asshole lightly.

"I am going to possess every part of you. Not now, but soon," he says confidently.

Before I can ask how that would even be possible, his lips are on me again as he slips two fingers inside my tightness. Before a climax can rock my body, he stops, stilling his fingers and beginning to kiss my thighs.

"Ian," I grate out.

"What is it?" he asks me innocently.

I moan when he puts his mouth back on my clit, sucking it gently. Then he releases me as he sees I am close to climax. *Asshole.*

"I can end your misery right now. You know what you have to do." He gets up, pulling down his shorts. Slowly, his cock slips out as if begging to be free. He grips it and begins stroking himself. *Oh my…*

Without a second thought I slide off the counter, going down onto my knees in front of him. He guides his cock into my mouth as I attempt to take him as far as I can. He groans as my tongue flicks the tip of his head, tasting his essence. I squeeze my thighs together and moan when I feel his hands in my hair as he finds a rhythm. Lifting my hand, I cup his testicles and relish when they tighten in my hand. He's close. I pause and let him go, instead placing sweet kisses on his stomach. He growls again in frustration, and I smile up at him.

I love having this power over him. I realize then that I want to possess him in every way possible as well. I guide him back into my mouth, using my hand to stroke him at the same time. He groans again and that encourages me further. He holds my head tightly as he fucks my mouth. He's relentless in his thrusting, causing me to gag a little, but that doesn't stop me. I am a girl on a mission. His cock twitches slightly, and my womanly instincts make me suck harder. I feel a gush of warm liquid fill my mouth. *Oh God, can I do this?* Taking one look up at him, I see his head thrown back in ecstasy and his mouth parted, his fangs protruding from his mouth. *Hell yes, I can.* I thought watching him stroke himself was sexy as hell, but this? His hair's disheveled, looking utterly and thoroughly fucked. I swallow every single drop of him until he softens in my mouth. I pull him out, kissing his thigh afterward.

"Fuck begging," he says as he lifts me up, just when I was going to beg him to fuck me. But he doesn't need to know that.

He sets me down on the bed, his body lying on top of mine, and he kisses me. A slow, lingering kiss. His cock begins to harden again. He kisses down my neck toward my breasts, leaving sweet trails down to my stomach. He kisses my thighs and I feel the tips of his fangs before he gently bites me.

"Ah," I moan from the pleasure and pain. I pull my fingers through his hair, holding him tightly to me as he drinks. He slips a finger inside of me. I moan as I clench myself around his hand. He pulls away after drinking, removing his hand. I don't even get a chance to protest the loss of him, because he fills me with one hard thrust of his cock. My arms go around him as I lift my pelvis to meet him thrust for thrust.

"Yes..." I whisper.

"This is what you wanted," he growls.

"Yes...oh yes," I whimper, staring into his eyes, digging my nails into his back.

He picks up his tempo, pounding deeply into me, and just like that I am floating high, screaming my release, staring into his eyes the whole time. The force of my climax makes him go into his own. Both breathless and still joined, we just stare at each other. The air shifts around us, and we both know that this was different. Something has changed between us. His hand comes up almost hesitantly and touches the side of my face. I am incoherent to anything that's around me. I am lost, and the only one I want to find me is Ian.

"Maylina, you are needed downstairs," one of the ancients, named Lucas, calls. I don't answer him; there's really no need to. I do what I am told. No questions, because I couldn't give a shit about the answer. I am a cold, stone robot. At least that is what I am used to being called. Being the only female now working for the queen, I feel I have to prove myself against everyone, even though there's not much really to prove.

Before working for the queen, I was an assassin. I was paid handsomely for what I did. I was the best in the business, and though it was a man's world, I ruled it. The queen gave me an offer I couldn't refuse. At the time, I felt like if I did refuse, she would come at me with full force. I pick my battles wisely, though. What did I really have to lose? Fuck the humans. Fuck the world. That's my motto. She said she needed me to take charge of the "security team" that she has surrounding her home; not only that, but I was to be the one overseeing the humans that are kept as prisoners, blood slaves. They are shipped from all over the world, hauled into the basement, and sedated, and tubes run any which way from their bodies.

Since taking charge, some of the men, and by that I mean Lucas, are not happy. He thinks he should have gotten that privilege, but he's a spineless fool. I can sense that a mile away. I feel it in his stare when he looks at me silently when I give a command to one of the ancients, and I feel it now as he follows behind me. He doesn't appreciate taking orders from a woman. Fuck him. What I wouldn't give to rip his jugular out. I just need a reason to do it. As I head downstairs, the air begins to thicken with the smell of blood and death. Going farther into the basement, I notice the men are all gathered, having quite a discussion.

"What seems to be the problem?" I ask.

John clears his throat first.

"One of the humans passed. Charles got carried away in his feedings."

I feel my anger begin to rise, but not for the human. A hungry vampire is a weak vampire. There's nothing worse than sloppiness. That's something I do not tolerate.

"Where is he?" I ask.

"He's being held in one of the rooms," Lucas speaks up.

"Good. He is not allowed out until I say so," I say, going to the doorway to assess the damage myself. "Did anyone check this out?"

They all shake their heads in unison.

"So what are your plans for Charles? What about his feedings?" Lucas asks.

"He can fucking starve for all I care," I say, entering the dark room and closing the door behind me.

Right away the darkness welcomes me. The only sound that greets me is a heart that is beating rapidly and the sound of a whimper. *Fuck, besides that asshole not controlling his hunger, he can't even fucking kill right.*

Switching on the light reveals blood everywhere. It looks like the fight got pretty nasty. I find her body and pause. The woman's lifeless body is surrounded by a pool of her own blood. Blood that now stains her blond hair. That isn't what gives me pause. Her clothes are in tatters, and her panties are below her ankles. Not even that gives me pause. What does give me pause—what causes my body to still with awareness—is when I see the reflection of the monster that I have become in the eyes of a young child. The child's small arms are wrapped around the dead body of what I can only presume was her mother. The child's alive. *Holy fuck! How did she get spared?*

"My mommy...my mommy," the little girl whispers to me, her big, soft eyes pleading with me.

The sound of her childlike voice makes me swallow hard. I feel something in the pit of my stomach. Ignoring that feeling, I grab the knife from my pocket and walk over to her. I should put her out of her misery. I walk over to her and kneel down. The sight of the blood doesn't bother me in the slightest. I learned from early on in my change to curb my hunger. It's a weakness, and I have none. I focus in on my target. Her hair's wet from her tears, and her pink dress is stained in blood.

"Come here," I whisper to her.

She lets go of her mother and stands. Her hair, I notice, is beautifully curled, and she's about three, maybe four, years old. She notices the knife in my hands, but that doesn't stop her from coming to me. *So trusting.* She wraps her small arms around my neck, catching me by surprise. The force of her hug makes me stagger back a little in shock. She smells of vanilla and cookies. She shivers from my coldness but nuzzles closer to me. I grip my knife tighter, ready to aim it in the small of her back, but again I pause. *What the fuck is wrong with me?*

"Please don't let those big men get me," she says, clutching me tighter.

I can't do it. I drop the knife, angry with myself, and hug her to me, gently stoking her back up and down as my mother did when she comforted me. I wonder if this is my human side, the one that I thought had died with me the day I turned. Even though when I was human, I never felt remorse, and that just amplified once my change began. I can't kill her, and I'll be damned if I let anyone hurt her.

"No, I won't let them hurt you," I tell her.

"You pinkie promise?" she asks me, pulling back from me a little.

"I pinkie promise," I say.

Holding her again against me, I begin to come up with a plan. I have to get her the fuck out of here. But first I have to hide her from the others. As I begin to stoke her hair, I realize I've found my first weakness.

25

I wake to the sound of a baby crying—or at least I think I hear that sound. Sitting up from the bed, I notice I am stark naked, and looking to the side I see that Ian is not with me. I feel a sting of disappointment that he isn't. I'm beginning to get used to waking up with him by my side.

I pick up the covers and hold them to my naked chest. I wince from the sting of the soft sheets on my aching breasts. Peeling the sheet off, I look down and notice that my breasts look huge. I was never small to begin with, but my nipples look darker. Bringing my hand up to cup one of them, I realize I am right. They feel heavier. Using my thumb, I graze over my nipple and wince again; it's so sensitive. I get up, wrapping the sheet around me, and head to the bathroom. I am startled by my reflection in the mirror. My hair's one knotted mess, and my skin's overly pale. I turn on the water, rinsing my face and loving the feel of the refreshing, cool water. Looking up, I am happy to see the color returning to my face.

I begin to brush my teeth. My stomach begins to turn, and my mouth salivates. *No, don't think about it. You're not going to throw up. Distract yourself. Think of ice cream. Yes. That's it.* But that doesn't seem to help as I begin to think of melting ice cream that's gooey and sticky. Turning the ice cream to old rotten milk, I turn just in time toward the toilet. Dropping to my knees, ignoring the pain, I begin to dry heave the emptiness in my stomach.

Shaking, I flush the toilet and just sit on the cold floor. I wipe my eyes. I felt so much better after Flora did her magic on me. Why do I feel like crap again? And why do I get the nagging feeling that Flora knows what's wrong with me? Now that I think of it, she's acting extremely suspiciously. I get up quickly but have to steady myself when a wave of dizziness hits me, making me see white flecks in my vision. Taking a deep breath, I close my eyes and wait until I feel steady enough to move. I walk out slowly, reminding myself not to move too fast. I dress in an oversized gray sweater and black leggings with my black combat boots. I tie my hair in a ponytail and don't bother with any makeup, since my cheeks are pink against the rest of my pale face. Flora's going to give me answers.

I go right to Hugo's room. Hugo answers on the first knock, wearing nothing but a pair of jeans. *Whoa, I can really see now why Flora was so possessive. Hugo's hot.* His hair's a sexy mess, and his soft brown eyes look at me worriedly.

"Scarlett, what's wrong?" he asks, letting me into his room.

"Where's Flora?" I ask, not answering him because I'm really not sure myself.

"Scarlett, how are you feeling?" Flora asks me, coming out of the bathroom.

She's wearing one of Hugo's T-shirts, and I feel a little uncomfortable knowing they may have just finished having sex. *I mean this is Hugo we're talking about.* I quickly close the door.

"OK, Flora, you can cut the act. What's wrong with me?" I ask.

Her smile drops a little. She looks uneasily at Hugo, who has the same questioning look in his eyes. I feel like a bomb is about to be dropped. My mouth begins to salivate again, and I walk over to their bed, having a seat at the edge.

"Scarlett, are you OK?" Hugo worriedly comes over to sit beside me.

I again look at Flora, silently begging her just to come out with it.

"Well, it seems that my magic over you was temporary. Whatever is happening, it's too strong for my magic."

"What are you talking about, Flora?" Hugo asks, looking between Flora and me.

"The missing prophecy spoke of two beings," Flora says.

I shake my head as she continues.

"Two new prophets. One coming from lightness. One coming from dark."

Hugo gets up, pacing back and forth. "No, that doesn't make sense. Are you saying what I think you're saying? That is not possible."

"Anything is possible. Look at Scarlett. She is living proof of that."

I gently put my hand to my stomach. *Can it be? One born of light and one born of darkness.* Hugo and Flora begin debating, forgetting that I am there.

"The queen is having a baby," I say quietly. *Born of darkness.* "She and Damian conjured up a spell with Opal. It's Chayton."

They both pause, looking at me.

"So it's already started," Flora says, looking like she wants to add more, but the look on my face must give her pause.

My stomach drops in dread. This can't be happening. This is so fucking wrong in so many ways. I get up.

"I have to go out," I whisper, needing to get air.

"I'll go with you," Hugo says, grabbing his shirt off the floor.

I look at him, thankful that I have him. What would I do if I didn't have him? I know I can't count on Ian. Oh God. Ian…I feel like I am going to be sick again.

"Come on," Hugo says softly to me, leading me out of the door, putting on his leather jacket. I feel his eyes meet Flora's, and she nods her head in understanding.

We walk down the steps quickly. It's morning out, and I know the others are most likely in the training center. I hurry out the front door and breathe a sigh of relief that no one stops us.

"Where do you want to go?" Hugo asks me tentatively.

"I don't know. Let's just walk. There is a small park not too far from here," I say, beginning to lead the way. The weather's cold. I know I shouldn't have left without a jacket, but the cold air's soothing to me. *Just like Ian's touch.*

"You're not cold?" Hugo asks me.

"No. Do you think it's true?" I ask. I can't bring myself to actually say it.

"I don't know. I can't sense anything different in you," Hugo says, his eyes looking puzzled.

"You can sense this?"

"Yes, but like Flora said, her magic's not strong enough to fend off your sickness. So whatever is going on may be too strong for me to detect."

"Great," I say sarcastically.

We find the park, but I keep an eye on the stores along the way. I spot a drug store and head in that direction, Hugo close on my heels. He opens the door for me, and we both walk in. The door chimes and the cashier greets us. An older lady with graying hair, the cashier, smiles at us warmly, and I return her smile. I know when I get my feminine products I see pregnancy tests right by them. Going to the feminine hygiene aisle, I look, and there are tons of them. I look at Hugo for help, and he seems as lost as I am.

"Do you need help with anything, honey?" the cashier asks me.

Hugo and I turn to her, rather guilty, and I can't help picturing myself asking her, "Yeah, I do. What would be the best pregnancy test for someone who could potentially be having a baby that's a vampire?" I burst out laughing in a hysterical giggle. The cashier lets out a nervous laugh, and Hugo excuses my behavior due to nerves.

"Well, you guys just holler if you need anything," she says, looking at us strangely.

I wipe my eyes, and Hugo seems at a loss for words.

OK. This shouldn't be too bad. They all do the same thing. I pick up one that looks familiar to me from commercials. A woman with dark hair comes on the television and says, "Do you think you're expecting?" I look on the back, and it says I can test before I miss my period. When was my last period? I don't even remember. I never felt the need to keep track, and I'm always irregular anyway. The tests come with two sticks. That's all I really need, right? Then I look over, and there are digital ones. Great, which one do I get? Spending another five minutes in the aisle, I just decide on getting my first pick. I go to the cashier, and she's waiting for me, smiling a womanly smile. She rings me up and charges me. Hugo hands her the money, and she puts the tests in a plastic bag.

"Good luck to you both," she says, handing me the bag.

Hugo lets out a laugh, which he tries to cover up with a cough, and I smile brightly at her.

"Thank you. But he's not the father; someone else is." Smirking at her shocked expression, I turn to Hugo. "Come on, baby, you know we have to plan our wedding." Putting my hand on Hugo's arm, we walk out of the store. I laugh as soon as we are outside.

"Well, it's good that you haven't lost your sense of humor," he says, laughing with me.

I stop laughing, very much on the verge of tears. My heart begins to beat rapidly, and I feel like I can't breathe.

"Scarlett, it's going to be OK," Hugo says softly.

He rushes me over to have a seat on a bench overlooking the park. He rubs my back so comfortingly, but why do I feel like something is missing? Yes, he's comforting me but...*it's not Ian.*

"Whatever happens, just know I will be here for you. I promise you that," he says, putting his hand over mine.

"I don't know what I would do if you weren't here with me. Flora is very lucky," I tell him.

"Well, next time I get her mad, I'll be sure to have you to remind her of that," he says, smiling.

Hugo in love. It isn't strange at all to see him this way. It's easy to see why Flora loves him. It's effortless to love him. I think of Ian and...it's complicated. I don't hate him. I couldn't. What would he say to this latest development? I am scared to even tell him. No, I can't tell him at least until I know for sure.

"Ready to go?" Hugo asks me.

"Yeah," I say, reluctantly getting up.

We walk the rest of the way home in silence, which I am happy about. My thoughts keep straying to Ian. Our time together is definitely affecting me. It's not just fucking. He knows that and so do I, even though I'm not ready to admit it out loud. We reach the house, and I head upstairs with Hugo close behind me.

"Do you want me to go in with you?" Hugo asks me as I open my door. I quickly peek in to make sure Ian's not there.

"Don't you think it's going to be just a little awkward, you standing there while I pee on a stick?" I ask, smiling at him teasingly.

"Agh. Sorry, I didn't realize what the test entailed," Hugo says, laughing.

"No, I'll be fine," I say, clutching the plastic bag tighter to me.

"OK. Once you take it, just call me over, and I will come to you."

I swallow hard, beginning to get nervous again. I want to laugh hysterically again, but I stop myself.

"OK," I say instead, softly closing the door behind me.

I take the test out of the bag and place it down on the bed as I begin to pace back and forth. My palms are beginning to sweat. I have to do it before Ian comes into the room. *Fuck it.* I grab the test and peel off the plastic, taking out one of the testing sticks. Reading the directions, I head over to the bathroom, sitting down on the toilet and doing my business where it told me to. Once done, I seal it and place it on the counter. It says to wait three minutes for the results.

I go into the bedroom and stop in my tracks as I see a folded black piece of paper lying against my white sheets. I would have definitely noticed that as soon as I came in. I walk slowly to the bed as the air begins to go still and a coldness spikes up my spine. Picking it up, I unfold the letter; it's written in red calligraphy. My nostrils flare as I catch the scent; it's written in blood.

Scarlett,

I think it is time we met in person. I have a friend of yours who is dying to see you. You know where Michael lives. Come meet me here. Leave your friends at home. If I sense them, which I will, I will rip Detective Alvarez limb from limb. I do hope you understand. I cannot wait to finally meet you.
Opal

All thoughts gone, I drop the letter to the floor and look at the time. It's nearly sundown. I go to my closet and dress for combat. My vision's coming to fruition. I put on my leather jacket, and then I pick the letter up and shove it into my jacket as I grab my sword case, wrapping it around my back. As I head out the doorway, I begin to run down the stairs, calling everyone to the meeting room. I wait for everyone to come, and all of them go quiet as they see I'm dressed for battle. Ian walks in; I avoid his penetrating stare. This is no time to get sidetracked.

"I got a letter from Opal. They're holding a human by the name of Detective Alvarez hostage. He knows about us," I say, holding their stares.

"A fucking human that knows about us. This should be interesting," Big Red states, his big arms folded over his chest.

"Yeah. He's not to be harmed or entranced. Opal is there." I look at Hugo and Flora. Her eyes flare in anger. "She doesn't want any unwelcome guests, so do you guys think you can pull the wool over her eyes?" I ask them.

"She is never going to see us coming," Flora says confidently before Hugo can say anything. I like the fire I see in her eyes.

"What do you want us to do, Scarlett?" Con asks me. He looks at me admiringly. I know he's proud that I'm taking leadership—even though I look to him to be our leader.

"I will call you to me once we have her cornered. The bottom and top floors are going to be surrounded by ancients," I say matter-of-factly. "I'll park my car a block away from the building; I will give you all a signal when to come in the building." They all nod in agreement and head out to get ready. I turn to head out, and Ian grabs me by the arm, turning me quickly into his arms, his mouth crashing down onto mine. I melt in his kiss, and just like that his lips are gone.

"Be safe," he whispers against my lips and leaves the room before I do. I want to say something to him, but the words are lost on me. Maybe it's my pride, or maybe it's fear. *Fear.* The voice in my head shouts to me to go after him. Tell him I want him to be safe too. But…I can't. I have to get my head in the game, because I know once I enter Michael's building things are going to get crazy.

I go outside. It's cold out. It's beginning to get dark. I get into my car, pulling out of the driveway with the Xs and Ian not far behind. I look back into my rearview mirror, and I can spot Ian's car. We are close; I park two blocks away from the building. Making the walk over, I take the letter out of my pocket. The scent of blood's evident, and I have to wonder if the scent I catch is of Bronx. I reach the front of the building, putting the letter in my back pocket.

"I will signal you guys as soon as I enter," my mind whispers to the group.

Taking a deep breath, I open the building door. The last time I was here, there was a doorman and security to greet me as soon as I walked in. But now it's empty. The hairs on the back of my neck stand in warning. Not taking the elevator, I head for the stairway, taking the steps up cautiously and constantly looking behind me. Opening another door that leads to the floor Michael's on, I peek out first and then begin the long walk down the hallway. It's quiet—too quiet. The lights began to flicker once I reach his doorway. My hand reaches toward the knob, and I close my eyes.

"I am going into the apartment now. The bottom floor is going to be surrounded with ancients. Flora and Hugo, meet me up here. I am going to need some magic."

Licking my lips, I turn the knob quietly. I shiver from the cold and see that the windows are open; once I enter, the lights begin to flicker earnestly. Opal is near. I go into the living room as the smell of blood becomes stronger. I realize then that the blood on the letter is not Bronx's—it's someone else's.

Bronx is tied up just like in my vision. His chin is resting on his chest, and his wrists are tied behind his back. Wasting no time, I rush over to him, taking out my dagger and cutting the ties at his wrists. He groans, coming to and lifting his head slowly. He's bruised and bloody.

"Shit, what did I tell you about getting involved, Bronx?" I whisper to him, ripping off the tape that's over his mouth, making him wince.

"It's too late. I'm already involved," he grunts as I help him up.

"Well, lucky for you I'm in the saving kind of mood." He puts his arm around my shoulder, and we begin to walk out.

"I find it fascinating you think you can save him," Michael's voice says from behind us.

Leaning forward so I can whisper in his ear but make it loud enough so Michael can hear me, I say, "I'll be right back. Try not to get into too much trouble." I turn toward Michael, smiling as I see that he has a bandage wrapped around his hand. *Let's see what I can do to the other hand.* I begin to walk slowly toward him.

"Wait a second. Come on, Scarlett. You are in my home, and I haven't introduced you to my friend. How rude of me," he says, smiling at me as if he has the upper hand, his eyes raking me from head to toe. From behind him, just as in my vision, steps out a young girl, a teenager maybe, with short hair that's perfectly cut. As soon as her presence is near me, the smell in the air changes; it reeks of death. The lights that were flickering turn off. Evil hides behind that look of a young child. Maybe this is Opal's idea of spitting on the innocent.

As if sensing my thoughts, she lets out a girlish giggle. Her face screws up, giving her a demonic expression as she lifts her palm, hissing out a chant. My body rises in midair before I can react. I am suspended for a brief moment. *Shit, this is going to hurt!* She chants again and brings her palms down roughly, slamming my body to the floor. My body lets out a whoosh. Before I can try to get up, she is over me, putting her foot down on my chest, holding me down effortlessly, her eyes turning white and revealing who she truly is.

"It is nice to finally meet you, Scarlett," she says, staring down at me, her eyes widening with open wonder.

"Opal," I say in greeting.

"You know who I am. Very impressive."

"I know a lot more than you think," I say.

"Come now, don't leave me in suspense. What would you know that I don't already?" she says sarcastically.

I grind my teeth together as I put my hands on her foot, trying to take some of the pressure off my chest.

"I know karma is a bitch. You chose the wrong people to fuck with. You'll die exactly how you should."

"Oh, yes? How is that, Prophet? How will you kill me?" she asks me, savagely ramming her foot deeper into my chest.

"No, I won't kill you. Flora will."

Just then, the lights begin to flicker again. I push Opal's foot off. Once I see that she is good and distracted, I roll away, and the doors open. Hugo walks in first, with Flora right behind him. Opal's eyes widen in fear as she turns to meet her adversaries.

"*Bronx, sit tight. Because if you thought knowing vampires was crazy, wait until you get a load of this.*"

I shiver from the cold as we all wait for the moment Scarlett lets us know when to enter the building.

"Are you cold?" Hugo asks, coming to me, wrapping his arms around me. I nestle into his warmth, resting my head briefly on his shoulder. I watch as the Xs all wait impatiently. Ian stands apart from the others, but I can tell he's just as impatient. Even though he remains closed off, I can sense his worry.

"Did you have trouble bypassing her shield?" Con asks us. Zayah is standing beside him.

I remember meeting them when Ezarbet married the king. I always stare at them with wonder, because they are the first vampires I ever met who were married in the sacred vampire tradition. I always found it romantic that vampires can sense their one true love with one look.

"The cover is set; she doesn't know we're here," Hugo tells the Xs.

I again focus on the building ahead, looking up at the floor that I sense Scarlett and Opal are on. I see the light in the window begin to flicker, and I know that our moment to go in has arrived. It's a sign; we all hear Scarlett's voice telling Hugo and me to meet her up there. We all run like our lives depend on it. The Xs go in first, and just like Scarlett had said, it's surrounded by ancients. Con and Big Red go in first, with Zayah and the others trailing behind them. Ian stands beside us.

"Quick, come! Take the stairs," Zayah yells as she kicks an ancient in the chest and beheads him. He falls to his knees.

"Stay close," Ian says as we walk in.

The ancients are everywhere. I know with one spell I can easily wipe them out, but that would threaten the Xs as well. Hugo's hand is protectively at my back as he guides me through the chaos. As we get to the stairs, an ancient approaches, and Ian is ready, kicking the dagger out of the ancient's hand, punching up so that he falls to his knees. Hugo wastes no time and touches the ancient's temple, releasing a spell. The ancient begins to shake as smoke comes out of his nose and mouth. We walk into the stairwell, not bothering to watch him as he turns to ash. We go up the steps and right to the apartment. Ian is about to open the door, and I put my hand on his sleeve.

"We should go in first. Opal is mine," I tell him.

He looks down at me at me briefly, and I catch a hint of his eyes assessing me with approval. He steps back, and Hugo leads the way, opening the door. As we step in, we walk toward the living room—and there she is. Even though she's disguised as a young girl, I can sense her. I can sense the evil that pours out of her. Scarlett's on the floor, and as soon as Opal sees us she gets distracted, her eyes widening in fear. Yes, fear. I actually relish in that. Scarlett shoves Opal's foot off and rolls away from her. Ian sees Scarlett and tenses. I hold my arms out, silently letting him know not to move.

Opal begins clapping her hands, her earlier surprise of seeing us wiped away as she assesses her current situation.

"Well, well…if it isn't the warlock and his main squeeze," she says menacingly, moving a little toward the windows. "You broke through my shield. How did you manage to do that?"

"It's easy enough. You are not as strong as you think you are, Opal," I say to her.

"Really? I wonder…what are you going to do about this?" She swings her hands to the left, grabbing Hugo in midair, quickly lifting him and slamming him to the wall and holding him there.

I pause in fear for Hugo as he grunts, trying to disengage himself from whatever magic she holds. As she does this, ancients run into the room all ready to attack. Ian steps in front of me and begins to fight. Scarlett, seeing this, tries to join him but is stopped by the man I assume is Michael Pearson. He has a gun to her face but gets tackled by another human, the detective Scarlett mentioned.

"Looks like it's just me and you," Opal says, and she laughs.

She places her palms together, and a purple light radiates from them. She begins to chant, blasting the light from her hands and directing it toward me. Before the light can hit me, I hold out my hand, holding onto the light with my palms, using all the power I have to halt it in its tracks. I take the purple ball of light into my hands, holding it steady. Sweat begins to gleam from my brow as I hold onto the light. I look up, and Opal's eyes widen once again. Stepping back, I throw the light back at her with full force, shouting in the process. The beam of light misses her as she throws herself to the floor, and the force of the light punches a hole through the wall. I scramble over to Hugo as her magic releases him. He falls over with a thud, but Opal blocks me. She opens her palm, and that makes me fly to the wall, slamming hard against it. I slide down to the floor as I briefly see stars dancing around my head.

"Look at you. Just like your mother," she hisses at me.

The rage that I feel is like none other. I fling myself at her, tackling her to the ground. That's when I realize I don't just need magic to defeat Opal…I need my anger, my hate for her. It consumes me. I have had so much taken away from me. My mother, my freedom. Now it's time to fight back. I get on top of her, balling my hands into fists and punching her in the face. She screams out in pain and tries to bring her palms up, but I stop her in midmotion. She tries to scream, but no words come out. Without uttering any magic or using my palms, I try to destroy her. I look up, and Hugo is staring at me. He is with me; we are connected. I put my palms to her head and conjure up a chant. Letting her go, I stand up. She rolls away from me. I look around and see the detective holding Michael down. Black ash is all around us as Ian and Scarlett defeat the rest of the ancients.

"What…what have you done to me?" Opal asks me, finally finding her voice.

I stare at her as she gets up. No longer disguised behind the form of the young girl, Opal's true, hideous form comes into view. She begins to blink several times, seeming to find it hard to talk.

"You are beginning to feel numbness in your body, and your vision is becoming weak. I suspect this is going to be quick," I say, watching as she drops to her knees. She tries to bring her palms together to conjure a spell, but she can't. Blood begins to pour out of her nose. I drop to my knees before her. I feel Scarlett and Hugo beside me.

"I took your power away," I whisper to her.

Opal shakes her head furiously at me. Again trying to conjure, she fails. She raises her hand to her nose and looks at the blood that is staining her hand. The blood that is now seeping from her eyes, I suspect, is tears.

"You're going to die, just like my mother. You took her from me so you and my sister could follow through with your dominance over the world. I will show you what that looks like. I will show you how this will all play out." I grab her shaking hand as she begins to whimper. "Scarlett, give me your hand."

Scarlett looks at me hesitantly, and I feel both Hugo and Ian tense.

"Trust me," I say to her.

She nods her head, giving me her hand. I let Opal touch Scarlett. I let her have her final moments of power. She begins to read Scarlett. She shakes her head back and forth furiously. She's moaning now, but I don't think it's only from the pain. It's from what she sees. Once I know she has seen enough, I take Scarlett's hand from hers. She falls back in an awkward position with her legs still folded behind her. Her white eyes close as her mind fogs and her whole body begins to shake. We all stand there as she dies a slow, painful death. The darkness that surrounds us leaves with her. I feel a weight lift from my shoulders, but I know it isn't enough. For now, yes. But there's one more person who needs vengeance. I look at Scarlett, who looks a bit pale and tired.

"Get the fuck off of me," Michael yells.

"Not on your fucking life," the detective yells back.

Scarlett goes over to the detective; he lets Michael go. The detective looks worse for wear, but I sense fierce bravery in him. Michael gets up and looks around at the wreckage that has been done. His mouth and nose are bloodied. A black eye is beginning to form. His eyes are wild as he looks at each of us. He's cornered and he knows it.

"What? What are you going to do?" he shouts at Scarlett and backs away a little as Ian moves closer to him.

"Hold it," the detective says, pointing his gun at Ian. "We just can't go killing people. Your kind, fine, but not mine. We can arrest this guy and put him away for a long time."

Ian smiles at him; Scarlett puts up her hand, easing Ian back. He grinds his teeth but backs off.

"And tell them what? That this guy's in cahoots with vampires? They'll think you're fucking nuts. And that's assuming your department isn't already corrupt. They have people everywhere working for them. He's one of them. Think about it," Scarlett says.

He lowers his weapon as he begins to realize the strength of her words. Scarlett's right. My sister has connections everywhere. It's all about connecting the dots—beginning with Michael. Without us realizing it, Michael grabs a knife from his back pocket, aiming it toward Scarlett, but before he can strike or anyone else can react, the detective fires his weapon, two shots to the chest. Michael's lifeless eyes are dazed as he drops the knife and falls to his knees, dead. His blood's already beginning to pool around him. The detective puts down the gun, seeming frustrated that it has to come to that. I want to reassure him, but there's really no point. He's now tainted, even though I suspect that he already was. I really want to get a read on him, but I sense I will soon enough.

"The Xs are safe, and downstairs is cleared," Scarlett says.

"Xs?" the detective asks.

"Long story, which I will share with you, Bronx. But for now, let's go," she says, walking toward the door but pausing by Opal's body. I know that she sought vengeance against Ezarbet; it's something I sought when going against Opal. It is something I seek when I go against my sister. I know without a doubt that I will help her. Even if that means killing Ezarbet myself.

26

Big Red shoves the ancient my way as my sword beheads him. He smirks at me.

"Just like old times," he shouts.

I smile back. Indeed it is. Battling with Big Red's always enjoyable. I quickly look to see where Zayah is, and she is safe. Even though I know she can hold her own, my eyes always wander over to her. I can't help it. She catches my eye and winks, silently letting me know she is thinking of me too. Another ancient comes charging at me with a big knife. I quickly twist the knife out of his hands, twisting it enough that I hear a few bones break. I kick his leg out, and he falls to the ground. He screams out in pain, holding his arm. I can see a bone sticking out.

"Con, you fucking traitor," he says, slobber coming from his mouth as he hisses at me.

I remember Desmond during our time working for the king. We were never close, but we had trained together. He looks different to me now, more bloodthirsty. I hardly recognize him with his long hair and fully grown beard. It looks like he's trying to fit the part. I wonder how dirty he had to get to succeed in that. I wonder how many innocent people he had to kill to do so. And now here he is, trying to kill me and my family.

"Traitor? You go against everything our people have set for centuries. And you have the nerve to call me a traitor." I reach down, grabbing the knife he tried to kill me with.

He laughs, spitting on my shoe. I don't hesitate to bring the knife under his chin, stabbing him up through the face to his skull and turning him to ash.

I look around as the ancients are eliminated. Zayah comes over to me and gives me a hug. I bring her close to my body, loving the smoothness of her chocolate skin as she wraps her long arms around my neck.

"I love you," she whispers in my ear.

"Say it again," I whisper back to her.

She pulls away from me, looking into my eyes. I wonder then if she has found my secret. I swear that woman's stare alone can bring any man to his knees.

"I love you, Con. Always." Her eyes get teary. I bring her in for another hug, swallowing hard. I feel my own eyes begin to glisten.

"I will never get tired of hearing you say that," I tell her.

Just then we all hear the voice we have been waiting for. *"Opal is dead,"* her mind whispers to us.

The Xs all let out a shout of victory. My arms grip Zayah tighter.

"It's clear down here. All the ancients have been defeated," my mind whispers back to her.

"Be right down," she says.

We all celebrate this victory, giving each other slaps on the back. It's a big one. We are now at a huge advantage. I have to wonder what will be the queen's reaction upon learning this latest news. Big Red comes over to me and slaps me on the back, and I grab him instead, giving him a bear hug.

"Whoa, what is this about? Zayah, I think you might have some competition," he says, laughing as I hear Zayah's beautiful laughter behind me. He returns my hug, again slapping me on the back. My eyes begin to glisten. Just then, from the glass doorway, I see a man I have never seen before, except in my vision. His eyes are focused on Big Red as his nostrils flare in the familiarity of his scent. He lifts his gloved hand toward his back, taking out a stake of some sort, and in what seems like slow motion flings it toward Big Red's back. I let out a shout of anger, pushing Big Red to the floor as the stake connects with my shoulder. I fall back to the floor as the force of the blow hits me hard. I hear the male laugh in the distance. The Xs, stunned frozen, see that I am not getting up. I should be getting up, but I can't. Big Red crawls over to me, holding my head in his lap and looking back at the doorway.

"Con," I hear Zayah's confused voice behind me as she scrambles to me.

Just then I hear the elevator ding open, and Scarlett is by my side, falling onto her knees.

"What happened? Why isn't he healing?" I hear her shout.

Zayah goes to remove the stake that is still in my shoulder.

"No!" Flora shouts.

They all look at her, confused.

"This stake is spelled with black magic. None of us can touch it."

"Can't you undo it?" Scarlett asks, looking between Hugo and Zayah, her eyes wide.

"The spell is binding. There is nothing we can do. I am sorry," Flora whispers, tears running down her face.

There is a deadly pause as they all take in what she just said.

"No. This can't be," Zayah screams.

"We can't leave it in there. Bronx is human—can he remove it?" Scarlett asks.

Flora puts her hand over the stake, careful not to touch it, nodding her head.

I wonder vaguely who Bronx is. Then I remember that he is the detective Scarlett mentioned. I remember him from a vision I had.

"Pull it out," Big Red screams at him, making him jump a little.

He goes onto his knees next to me. He looks at Zayah sadly as she cries, holding my hand. He reaches over hesitantly and grabs onto the stake, pulling it out as I howl in pain. God, the pain. I feel excruciating pain. I feel hot as if in fever. I'm dying. Not dying a quick death, but a slow, painful death. The only thing I'm thankful for is that at least I get to say good-bye. I get to say good-bye to my family. I look at each of them; yes, we came from different backgrounds, but they are my family. I have a family. I look at Zayah first. My one true love. My life, my heart, my everything. I love her with everything that I am. I take my hand out of her tight grasp, touching her face. She leans into my touch, her tears coating my hand.

"Say it again," I tell her.

She cries harder, shaking her head in denial of my words.

"Say it again, my love," I whisper to her.

"I love you, Con. Always and always. You can't leave me," she begs as Flora wraps her arms around her shoulders.

"Zayah, I love you. I will always be here with you." My fingers weakly trail to her heart.

She nods. I look up at my brother, Big Red. He is breathing as heavily as I am. He is shaking his head back and forth. "My brother," I whisper to him. I don't have to tell him; he is nodding his head, looking pained.

I look to Scarlett. Scarlett...She reminds me so much of her father. She looks pale and shaky.

"What will I do without you?" her mind whispers to me.

"Lead. You will lead. Be the person you are meant to be."

I look at Ian, who is standing right behind Scarlett. His eyes look stoic, his expression giving nothing away. "Take care of her," I whisper to him. He nods his head, silently promising me.

I feel my body begin to shake as my insides flare in blackness. I can't take anymore. The pain is overwhelming me. I faintly hear a prayer being said. It's the detective.

"God, our father, your power brings us to birth, your providence guides our lives, and by your command we return to dust. Lord, those who die still live in your presence; their lives change but do not end. I pray and hope for my family, relatives, and friends, and for the dead known to you alone. In company with Christ, who die and now live, may they rejoice in your kingdom, where all of our tears are wiped away. Unite us together again in one family, to sing your praise forever and ever. Amen."

My vision is going hazy, but behind Zayah I can see Edrick. I smile through my pain. I always knew he would be an angel. Taking my final breaths, I stare at Zayah. I hate to see her misery. I hate to see her crying. But I know one day she will smile again. She will live her life without me, and she will be happy despite it. I try to tell her this, but the words are lost to me as I begin to see a white light beckoning me to come forth. I want to stay here a bit longer to reassure my family that all will be well again. But I begin to fade, starting with my feet and working its way up. I choke out my final words to Zayah.

"I love you. Always."

Only then do I let the white light take me.

He begins to fade in my hands. I hear Zayah wail beside me, but I feel lost. *This can't be happening.* I shake off the hand that's at my shoulder; I think it's Hugo's, but I'm not sure. I don't want to be touched or consoled. I want my brother back. *Con's gone.* I swallow hard at those words. I feel like another part of me is gone. He saved me. I remember the man who threw the stake. He looked at me before he took off. He knows me, but I don't know him. As the sadness leaves my body, rage begins to set in. I get up, everyone watching me closely. I look down at Zayah, who is being held by Flora. It should have been me that died. I have nothing to live for, when Con did. I feel like I have no right to be in Zayah's presence. I have no right to be here. Without Con, I am not part of the Xs. I take off my metal shield, leaving me only in my black shirt and pants. I pick up my sword, letting it hang loosely. I begin to walk out, maybe even in a daze. I need a kill. I need to find that motherfucker. I hear my name called in the distance. Hugo is calling me back, but Scarlett stops him.

"Let him go," I hear her say.

I go without looking back. It's cold outside, but all I feel is the heat. I feel hot rage burn within. It begins to leak out of my pores. I sense them; they're not too far. They are running. *Fucking cowards.* I go into a dark alley, letting my sword drag along the ground. I want them to hear me. The first ancient stops, running back toward me. They know I am alone. He comes at me quickly with his sword, but I easily block him with mine, kicking the ancient in the chest, spinning my sword, and slicing his head off. The other five ancients come forth and surround me. I release my sword, dropping it to the ground, making a loud clinking sound in the quiet alley. I lift my hands as if I am surrendering, but instead to their surprise I ball my hands together, flipping them the bird.

"Come on, you fucks!" I yell at them.

They begin to laugh at me for my stupidity. *If they only knew who they were fucking with.* They all attack at once. Being a skilled fighter, I am quick, uppercutting the first one and making him fall to the ground with a grunt. I get a savage joy from watching him spit out a few teeth. The other ancient grabs me by the arms, trying to hold me, while another with a dagger comes toward me to aim at my heart, but I jump upward quickly, my legs going around his neck and snapping it, making him turn to ash. The ancient with his arms around me loosens his grip, and I take advantage of it by spinning, grabbing him by the neck, and snapping it. The other three ancients attack, but I am like a caged animal waiting to be released. I am thirsty for death. I finally grab onto my sword and stab one of the ancients through the chest, aiming it perfectly at his heart. The other ancient grabs his sword, taking a nice swipe at me but missing me by mere inches. I turn in the nick of time and cut his arm off. He screams in pain, falling to the ground. The last of the ancients runs toward me. I swiftly pull out a dagger from my back pocket and fling it with all of my might, turning him to ash midrun. I feel lost in the moment. I'm not even out of breath. I want more. I then notice the screaming ancient not too far from me. His arm's missing. Walking over to him, I drop to my haunches slowly.

"What's your leader's name?" I ask him quietly.

"Fuck you, traitor," he screams at me.

Saying nothing, I stand back up and grab my sword, wiping off the blood with my fingertips. The ancient freezes, his eyes going wide with fear as he sees the sword in my hands.

"Fuck me, you say?" I whisper.

I lift my sword, and, without a moment's thought, I bring it down hard, cutting off the ancient's left leg. The ancient screams again, crying, begging me. I hear his pleas of mercy; I am unfazed by them.

"I am going to give you one more chance. Who is your leader?" I ask.

"His name is…his name is Matthias. Matthias is his name!" he screams at me, flipping onto his stomach, his armed hand reaching up, clawing the ground, trying to get away from me.

"Matthias." I whisper his name. I now have a name. I get up, turning away for a moment, and then I stop, turning back toward the ancient.

"Too bad for you, ancient—I don't give second chances," I say before raising my sword once more and chopping his head off, turning him to ash. I then allow myself to drop my sword, spent from this small battle. I drop to my knees hard with my head bent. I bring my hands up and notice they are black from Con's ashes. I finally let my emotions wash over me. Balling my hands into fists, I pound on the cold cement ground so hard that I draw blood to my knuckles. But I feel no pain. My body shakes with uncontrollable anguish. But I still feel no pain. I remember Matthias's face, his amused smirk and the laugh he gave as he knew Con would die. Con...I let the pain take me. I let the tears come as I cry for my brother. I am alone now. I will seek retribution at whatever cost. Matthias *will* pay. My scream of fury and pain echoes throughout the empty alley.

"I hate Scarlett. I hate her," I repeat over and over again in my head.

I am bound, hanging up as if I were cattle. My arms are above my head, as I dangle on tiptoes. There is a gag in my mouth, and I am beginning to find it hard to breathe. I am tired, but I refuse to sleep. He is coming back just like he promised. There are other girls here who look strangely like me, all fair-skinned with blond hair, but for whatever reason he seems fixated on me. The last time he was here, he brought a young girl with him. Through my gag, I begged her to help me, but she just smiled at me evilly, taking out a knife and stabbing my hand. As the blood began to pour, she put it in some type of porcelain bowl. I screamed and screamed from the gruesome pain to the point of blacking out. I woke to find him licking my hand, his tongue lapping my wound. I tried to swing my body away from him, and that seemed to excite him more.

He's a monster. They all are. I tried to get the other girls' attention, but they don't speak. I suspect they are drugged. What does he want with me? I hear the door begin to open, and I quickly lower my head, closing my eyes and pretending

I am unconscious. I feel someone in front of me, and a single finger touches my face. I try not to shiver repulsively from the touch that I am beginning to grow accustomed to.

"Is this the game you want to play?" he asks me.

I have no idea what he's talking about, so I pretend I am still sleeping. Yes, it's safer this way.

"I finally met the man whose scent was all over you," he whispers, leaning in close so that so I can feel his breath on my skin.

I go still at his words. I have no idea what he's talking about.

"What do I have to do to prove to you that you are mine?" His fingertips trail against my arm.

He knows I am awake. I try to hold back my tears of fear, but I can't. He terrifies me and he knows it. He lets me go, and I breathe a sigh of relief. He goes behind me, removing my gag.

"Please, just let me go," I begin.

"Shhh…let me prove to you that you are mine," he shushes me.

My lips begin to tremble as I see him cut loose one of the girls, placing her in direct view of my vision. She seems dazed. Long, blond hair and pale, blue eyes—we could have been sisters. I watch in horror as he takes a knife out of his pocket, touching her arm with its point and trailing it up and down. She doesn't move or flinch.

"Stop…" I whisper.

"I want you to tell me," he says as he begins poking at her arm with the knife's edge, gently at first but then digging deeper.

"Tell you what?" I am confused. *This can't be fucking happening. This is a bad dream. You're going to wake up any minute, Jewels, and see this was all a dream. All a fucked-up dream. Wake up, Jewels. Wake up!*

"Tell me you are not his!" he screams at me, making me jump. The veins began to pulse from his neck. Blood begins to spill from this girl. Still no reaction from her. Not a scream or wince of pain.

"I am not his," I stutter. I have no idea who the hell he's talking about, but at this point I am going to say anything he wants.

"You're mine. Tell me you're mine." He brings the knife to the girl's throat this time.

"I'm…I'm yours…please don't hurt her…please…" I beg over and over again.

He smiles at me, a sick genuine smile. As if my proclamation is the best thing he has ever heard. "I am so happy to hear you say that," he says.

I nod my head rapidly, hoping just to settle him enough so he will get away from the girl.

"Nothing should come between us. Not even her." Just then, he takes the knife and slices the girl's throat. I scream in horror. The girl makes a gurgling noise, slumping forward, as her blood spills everywhere. I think I scream until I can't anymore. Vomit runs down my chin as I attempt to turn my body away from him, the rope cutting into my skin. I hear his footsteps as he nears me, and I flinch from his cold touch. He likes that. I can almost feel his smile. He's sick. A truly demented soul.

"Look at me," he whispers in my ear.

I close my eyes tighter. I know what's coming. I've seen him do it to the other girls. He is going to make me his puppet.

"Look at me. You don't want me to get angry and take it out on the others, do you? Perhaps we are two of a kind, and you enjoy it as well." He lifts my chin, cleaning me off.

I want to yell at the top of my lungs that we are nothing alike, but I don't want to see anyone else hurt, especially at my expense. I slump my shoulders in defeat. I slowly open my eyes, turning my head so I can look at him.

"He's going to come after you," he says softly.

I open my mouth to ask who, but he places a finger over my mouth, silencing me. *Yes, please come save me, whoever you are—please help me.*

"But you won't go with him," he tells me.

His eyes probe mine deeply, and I begin to get lost. My body begins to relax under his gaze.

"You won't let him take you from me, will you?" I feel fingers graze my face, but I only focus on his words.

"I won't let him," I say.

"You will kill him if he does. You are mine, only mine," he whispers to me, sealing his words with a rough kiss. His lips move over mine roughly. He bites down on my lower lip, drawing blood. I gasp from the sting, but he disgustingly laps it up.

"Yes," I whisper as he pulls away. He smiles, satisfied.

Yes, I am his…wait…no, you need to get out of here. What the fuck is wrong with me? Why am I agreeing with this guy? I can't control anything that comes out of my mouth. I am repulsed by his kiss, but I let him. I wonder how long it will take for him to rape me—or will I willingly let him have sex with me? I close my eyes again, feeling sickened. He will have to kill me first. I know now that I will probably die here.

"Scarlett, whoever you are…I fucking hate you."

27

My body jolts forward as the link between Opal and me is broken. I put my hand over my mouth, too stunned to speak. Opal is dead. The woman who backed me, who was loyal to me, was dead. If I had any type of emotion, I would probably cry. Not in remorse, but because my plan is momentarily stalled. I will need a new witch, and fast. I close my eyes, trying to absorb everything that took place. Flora. It has to be. Her and that fucking warlock. I get up, going over to my mirror, and I toss everything off my vanity in a fit of rage, finally letting out a piercing scream. *I should have killed that bitch when I had a chance!* Entering our room in a rush, Damian comes to my rescue.

"Opal's dead." I whisper my explanation for the mess.

He nods his head in understanding. He is the exact opposite of Abel. Abel would bend like a dog for me, but Damian… he is in a league of his own. He is a true dominant. I don't think any other would do for me. *Well, with the exception of Ian. But let's not get ahead of ourselves.*

"I just heard from Matthias. Con is dead, and they captured one of Scarlett's human friends. And Michael Pearson is dead."

I reward myself with this victory. Con's dead. This is huge. I wish I could've been there to see all of their broken faces. How did their leader react? Michael Pearson being dead is not an issue to me anymore.

"Put Matthias on the phone for me. It's time to move to the next phase," I tell him, turning my back to him.

He leaves the room without another word. I glance at myself at the mirror. I am beginning to show. I place my hand on the small swell that's beginning to form, trying to squeeze my stomach in. *I am going to be fat.* By no means was the reason for the spell to conceive a motherly aspect. It was to conceive a new species. I was a week or two along when I first felt him move. He's strong; he's beginning to suck the energy out of me, which I don't like at all. I don't have any morning sickness, but the need to drink is powerful. He's already insatiable. *Just like his father.* I comb out the hair from my face, wondering if he will have my family's famous red hair. I hope not. I think of Flora again and I grind my teeth. *Who the fuck does she think she is?* I can break her. I did it before; I can do it again. I move to the window to look outside. We are surrounded by trees and are not too far from the city's hustle and bustle. I had decided I wanted to be up close and personal with the action. Yes, while Scarlett went on her little scavenger hunt, I had decided it was time to come here.

Now I am just under her nose, and she doesn't know it yet. Even though I know Damian's against traveling due to my "fragile" state, it matters not. I have to take out Scarlett. Besides—there are a few things that need to be ironed out. One of them is moving some accounts around. I knew Michael would became a liability and begin to get sloppy with the club's extracurricular activities. If I can't get my hands on Scarlett now, I will take out her team one by one if I have to. I will take joy in her pain; I will swim in her tears of misery. I have a flashback to Michael calling me, frantically saying that Scarlett knew about him. I remember getting irritated with him and telling him to quit being a pussy. That shut him up. But he told me Scarlett mentioned a name—someone Scarlett thought I knew. I ponder that a moment, thinking back to what I saw when I drank from her. I feel my throat constrict from the remembrance of her taste, but something else is beginning to plague me. Curiosity's starting to set in as I place my hand over my stomach, irritated by the movement that I feel. What's his name again? This pregnancy's fucking with my mind along with everything else that's happening. Then, like an epiphany, the name comes to me. I smile lightly as I think of the name of my son. Damian picked it out. I honestly didn't care what we named him. We can call him Beast for all I care. But the name I do like. Yes. I can just picture it now: *King Dominic.*

We enter my room in silence, hand and hand, seeking comfort from each other's warmth. We had dropped off Zayah in her room. We had spelled her to sleep, knocking her out for the remainder of the day—or what was left of it. We stood by her side the rest of the night, neither of us sleeping.

What time is it? I should go to Scarlett. She seems as lost as I feel. There's nothing that can be done about the loss of one of our own. As soon as I saw him on the ground, I knew the blood on my hands was his, no matter how strong Flora's connection was or the powerful connection we shared. Con's fate was written in stone as surely as Scarlett's was. I look at Flora, who sits on the bed now, her eyes furrowed in deep thought, biting her lip. My fate's written in stone too. I knew that as soon as I saw her, even though I fought those feelings tooth and nail. I don't want to waste another moment not being close to her. I walk over to her, going on my knees so that I can lean into her. Her arms welcome me as we hold each other.

"That could have been me, you know? Or it could have been you," she whispers brokenly. "I don't think I could bear that."

She's right. It could have easily been any one of us. The thought of losing her…I swallow hard at the thought. There are no promises of tomorrow I can give her, but what I can do is live in the moment with her. Every day, live in the moment together. The thought of the future is muddled, but I have hope. She has given me hope. I unlink her arms from around me, grabbing her face between my hands and kissing her gently on the lips.

"I love you," I whisper against her lips. She smiles, and I catch the tear that begins to fall down her cheek.

"I love you too." She pulls away a little, reaching down, grabbing her locket, and opening it. I feel a hint of jealousy as I look at the picture of the male still inside. "I never told you, but there is an urban legend that goes with this locket." She starts smiling. "This was my grandmother's locket, and it was passed down to me. For the life of me, I've never been able to open it. My mother said that only my true love would be able to open it."

Realization hits me. It's her grandfather's picture. I chuckle as I remember her anger when she discovered I had opened it. I can see why that would piss her off; I wasn't very nice.

"I'm sorry," I start.

She shakes her head at me, touching the side of my face. Her touch alone is enough for me. She's everything that I didn't think I needed, balancing me in perfection. *The warlock and the witch.* Who would have thought we could both give our ancestors something to think about? It no longer matters who brought the war between our people. It stops now, ending with us. We are redefining history. There's no magic needed, no spells to be cast. This is true love. I bring her closer to me, kissing her softly on her neck.

"My sister's right about one thing, you know," she whispers huskily in my ear.

"What's that?" I whisper back, getting caught up in her softness and scent.

"I did fall in love with a warlock..."

28

I walk and walk until daylight breaks. I know Ian wanted to follow me, but he reluctantly stayed behind. I guess he respects the fact that I just need to be alone. The lonely streets of New York give me solitude. I don't even remember getting in my car or driving home. The memory of Con is imbedded in my head. *Why didn't I see this in a vision? Could I have stopped it somehow?* I ask myself over and over again. I pull up in front of our home, closing my eyes as I feel the sadness I am trying to contain wash over me. How can I possibly walk in there and try to act like everything will be OK? I get out of the car numbly and walk in. The warmth of the home greets me. I feel so cold inside and out. I climb the steps slowly, and once inside the safety of my room, I let myself begin to feel...feel for the first time in a long time. I take off my jacket and drop it to the floor. I drop onto my knees in front of the fireplace, picturing Con there with me when he last talked to me. I am trying to apologize, and he shakes his head in understanding. My lips begin to tremble at the memory.

"Let all that anger, that hate...let it out. Feel."

I remember telling him how it's safer not to. But is it? I look at my hands, which are marked with Bronx's blood and Con's ashes. I finally let myself release. I let out a scream as all my emotions fight each other. I cry and I cry. And, God, does it feel good. I cry for Con. I cry for Zayah. I cry for my family. I feel released in some ways. I am accepting who I am. This is who I am. I am not a vampire. Partly, yes. But I am a human. I feel. I love. I hate. All these things make me who I am. I put my hands over my face as I sob for my friend.

"I'm sorry," I whisper over and over again, wishing there was more I could have done to prevent it.

I have to wonder if he knew. The vision I have of Big Red is on a summer's night. But once I feel his rage, I know that it's the heat I feel in the vision. I feel his hate and pain. Again I begin to cry as I think of Big Red. I know he will be lost for a while, but he will come back; it'll be in his own time and on his own terms, but I know he will. I hear the door open; I don't bother to turn, as I know it will be Hugo. He's always there when I need him. I absently remember the last battle; it kind of ended the same way: me on my knees crying as he comforted me. I begin to cry harder if that's even possible, putting my hands over my face. He kneels in front of me. I feel his arms going around me hesitantly, and I sink into his embrace. I shiver from the cold, and the hands going up and down my back comfortingly are not those of Hugo; it's the touch of Ian. Ian. This man I tried my damnedest to hate. This man who weaseled his way back into my life. I don't hate him. I can't. Because I am irrevocably in love with him. I love this man. For all of his faults and dark confessions, I love him even more for them. I sink into his embrace further, wrapping my arms around his neck and laying my head on his shoulder.

What if I lose him? I remember the vision I had of him as he turned to ash in my arms. I hug him that much tighter. No…I can't lose him—that is not an option. I have to do something. I just don't know what. If it's the last thing I do, I will find a way. Because now that I have him, I will never let him go. I wash those thoughts away as I focus on his hands rubbing up and down my back, now going into my hair. I seek comfort in the man who doesn't know how—the man who, even though he doesn't say it out loud, loves me. So I take what he gives so freely. I take his comfort and—unbeknownst to him—his heart.

SPELLBOUND

Playlist

Too Close- Alex Clare
Adore You- Miley Cyrus
All of Me- John Legend
Breath of Life- Florence + The Machines
Colorblind- Natalie Walker
Corner of Your Heart- Ingrid Michaelson
Dark Horse- Katy Perry featuring Juicy J
E.T.- Katy Perry Featuring Kanye West
Eyes on Fire- Blue Foundation
Foolish Games- Jewel
In for the Kill- La Roux (Skrillex remix)
Jar of Hearts- Christina Perri
Stay- Rihanna featuring Mikky Ekko
Radioactive- Imagine Dragons
Sail- AWOLNATION
Say Something- A Great Big World & Christina Aguilera
Scary Monster and Nice Sprites- Skrillex
Team- Lorde
Unconditionally- Katy Perry
Wrecking Ball- Miley Cyrus
You Were Meant for Me- Jewel
Chandelier- Sia
Not About Angels- Birdy
Stay With Me- Sam Smith
Start a Riot- Jetta

Landfill- Daugher
Life Support- Sam Smith
Latch- Sam Smith (Acoustic)
Waves- Beth (Tribute to Mr. Probz)
Breathe Me- Sia
Yellow Flicker Beat-Lorde
Haunted- Beyonce

AUTHOR'S NOTE

I wanted to take this time to thank you for reading Spellbound. I hope you enjoyed reading it as much as I enjoyed writing it.

If you have time, please leave a review on Amazon.com, B&N.com, Goodreads.com, OR send me an email (Rebeccas.1003@gmail.com) so I can personally thank you.

For sneak peeks follow me on Instagram: Rebeccas_author
Facebook: www.facebook.com/RebeccaSenthralled

Rebecca S.

www.ingramcontent.com/pod-product-compliance
Lightning Source LLC
Chambersburg PA
CBHW051945240626
47153CB00005B/1638

* 9 7 8 0 6 9 2 3 7 9 3 0 1 *